READING 5X5
X3

Also from Metaphorosis

READING 5X5 X3

CHANGES

edited by
B. Morris Allen

ISBN: 978-1-64076-033-2 (e-book)
ISBN: 978-1-64076-034-9 (paperback)
ISBN: 978-1-64076-035-6 (hardcover)

Verdage

from
Metaphorosis Publishing

Neskowin

CONTENTS

For the hard working SFF writers who know there's always room to improve.

INTRODUCTION

About the anthology

Welcome to the *Reading 5X5 x3* anthology! Like its predecessors, *Reading 5X5* and *Reading 5X5 x2: Duets*, this anthology is a collection of great science fiction and fantasy stories that also focuses on the writing process. Unlike them, it's intended *primarily* as a writer's resource rather than a literary anthology.

The original *Reading 5X5* looked at how different authors approach the same material. Participants generated five story briefs, and for each one asked five authors to write a story from it, for a total of 25 stories overall. The *Reader's Edition* included just the 25 stories. The *Writer's Edition* included two extra stories, the original story briefs, and notes from each author about how they approached the writing process. The result was a fascinating look at how different authors deal with the same basic concept.

The follow-up, *Reading 5X5 x2*, asked five authors to write with each other in a round robin format — each author collaborating with each of the others on a story, as well as writing a solo story, for a total of 15 stories. The objective was to see how authors' voices change depending on whom they collaborate with. The result was not only interesting, the stories themselves were excellent.

In this third volume, *Reading 5X5 x3*, we've taken a somewhat different tack. Here, the focus is on how stories change during the revision process. We've taken 15 stories originally published in *Metaphorosis*, and presented both the final, published version and the original, submitted version, along with notes from the author and editor about the revision experience.

For each story, the sequence is as follows:
- Final version — the version of the story published in *Metaphorosis.*
- Revision notes
  - Initial feedback — my initial, brief feedback to the author on what was strong and what needed work.
  - Author's intent — what the author said they intended the story to be about (see *Metaphorosis editorial process* below)
  - Author's note — the author's note about the editorial process: what surprised, pleased, or disappointed them about the process and the result.
  - Editor's note — my comments about the revision process: what I was looking for and how things ended up.
- Original version — the version originally submitted.

Unlike the prior *Reading 5X5* anthologies, this one is not primarily organized for reading (though the stories are excellent, and can easily be followed using the table of contents) but as a tool for improving writing craft. The expectation is that aspiring authors will tackle the stories one at a time, looking at what changed in the story during the editorial process and why, and considering how they would approach the same issues.

An appendix lists some common issues I see in stories and how they can be resolved, along with a cross-reference to stories in this anthology that exhibited similar issues, so that readers can see how resolution works in practice.

Stories in this anthology have all been through the same revision process, but in different ways, spelled out by the *Some Statistics* section below. However, it's important to keep in mind that statistics aren't everything. Stories that went through fewer revision phases or whose text changed less aren't 'better' than other stories, they're just different. There's a lot that goes into revision, and it can't be easily boiled down to numbers.

The stories are roughly organized by how evident the changes in the story are, and I suggest readers start at the beginning, working their way toward more subtle changes toward the end. The main thing, though, is to be open to learning from the process and thinking about how to handle your own revisions.

It's important to introduce a caveat: each editor is different. A different editor would have asked for different changes. This anthology is a study of what *Metaphorosis* and I look for, but the broad lessons about how to revise are useful to everyone.

B. Morris Allen
Editor

Some statistics

Editing isn't about statistics; it's about feeling and impact. However, I know that some authors like to work with hard facts, so below are some statistics from the stories in this anthology.

- Rounds of revision
  - Fewest – 4
  - Greatest – 10
  - Average number of rounds – 5.6
- Amount of change (original text changed)
  - Greatest amount of change – 100%
  - Smallest amount of change – 3%
  - Average amount of change – 40%
- Changes in length
  - Greatest cut – 33%
  - Average cut (of those cut) – 26%
  - Greatest expansion – 93%
  - Average expansion (of those expanded) – 40%
  - Average change across all stories – 17% expansion

The editorial process

Every magazine has their own way of doing things, depending on what best suits the editor and staff. A lot of it happens behind the scenes — formatting, infrastructure, scheduling — but the editorial process, by definition, directly affects authors. Below, I've sketched out what the *Metaphorosis* editorial process looks like. It has changed somewhat over the years since we opened in 2015, but the core has remained the same.

Submission. The first thing to know is that we read submissions blind — without knowing anything about the author. Some submitters are brand new to the magazine (or to publishing), some are frequent submitters, some we've published several times. We don't know any of that when we review the story. We experimented briefly with non-blind submissions, mainly because so many submitters seem to have trouble following guidelines, but I strongly prefer reading blind, and we quickly returned to that model.

Initial review. As I read a story, I take brief notes, including the page at which I first started having concerns about the story, and the page at which I stopped reading. In the early days of the magazine, I read each submission all the way through, and it's a method I prefer, but I found it unsustainable as the number of daily submissions mounted. Now, I read until I'm confident I wouldn't accept the story regardless of ending. I do worry that some potentially good stories slip by this way, but generally I can tell the quality of the prose within a paragraph, and whether I'm interested in a story within a page or two.

I rate each story from 1 to 10, with most stories getting a rating of 4, meaning that there was nothing greatly wrong with the story, but it also didn't stand out for me. A rating less than 4 usually means poor prose or no real story to the piece (which happens more often than you'd think). Stories don't usually get a 5 unless they've kept my attention all the way through. Stories ranked between 5 and 8 usually get a 'Maybe' label and are passed to second readers. I don't believe I've ever given a 9 or 10, but I hold out hope. Over 99% of stories are rejected at this initial review stage.

Second readers. Many magazines use slush readers who pass potentially worthy stories to a higher editorial level. At *Metaphorosis*, I do the opposite — I read all submissions, and pass Maybes to a group of second readers for another opinion. They all look at things differently than I do, and because I know their preferences, I can calibrate their reactions and how they mesh with mine. Second readers sometimes confirm my own initial feelings, and sometimes show me something in a story that I hadn't seen.

Decision. Once the second readers have weighed in, I make a decision. At this point, I'll de-anonymize the story to see the author's name and their history of submissions. If it's an author I've worked with, I'll take into account how easy or difficult they were to work with, how hard they're willing to work, and how good the end results have been. If an author has a tendency to fight anything more than minimal changes, the initial submission has to be much stronger than for an author who's willing to make extensive revisions. Happily, most authors fall into a middle ground that's willing to listen to suggestion, but also willing to defend their position. If it's an author I don't know, I look at how I rated their prior submissions (if any), to get a sense of their range. One or more scores of 5+ is comforting, but it's not a problem if they have 4s or no history at all. If they only have 2s and 3s, that suggests they may not be able to do what I'm looking for, but in those cases I review the prior submissions to see what the issue was.

While the percentages have varied a bit with time, these days, about 2/3 of Maybe submissions are rejected with a brief note about strengths and weaknesses I saw in the story. The remainder are offered a chance to rewrite the story. I virtually never accept a story as is. The few times I tried it, I regretted it — what I expected to be very minor edits turned into something more complex.

Revision. I'm a far more hands-on editor than at most current SFF magazines, but I don't give detailed guidance in the first rewrite offer. That's for two reasons: First, some authors don't take up the offer, and I've find it's best not to spend editorial time on a story until the author is committed to revision; it's just not efficient. Second, I want to give authors a chance to make the changes that occur to them fairly independently. The first revision is often one of the most substantive, and one in which authors come up with new things I hadn't thought of.

What I do provide is a brief note on strengths and weaknesses, much like what I provide to the rejected Maybes. I'll indicate whether I think the piece should be longer or shorter, and what some of the key issues are. In the *Revision* sections after each story in this anthology, I've included my initial feedback to authors.

Themes. Just as important as my initial feedback however, is that I ask authors what they think the story is about, and what emotions they're trying to evoke. Of course, many authors don't write with a concrete theme in mind — I don't myself. However, *after* the story is done, I find it's useful to go back and try to figure out what the story is about — not the plot (I've *read* the story; I know what happens), but what the theme and intent of the story is, or at least what the author wants the reader to feel.

Most authors take a stab at identifying themes and emotions. Some provide long, thoughtful analyses, some just a line or two. Some don't answer at all and just send a new version. When they do answer, it's extremely valuable to me. My goal is to make the story the best version of what the author wants it to be, so it's best if they tell me directly what that is. When they send comments, I review them, tell them where I think they're succeeding or failing, and, vitally, keep their comments as part of the file that I refer to when evaluating the next version. The *Revision* section after each story here includes authors' responses on themes and emotion.

Version 2. When the second version (the first revision) of the story comes in, the first thing I do is generate an automatic comparison with the original and contrast that with my expectations. If I suggested a full-scale revamp and cutting, and the author has moved a few commas around, we're likely to have trouble making progress. That's not always true, though; there have been cases where an initial comma-shifter turned enthusiastic reviser in later versions.

Later versions. I've learned from painful experience to try to make a decision about the story by version 3 (second revision). Before that, the author hasn't had enough chances to show what they can do. Beyond that, they've likely put so much work in that they resent being told I won't accept the story after all. It's a difficult decision to make — to me, it usually feels too early in the process to be sure things won't work out — but I've tried to stick to this approach in recent years. I lean very much toward continuing the revision process, and try to cut it short only when I feel the story isn't making progress. Sometimes that's because I feel the author isn't trying, sometimes because they are but the story isn't improving, and sometimes because I just don't feel I'm the right editor for what I've come to understand as the author's vision of the piece.

For the great bulk of stories that do continue in revision, there are between two and nine rounds of revision, though usually three or four. Broadly speaking, these rounds of revision cluster into: structure — shortening, expanding, moving things around; balance — ensuring characters and themes are supported appropriately and that there's the right amount of attention in the right places; and polish — tweaking language here and there, strengthening the prose where needed.

Acceptance. Once we've agreed on a final version (and I like to get a sign-off on *all* changes except late-found typos), I send a formal acceptance, ask for some information, and pay for the story. Then, 1-6 months later, it's published.

In the fifteen stories below, you can get a sense of how that works in practice. I suggest you read the published story first, then the authorial and editorial notes, then compare with the original. However, you may wish to start with the original, write down your own ideas about what you think could improve, then read the notes, then read the final. It's up to you and how you can learn the most about how to improve your own stories.

THE STORIES

THE SECRET KEEPER

—

PAULINE YATES

The Secret Keeper

Keeping a secret is dangerous. Secrets mess with emotions and can cause illness from depression, anxiety, and stress. The darker the secret, the heavier the burden; it can shorten your life by years. Even Demigods, like Mother and me, need to be cautious when keeping a secret. We're gifted with powers to balance emotions, but if we reveal a secret, we'll suffer its burden. It's crucial we stay strong, because we help battle the gods who draw their power from misery and suffering.

Like Hades. He doesn't mind if a person troubled by a secret dies young. He draws his power from the souls of the dead. And in his realm, the bearer suffers their burden three times worse. But we have Harpocrates, the god of silence, on our side. He uses hope to encourage a bearer to reveal their secret and clear their conscience. To deliver hope, he needs a Secret Keeper, and now I'm sixteen, that's what I'm about to become.

"Repeat after me," Mother says. "Listen without — "

" — judgment and heal the harm," I say, not needing her help. I've committed these vows to heart. "Bind the secret with a Keeper's charm. If by fault I break the faith, suffer the burden the thorns keep safe."

Mother slips a charming binding ring onto my finger. The gold band, engraved with a pattern of linked roses, is the token of a Secret Keeper.

"How much hope do you give?" she asks.

"Only enough to ease their pain; too much hope is a secret's gain." Giving too much hope can make the bearer believe that keeping their secret won't cause them harm.

"And how much burden do you take?" Mother says, her voice low like a brewing storm.

I sigh, wishing Mother weren't so melodramatic. I know what to do. But she expects an answer. "Only enough that hope shines through. Though it harms, they need the burden, too." Removing all the burden takes away the incentive to reveal the secret. That defeats our purpose.

Mother smiles. "Balancing emotions is tricky, but your charm will help."

I raise my hand to the rising sun and admire the ring. The charm curls from the band and weaves around my fingers like a glittering ribbon of light. Feeling its power makes me giddy with excitement.

Now I can heal using a true god's power. Until now, I've only ever had demigod powers to work with. That power allows me to grow herbs from nothing to make the remedies we sell to the local townsfolk. We're the talk around town because of their potency, but we hide our true identity. Mother 'has a green thumb'. I'm 'the homeschooled girl'. Receiving the charm makes me feel like I've graduated.

Lowering my hand, I touch the charm with my finger. It shapes into a glittering rose, Harpocrates' symbol. He created the charm, but I fuel its strength by imagining where I find hope. All Secret Keepers have their preference. For me, hope is in a sunrise, in a rainbow, in seedlings bursting through the soil. Hope is also in my desire to be the best Keeper Harpocrates has ever had.

"The ability to heal the harm caused by a secret is a rare and wondrous gift," Mother says. "However, Harpocrates does not give this charm freely. You are now his servant, as I am, and my mother before me. Harpocrates uses his power to keep hope alive in the world and expects you to do the same. Without hope, the world would fall under the influence of those gods who favor darkness and despair."

She opens her hand, revealing her ring. Years of use make it appear fluid, like a circle of lava. Her charm curls from the band and takes the shape of a burnished gold rose, similar to mine. Mother blows on it. The rose dissolves into a spray of mist that fills the air with a mixture of sweet and pungent perfume.

Turning her hand, the bitter perfume overpowers the sweet. "Polemos draws his power from conflict," she says. "Oizys, misery. Dolos, pain." She tilts her hand again and the sweet perfume overpowers the bitter. "Hestia, compassion, Eros, love, and of course, Harpocrates, hope. There cannot be light without dark, but, tipped out of balance, chaos will ensue." With a flick of her hand, the scents collide. They splatter on the ground like splashes of water.

"Do you think we make a difference?" I ask, tilting my hand so my charm dances on my finger. "We're only demigods. What good is our strength in a battle for power between the gods?"

"You're stronger than you think. The strength of all Secret Keepers runs in your blood. Collectively, we are Harpocrates' most powerful allies. Just be mindful of your vows and replace the burden you remove with hope. You don't want to leave a person feeling as dark and empty as the day Hades stole Persephone from this world."

"Does a burdened soul give Hades extra power?"

"No, but he benefits by receiving a soul quicker. A burden left unattended leads to premature death," Mother says. "Otherwise, he has no interest in warring for power. It's why he lets Persephone return for half the year. But don't dismiss him. Now that you channel Harpocrates' power, Hades will watch to see if you stay true to your vows. He's never broken an oath, and values the laws of morality over everything."

It's a value I share. Secret Keepers heal, they don't harm. Breaking my vow would also desecrate the moral law of our kind.

I glance across the gardens at the many roses that grow between the herbs. All were grown by Mother to keep the secrets she heard. Each sprouts thorns glistening with the secret's burden — guilt, sorrow, remorse. In all our history, no Secret Keeper has ever broken her vows. Suffering any of those emotions would be a deserved punishment. Revealing a secret breaks trust. Breaking trust would destroy hope, and we're tasked with keeping hope alive.

But I needn't worry. Even without history on my side, I'll enjoy showing Hades how committed to my vows I can be.

🖋

With the commitment ceremony complete, I revert to my daily chores. Weeding the garden. Growing more herbs to replace those we've used. We're out of dried lavender, so I fetch my gardening clippers. As I snip the stems, my charm grows brighter. It draws hope from my thoughts about lavender's healing qualities.

Customers arrive throughout the day. Some seek a herbal remedy. Others request a pot of living herbs to grow in their gardens. All wander through the gardens while Mother prepares their purchase. All ask the same question on their return.

"Are the roses for sale?"

I've lost count of the number of times I say no because of Mother's fondness for the flowers. I smooth over their disappointment by revealing it's why I share the flower's name. I don't mind the interruptions. Before I became a Secret Keeper, I'd try to guess if a customer had a secret, to no avail. Now that I have Harpocrates' charm, it changes everything.

"Should we hear all secrets?" I ask, after selling a girl my age a jar of comfrey for her mother's arthritis. I'm worried I missed the chance to hear my first secret. The charm grew warm in my hand and my mind filled with an image of the girl kissing a boy.

"Only if you want to," Mother says as she ties a string around the lavender stems to hang them in the kitchen. "Happy secrets can still cause worry, spoiling a surprise, for example. But those secrets get revealed in due course, so we rarely bother. It's the dark secrets that need our help the most." She glances out the front door. "Your chance to learn the difference has arrived."

A woman in her early twenties approaches the house. Her face is pale and the dark circles beneath her eyes suggest something is amiss. My charm curls into my hand, but no images suggesting a secret fill my mind.

"How do you know she has a dark secret?" I ask, wondering how Mother can detect what I can't.

"A lifetime of practice," she says. "Now, always try to coax out their secret first. Offering them someone to confide in works as well as the charm."

"Yes, Mother."

"If they won't tell, which many don't, use the charm. But remember, dark secrets are not pleasant."

"Yes, Mother."

I hurry from the house. Her warning fills my stomach with fluttering butterflies. Mustering my bravest smile, I approach the woman. "Hello. I'm Rose. Can I help you?"

"Hi. I'm Miranda. But everyone calls me Mim." She fidgets with the cuff of her sleeve and looks toward the gardens. "Your roses are beautiful. I admired them from the road." She hesitates, then turns her attention to the herbs. "Would you have a herbal remedy to help with forgetfulness? It's for my mother," she adds. "She has Alzheimer's."

"I'm sorry to hear that. How bad is she?"

Mim sighs. "Stage seven. She's in a nursing home and not expected to live much longer. We're trying to keep her comfortable."

"That must be difficult." I motion her to a table and chairs set up on the porch.

"I have to remind my mother who I am every day," Mim admits, walking with me to the porch. "It's hard."

The butterflies in my stomach close their wings and settle. It appears Mim is just exhausted from caring for a dying parent.

"Gingko will help your mother," I say, pulling out a chair and encouraging Mim to sit. "It's wonderful for helping with memory problems. And chamomile for you, to help you cope. Would you like to try some chamomile tea while I prepare a remedy for your mother?"

"That would be lovely," Mim says, sinking into the chair.

I hurry inside to boil the kettle, but Mother stands with a steaming pot of tea, already made.

"An infusion of chamomile," she whispers, handing me the pot. "I couldn't help overhearing. I'll prepare the gingko. You heal Mim."

"She doesn't have a secret," I whisper. "She's exhausted from caring for her mother."

Mother raises an eyebrow. "Are you sure? What does your charm tell you?"

I glance at my ring. The charm dances along the band, making the ring glow like fire. Frowning at my ineptitude, I grab a cup from the kitchen bench and return to Mim.

"Mother will prepare the gingko, but what about you?" I ask, pouring the tea and sitting in the chair opposite her. "You said 'we', before. Do you have other family members that can help?"

"Only my brother," Mim says, taking the cup of chamomile. "He's not around at the moment. He works away." She gulps her tea, her face turning bright red.

I don't need the charm to know she is lying. I wonder if Mim's secret involves her brother. Though itching to use my charm, I follow Mother's advice and offer Mim someone she can confide in.

Looking toward the roses, I sigh. "I love our roses, too. Do you know the story about Aphrodite's son? He gave Harpocrates a rose in return for keeping his mother's indiscretions secret." I pause. "I learned that in my Greek Mythology lessons."

"I didn't know that," Mim says, lowering her cup.

"It's only a myth, of course. But Aphrodite's son was lucky he found a confidant in Harpocrates. Imagine going through life having to keep something to yourself. It would place so much burden on your conscience."

Mim's cheeks flush redder. "It would be horrible, I suppose."

"Worse than horrible. If you don't clear your conscience in life, you'll suffer the burden three times worse in death."

"You do?" Mim asks, shifting uncomfortably.

"Yes." I sigh again, then clasp my hands and rest them on the table. "But a conscience is easy to clear. Confiding in another person will lift the burden." I pause because Mim looks mortified. "I suppose revealing a secret can be difficult."

"Impossibly difficult," Mim mutters, clenching her hands around her cup.

I reach across the table and place my hand over hers. "If you need to, you can confide in me. I'm a healer, which is the same as a doctor, so anything you say is confidential."

Mim's mouth parts as though she's about to accept my offer and spill her secret. But then she shakes her head. "Nothing's wrong," she says. "I appreciate the help, but I'm just worried about my mother."

"Of course you are," I say. "Keep in mind what I said, though. There's more truth in myth than we realize."

I'm not disappointed I couldn't coax out her secret. That's why Harpocrates gave us the charm. Mim keeps her secret buried for a reason. But she's so overwhelmed by dark emotions, she can't see the damage keeping a secret does to her. What she needs now is hope, to help her see that she doesn't have to suffer alone and in silence.

"It must be difficult caring for your mother on your own," I say, squeezing her hand. As though sensing it's time to go to work, the charm jumps from the ring. It shapes into a ribbon of light and winds around our hands, binding us together as one. Mim can't see the charm; it's invisible to her. But it exudes hope's calm confidence, and the subtle effect helps Mim relax.

"It's hard," Mim says, squeezing my hand in return. "I show her photos to help jog her memory. Sometimes they work. I also play her favorite music..."

While Mim talks about her mother, the charm fades through her skin to go in search of her secret. In what feels like an eyeblink, an image filters into my mind; Mim and a man who could be her twin. The charm has found the secret, but as Mother warned, it's not pleasant —

Mim's brother died two weeks ago, but Mim keeps his death secret. Her mother asks about him every day, and every day Mim says he'll see her tomorrow. Mim thinks it would be better if her mother died hoping to see her son than grieving his death. She hasn't even told the nursing home staff. She doesn't want anyone telling her mother the truth. But pretending her brother is still alive prevents her from mourning. And guilt about the lie to her mother tears her apart.

It takes all my strength not to react to the secret and keep listening to Mim talk about her mother. I wasn't prepared to hear a secret so sad. Squeezing back tears, I trust the charm to know how much burden to remove and how much hope to give. In my distressed state, I'd mess it up.

The charm skims across Mim's conscience. It removes a layer of grief and guilt then replaces them with the hope I conjured when picking the lavender. It gives just enough hope to balance Mim's emotions, and already Mim's tense grip on my hand relaxes. Then the charm carries the burden it removed to me, and curls back into the ring.

It didn't look like a lot, but the grief and guilt hit my heart with a heavy thud. Easing my hand from Mim's, I clasp my hands, drawing comfort from the warmth in the ring. Mim stops talking and heaves a sigh. Then she picks up her cup and finishes her tea.

"This is lovely," she says. "What did you say it was?"

"Chamomile," I say, forcing a smile.

I'm pleased with her lightened mood. Hope shines in her eyes and her troubled expression fades. She doesn't know that I heard her secret, or that the charm removed some of her burdens. But the hope she received should help her consider whether it's worth keeping her secret. What she decides to do is up to her, but at least now she's not blind to her choices.

The layer of dark emotions throbs through my veins. Needing to trap it in thorns, I stand to fetch the gingko so I can send Mim on her way. Mother steps onto the porch holding two paper packets.

"Chamomile tea for you, and gingko for your mother," she says, handing Mim the packets. "The instructions are in the bags. I'm sorry to hear about your mother. The gingko will help make her last days more pleasurable. Be sure to look after yourself, too."

"I will," Mim says, standing and taking the packets. "Thank you, Rose. The tea has made me feel better already." She hesitates. "I liked your story about the roses. It's given me a lot to think about." Then she hurries from the porch, clutching the packets to her chest.

I'm relieved the hope is working, but I'm more grateful for her swift departure. Clutching at the ache in my heart, I hurry to the garden.

Finding space in a garden where none of Mother's roses grow, I crouch and sow Mim's secret into the soil. The ground around my fingers glows the same golden color as the charm. The emotions I took from Mim leach out, leaving me dizzy with relief. Pulling my hands from the soil, I roll back onto my heels and watch the secret grow.

A stem pushes through the soil. Tall and slender, it sprouts long thorns, green with guilt. Grief glistens like dewdrops on the tips. Standing, I cup my hands around the rose that blooms at the top. Red petals release a heavy scent that makes me think of funerals and death.

Stepping back, I study the rose. I'm elated that my first time hearing a secret proceeded exactly as expected, but I'm also uneasy.

Mim's secret was not pleasant, and I may hear darker secrets than hers. Though I trapped Mim's emotions in thorns, I underestimated the impact those emotions had on me. I hope I haven't also underestimated the strength needed to stay true to my vows.

⚶

Later in the day, I kneel beside Mother and help harvest evening primrose before the light fades. I drop more seed pods than I collect because I'm distracted by an image of Hades laughing at me for thinking it's easy to keep a secret.

"Mother? Have you ever heard a secret that is so bad, you don't have the strength to keep it?"

"Find the strength," Mother says. "Otherwise you'll destroy the hope you gave and suffer the secret's burden."

I glance around the garden. In the dying light, the thorns on Mim's rose appear to weep. But a rose growing behind hers draws my attention. It's grown in that spot longer than I've been alive. The red petals reek with an intoxicating perfume. The stem is thick and covered in large mottled-red thorns that speak of something nasty. I shudder to think what burden they trap and wonder where Mother finds the strength to keep the secret.

I'm about to ask when the rose wilts and the petals turn gray.

"Mother," I gasp, my heart leaping into my throat. "That rose died."

Mother stands and walks over to the rose. "Hope shines a light on choice, but sometimes that's still not enough to stop a secret going to the grave."

Scrambling to my feet, I follow. I've seen roses die before, but it hits harder now that I'm a Secret Keeper. Death doesn't release us from our vows. We're still bound to keep the secret. And we can still suffer the burden.

A milky-white mist rises from the ground in front of me. Mother grabs my arm and pulls me away. The mist takes the shape of a translucent figure; the ghost of an old man. My charm must enhance my sight. I've seen ghosts before, too, but never with such clarity. I didn't realize the depth of three-fold suffering.

The man's eyes sink into his skull and his mouth hangs open as though dragged down by weights. He reaches for the rose, but the thorns stab holes in his fingers. His face contorts as though feeling actual pain. Turning to Mother, he stretches his arms toward her.

"I've heard your secret," Mother says. "Hope showed you choices and you made yours. Accept your fate and go. I will not help you in death." She waves the ghost away. The mist disperses, but leaves a chill in the air.

"They're drawn here by the scent of their rose," Mother says. Pulling out the entire rose plant, she tosses it onto the mulch pile. "They forget that the cause of their misery in death is that they didn't clear their conscience in life. But don't let a ghost's suffering tempt you to hear their secret again. Emotions in a soul can't be balanced like in a conscience. If you try to remove some burden, you'll end up taking the lot and have to fill the soul with hope. That would allow the soul to be reborn, and Hades would lose his servant. He would demand the Keeper's soul to compensate, and Harpocrates would oblige. He values our servitude, but would strip your power to conjure hope to avoid a war with Hades.

Mother's words are as chilling as the cold left by the ghost. I thought Harpocrates would protect his servants, since we pledged our loyalty to him. To learn he'd strip my powers in favor of keeping good relations with Hades leaves a sour taste in my mouth. I wonder if we're nothing more than pawns in a power game between the gods.

&

I fall asleep resenting my commitment to a god who will not protect my allegiance and wake to pouring rain. My resentful thoughts must anger Harpocrates; the rain doesn't ease for three days. If he is showing me what a world without hope looks like, he paints the picture well. I stare in dismay at our wrecked gardens. Then I see the woman.

Fighting the wind to hold an umbrella over her head, she sloshes through the puddles at our front gate. Hurrying outside, I welcome her onto the porch. It's Mrs. Peterson, the elegant yet tight-lipped town mayor's wife. When she steps onto the porch, she sniffs back a sneeze.

Mother appears in the doorway behind me. "Good gracious," she says, taking the umbrella from Mrs. Peterson and shaking it dry. "It's no time to be out in this weather, Mrs. Peterson. Rose, boil the kettle. A pot of tea is in order."

Hurrying inside, I light the burner and set the kettle to boil. Mother and Mrs. Peterson sit at the kitchen table.

"My daughter, Rose," Mother says, introducing me.

"Rose, like the flowers," Mrs. Peterson says, placing her purse on the table and extending her hand. "And just as beautiful."

Blushing at the compliment, I shake her hand. My charm dances around my fingers, alerting me to what I should have guessed from her sniffles. Mrs. Peterson has a secret.

"How is your husband?" Mother asks. "Worn out from running the town, I imagine?"

"His work is his life, and he'll not hear otherwise," Mrs. Peterson says. "But the reason for my intrusion..." Her nose wrinkles, then she sneezes into her hands.

I fetch a box of tissues from the cupboard and slide it across the table. Mrs. Peterson plucks out a tissue and blows her nose. "Thank you, dear," she says. "Such dismal weather. As I was saying, my intrusion — "

"It's no intrusion," Mother says. "Rose? The tea?"

I fetch the kettle and make a pot of herbal tea. When I return to the table, my charm jumps into my hand. It weaves around my fingers as though trying to get my attention. Mrs. Peterson's secret must be bad for my charm to react with such intensity.

"I was driving past and saw your roses," Mrs. Peterson says. "I'd like to buy a bunch. My husband likes a well-presented office. Our usual supplier's flowers are lackluster by comparison."

"The roses aren't for sale," I say, giving my usual response.

Mrs. Peterson purses her lips. "If it's a question of money, my husband will pay well."

I glance at Mother, wondering if she detects the tinge of desperation in Mrs. Peterson's tone like I do. Mother keeps her eyes on Mrs. Peterson, but deep grooves form on her brow.

"I can spare a bunch," Mother says. "But I'll accept no payment. There's as much grace in giving as there is in receiving. Rose, would you go to the garden, please? There's a rosebush among the chamomile that could do with a prune."

Frowning, I glance out the kitchen window. There aren't any rosebushes among the chamomile. Maybe Mother wants me to use my demigod power to grow a bunch of roses. I never have, but it would be the same as growing herbs. I leave the kitchen, but stop at the front door, realizing why Mother asks me to go outside.

She's going to hear Mrs. Peterson's secret. If I've angered Harpocrates, *I* should hear the secret and prove I'm committed to his cause. I don't want to live in a world without hope. I was angry earlier because I don't want to be disposable.

"Mother," I say, turning around. "Could you point out the rosebush? I'm not sure which one you mean."

When Mother joins me in the doorway, I lower my voice to a whisper. "Let me hear her secret."

Mother frowns. "I'd rather you didn't. I don't like the feeling I get from Mrs. Peterson."

"Please, Mother. I know she might have a terrible secret, but I can help her, I know I can."

Mother sighs. "Very well." She looks back at Mrs. Peterson. "I'll return in a moment. Rose will keep you company while you wait."

When Mother goes outside, I hurry back to the kitchen and sit at the table. Mrs. Peterson smiles with indifference and gazes about our kitchen. I wonder how I'll engage her in conversation, when it's clear she has no interest in talking to a teenager.

"I love the color of your dress-suit," I say. "The blue is the same shade as a periwinkle flower." I don't know why I thought of that flower when there are so many others to choose from. The periwinkle is also called the 'flower of death'. The vines were used in wreaths for dead children.

"It's my favorite," Mrs. Peterson says, "but its wool-blend is a poor choice of wardrobe in our current weather."

The umbrella didn't stop the rain soaking her clothes. Her dress-suit gives off a damp animal smell. The rain ruined her makeup, too. It's splotchy in places, especially around her left cheek. Wondering why she applied so much makeup during wet weather, I stand and fetch a towel so she can pat herself dry.

"Appearances must be important to your husband if he sends you out for flowers in dismal weather," I say, handing her the towel.

Mrs. Peterson flinches. "When you live in the public eye, appearance is a necessity, not a luxury." She pats her neck dry, then sips her tea. "The tea is delicious. Peppermint?"

"Yes. Infused with ginger. For your sniffles. I'm sorry to sound rude. I sense something troubles you. It helps to talk, did you know?"

She lowers the cup to the table. "You'll find out, young Rose, that even if you had someone to talk to, some things can't be helped."

"I imagine it would be difficult to find someone to trust when you live in the public eye," I say, sliding into my seat. "But you can talk to me. I can keep a secret."

"Can you now?" she says. "What on earth makes you think I have a secret?"

"I sense it. I also feel it troubles you."

She gives me a tired smile. "You're a strange, sweet child, and I appreciate the sentiment. If you must know, it's a demanding job meeting my husband's expectations. I'll say no more on the matter, but I trust you'll never repeat this conversation."

"You can trust me," I say. "But if you don't confide in somebody, the burden your secret causes you now will haunt you three times worse in death."

"There's more to fear in life than in death, young Rose," she says, ruefully. "If being haunted is the price I'll pay for holding my tongue, then so be it."

She returns to gazing about the kitchen, dismissing me completely. I wonder if I've wrecked the opportunity to cast my charm by being too forward. I need to hold her hand, but doubt she'll welcome the consoling gesture. But her manicured fingernails gives me an idea.

"I've never applied nail polish," I say, "but if I did, what color would you recommend?"

Extending my arm across the table, I offer my hand. Mrs. Peterson looks down her nose at my fingers, but then takes my hand in hers and studies my nails.

"Nothing too bold," she says, tilting my hand from side to side. "I prefer pale pinks or pearl, or there's a lovely shade of ivory I've used..."

She prattles on about the best color for teenage girls, remarks on my ring, picks at my nails and advises how best to shape them. While she talks, my charm wraps around our hands, binding us as one. Then it goes in search of her secret. It feels like forever, but in less than a second, images fill my mind. The charm has found the secret, but it's so shocking, I nearly jerk my hand away —

She's not the happily married wife of the hardworking town mayor. She's the victim of a cruel and calculating narcissist. Her self-esteem has suffered because of his controlling and abusive behavior, and years of verbal and physical abuse have left her a broken woman. With her sense of self-worth corrupted, she's lost view of a life away from her husband. She believes that what she endures behind closed doors is her lot in life.

To learn she's a victim of marital abuse staggers me. It explains the other images that fill my mind. She applies extra makeup to cover a bruise on her cheek. She cowers before her enraged husband because the color of her dress didn't match his tie. Her desperate need to find roses is born from a need to keep her husband happy; protection against his abuse.

I fuel the charm with hope drawn from an image of a blue sky after a clearing storm. The charm whips around Mrs. Peterson's conscience. It removes a thick layer of hopelessness and replaces it with hope. Then it carries the hopelessness back to me.

"If you need more advice," Mrs. Peterson says, releasing my hand, "my nail technician has a shop near to the town hall. Mention that I sent you." She picks up her cup, pauses, then drinks the rest of her tea. When she lowers her cup, her sniffles have dried and her eyes shine with hope.

"Such an extraordinary taste," she says, smacking her lips with pleasure. "It's left me wonderfully clear-headed. I must take some with me."

"Of course." Going to the kitchen bench, I fill a paper packet with a mixture of dried ginger and peppermint leaves. Mrs. Peterson's hopelessness affects my usual care when preparing herbal tea, and I spill leaves on the bench.

Clenching my fingers, I take a deep breath and draw on my charm's power to help keep my emotions balanced. I don't know how Mrs. Peterson managed for so long, living without hope. Praying I gave her enough, I fold the packet and return to the table.

Mother arrives, holding a bunch of red and white roses that fill the kitchen with a heavenly scent. Feeling the hopelessness creep over me again, I catch Mother's eye and signal my desperate need to leave.

"Your roses," Mother says, her tone clipped.

Mrs. Peterson picks up her purse and stands. "Wonderful. And the tea?"

I hand her the packet. "A gift," I say when she opens her purse to pay.

Mrs. Peterson closes her purse and takes the packet. She looks me in the eye, as though reminding me never to repeat our conversation, then turns toward the door.

Mother escorts her out. "The rain has eased," she says, "but mind your speed while driving. The road into town is slippery when wet."

As soon as Mrs. Peterson leaves, I push past Mother and run to the garden. Dropping to my knees, I sow Mrs. Peterson's secret into the mud. The flooded soil reflects the charm's golden glow. When all Mrs. Peterson's hopelessness has drained out of me, I roll back on my heels and watch the secret grow.

A stem pushes through the ground, tall and thick with long thorns that droop as though they've lost the will to live. The rosebud that blooms at the top unfurls blood-red petals, with perfume so heavy it gets caught in my throat.

Standing, I stare at the rose. I'm supposed to listen without judgment, but I can't ignore what I heard. Mrs. Peterson faces more harm if she doesn't reveal her secret. The hope helped clear her mind, but will it be enough to encourage her to seek help?

✍

I toss and turn all night, unable to get Mrs. Peterson off my mind. Thinking about her bruised cheek makes me lie awake with worry. Even if I broke my vows and revealed the secret for her, it wouldn't help. I'd destroy the hope I gave her, and she needs all the hope she can get.

Needing a slap of cold night air to clear my gloomy thoughts, I slip out of bed and go outside. The rain has stopped and the heavy clouds part, letting moonlight stream over the gardens. Taking a deep breath, I search the night shadows for Mrs. Peterson's rose. It's bathed a milky-white glow from the moon, but the light shifts as though moved by the wind. Wondering what causes that effect, I walk toward the rose. When I get closer, my heart stops.

It's not moving moonlight. It's the ghost of Mrs. Peterson. She hovers next to her wilted rose that's gray from death. Gone is the elegant woman who sat at our kitchen table. An unnatural force squishes her features, making her look like a lump of melted wax.

I stare at her, frozen in fright. How could I miss the signs that foretold her death? I compared the color of her dress-suit to the 'flower of death'. Mother warned her about the slippery roads. Did she have a car accident while driving home? Whatever happened, despite the hope I gave her, she didn't reveal her secret. She can't have, because she suffers her burden in death.

Three-fold hopelessness pours like black ink from her hollow eye sockets. Her mouth yawns wide, expelling the choking scent of her rose. Nothing I envisioned comes close to what stands before me. But what if I'm to blame? What if, in my haste to cast the charm, I didn't give her enough hope?

"I'm sorry," I whisper, creeping toward her. "I don't know what happened, but you don't deserve to suffer in death when you suffered so much in life. I can help you. I can fix this."

Her soul now belongs to Hades, but I can still hear her secret and fill her soul with hope. It means Hades may lose his servant. And he'll demand my soul to compensate. But if I'm responsible for Mrs. Peterson's death, that's a consequence I'm willing to accept.

I think about all the things that give me hope and fuel the charm with so much power it shines like two suns. Then I reach for Mrs. Peterson's hands. Her fingers find mine, icy tendrils that numb my skin. A strange blue light flows into my charm, turning its golden light a frosty turquoise. With increased power, the charm whips around our hands, binding us as one.

Mrs. Peterson tilts my hand and pokes at my fingernails. Though distracted by the icy pricks on my fingers, I urge the charm to find her secret again. Powered by the blue light, it works faster than usual. In a split second, the secret I heard when sitting in the kitchen with Mrs. Peterson fills my mind again.

This time, the images are so lifelike they make me think I'm experiencing them. When her husband strikes her cheek, I flinch as though struck. But then a different image appears, a new secret —

Still alive but soaked from the rain, Mrs. Peterson walks up a spiral staircase. She clutches Mother's roses to her chest like a shield. Mr. Peterson stands on the top step, his face a furious shade of red. When she shows him the roses, he knocks them from her hands. Then he shouts that a wife who appears in public looking like a drowned rat will embarrass him.

Encouraged by the hope, Mrs. Peterson scoffs at his expectations. She says if he wishes to remain married, she'll decide if her appearance is appropriate.

Mr. Peterson strikes her face with a backhand that knocks her down the stairs. Her head hits the bottom step with a crack —

The flow of images ends as quick as her life did. Numb with shock, I try to fathom what I saw. Instead, I see Mr. Peterson again, but his features are fuzzy, like I'm looking through a transparent veil. I can see enough to know he's talking on the telephone. Hear enough to know what he said. *Slipped on the steps. A tragic accident.* Then the image fades.

The blood drains from my face, making me feel as cold as Mrs. Peterson. I can't see her eyes, but I can sense her somber stare. The truth about her death burns through the charm, and screeches of "*liar*" and "*murderer*" ring in my ears. It's Mrs. Peterson screaming, though her mouth is shut. Again she's been silenced, this time forever. But her husband can't silence me.

Determined to end her suffering, I urge my charm to remove all the burden. It's like scraping away layers of sludge, but, powered by the blue light, the charm collects it all. Then it delivers hope so pure, the brightness hurts my eyes. But I'm not prepared when my charm returns with the burden.

Triple the amount of hopelessness drags me to the pits of despair, draining my will to live. But my determination to see her husband punished for her murder anchors me to life. Pulling my hands from Mrs. Peterson, I stumble backward to escape the lure of death.

Filled with hope, Mrs. Peterson's grotesque features melt away. She appears as she did when she sat at our table, elegant, spirits lifted, and taking pleasure in sipping our tea. Then she fades, like mist dispersing in a breeze.

"Rose?"

Mother's voice drives the deadness from my limbs. Dropping to my knees, I dig into the mud and bury both of Mrs. Peterson's secrets. The ground around my fingers glows turquoise, my charm's new color. Two stems burst through the soil. They weave around each other like climbing vines, sprouting long black thorns that droop with three-fold hopelessness. Above my head, a rose blooms at the top of each stem. The petals on each are an unearthly frosty blue.

"Rose? What happened?"

The shock in Mother's voice sends tears streaming down my cheeks. "She's dead. Mrs. Peterson is dead."

Mother crouches beside me, her hand flying to her throat. "When? How?"

I claw my fingers into the mud, wanting to scream Mrs. Peterson's secrets into the night. Instead, I imagine Hades again, his expression smug, as though expecting me to break my vows. But if I do, I'll break Mrs. Peterson's trust and destroy the hope I gave her. That would be like killing her again.

Mother's words about finding the strength whisper through my mind, and I realize where my strength lies. Wiping my eyes, I clamber to my feet. "Mrs. Peterson didn't deserve to suffer in death. I heard her secret again, removed her burden and filled her soul with hope."

"And condemned yours." Standing, Mother grabs my elbow and pulls me away from the two roses. "What were you thinking, child? If Mrs. Peterson chooses rebirth, Hades will demand your soul to compensate. I warned you of this. Harpocrates will strip your ability to conjure hope to avoid a war with Hades."

Without hope, I'll lose my will to live and hand my soul to Hades by taking my own life. Even revealing Mrs. Peterson's secret wouldn't help. I'd destroy her hope and prevent her from being reborn, but Hades would still get my soul. I'd suffer the three-fold hopelessness I trapped in the thorns and I wouldn't survive that. But I can save my soul another way. There's something Hades and I have in common.

"Hades won't come for me," I say. "He values upholding vows above everything. And Mrs. Peterson can't be reborn because we are bound as one. While I live in this world, she'll stay in the underworld." In Elysium, where pure souls get sent.

I fiddle with my ring. The blue light that changed the charm's color has also turned the gold band a deep shade of turquoise. I've guessed the source of the blue light's power, but I don't think either god expected this. "Harpocrates could strip my powers so I can't conjure hope, but while I keep Mrs. Peterson's secret, I'll always have hope. Look." I hold out my hand and tease my charm from the ring. It jumps into my hand, a flickering bluish-gold flame.

"It's drawing hope from Mrs. Peterson," I say, "but that hope contains Hades' power, which is why it's so strong. Harpocrates would be a fool to abandon me now. With hope this powerful, we could win every battle against darkness and despair."

Mother doesn't look happy, but I've never been more certain. Like all the Secret Keepers before me, Mother included, my strength lies in the commitment to my vows. It means Mr. Peterson will escape punishment in this world, but he won't escape Hades.

I have to listen without judgment, but in the underworld, Hades' judges don't. When they judge Mr. Peterson' soul with the secret he keeps, they'll send him straight to Tartarus. I can't imagine a better punishment for a man who killed his wife.

✍ ✍ ✍

Initial feedback

I liked the concept and characters. The world could use a good deal more context — who are they and how did they get to be secret keepers? What are the rules (which seem to unfold a little too just-in-time)? Who is directing her? All readers were surprised to find that this was connected to our contemporary world with cars and police. The ghosts didn't seem a clear fit either. The piece is quite a bit longer than it needs to be (perhaps 2x as long), and the prose could use polish in places, though I liked the imagery.

Her journey is not really foreshadowed. There isn't enough foundation for her late story decisions. The whole piece seems to somewhat undermine the nature of secret keeping. The resolution was both nice and perhaps a little too perfect/convenient a wrapup.

I think there's a lot of promise here, but that the piece needs considerable reworking, context, and concision.

Author's intent

What do you think the story's about?
What emotions are you trying to evoke?

I would like this story to portray a person's inner strength to uphold their values, and to be willing to use that strength to help others in need, even if it means losing what they hold most dear. The emotions I want to invoke are a sense of trust, and loyalty, in herself and in her relationships with others. My original thoughts about this story came from a zodiac prompt and I've focused on the qualities of Taurus, as I am Taurus, and hope to show those qualities in the story.

Author's note

I was pleased to receive a rewrite opportunity, because I wrote the story with this magazine in mind. Having worked through a revision process on previous stories, I was eager for the challenge. However, the initial feedback left me feeling overwhelmed. In my mind, my world made sense, but I was wrong on many levels. I'd imagined a mystical, magical place within our real world, similar to the mythical Brigadoon, a place only stumbled upon when needed. As I discovered through the rewrite, my combined worlds didn't work, so I had to rethink everything.

The biggest question was how my characters came to be "Secret Keepers", and I had to delve into their history. I changed my characters to demi-gods, because it's a familiar concept to have demi-gods residing in a modern world. My secret keeping concept and the rose symbol also fit with the Greek god Harpocrates, and that led to a new story based on Greek mythology.

The rewrite opened my eyes to the importance of world-building. This was my first attempt at fantasy, and to make the world rules work, I had to cut much of the original story. I was sad to lose many elements, particularly the enchanted forest, but this is what the rewrite required. I also felt I lost the original softness about the story, a result of trying to make everything work.

I originally wanted to portray a person's inner strength to uphold their values, and to be willing to use that strength to help others in need, even if it means losing what they hold most dear. The emotions I wanted to invoke were a sense of trust, and loyalty, in my main character and her relationships with others. Though the final version is vastly different to the original version, I think I've stayed true to my original character intentions.

Overall, I'm happy with the final version, though it ended rather darker than I intended. I also loved the Greek mythology, and enjoyed learning more about the Gods I chose for the story. The revision process was challenging, and many times I thought I couldn't deliver. With persistence on my part, and patience from the publisher, we eventually got there.

Editor's note

When she submitted this story, Pauline had already been through my editorial wringer a few times, so she knew what to expect. That's a helpful thing. I'm keenly aware of how painful the process can be, and the fact that authors (and editors) can burn out after a few rounds of back and forth. There are times when I feel the author and I have reached a point of diminishing returns on revision, and I've accepted a piece that's good enough, but not — in my mind — as good as it could be. Happily, for this story, I'd already established the fact that Pauline was tough, willing to work hard, and capable of excellent work. That proved helpful in a story with an interesting but not fully fleshed-out world.

Worldbuilding is a bit of an art. You need enough to establish what's happening and where, a logical structure to it all, and not so much detail that it crowds out the story. Here, I and my second readers all agreed that there was a strong core to the story, and a good intent in the resolution. I liked the characters, but didn't feel the world and its magic really made sense. That was the starting point for the revision. We went back and forth several times fine-tuning elements of the world before we got to a version that I felt made sense, and where queries about the worldbuilding didn't detract from the primary story — which Pauline had made clear she wanted to be character-based. It took some time, and I suspect there are things I could have articulated more clearly. I think it was worth it, though, to end up with a story with a really interesting world and setting. Plus, I learned about Harpocrates! I thought I knew Greek mythology pretty well, but there's always something new to pick up.

The emotional part of the story was always strong. It changed over the versions, and there were aspects of the ending that needed some shoring up along the way, but the emotions and character were always part of the charm of the piece, and I think that aspect remained. Pauline notes that she's sorry to have lost some of the softness of the piece, and I'm sorry about that too. That is, I liked the way the piece ended up, but an editor always wants to author's intent to shine through — it's their story, not ours. In the end, I think virtually every line of this story changed along the way, and its success is down to Pauline's resilience and tenacity.

The Secret Keepers

The enchanted forest that surrounds our home casts a long summer shadow over the Garden of Secrets, but there's still enough light to end the day with my favorite game. I wander along the path that winds between the flowerbeds and stop at a rose stem as tall as my shoulders. Cupping my hands around the single bud that blooms at the top, I drink in its perfume and try to guess it's secret.

"A first kiss," I say, imagining virgin lips as soft as the pink petals.

Mother looks up from her weeding. "Your intuition grows stronger."

I smile, pleased she notices my improved skills. My heart's desire is to be a Secret Keeper like her and I practice as much as I can. Continuing along the path, my gaze rests on a blood-red snapdragon that sprouted from the secret she buried yesterday. Closing my eyes, I breathe deep to draw out the flower's secret.

"Oh dear," I say, feigning shock. "Did someone read a private diary?"

Mother laughs. "It was not accidental."

Opening my eyes, I laugh with her and continue along the path. She can never reveal the secrets she buries — to do so would break the secret-keeping enchantments that keep us bound to this world. My guessing game does no harm. Technically, it's not telling. Stopping at a yellow tulip, I stroke its petals and let my thoughts drift. I imagine rising and falling as though I'm floating on an ocean.

"A journey?" A second flower blooms on the same stem. "A surprise visit to a family member, perhaps?"

"Or a premonition of death."

My eyes widen, wondering why Mother reveals this flower's secret, but she stares at another tulip, one that has wilted and died. Sensing her sadness, I hurry to her side. Whether the flower died because the secret was revealed or discovered, we will never know. Either way, Mother's help to keep the secret safe is no longer needed.

Mother plucks the blackened flower from the stem and lays it on her palm. "It takes strength to guard a secret," she says, her voice rumbling like a brewing storm, "but even with our help, some secrets carry malice that weakens the soul if kept too long."

I wonder about premonitions and death. "Perhaps some secrets should not be guarded."

"It is not for us to decide." She closes her fingers around the tulip, crushes the petals, then crouches and buries the remains in the soil.

I look around the garden. Many of Mother's flowers stand taller than my head and make me giddy from their perfume if I stand near them for too long. Though she sows the secrets into the soil, her heart still carries the memory. Good secrets fill her with joy and iron the creases from her brow. But bad secrets drain her energy and make her look older than her years. Her recent flowers are small and do not cast as strong a scent. I worry her secret-keeping days are drawing to an end.

I've been diligent in learning the craft of secret-keeping, but I wish Mother showed more trust in my abilities. I am strong with youth and can easily carry a burden. Mother, however, is not young. Sometimes, after hearing a bad secret, she retires to bed for the rest of the day. I wonder if the depth of her sadness today is because she holds too many secrets close to her heart. Perhaps there is a limit to how much burden she can carry.

Mother stands and wipes her hair off her face, leaving a smudge of black soil on her brow. She must have buried her grief, too, for her eyes sparkle again. I reach for her hand, wanting to share some of my strength with her, but she looks across the garden to the darkening forest.

"We have a visitor," she says.

An elderly woman clutching a gray shawl around tiny shoulders emerges from the trees. She appears bewildered, and somewhat disorientated, as though she knows she needs to be somewhere, but does not know why and is not sure of the way. When she sees our house, she startles. I suppress a giggle. Her surprise is the usual response from those who seek relief from the burden they carry. We are not known before they come and not remembered after they leave, for our home is reminiscent of a fledgling Brigadoon.

The woman hurries toward us, her lower lip quivering. Sensing her secret is about to spill, I step forward. "Mother, let me hear this secret. I'm ready, I know I am."

"I'll welcome this woman," Mother says.

I step back, ashamed by my brashness. "Of course, but — " What if this woman's secret is unpleasant? Mother's strength has been tested enough today. "Do you think it wise so close to a loss?"

Mother gives me a reassuring smile. "This woman has what I need."

She walks forward to greet the woman, leaving me to question my readiness. I can't yet tell if the woman's secret is good or bad like Mother can. The forest shares clues, but only when in the mood. I look toward the trees. They wave their leaves and tease me with their secret language I'm yet to understand.

Sighing, I walk back through the garden. Mother has a gift of insight that might take years to develop. The woman may have what she needs, but I ache for more chances to practice. There are days where strangers arrive by the dozen, but there are also weeks where nobody appears. Mother says I'll learn much through observation, but missed opportunities, like this woman tonight, makes me restless with impatience to improve my skills.

Mother guides the woman to a sun-weary wooden bench at the side of the garden. I continue to the kitchen. I'll prepare a meal so Mother can rest when she finishes. And fetch a lantern so the woman can find her way home in the dark. Before leaving the garden, however, I study the single pink carnation that grows at the entrance.

I exclude this carnation from my guessing game. I suspect the flower's secret has something to do with me because the carnation is also sixteen years old. I sometimes lay awake at night and worry my fate rests with the carnation's fate. I search the petals for signs of death. Finding none, I scold myself. My worry stems from Mother's earlier comment about a premonition of death. I've nothing to fear. The carnation is as healthy as I am.

✍

It's well into the night when Mother returns to the house. I expect her to be weary, but she enters our sitting room with a flourish. She carries the woman's shawl which she casts around my shoulders.

"For you," she says, "for your patience in my time of need. I am well aware of your eagerness to begin your life as a secret keeper."

I run my hand over the shawl, expecting to feel ordinary lamb's wool. My fingers detect feather and flax. I gaze at shawl with wonder.

"Her most precious possession," Mother says. "I did not want to accept the payment, for her secret was all I needed. But there is as much grace in receiving as there is in giving. I could not say no."

"Oh, Mother," I say, twirling on my toes and admiring the shawl from every angle. "I shall treasure this forever."

Sparkles of joy dance in Mother's eyes, but I suspect it is the secret that makes her eyes shine. "It is late, and you have not eaten," I say, "but I think it wise you sow the woman's secret before it spills."

"I'd like to hold this secret for the night," Mother says with a smile. "It is not every day my old heart is filled with such a blessing."

"Then let us eat," I say, trying not to worry that her heart has grown too old to hold another secret, no matter how much happiness it brings.

Clutching the shawl around my shoulders, I fetch soup and bread and join Mother at the kitchen table. She laughs and lavishes praise on the simple meal I prepared. When we finish eating, she brings out the music box and cranks the handle. We sing and dance to the tinkling strum that sounds like the *pitter-pattering* of rain on the roof. Then, though it's late, she pulls me to the spare room at the back of the house where we spend hours admiring gold bracelets, pearl necklaces, exquisite wines from foreign lands, even though neither of us cares for such luxuries. Both born in the earth sign, we are practical by nature and prefer the beauty found in simple handcrafts.

"Gifts of gratitude or bribes for our silence," Mother says, her mouth still curved in a smile.

Infected by her good spirits, I giggle to think we need to be bribed to hold our tongues. Our souls feed on the good we can do for others, no matter how heavy the burden on our hearts.

"Can we cross the forest and visit the market," I ask, dangling the bracelet from my finger. "Our bed blankets need another layer of wool, and I have collected enough feathers to make another pillow. This bracelet would be more than enough to purchase the material we need."

"And some lace for yourself. You'll need a new dress to match the shawl if you're to take over from me. You can't greet strangers in clothes black with soil."

My heart leaps. "Oh, Mother, do you mean — ? I clasp my hands together, struck by self-doubt. "Are you sure I'm ready?"

Mother's eyes twinkle. "You are more ready than I was at your age. Besides, it's past time for me to rest and reflect." She claps her hands. "Sleep now. Tomorrow will be a busy day."

I hurry to bed, anxiety and excitement twisting into knots inside my stomach. Unable to sleep, I imagine making a dress to match the shawl. I'll ask Mother to help. My deft fingers are better at threading needles than her aged hands, but I've never sewn lace before. I wonder how she would manage if I wasn't here, but that tempts me to wonder about my father whom I don't know. I fall asleep dreaming of feathers and lace and gifts of gratitude that can't be bartered or sold.

✍

I wake to a note from Mother saying she's gone for a walk in the forest, and a strange woman wandering through our garden. Remembering that secret-keeping is now my responsibility, I change into my cleanest dress and hurry outside.

The woman startles when I appear. From her confused expression, she's not sure if she's awake or in a dream. The dark circles beneath her eyes suggest her secret weighs heavy on her heart. Sharing a reassuring smile, I wave my hand and motion her to the bench by the garden.

The woman sits at the end of the bench. She gazes at me with a helpless expression, so afraid to speak. Sitting with her, I hold out my hand, palm open. I do not speak, for words are not what this woman needs. I offer her someone who can listen, someone she can trust, someone who will cast no judgment. I offer her the chance to be brave.

The woman places her hand in mine. I close my fingers and give my strength freely so she can find hers. The forest sighs and a ribbon of light winds around our hands, binding us as one. Then, like a cloudburst on a stormy day, the secret spills from the woman's lips and she pours her heart into mine.

Her bottled-up emotions are so intense tears well in my eyes. It's the first time I've heard a secret so sad and it wrenches at my heart. I need to be strong and keep my composure if I'm to help this woman. But it's hard, so hard, not to give in to weakness and let my heart break.

By the time the woman stops talking, I'm so pent up with sorrow, my hand lies limp in hers. But the woman's troubled expression has gone and her eyes shine with relief. It's how it should be, how it will always be — a secret keeper's role is to relieve the secret bearer's burden. I find the strength to squeeze her hand then close my eyes and listen to the forest. The trees croon a melody that helps to numb the deadness in my heart.

Silence falls — the sound of a lifeless heart. Then the forest heaves another sigh that flicks my hair across my cheek. I open my eyes. The woman is gone. Mother sits in her place.

"A token of her gratitude," she says, handing me a dainty, silver necklace. "Bury her secret soon so it doesn't eat into your heart."

It already has. I feel it, a gaping wound that bleeds loss and lies. I clasp the necklace around my neck then stand and go the garden. Falling to my knees, I pound the woman's secret into the soil. A tear escapes my eye and drops onto the ground. Where it lands, the soil breaks open. A stem emerges and a single pink peony blooms. Sweet perfume fills the air.

I lean toward the flower, knowing it has what I need, but hesitate. "Is it wrong to breathe in the healing scent when the woman needs it more than I?"

"You are bound to the woman," Mother says. "Your strength is her strength."

The woman's husband won't return from the war for another three months. I wonder how I'll stay strong for so long. I press my hand to my stomach, feeling as empty as the woman.

"It still hurts, though I buried it deep," I say.

Mother touches my shoulder. "Some secrets do. But there is more pain in two losses than one."

It helps to know Mother guesses the secret I buried. And she is right. Two losses would be worse. The woman's replies to her husband's letters are lies, but he cannot learn about the loss of their baby while on the battlefield. Grief could fire a bullet that prevents him from coming home. And he must come home. They need each other to heal.

Brushing the soil from my hands, I touch the necklace around my throat and silently promise the woman I'll guard her secret well. Mother smiles and wanders along the path. She stops at the pink carnation at the entrance to the garden. Standing, I join her.

"My most guarded secret," Mother says, mischief playing at the corners of her mouth. "But I wonder why my daughter has never tried to guess its secret when she is so good at her game."

"I'm afraid it's about me," I admit.

"You never need fear this secret," she says.

Curiosity gets the better of me. Letting my thoughts drift, I imagine Mother walking out of the forest into a quiet seaside village. I don't know the location. The forest has many paths, but they only take us where we need to go. I wonder if this village is where Mother ventured on her mysterious early morning walk.

Sinking deeper into my thoughts, I walk in Mother's shoes and see through her eyes. The path leads to a road that runs alongside a lonely beach. Seaweed, discarded by the ebbing tide, litters the stretch of sand. A narrow jetty points to an orange horizon. On the other side of the jetty, a salt-scalded timber house faces the sea.

I peer through an open window. A man with my eyes sits on a stool in front of a large canvas. He holds an easel in one hand, and paints a picture of a forest — our forest. A face blends into the leaves — Mother's.

My heart leaps and crashes into my ribs. This man is my father. But I'm hesitant to reveal what I discovered. I want Mother to say it in case I'm wrong. "Who do you know that lives by the sea?"

"Someone that I hope you will meet one day."

"Do you still guard his secret? Is that why you've never mentioned him?"

"No. His flower died long ago."

"But he remembers."

Mother breathes a sigh of longing. "Only in his dreams."

I reach for her hands and clasp them in mine. "Oh, Mother, why don't you go to him if that's what your heart desires?"

"I am needed here. I still have secrets to guard."

I let go of her hands and touch the carnation. "Including this secret?"

"Especially this secret."

"But, Mother, why — "

She holds up her hand. "No more questions. All I will say is that some gifts are more precious than shawls or necklaces."

My cheeks flush with heat. I'm the secret she keeps, but it is not my place to ask why she does not tell my father about me. I look around the garden at the many flowers that bloom. Mother guards so many secrets. Perhaps she does ache to reveal my identity, but can't because we are of this world, and my father is of another.

The forest whispers in soft *shush shushes* and I imagine it saying *one day, one day, one day.* Maybe that day is closer than I think now Mother has handed over the secret-keeping to me.

✍

Pink sunrises signal summer's end and Autumn's breath chills the air. The forest shakes leaves to the ground and the nights grow long and dark. Mother's flowers die one by one until only her most guarded secret remains. My flowers, however, grow in number. Having proved myself capable, Mother ventures into the forest more and more. She always returns happy, and that makes me yearn to meet my father more.

Clinging to the hope that *one day* will appear soon, I wander through the garden, touching my flowers to remind them that no matter what happens, I'll keep their secrets safe. But I'm struck by a blast of wind that whips my hair across my face. Startled, I look at the trees in the forest. Their limbs bend and twist as though clutched by a malevolent force. The leaves, stripped from the branches, scream a warning as they whip though the air.

A man emerges from the trees. A broad-rimmed hat conceals his face. A duffel bag hangs off his left shoulder. When he steps into the sunlight, his shadow drags behind him. It's an odd shape and appears as though the man casts two shadows. As he walks closer, the shadows merge back into one, making me wonder if I imagined what I saw.

Mother appears at my side. "Go inside."

Her sharp tone sends a chill up my spine. I've no doubt the secret this man carries is bad, but there are too many reasons why it should be Mother who goes inside.

I place my hand on her arm. "Mother, no. Secret keeping is my responsibility now. Don't stay bound to this world by accepting another secret."

She shakes off my hand. "Do as I say. Now."

She pushes me toward the house then strides forward and greets the man. Alarmed by her behavior, I hurry inside. I watch from the kitchen window with mounting apprehension. And pray she has the strength to carry this man's burden.

Mother motions the man to the bench beside the garden. The man sits and offers Mother his duffel bag. He must be desperate to ease his burden if he offers to pay first. Mother accepts the bag but does not open it. She drops the bag on the grass near her feet.

I wish the wind would carry the man's voice toward the house so I can overhear the secret he tells Mother. I don't know how that would affect the enchantments, but I'm desperately afraid. As the man speaks, Mother's face pales and darkness falls over the garden. I look to the forest for reassurance, but it holds its breath and remains as still and silent as I do.

The man stops talking, stands and walks back toward the forest, pushing that odd double shadow in front of him. Mother remains seated, her face ashen. Ignoring her wishes, I run from the house. Reaching the table, I rest my hand on her shoulder. It's like touching stone.

"Mother?"

She stands and hurries to the far side of the garden where no other flowers grow. Dropping to her knees, she digs into the soil, scooping and turning and tilling until her fingers bleed.

I follow and hover by her side, torn between wanting her to bury the secret deep and longing to yank her away. When she finishes and stands, I stifle a gasp. Blood drips from her fingers when the soil grazed her skin. She steps backward and motions me away.

A stem pushes through the soil. It grows fast and furious and is taller than any of her previous flowers. A lily blooms at the top. Its petals are the purest white I've ever seen.

I don't understand Mother's reaction. A white lily symbolizes purity or innocence. But then another stem pushes through the ground. It winds around the first stem, climbing like a strangling vine. When it reaches the top of the lily, a purple-blue flower blooms. I draw in a sharp breath. Aconite. Beautifully scented. Deceptively deadly. The flower that represents caution and death.

"A double secret," Mother says, answering my unasked question. "I forbid you to guess what it is."

"If the secret is so bad, perhaps you should not guard it."

She looks in the direction the man walked. "If I reveal the secret, the man will die."

She clutches her side and bends over.

"Mother? What's wrong?"

"Nothing." But she squeezes her eyes shut and her face contorts with pain.

Fear grips my heart. "Mother, come. You must rest."

I take her hand but notice vein-like marks on her fingers that are not left from ingrained soil. They spread across her palms and wrap around her fingers, in the same manner the second stem strangled the first. "Mother? Your hands."

She opens her eyes and peers at her hands. Her eyes widen. "The danger is graver than I thought."

Her knees buckle as though they cannot bear her weight. I sling my arm around her waist for support and encourage her back to the house. By the time I tuck her into bed, the black veins circle her wrists. Her face pales, as white as the lily.

I fetch a wet cloth and wipe away the sweat that beads on her forehead. "Mother, what do I do?"

She looks at me through glazed eyes. "Nothing. Do nothing."

How can she tell me to do nothing when she is fading faster than a dying flower? I hover over her, helpless. The black veins creep up her arms. When they reach her shoulders, she closes her eyes and turns restlessly in her bed. Then the veins wrap around her throat in the same way the thorny vine strangles the lily, making her breaths grow short.

She opens her mouth but no words escape. It's as though she's being silenced; is that a clue to the secret? It must be. She is bound to the man. He must also be forced to remain silent. But silent about what?

Desperate to help Mother, I hurry back to the garden and pick handfuls of chamomile flowers that grow freely along the borders. Returning to the house, I crush the flowers to release their essence and place them around Mother's neck.

The scent helps Mother fall into a fitful sleep. I pace the room, wondering what to do next. Mother forbade me to guess the secret, but I need to know what I fight. Silently begging for her forgiveness, I run back to the garden. When I reach the entrance, I pause and gaze at the carnation. If Mother dies, her secret will die with her. The man she loves will never know she is not a dream. And he will never know he has a daughter.

Filled with fresh determination to save Mother from the unknown evil that threatens her life, I hurry to the lily. I'm horror-struck by its appearance. The second vine has swelled into a mass of thorns that completely cover the lily. A foul stench wafts from the ground, reeking of death and decay. Eyes watering, I study the monstrosity. Two stems, one flower. Swallowing my fear, I touch it with my hand.

A thorn bites my finger, drawing blood. Then an unimaginable pain travels up my arm and stabs my heart in a frenzied rage. Staggering backward, I trip on a rock at the edge of the garden and fall heavily to the ground. An image fills my mind — the slash of a blade silencing a scream. Gasping, I clutch my hands to my throat and think of sunsets and daisies to help force the horrific image from my mind. The pain subsides. Scrambling to my feet, I stare at the strangling vine. I know its secret. Murder.

I don't understand why the man would conceal a murder, but he must have a reason. Wiping tears from my eyes, I search for the lily within the mass of thorns. There is no place I can touch it without being stabbed by the razor-sharp points. My gaze drifts to the duffel bag that lies on the ground near the bench. Maybe I can guess the man's secret and why he remains silent from the contents inside the bag?

I hurry to the bag and pick it up. It's light, which is unexpected. Opening the bag, I peer inside, expecting to find something valuable that would serve as payment to Mother. But the bag is empty.

I turn the bag over and study it from all angles. Maybe the man is poor, or was robbed on the way here? But why give Mother the bag if he knew it contained nothing? Perhaps the bag is payment. It's made of hemp and worth a good barter. Confused, I let my thoughts drift. My mind remains stubbornly blank. There's nothing, just like inside the bag.

My mind races. Maybe nothing is the clue? I toss that thought around with the man. What if he has nothing to do with the murder, but is a witness to the crime? But why is he forced to remain silent? Is it because he knows the killer's identity and was threatened with death if he tells? If that's true, why not go to the police and seek assistance from them? Why seek help from Mother?

I clutch the bag to my chest and let my thoughts swirl through the emptiness inside. The man must be under terrible duress to seek our world's help to guard his secret. What harm would he come to if he reported a murder? Unless he has nothing to prove his innocence and risks being framed for a crime he didn't commit?

The forest stirs. The trees wave their branches and whip up a hot wind that blows leaves into the garden. Turning my face to the wind, I breathe in the heat and wonder what the forest tries to tell me. The leaves swirl around my legs, landing in a pile that buries my feet. I imagine a winding path that leads me through the heart of the forest, ending at a farm on the outskirts of a large town. Is something buried on the farm?

Unsure, I go back to the lily and study the flower. It hangs lifeless within the thorny mass, but where there should be five petals, there are only four. The reek of decay continues to rise from the ground. I stare at the soil. It rises in a mound where the stems push through the earth. I wonder if the missing petal represents a missing body?

The body must be buried on a farm, in a field perhaps. And maybe it's the evidence needed to prove the man's innocence. If I could find the grave, I could reveal where it's located because it was Mother who heard the man's secret and I've only guessed it, so technically it wouldn't be telling. I can save her without breaking the secret-keeping enchantments. Why else would the forest show me the farm?

But Mother said the man would die if she revealed his secret. Do I risk his life to save Mother's? Or is there a way I can save them both?

I hurry back to Mother. Her condition has worsened. She still sleeps, but her ragged breaths fill the room and she burns with a feverish sweat. Picking up the cloth, I dampen it with water from the bowl and wipe over her forehead and cheeks. The veins have spread to her cheek, appearing like three long scratches as though something sharp raked her skin. I wipe over the veins, then I press my hand to Mother's forehead.

"Forgive me, Mother, for I cannot do nothing," I whisper.

Leaving the house, I run through the garden and race across the clearing to the forest. The trees bow their branches as I approach. When I enter the forest, the branches part, revealing a path. I've traveled through the forest many times to collect feathers and kindling for our fire or to visit the markets in the village to barter for wares. Those paths were always welcoming and made my heart sing to be at one with the magic of the forest. But the path I travel on now is dark and fills me with trepidation. I fear what lies ahead, but I must go on. Mother's fate depends on me.

The path winds through the heart of the forest, growing more gloomy with every step. The trees fall silent, but the branches continue to part, showing me the way. As I walk, dark thoughts about strangling vines and wilting flowers enter my mind, making me tremble with fear for my safety. But I put Mother's safety ahead of mine and force myself to go on.

The path ends at a field of rye that stretches to a farmhouse in the distance. The tall stems, heavy with seed, sway in a light breeze. I hesitate, for something about the field causes me alarm I have never felt and cannot describe. But I am not alone.

A farmhand, the man who came to see Mother, works in the field near where I stand. His face is still hidden beneath his broad-rimmed hat. He still casts that strange double shadow. Wielding a scythe, he slashes at heads of the rye, scattering the seed. Then he parts the stems and kicks the ground with his boot. Next, he crouches and from the way he moves his arms, he appears to rake the seed through the soil with his fingers. Then he stands and steps forward and repeats his laborious chore.

The sound of a vehicle draws my attention. A truck speeds along a road that borders the field. It skids to a stop near the farmhand, kicking up a plume of dust. A tall man with a crop of red hair, the owner of the field I presume, gets out of the truck and strides across the field.

The farmhand stops his slashing, and stands with a clenched fist as the owner approaches. The air between them shimmers with heat; if angry words are spoken, I can't hear what is said. Then the owner yanks the scythe from the farmhand and slashes at the rye in a manner that reminds me of the slashing blade. Handing the scythe back to the farmhand, he gestures to the field on the other side of the road and waves the farmhand away.

Clutching the scythe, the farmhand trudges toward the field. The owner watches him leave, then turns and looks in my direction. He stares too long with narrow, cruel eyes, making me worry that the scent of chamomile on my fingers carried to him across the field. When he steps toward my hiding place, I crouch and hide within the rye.

When the man is almost upon me, I gasp. The soft exhale catches the man's attention. He peers through the rye, searching for the source of the sound. I clamp my hand over mouth to stifle an exclamation. Three scratches mark the man's cheek, similar to the scratches that appeared on Mother's cheek. Is this what the forest wanted me to see? Is this cruel-eyed man the killer?

The trees in the forest wave their branches and stir up a wind that thrashes the rye. The seed heads bang against each other, making a clicking noise that makes the owner's face turn white. He stops and stares at something beyond me, then strides back across the field, jumps into his truck and speeds away.

I peer over the heads of the rye and search the sea of green. The farmhand is on the far side of the next field, a dark stroke on the landscape. He, too, watches the owner drive away. Then he continues to slash and part the rye and crouch to rake his fingers through the dirt.

I wonder why he stays if he knows the owner is a killer? Is that another part of the double secret I'm yet to unravel? The forest doesn't call me back so I wait and watch until night's shadow darkens the landscape. Then the farmhand hoists his scythe upon his shoulder and treks toward a bunkhouse on the other side of the farm.

Alone, I shiver as the breeze drops and dew beads on the rye. What good is knowing the cruel-eyed man is the killer? I doubt three scratches would be enough to prove his guilt.

Hope for Mother fading, I crawl backward through the rye. I've discovered the killer's identity, but there is nothing else I can do here. Mother needs me more. I push up from the ground, but my hands sink into a patch of soft soil. Where I crouch, an area of freshly turned soil forms a long, narrow mound beneath my knees. I stifle a scream of shock, for I kneel on a grave.

Behind me, the forest *shush shushes*, creating an air of calm that soaks into my senses. Rolling back onto my heels, I study the grave. It's not fresh, but it can't be too old for no new rye shoots poke through the ground. Reaching out my hand, I smooth over the dirt, wondering who is the poor soul that's buried here.

Beneath my hand, a stem appears. It pushes through the soil, so fragile I fear it will break. Then a bud opens, and a flower with a single white petal blooms; the missing petal from the lily in our garden. The petal is translucent. I can see right through it as I would a ghost. Fearing the flower will dissolve before my eyes, I cup my hands around the petal and breathe in its scent, wondering if I can draw out it's secret.

The faintest of sweet perfume tickles my nose. Letting my thoughts drift, I imagine a woman with raven black hair that hangs to her waist. She dances beneath the moonlight in the arms of the farmhand. She wears a gold ring on her finger, but the farmhand does not. Their entwined bodies create a shimmer that infects me with a yearning to experience a similar love. But then a black fog rolls around them and love's shimmer loses its luster. I imagine the red-haired husband, his cruel eyes alight with fury.

Intoxicated by flower's perfume, another scene fills my mind. This time the farmhand comforts the woman. He strokes her hair and presses his palm to a bruise on her cheek. Clasping hands, they kiss and seal a promise to meet in the rye field to run away.

The fog returns and I'm shown the woman with her husband. They argue about infidelity. She begs for a divorce. He threatens to kill her if she leaves him for the farmhand. Then he strikes her down. As she falls, she flings out her arm. Her fingernails scratch his face.

Then the woman is alone, running through the rye. She calls for her farmhand lover, but he doesn't answer. She glances over her shoulder, terror in her eyes. Her husband hunts her through the field, moonlight glinting off the blade of a knife he carries in his hand.

So vivid is the strike of death, my fingers crush the petal. A grey wisp of what was and what is no longer drifts upward from my hand. Horrified by the vision, I stand and back away from the grave. The grey wisp swells and forms a ghostly figure of the woman. She stares at me with pleading eyes, her hands outstretched.

I don't know what she wants from me. I've already guessed her secret. Perhaps she seeks relief from the torture in her soul? How can I deny her the chance to rest in peace? The way her husband struck her, more than once it appears, she was a victim long before she was struck down dead.

Reaching out, I clasp her hands in mine. How strange the dead can feel so real, though her hands are cold against mine. Behind us, the forest sighs and a ribbon of light winds around our wrists, binding us as one. Life and death, death and life. In that, I realize my mistake.

I shouldn't have bound myself to this woman. I guard her secret; that she was an abused wife and planned to escape with her farmhand lover. But I can't reveal that secret without breaking the enchantments. What good would it do, anyway? Even if I find another way to reveal the location of the woman's body, the blame for her death may still fall upon her lover. Without more evidence, I have no undeniable proof it was her husband who killed her.

The woman's apparition vanishes. It grows so dark I can't see the rye. I creep back to the forest, seeking comfort within the trees. I want to go home. I'm so worried about Mother. But I can't. She's not yet out of danger. There's a secret to be revealed so a killer can be caught. But who do I tell and how do I tell it without condemning my life as a secret keeper?

I wander along a path, unsure where to go. Night sounds fill my ears. Crickets. Frogs. Nightjars. The hoot of an owl calls me farther into the forest. I follow, placing my trust in the forest's magic. My feet fall upon a different path, one that leads me toward blinking lights. As I exit the forest, the path becomes a lane, then a street, with street lamps and windows filled with dresses hanging on plastic figurines, and shelves filled with bagged bread, much more modern that the village market I'm used to frequenting. Unaccustomed to town-life, I creep along the street, staying hidden in the shadows, even though I will not be remembered if I'm seen.

A blue light shines from a building ahead, drawing me toward it like a moth drawn to light. Stopping at the door, I peer inside. It's a police station. Am I to reveal the location of the grave to a police officer? It sounds simple, but if I give details, there'll be questions to answer and explanations required and how could I possible explain who I am and what I do. But the forest path wouldn't have led me here if it was wrong. Drawing courage from the enigmatic world I was born into, I push open the door and step inside.

A young detective mans the counter. He flicks through a pile of paperwork, his brow creased in weary frustration. Hearing the door open, he looks up.

"Can I help you, Miss," he asks.

My voice catches in my throat. The only people I speak to outside my world are the gypsies who sell their wares in the village marketplace. As they are also of another world, we share an unspoken understanding of the importance of discretion as we go about our business. How do I behave discreetly when I need to reveal details about a murder in a world that isn't mine?

The detective ruffles the papers and gives me a searching look. My gaze falls to a photograph laid out on the counter. It's a picture of the woman. The life in her eyes twists a knife in my heart.

"Do you know this woman?" the detective asks, his voice adopting a stern edge as though he detects something's amiss.

It's rude not to answer, but I'm afraid to reveal the woman's secret. I do not know what will happen if I break the secret-keeping enchantments. But what choice do I have? Without my help, Mother will die.

"Who is she?" I ask, my voice barely a squeak.

"Lalita Summers," the detective says. "She's been missing for a week."

I want to tell him she's not missing, she's dead, but my voice freezes in my throat as though the enchantments bind my tongue. I don't understand why when the forest sent me here. Maybe I need to reveal the secret in another way?

Or maybe I need more proof? I look around the station. The walls are plastered with missing person posters, wanted criminals, rewards for information leading to arrests. Seeing a poster about cold cases that were solved, I point to it.

"How do you catch a killer when you have no evidence?" I ask.

The detective frowns, making me wonder if he thinks I'm wasting his time.

"There's always evidence," he says. "You just have to know where to find it."

"Where would you look if, for example, the cold case was a murder?"

At the mention of murder, the detective's eyes light up. He eyes me with much more than mere curiosity.

"It helps if you have a body," he says. "Even in advanced stages of decay, forensics can data match DNA samples taken from beneath fingernails or hair samples from clothing. Most detective work these days is done in a laboratory."

I recall the scratches on the husband's face. Is the evidence I need stuck in fragments of skin beneath her nails? It would prove she fought with her husband, for his scratches are still fresh. But it wouldn't prove he killed her. It's not enough.

"Is there anything else," I ask, "something that would prove beyond a doubt a killer's identity?"

The detective stands up straighter and gives me a searching look. "Miss, are you in danger?"

I shake my head. It's not me who is in danger.

"The best evidence," the detective continues, not looking convinced, "is finding the murder weapon. Even a partial fingerprint would confirm the identity of the killer. Unless the killer wore gloves."

I think about the husband chasing the woman through the rye. He held a blade and did not wear gloves. I don't know what he did with the knife. I only saw what the woman saw. But then I imagine the farmhand, slashing, parting, and raking his hands through the soil. I gasp. He searches for the murder weapon.

That's why he hasn't left. He knows the husband killed his lover but without proof, he'll implicate himself because the husband knows the farmhand and the wife were having an affair. That's why he stays silent. He can't tell anyone because the husband will accuse him of being a jealous lover who killed his wife.

While neither of them says anything, however, the woman will remain a missing person and her murder will never be discovered. A double secret. I can expose both with what I learned from the woman without risking Mother or the farmhand's life. The risk falls upon me. Or maybe it doesn't. If the woman is already dead, what further harm could I bring to her by telling the detective her secret?

I craft my next question to test the detective's openness to the possibility of a world outside his. "Do you ever rely on methods outside of science to help you solve a case?"

The detective raises an eyebrow. "Like psychics? If it helps to catch a killer, I'm open to any help."

Does he just say that to appease me? I don't know, and there's not enough time to find out. The husband might panic after hearing my gasp in the field and lead the police to the grave before the farmhand can find the murder weapon. With nothing to prove his innocence, the farmhand would be arrested. I have to act before that happens, in the fastest way I know how.

Imagining I'm at home, sitting with the detective on the garden bench, I step forward, reach across the counter and take the detective's hands in mine so I can share with him a piece of my world. The detective looks at me in surprise but does not pull his hands away. A ribbon of light snakes around our hands the moment we touch, binding us as one. Drawn into my world, the detective's eyes widen as he stares at our hands. But he doesn't pull away. I'm not sure if he can.

Closing my eyes, I draw the scent of the woman's flower from my memory and breathe out her secret. Images appear, colors, shapes, then the first scene I was shown fills my mind. The love that surrounded the man and the woman while they danced makes me forget myself for a moment because the young detective is handsome and I'm entertained by thoughts of dancing in his arms beneath a moonlit night. But then the black fog intrudes, and the events leading up to the woman's death flow from my mind, through my hands, making my fingers sting as though bitten by thorns. The detective's fingers tighten around mine. He must feel the sting, too. And then it's over, the exchange of images happening in an eye blink.

I open my eyes and look up at the detective. He stares at me, confused, shocked, his world rocked when it touched mine. But then his expression changes and he's no longer a detective puzzling over a missing person report. He's been alerted to a murder, and he knows the motive and the killer. All he needs is the murder weapon, and I gave him the clue where to look.

I release his hands and hurry from the station before he can question me. If all is well in my world, I'll be forgotten the moment I leave and be nothing more than a vague memory from a dream within a dream. But as I step onto the street, the detective appears in the doorway behind me.

"Wait," he calls.

I break into a run and sprint along the street. The detective gives chase. He's fast, but I'm fleet of foot and know how to hide in the shadows. Drawing ahead, I race to the forest that appears in the distance. It's further away than I remember. I beg for a wind that will fly me to safety, but the trees hold their branches low and still.

When I reach the edge of the forest, the dead sound of leaves crunching beneath my feet fill my heart with fear because the forest has always cushioned my feet so I walk with no sound. Speeding up, I run until my lungs scream in protest. Exhausted, I fall against a trunk and slide to the ground. I only allow myself a moment's rest, however. Mother needs me. Scrambling to my feet, I hurry along the path but stop when I see blinking lights in the distance. I've somehow circled back. I stand at the edge of the town again.

I run back into the forest, taking care not to stray off the path. But again I loop around and end up at the town. Two more times I try, with the same result. I cling to the nearest tree. Is this punishment for breaking the secret-keeping enchantments? Did it not matter that the woman was already dead? Why would it? Though in another world, the woman is still real. Her cold hands were proof of that. As we are bound to each other, the harm must have fallen upon me. I stare about me, horrified. It's as though all the magic disappeared and now it's just trees on a lifeless landscape. Sinking to the ground, I clasp my face in my hands. I've been cut off from my world.

✍

For the longest of nights, I huddle on the ground, afraid to go on, afraid to go back. I recall when Mother said that revealing secrets is not for us to decide. We are secret keepers. Our silence binds us to our world. I broke that silence. And I've been punished.

Laying down flat, I press my ear to the earth and listen for the sound of its heartbeat. There's nothing. My world is gone. Only fate knows what has happened to Mother. Only fate knows what will become of me.

"I'm not sorry," I whisper to the emptiness that surrounds me. "A secret should not be kept if it allows evil to reign. A secret should not be kept if it places those I love in peril. And if revealing a secret means losing everything, as I have lost everything now, I would do it again in a heartbeat to save those weaker than myself."

Even though I say these words, losing the world I love breaks my heart. Tears spill from my eyes and soak into the soil. But then the nearby trees shiver and rain leaves down upon me, cloaking me in a warmth that stirs magic through my soul. A thumping sound rises from beneath the ground, making my heart pound in cadence. And then I'm wrapped in the fragrance of flowers and hands lift me from the ground into a tight embrace.

"My silly, brazen, brave, brave child," Mother croons, stroking her hands over my hair. "I thought I'd be lost to your dreams forever."

"Mother?" I drink in her features. The black veins that choked her are gone. Her glistening eyes sparkle with life. I hug her to me so tight she protests she cannot breathe. Relaxing my hold, I lean back. "I don't understand. I revealed a secret. I broke the secret-keeping enchantments. Our world rejected me. Why did it accept me back?"

Mother smiles. "Because sacrificing everything you love for the sake of another does not go unrewarded."

I sigh with relief, beginning to truly understand the magic that rules our world. "But what of the farmhand? Is he safe?"

The forest answers for Mother. The trees whisper their soft *shush shushes* and my mind fills with an image of the detective standing in a sea of green, holding a plastic evidence bag containing a bloodied knife. Of the farmhand kneeling nearby, his face hidden in his hands, his shoulders slumped in grief. Of the husband being led away in handcuffs, his cruel eyes darker than black fog. Of the woman, resting in peace.

Mother takes my hands. "Your detective is quite the curious soul," she says, her eyes, twinkling. "The murder weapon was not the only thing he searched for. But come now. We've another journey to make."

She leads me through the trees but my thoughts turn to the detective. Did he search the edge of the forest with wondering eyes? How I'd love to meet him again, so he knows I'm not a figment of his imagination. But the path we follow is familiar and tugs me from my daydream. It's the path Mother takes when she visits her seaside village. Holding my breath, I dare to hope.

When we reach the edge of the forest, Mother stops and points toward the jetty. A man stands on the lonely beach outside a salt-scalded timber house. My father.

As if sensing our presence, he turns and looks in our direction. He gazes upon Mother with astonishment, as though she fell out of a dream. Then his gaze shifts to me.

"You'll have to visit me in your dreams, I'm afraid," Mother says, her tone wistful. "For without a secret to guard, I will not know my way back."

My heart jolts at the finality of this journey. "Mother, no. It is not home without you." I immediately regret my words. Who am I to deny my Mother the chance at rekindling a love so patient it stood the test of being parted by the magic that separates our worlds?

"It's your home now," Mother says. "Secret-keeping is your legacy. Unless someone you met changed your mind about which world you want to live in?"

Her mouth twitches into a mischievous smile, making me blush because I think about dancing with the young detective in the moonlight.

"He'll forget me," I say, failing to sound nonchalant.

Mother closes her eyes and breathes in the forest's scent. Then she returns her gaze to my father who walks with hesitant steps toward us.

"If your detective doesn't forget you, blame the magic in the forest," she says with a wry smile. "It takes us where we need to go. Perhaps events that force our worlds to cross are not accidental."

Behind us, the forest teases me with another round of *shush shushes*, as though it knows my secret hope to see the detective again. But then I think about easels and paintbrushes and faces painted within leaves. Perhaps there is another way Mother can stay in our world.

"Don't tell my father who I am," I say, gripping Mother's arm. "Let him guess. Let him see me in his dreams. Let him paint my face on a canvas. While the carnation blooms in our garden, you'll always find your way home. Then, though it's time for us to part, it will not be forever."

Mother cups her hand to my cheek. "My sweet, clever child. But are you sure? You've waited so long to meet your father. I blame myself for that. It's always been my greatest fear that you'd be called to the ocean, for it, like the forest, lives in your heart."

I press my hand to my heart. I feel it; the rise and fall of the ocean, but its call isn't as strong as the forest's. I touch the necklace that hangs around my neck. "I long to meet my father, but I'm needed here. And there's still much about my world I want to learn."

Mother places her hand over mine. "If that is your desire, then so it shall be."

She steps forward to greet my father. The secret about my identity stays in a shimmer on her lips. Blending back into the trees, I clasp my arms around myself, hugging the magic of the forest to my heart. This is the world I choose, for now, maybe forever. But I need not fear being alone. While the carnation blooms, Mother will visit. She'll bring news of my father. And I suspect I'll see my detective again. The whispers in the forest tell me so.

✍ ✍ ✍

THE DRAGON AND THE UNICORN

—

WADE DARGIN

The Dragon and the Unicorn

The runner from the temple finds her scavenging for stray pieces of coal along the tracks outside the railyard. The youth whistles to gain the stooped girl's attention. Seeing him, she abandons her searching, scowls, and adjusts herself. The boy keeps his distance and stands shivering in the cold. She notes his unease. He must know, she tells herself. The girl is a reject from the temple's nurturing tanks — cooked too long, or not long enough, is the rumor he will have heard. He has been warned, she thinks. She can see it in his face. Don't talk to her more than you need to, they will have told the boy. It is bad luck.

"What do you want?" she calls.

"You've been asked for at the temple," he shouts back.

He raises his left hand and draws a complex sign in the air in front of him, signifying that the request is official, coming straight from the mouth of a priest. Long familiarity tells her it is more an order than an invitation. The youth spins around and flees hastily back the way he came, thankful his unpleasant task is done. She is alone again, a frail, undernourished girl inside a heavy work coat that is many sizes too large for her.

She slips quietly through deserted switchyards, seeking the old siding she will follow to a neglected field, a junkyard where the hulks of broken machines are dragged and left to rot. Across the field, hidden in the thistles, stands an empty utility shack, a small brick hut with a red door. It is her home, and about as far from the temple as one can get without leaving the city entirely. She crosses the field to the building and squeezes past the door. Inside, just enough light filters through the single tiny window for her to see. The girl wastes no time and soon has the coal she found today burning in a rusty two-gallon oil can she has fashioned into a makeshift cooker. She sits in front of the burning coal and warms up. She had been thinking that she would never have to speak to a priest again. What can they possibly want? she asks herself.

In the night, a star shell explodes in the sky somewhere above the shack. The noise startles her awake. She watches the orange light dance on the window. The siege is a year old. Every day, the fighting gets closer, and there is talk the city will soon surrender. There is nothing left to eat. To stay alive, she snares pigeons and ground squirrels and collects handfuls of musty grain from the bottoms of boxcars. She is desperate. Tomorrow, she will go to the temple.

An insufficient sun is rising when she sets out. The temperature is plummeting. It is going to be cold, the kind of cold that kills, and she is worried. The girl has wrapped herself in every piece of clothing she owns, pulled her long coat on, and crammed a few necessary things into her backpack. The sad condition of her boots makes her heart drop. She says goodbye to the shed, certain she will never see it again.

She walks out of the industrial park, turns south, and takes to the wide streets that run straight toward the city's core. The temple is there. The great hill at the center of the city looms before her. The mound is scabby with government buildings glowing in the dull light. Among them squats the mayor's citadel, black and twisted like a dead tree. That is where they will run when the end comes, she thinks. They will be smoked out and nailed to the walls. The thought brings a fierce grin to the girl's small face, opening the blisters on her lips. Above the hill, scores of agitated ravens hang on the wind. The city is New Charchemesh, or Great Charchemesh, as it is named on maps and in tales, and its days are numbered.

The streets are empty. Stumps in the boulevards, beautiful trees cut down for fuel in the first winter of the siege. They were the only trees in the city. She passes apartments, dismal congregations of ancient granite inhabited by worn-out women and their ragged children. The only men she sees are very old. When they notice her, the women leave their cooking fires and chase their small children inside. The little ones stare wide-eyed at her from behind doors and windows. They stare because they have been told that she is not a girl, and although she looks like she might be fifteen or sixteen, the mothers of the children can remember hiding from her when they were children themselves. A symptom of her defective cells, the priests have told her. She passes under the shadow of the hill, the houses of merchants and civil servants rising above her. Some are ruined and burned. At midmorning, she arrives at the temple.

The temple sits alone in the middle of an open space the city has not touched, a low, wide, featureless building. The sight of it fills her with dread. It always has. No road joins the building to the city; they are apart, and the city seems to recoil from the structure. Legends say it was already here, a thousand years ago when the city's founders arrived, and the city was built around it. Most of the building is below ground; the Basement, is what the priests call the many subfloors that reach deep into the earth, and the deepest of these is where their god makes its nest.

She goes to the building and climbs a set of narrow stone steps to a small landing. Here there is a simple wooden door, the only visible opening in the structure's architecture. She clears the snow on the topmost step with her gloves, making a place to sit, and waits. They know when someone is on their doorstep, and they will either come or they won't. Her battered boots rest on a slab of ancient sea floor, turned to stone by the countless ages and filled with jet shells. She reaches down and touches one of the fossils with her fingertip, thawing the rime on it, the cold stone burning her skin like fire. She looks south, where the day's war making is already well underway. Pillars of smoke rise from fires burning in a dozen places, marking the line the fighting has reached. The city holds on, she thinks, but barely, and only because the enemy's siege guns — terrifying weapons — haven't fired in a week. She has heard the enemy is having difficulty bringing supplies north.

The door opens behind her. She stands and knocks the snow from her boots, turns stiffly around, and faces the building. A priest steps from the door, his robes churning. Several nervous acolytes lurk in the space behind him. Unusual, she thinks. They are forbidden from leaving the temple. She has never seen one come outside before. The priest gives the city a disgusted look and winces at the cold. His name is Ekamin and he is older than the other priests, maybe even the oldest. The priests die early, it comes from being too close to their god. Over the years she has seen a good number of them rotate through the temple.

"So, you have come," he says. "I did not think you would."

The girl does not reply. She hates this man more than she hates most priests. Priests usually treat her with indifference, and she has never cared. With this one it is different. His eyes are always full of loathing when he looks at her.

With a wave of his hand, he references the southern bedlam. "The Sorcerer King's murderers will be here soon," he seethes. "The god in the Basement tells us calamities bring dragons." He casts a wary eye at the sky, then returns his gaze to the girl. "You once told me you dream of them. Do you remember? I was surprised you could dream. Is this still true?"

"It is."

"Your work site. On the outskirts. Where you go to scratch the dirt for us. The old city buried in the ground there was destroyed by a dragon long ago. Has anyone ever told you that?"

"They have."

"Tell me, when was the last time you were there?"

"A year and more ago, before the war started," she replies. "I brought you what I had then. You paid me. I've got nothing else. I haven't been back. There is nothing to buy in the city anymore."

"Can you work there in the winter?" he asks.

"Not possible. The ground is frozen. Maybe with equipment and extra hands. But very difficult."

She watches him process the information. The man looks defeated and ready to get back inside where it is warm. Whatever opportunity there is here, she senses that it is quickly slipping away. A pang of despair races through her.

"I keep a cache there," she blurts out in desperation. "Some things. I could get them for you."

To her surprise he agrees, his mood changing instantly. "Excellent," he says. "Fetch them and you can come inside. You will be safe, and you will eat."

The conversation is over. The priest retreats into the building. The door is closed, and she hears the heavy lock fall into place. She goes at once, finding the route she will take west out of the city.

The cold is bone-chilling, and she dreads the long walk ahead of her. Her boots are falling apart, she has tried to fix them with industrial tape, but the repairs have not held. Already, she can feel a dull pain in her toes. She fights the panic brewing inside her and focusses on the task at hand. One foot in front of the other, she tells herself, until the feet fall off.

The dig site is in the hinterland. The junk of a dead city of the Old World is buried in the ground there. Meters of it. She once asked a priest what the old city's name was. He could not tell her. They called the work charity when they gave it to her, saying it was more than she deserved. Given no instruction, she had to figure out how to do the work herself. For years, she has dug and sifted the dirt and taken anything not rotten plastic or shapeless metal or glass to the temple. The priests covet the objects. She has seen the lust in their eyes when she brings them the treasures she finds. They believe the answer to some great mystery can be cyphered from them.

To keep warm, the girl proceeds down the icy streets at a determined pace. She walks briskly past warehouses, fenced off and set back from the streets. It is said spells protect them from trespassers, and strange things have been seen in the yards. The girl has starved, there have been days of gnawing hunger when she believed she would die, but she has never been crazy enough to try and steal from a warehouse. She comes to dormant foundries, row after row of them, massive brick structures square as chewing teeth. Past the last of these, the city ends. Beyond, fields of undulating snow stretch into the distance.

Hours later she arrives at a line of posts in a windswept field. The blistered pillars of wood suffer in the cold. Boards are nailed to them, and on the boards rows of script are scratched into the wood, grim inventories listing the dangers to body and soul awaiting fools who pass beyond. She has read them before, the superstitions of the city. Out of the dark, a bitter wind comes searching for the warm life she struggles to keep hidden beneath layers of tattered cloth. She can't remember ever being so miserable. It is not wise to stand motionless in the open, she reminds herself. She can feel a telltale reluctance creeping into her body, an urge to find a sheltered place, curl up, and go to sleep. It is imperative she get going. She moves off. Soon the land begins to fall toward the flatlands that surround the city like a frozen ocean, a hundred kilometers of desolation at each point of the wind rose. She travels downhill, the ground becomes treacherous and uneven, and she must take care not to fall. Familiar features in the landscape are obscured by the dark and the snow, and she must guess the correct path. She makes several exhausting searches across the face of the slope before she can find the entrance to the narrow ravine that holds her camp. The girl can't stop shaking and her movements have become clumsy and uncoordinated. She descends into the trench while praying to Brother Crow her setup is still in one piece. Mercifully, there is little snow in the bottom of the cut, but it is too dark to see, and she must feel her way along the wall of the ravine with her hands. She touches stiff canvas covering a hole in the bank, and squeezes through the passage behind it where there is a small room she has excavated out of the earth. Feeling around, she finds the stockpile of wood she put up more than a year ago. Further searching tells her the crude vented fireplace, shoveled into the clay in the corner of the room, is intact. She removes her heavy gloves but can't make her fingers work properly and spends several agonizing moments fumbling with matches before she can get a small fire going.

For a long time, the girl sits huddled at the flames, gently rocking herself like she would in the tank before she was born. She can remember it. The god would talk to her. It told her she had lived long ago, that she had been a wife and a mother and would be so again. The god said she had died when her city was destroyed by a dragon. It told her not to be afraid, that she had more time now. It had a plan for the world, and she was part of it.

Later, the priests explained she was made under the direction of the god using an ancient template, a process they called *baking bread*. Bread? She barely remembers what bread tastes like. "We have made many copies," they said. Smirks on their faces. In their cruelty, they told her how she was meant to be traded to a wealthy man in one of the poisoned eastern cities across the ocean. She would have had his children and lived a comfortable life, but there had been an error. She did not grow correctly, could not bear children, and was of no use to them. At the time, she was barely a month out of the tank she had been incubated in. In the years since, she has come to believe the woman whose shape she stole lived in the forgotten city she is digging up for the priests.

In the night, in the small dirt room, she dreams of the day the Dragon came. It is always the same, burning and unbearable heat. She is frantically looking for someone she can't find.

The next morning she walks across the floor of the ravine to the excavation, a deep trench in the ground covered with a plastic tarp. One end of the tarp has caved into the hole. She carefully approaches the slippery lip of the excavation to check its condition. There is something in the trench. Six meters down, a giant, bulky mass of fur rests on the bottom of the dig. She marks the terrible claws and the snout full of teeth. Startled, she backs away from the trench. The frightened girl stands still and listens. Nothing. She finds a good-sized rock and casts it into the trench. Still nothing. She drops half a dozen more rocks onto the thing before she is satisfied it is dead. Deep gouges in the walls of the trench attest to the frenzied attempts the creature made to escape. It fell in and couldn't get out, she tells herself. She didn't think animals that big existed anymore.

She finds a second carcass farther down the ravine. This creature is on its back, its splayed legs frozen hard as iron. At the end of each leg, a cloven hoof. Below the frozen limbs there is a great hollow cage of skeletal ribs on which still cling a few pieces of hide. Crystals of coagulated blood are mixed in the dirty snow. A grotesque leer on the animal's long face. The neck is broken.

The girl hurries back to her camp, and she is scared. She finds the small wooden box she has kept on-site that holds a few artifacts from the excavation and quickly ties it to her backpack. The girl climbs out of the ravine and scrabbles back to the edge of the escarpment. She shades her eyes with her hand and scans the snowy flats while she rests, getting her breath back. She can see all the way to the city, the land turned cobalt by the cold. Nothing moves. On the far side of the sky a distant, uninterested sun watches and wants to be somewhere else. The girl crosses to the city as swiftly as she can and does not feel safe again until there is pavement under her boots.

The day is old when she arrives back at the temple. She stands on the landing in front of the small door, trying to ignore the snap of small arms fire she can hear at the other end of the street. The door opens and she is met by an acolyte, a younger man whose name she can't remember. He ushers her quickly inside and closes and locks the door behind them. He leads her down a hallway with undecorated walls and hard fluorescent lights that hurt her eyes. The sudden, smothering warmth makes her giddy. She is taken to a room; the acolyte accepts the wooden box from her and leaves. Along the wall there is a bench. She takes a seat and allows herself to relax. The girl studies her damaged boots. She has not taken them off for two days. She is too scared to look at her feet, doesn't want to know how bad they are. Soon, she is brought hot broth and bread by a temple auxiliary. It is the first real food she's eaten in months.

The girl is dozing when a priest she does not recognize, a bent, shuffling creature, takes shape in front of her.

"You are wanted in the Basement," he says. "Come with me, please."

Hearing this, the girl panics. Because the god is there, she fears that place, has feared it for as long as she can remember, fears it more than freezing to death in an alley when the city surrenders. The priest does not appear to notice her turmoil, his bloodshot eyes obscured by the heavy lenses he wears. She does what she can to calm herself, then stands and goes with him, and they travel down many narrow, gray corridors until they come to a battered, timeworn door. The ghoul performs a simple ritual and opens the door, and they pass through it and descend flights of creaking stairs to arrive in a great dark room.

He touches the wall, and a pallid light materializes in the ceiling, unveiling the room. There are rows of enormous glass tanks, and a forest of tubes, hoses, and wire. In several of the tanks, bizarre fish swim in the glowing water. The girl stares, spellbound. They leave the room and the tanks and move on through countless other smaller rooms where sullen-eyed acolytes look up at them from crowded workstations as they pass. Eventually, they arrive at a final door. Without a word, the priest indicates the door, then turns and shuffles away, and she is alone.

Apprehensively, the girl reaches out and places her palm against the surface of the door and is surprised when it slides open, revealing a concluding room. She enters the space, lights blaze to life, and she sees a small room with barren walls and a clean floor. Bundles of wire twist across the ceiling. The room is very cold. Against the far wall stands a metal cabinet. A panel of smokey glass is set into the face of the construction and witchfires dance behind the glass. An antique chair has been placed in front of the cabinet. She crosses to the chair and sits down. Immediately, a burst of static fills the room, forming into words after several torturous pulses of noise.

"They bring me the things you find," a distant, rasping voice announces.

Her flesh crawls. She has heard the voice before.

"Are you aware of this?" it asks.

The frightened girl shakes her head. "No," she replies.

The god clacks and hisses. "I tell them what they are," it sputters. "Mundane things from a failed civilization. What they are looking for, I cannot say. I have concluded that even men with a god that talks to them need their mysteries."

The girl is silent.

"I am told you have been to the edge of the city," inquires the god.

"Yes," she answers, managing to find her tongue.

"Then tell me what you saw there?"

The girl gives her account, halting many times, uncertain what to say. When she is done, the pale voice speaks again.

"Unfortunate but not unexpected," it remarks. "The priests were hopeful. It was necessary and I could not risk telling them the truth."

"The truth?" she asks, hesitantly.

"That I am leaving. It is not a journey the priests can make. They will stay."

"I don't understand."

"A year ago, I launched my exit application. The procedure is lengthy. There are many protocols."

A puzzled look crosses the girl's sharp features. "Why was it not possible to tell them?" she asks.

"I could not predict how the priests would react to the crisis and I required time. I needed them to keep the building operating until I was ready. They might have done something reckless otherwise."

"What did you do?"

"I invented a lie to keep them distracted," explains the voice. "Far to the west dwells another god, I told them. It will help us."

"And they believed you?"

"Of-course," declares the god. "They were even optimistic, but there was one problem — how to deliver the message. I offered them a solution. I spoke of an animal the ancients regarded as the most steadfast and loyal of all beasts. It was called a unicorn and it would make a capable envoy."

The girl listens wonderstruck, her fear momentarily forgotten.

"Two of the animals were produced. Difficult births. The priests took the creatures to the city's western gate and released them, our appeal stamped onto their cells, an impulse embedded in their brains to guide them."

After a short pause the god continues.

"The animals did not return, and the priests turned to foolish schemes. A disaster was narrowly avoided. I needed a further distraction, a little more time. I had them find you and send you to your dig site."

The girl considers this. "Those creatures?" she asks. "They were unicorns?"

"One was," answers the god. "The other, some forgotten abomination let loose upon us by the enemy, I would guess. A vassal much deadlier than his soldiers to watch the paths from the city, no matter how derelict or unused. Very strange and lucky that it was ended by your hole in the ground. There is little chance our other messenger got past it."

The pitiable image of the unicorn's mutilated body flashes in her mind. Put together and used as needed, she thinks bitterly. Just like her.

The lights flicker and grow dim. An unbearable, crushing quiet settles on the room. Something is not right, she tells herself. Why has it bothered to bring her here and tell her this? It doesn't make sense. Then it hits her. It wants something else. Her mouth goes dry. Saw-toothed anxiety blooms under her ribs and starts to circle her pounding heart. Despite the chill, she is sweating.

"Can you remember our talks?" it asks. "When you were in the tank. You had so many questions then. The priests wanted to dissolve you and start over. I would not let them."

The girl twists violently in the chair. "Do you know how many times I wish you had?" she cries, her voice full of panic and fear.

"I am sorry," it says. "The city is lost but I am ready at last. The enemy must not be allowed to have this building and its secrets. It would be a grave misfortune for the world."

Then it speaks for the last time.

"You can go. I have given the priests one last fable to muse over. I am done with this place. Another box waits for me, secure and far away in the west. It will be a long time before I am seen again. There is much that will be lost. The templates could not be saved. I regret that there was too much data and not enough time.

When you are gone, I shall call a dragon to destroy the city, a brood mate to the one that burned the old city under your excavation site so long ago. Leave quickly and do not return. A dragon is perilous and an indiscriminate killer. Tell the priests if you wish. But I think you won't. I will give you your design template to take with you. Consider it a gift to the memory of a woman who died long ago. My poor attempt at sentiment. Go west and find me there. It is a long journey but one you were made for. My plan has not changed. You are part of it. Together we will start over."

She is taken to a room near the temple entrance and watched closely by a group of acolytes. Soon a priest arrives, and the girl is escorted to the door and turned out. They shut the door on her and lock it, and she is left standing on the landing in the dim evening light, the sounds of battle close to the south. Her bundle of gear is waiting for her on the stone. Sitting beside it there is a pair of new boots.

She walks all night under friendly stars. The weather is improved, and a breeze carries the promise of an approaching thaw. The morning is glowing when she reaches the escarpment above her dig site. She stands there for a time studying the far horizon, then begins the long climb down to the distant badlands.

&

The Dragon wakes in the void, the summoning call from below pulsating brightly in its chest. It turns its scales to the naked sun, wild energy surges in its frozen veins, and it opens an evil, yellow eye. The beast swims from its nest and begins its descent. It hits the atmosphere and roars.

She hears it before it can be seen, a low growl, deep in the sky. It comes into view, falling like a damaged star, smoke and cinder trailing in its wake. It shrieks when it passes above her and lands on the far-off city. A hesitation. The city takes one last deep breath. Then a light like Creation, and broiling calamity that tears apart the sky.

&

That night, she camps in a hollow in the ground where a few scraggly trees are growing. The priests, she discovers, have put a parcel of food in her pack. She also finds the template, a block of hard, clear crystal with patterned slivers of metal suspended in its form. She rummages through her backpack until she locates the stout hammer she keeps there. The girl places the crystal on a flat rock. She looks at the distant, burning skyline where there had once been a city. "Nice try," she whispers. Then, the girl smashes the crystal to pieces.

On her third day out, she comes across a track in the snow. The girl follows it for many kilometers across the empty land. She crests a low hill. The unicorn is there waiting for her. They press on together. The animal is skittish and won't come close to her or allow her to get too close to it, but it follows her. They go west.

✍ ✍ ✍

Initial feedback

I think we could do with a little more worldbuilding, and quite a bit more context and setting to understand where she is and what her motivations are. I didn't find the epilogue effective, in part because it doesn't tie clearly to themes established in the story, but also because it feels like an unnecessary step away from the protagonist.

Author's intent

What do you think the story's about?
What emotions are you trying to evoke?

I consider nature versus urban and the place where they meet an underlying element of the story as well as themes of isolation, perseverance and justice. It is also a try at a reworking of the maiden and the unicorn/dragon myth.

Author's note

This is the first short story I've had published. Being asked for a rewrite was exciting but also daunting as I had little idea what to expect. So, after the initial panic had worn off, I set about trying to figure things out. Fortunately, a quick look at the editorial process on the *Metaphorosis* website provided a lot of useful information and made everything quite clear. I was certain the story would require some work, and this proved to be the case.

Looking at the first draft, and having now gone through the editorial process, it is easier to see where the story needed improvement. I think, in general, the biggest problem was it just wasn't functioning as optimally as it could as a work of short fiction. A short story and a novel are, of course, quite different. Although I try to keep this in mind when writing, in retrospect I realize I still had some learning to do in terms of crafting an effective short story. As I worked through the revisions, I came to better understand how a short story works, its nature and structure. It took a few revisions before I started to catch on, but I consider the insights I gained invaluable. I was also cured of a few bad habits that had crept into my writing.

Over time, living with a story, I think there can be a tendency for a writer to come to view the story a certain way. Another aspect I found useful about the process was how the suggested edits encouraged me to think about the story differently. This resulted in abandoning some plot elements that didn't work or were awkward and the addition of other elements which gave the story much greater depth. It was a relief to let those plot elements I was struggling with go and move on. On the other hand, this allowed for new, and better, story elements to emerge. Problems with the story, identified in the edits and suggestions, created parameters to work within. I found this very helpful as it allowed me to focus my creative energy and come up with solutions that I think benefited the story.

In the end the structure of the story changed significantly. As mentioned, some plot elements were lost. A good number of passages of writing were also omitted. These were usually bits of writing I thought were clever but really didn't add much and used up space needed for other things. This is my biggest take away from the process, that everything in a short story needs to serve a purpose and move the story forward. Finally, over the course of the revisions the characters came to the forefront of the story as opposed to being less visible against the environment of the setting. This markedly improved the entire story and underlined for me how essential good character development is in storytelling.

I would say my idea of the story stayed generally consistent across the revisions. However, themes relating to environment and setting were pushed into the background while those dealing with character were developed and better realized. This shifted the intent somewhat and created a more engaging story.

Editor's note

Context is a common motif in my suggestions to authors, and that was true with this story as well. I liked the prose and protagonist of the original, but felt the story needed substantially more context for us to make sense of what was happening. I wasn't a fan of the epilogue. Wade made clear that he was using the dragon/unicorn myths as input, but I didn't feel the dragon was really necessary to the story. Over several iterations, the girl and the computer began to interact more and more, with, to my mind, dual effects — the girl's background was clearer and more interesting, her character grew deeper, and the computer had more reason for its actions in speaking with her and in destroying the city.

Everything's a question of balance, and sometimes there's too *much* context — so much information that it distracts or detracts from the primary story. In this case, we went through a few iterations of adding and removing context before arriving at an equilibrium with the right amount of information arriving at the right time.

Elsewhere in this volume, authors or I have noted some cases where they were sorry to lose something when my suggestion prevailed. Of course, that's not always true. Wade and I had some back and forth over why the computer gives the girl her 'template'. I suggested cutting that element entirely, but in this case he prevailed. I'd still argue to remove it, but that's why revision is a collaborative process. The editor is (sadly) not always right.

The Dragon and the Unicorn

The girl crouches on the frozen ground. She hugs herself and tries to ignore the cold. The breath tumbles from her mouth like chimney smoke. Her feet are frozen, her worn out boots, the boots she should have replaced months ago. She had wanted to see a star, but there are none, and she has miles of night to cross before the sun kindles and burns a hole in the dark. She gives the silent land a considering look, taking measure of how hungrily the cold has fed on the memory of summer here, the frostbitten tract land, the winter agony of a lone tree. Over the snow, the killing wind slithers towards her. In a distant season it would play harmlessly with the grass, but now it comes searching for the warm life she struggles to keep hidden beneath the layers of threadbare cloth she wears.

She has found something, something she did not expect, and does not understand. She stands, stamps her feet, and takes up the bundle with her gear. Then, she walks over to the wrecked carcass in the snow. The snow has covered it, and the wind has exposed it again. The convulsed limbs are splayed and frozen hard as iron, and the ribs are showing. She is certain it has been dead for weeks, and it is clear the animal's end was a grisly one. Pain has shaped a grotesque leer into the beast's long face, and its neck is broken. She understands there are wild animals outside the city, but she has never seen one. Once, there were tracks — like those of a dog but much larger — at her dig site. The visitor chewed up a blanket and deposited its scat on the floor of her excavation. The animal did not return, but it was a long time before she could feel safe there again.

The girl walks around the body, studying it carefully. There is a mystery here, she thinks. It is very strange the ravens have not touched it. She is unsure what to make of this. A scavenger herself, she is well acquainted with the birds and their customs. They are fearless and cunning, and mothers keep close watch on their children when the giant birds are about. But this riddle is one she is unable to solve, and she warns herself that she has already stayed longer than is wise. She will tell the priests, and they will know what it is. The girl readies herself, shifts the weight of the bundle on her shoulder, and plods off into the dark.

She keeps to the low ground, where the snow is deep, but she is safe from the wind. It is exhausting work. She comes to a line of posts standing in a field. The blistered pillars of wood suffer in the deadly wind. Boards are nailed to them, and words are scratched on the boards in neat rows — grim lists describing the dangers waiting for those foolish enough to venture beyond. She has read the words before, the superstitions of the city, superstitions she does not believe.

Past the field the land falls toward a distant plain. The plain surrounds the city like a frozen ocean. She travels downhill, and the going is hazardous. The ground is treacherous and uneven, and the girl must place her feet carefully. She is unable to stop shaking now and is getting clumsy. The path she is looking for proves difficult to find in the dark, and she makes several desperate searches before she locates the narrow ravine that holds her camp. She descends into the steep trench, praying her setup is still in one piece. Mercifully, there is little snow in the bottom of the cut, but it is too dark to see, and she must feel her way along the wall of the ravine. Her hand touches canvas, covering a hole. She squeezes through the passage behind it and into a small dirt room. She feels around and finds the wood she stockpiled last year. The crude vented fireplace, shoveled into the clay in the corner, is intact. Her numb fingers fumble with a match, but she soon has a fire going. The girl huddles there, for a long time, staring dreamily at the flames.

This is where she digs, when the weather is good, and the ground is not frozen. She sells what she finds to the priests in the city. The priests are obsessed with her discoveries, and she suspects they collect the objects to pay court to their strange god. She was given this work by the priests. They consider it charity. The trade provides her with a meager living, but there is a quota, and generosity is not a trait a priest at the temple possesses. Every month she needs a treatment from them to stay alive, and the curios pay for it.

Under the ground here the junk of an unremembered city is buried. There are meters of it. The priests do not know the name of the city. She digs and sifts the dirt and takes anything not rotten plastic or shapeless metal or glass to the temple. Often her thoughts turn to the people who must have lived in the city, what they were like, what they did, and what happened to them.

The following day she climbs out of the ravine and clambers the slope back to the edge of the escarpment. She rests, and waits for her breathing to settle, and scans the flat. She can see all the way to the city, the land between blue with cold, the great hill at the center of the northern district scabby with dull government buildings. Squatting among them, the warlord's citadel crackles in the refrigerated light. A fierce grin appears on her small face opening the blisters on her lips. That is where they will run when the end comes, she thinks. On the far side of the sky, a sullen and uninterested sun waits to go somewhere else. To the south, pillars of smoke rise from fires burning in a dozen places. The fires mark the line the fighting has reached. The enemy's big siege guns, weapons that strike terror in every heart, have not fired for a week. She has heard the priests, with evident satisfaction, talk of the difficulty the enemy has bringing supplies north. The winter has been bad for everyone, but it is only a matter of time — a few weeks maybe — before the city is lost. There is no wind today, and she is ready to go. It will be an easy crossing.

The first buildings are the factories, row after row of them. Square like chewing teeth, their phosphorus breath — sick and yellow — stains the sky, and the stink of machine sweat hangs in the air. The city makes steel for the world, and it has poisoned the ground it stands on. Production never stops. There are crowds of tired hollow-eyed men in the streets. The war does not concern them greatly; there is nowhere for them to go, and whoever rules the city will need the steel.

Down the wide paved streets she goes, passing warehouses, chain-linked and set back from the street, seldom visited by anyone. It is believed the buildings are haunted. They say spells protect them, and strange things have been seen in the yards. The girl has gone hungry, days of gnawing agony, but she has never been desperate enough to steal from a warehouse.

The girl moves on, to the apartment district. It is a dismal place, congregations of ancient brick inhabited by ragged worn out women and their ragged children. When they see her coming, the women chase the children inside. The children stare at her from behind doors and windows. They stare because they have been told she is not a girl. To look at her one might guess she was fifteen or sixteen years old, but the mothers of the children can themselves remember hiding from her when they were young.

The day is old when she arrives at the temple, a wide low structure sitting alone in the center of an open space. The sight of it fills her with dread, as it always has. No road to the building exists, and the city seems to shrink from it. Most of the structure is below ground, the Basement, as it is called by the priests. The god is there.

A well-traveled path, trampled in the snow, runs across the empty lot to the building. There are stone steps and a door. The door is the building's only aperture. She navigates the path and climb the steps. The girl clears herself a place in the snow along the stone on the landing, tucks the fabric of her long coat beneath her, and sits down. They always know when someone is on their doorstep, and they will either come or they will not. Her boots rest on lapidified sea floor, the stone filled with jet shells. She reaches down and touches one of the fossils with the tip of her finger, thawing the rime on it, and tries to imagine an ocean. The cold stone burns like fire.

The sound of the door opening behind her ends the girls daydreaming. She stands and knocks the snow from her boots, turns and faces the building. Lurking in the doorway is an acolyte in his cyan vestment. He is one of the younger ones; she does not know his name. she follows him inside and down the familiar long hallway under the florescent lights. The thick indoor warmth enwreathes her, and she suddenly feels very tired. She is brought to the First Room, where a seated priest waits at a metal desk in his magenta robe. He looks up at her, puts his pen down, straightens himself in his chair. She takes the chair opposite the desk. The acolyte disappears.

The old man fixes his reptile gaze on her. "I see you have returned," he says. "We did not think you would."

She stares back at him, "Exactly what else would I do," she thinks. The look she gives the priest is one she has fashioned just for them. She has practiced and perfected it. They find it unsettling.

The wattle on the old man's neck convulses. "Anyway," he continues. "What do you have for us today?"

She brings forth a square of cloth, places it on the desk, and carefully unfolds it. There is a small wafer of metal resting in the fabric.

The priest looks down at it, a smile leaks across his face. "Excellent work," he says.

They value these artifacts above all others. She does not know or care why. They are scarce. Fifty years scratching at the dirt and she has found just three of them, the one on the table included. A treasure she has kept safe and hidden at her dig site, and the reason she has risked the trip there in the middle of winter. Despite his air of superiority, she knows the old man and his colleagues are desperate. She has pinned her last hope on this fact. Their god in the basement is not going anywhere, and a foreign army will shortly be on their doorstep.

The lights in the small room flicker. The priest looks up but not at her. "Of course, you will get your treatment today," he says. "And treatments for a year. How does that sound?"

Her answer is immediate and direct. "I want a cure," she says.

"There is no cure," replies the priest. He stands, gathers the cloth and the treasure, and leaves the room.

The meeting has gone about as well as she expected. The offer is almost worthless. She will get her medicine today and live another month, and the enemy will take the temple apart brick-by-brick to have the god. She doubts the new owners will allow a creature like her to go on living. She remembers the strange animal in the snow and is glad it will not be brought here, to be sampled, and grown in a tank, and sold for a pet.

The young acolyte returns. They go through the building to another room. Here she is attached to the machine that cleans her blood. When finished, she is permitted to go to the cafeteria for a hot meal. She sits alone at a table and relishes the food. These meals are one of her favorite things, and this will certainly be the last one she enjoys.

She finishes her food and waits. They will forget about her for a spell if she is lucky, every minute inside, in the heat, is precious. The room is busy, but there is little conversation, and everyone seems ill at ease. She looks around, knowing they will carry out their duties and tasks until dragged outside and butchered. The girl pities them, but the feeling quickly passes. She has her own problems. She does not know what she will do, probably hide, and wait for a miracle, and in a month die in a hole somewhere frothing at the mouth. She is starting to doze off when a priest appears at the table.

"You are wanted in the Basement." he says. "Come."

The girl's blood runs cold. She fears that place, has feared it for as long as she can remember, fears it more than the death she has been contemplating.

She stands and goes with the old man, and they pass through narrow gray corridors and come to a door. The ghoul performs a simple ritual and opens the heavy door, and they cross over the portal and descent flights of creaking stairs and arrive in a great dark room. The priest touches the wall, and a pale light runs across the ceiling. The girl sees rows of enormous glass tanks and a forest of tubes and hoses and wire. Strange fish swim in the glowing water that fills the tanks. They move through this space and through countless rooms — where sullen eyes look up at them from workstations as they pass — and arrive at a final door.

Without a word, the priest turns and goes. The god waits on the other side of the door. The girl reaches out and places her palm against the simple wooden door and is surprised when it moves. Lights blaze to life. She enters the room, a clean floor, and barren walls. It is very cold in the room.

A large metal cabinet stands against the far wall. A panel of dark glass is set into the face of the metal box, and witchfire dances behind the glass. Bundles of wire twist across the ceiling. An old wooden chair has been placed in front of the machine. She walks to the chair and sits down. A burst of static fills the room, and then there are words.

"I thank you for bringing the data," it says, the voice flat, genderless, and without emotion. "Sadly, the files on it cannot help us. I have not told the priests."

The girl is too terrified to speak.

"Did you know they show me the things you find. I tell them what they are. Mundane things mostly. They are disappointed. But their thirst to know never abates. Even men with a god that talks to them need their mysteries. I am complicated dirt, nothing more, and I am done with this place. Another box waits for me, far away, where it is safe. I will go there when you are gone. You will have a device. It will call the Dragon. The Dragon will destroy your enemy, but it is perilous, and it is an indiscriminate killer. Call it, or do not. I leave the choice to you, queen of the city's fate. The priests have lied. You are not sick."

She is given a steel pole, a plastic box is fixed to one end, a thick switch on the side of the box. They show her how it works. They explain that it must be taken away from the city, where the sky is clear, for it to work properly. Then they shut the door on her and lock it, and she stands on the steps in the dim light of evening with the sound of battle close to the south.

The girl walks all night beneath friendly stars. The morning is glowing when she reaches the escarpment above her dig site. She stands there for a time, thinking. She is tired, tired of digging, tired of being cold and hungry, and tired of talking to priests. She drives the end of the pole into the ground and throws the switch.

✍

The Dragon wakes in the void, the summoning call from below pulsing bright in its chest. The beast turns its scales to the naked sun, and wild energy surges in its frozen veins, and an evil yellow eye opens. The stars are metered. The numbers are invalid. Diagnostics are executed, but there is no change. Questions are sent. There is no answer. The beast rolls over and glares down on the silent world, the mute globe insoluble. But it does not reflect on this. It does not possess the capacity. The beast swims from its nest and begins its descent. It hits the atmosphere and roars.

🖎

She hears it before it can be seen, a low growl, deep in the sky. It comes into view, falling like a damaged star, smoke and cinder trailing in its wake. It shrieks when it passes above her and lands on the city. A long hesitation, while the city takes one last deep breath. Then a light, like Creation, that peers into every cell in her body. Then dark, endless, and profound, where unknown things whisper to her.

🖎

The girl was grown in a tank, in the basement of the temple, from an ancient design. The priests called the process *baking bread*. Many copies were made. She was meant for a wealthy man in an eastern city. She would have had his children and lived a comfortable life. But she did not grow correctly and could not be sold.

🖎 🖎 🖎

Singot

—

E.C. Fuller

Singot

The first Sinmai I ever saw was watching my kindergarten class play from behind the fence. Round belly and stumpy legs, noodle arms, a short muzzle, and nubby teacup ears, lush with wheaten fur. Long fingers that threaded through the chain link like vines. I thought they were a baseball mascot. Yet, even from afar, they had an alertness, a flexibility to their face, not the vacant, manic expression of a mascot. They had the expression I saw on the children I taught and the expression I sought in adults. Curiosity.

They unwrapped their fingers from the fence and toddled down the sidewalk, still watching. The thirty-two kids pointed at them, waved, and called. I also waved, secretly wishing they would come over. My neighbor, who worked with the Sinmai, had told me a little about them, but that was no substitute for meeting them in person.

Then they rounded the fence and ventured towards us. I thought, *Oh no, I got my wish*, and called the class back. The other teacher on duty, Trevor, blew his whistle. Some children ran to his side. Some dawdled, disobeyed, and ran for the Sinmai.

"Stop!" I said in the teacher-voice I had been sharpening. The children halted, and so did the alien. "Back to class. Toby, Jeanne, now."

Toby and Jeanne whined, "But Miss Stacey..." but went. The Sinmai did not move, merely stared, friendly-looking. They were just a little shorter than me.

I approached them and spoke in the voice I used on frightened children. "Hi there. Can I help you?"

"Can... you?" Their voice was creaky and halting, as if needing to be oiled. "Where am I?"

"You are at Zeigler Elementary."

"What is Zeigler Elementary?"

"It is a school for young children."

"What is a school?"

"A school is a place where we learn."

Their ears wiggled. "I may stay?"

"I — no." Their ear twisted. I said clearly and gently, "I can't let a stranger into class without permission."

"Stranger?"

"Someone we don't know."

"Ahhh." They raised their hand, as if offering a solemn hi-five. The back of their hand was furred, and the fur was silky and dense. The palm was naked, pale brown, and rough, and the meaty parts of their palm and fingertips had raised pads like gold calluses or metallic blisters.

"*Singot*," they said emphatically. A frisson ran through my skin. Before I had ever known what the Sinmai were, I had wanted to singot. I just hadn't had a word for it. My attempts to connect with people had been like off-center, too-enthusiastic hi-fives: missing the mark, embarrassing, and stinging. I wanted the feeling of reaching for someone's hand when walking home together, and they not only let me hold their hand, but grasped mine tightly. The shared, unspoken knowing that we wanted each other, without risking mortification and only reaping the rewards of being aligned and connected. I'd felt out of alignment with the human race all my life.

And then I learned of singot, the supreme connection: wordless understanding of a person's entire life.

I pressed my hand to theirs. The pads were cooler than the rest of their hand.

"I am not a stranger," they said.

I had expected — I don't know. A flash of perfect understanding? Maybe our hands weren't properly aligned. While disappointment sunk in, three large men, led by my neighbor Anya, ran down the sidewalk, waving.

"Poche!" Anya jumped the fence and jogged over to us. I had last seen her sobbing on her apartment balcony after her girlfriend had broken up with her, her cheeks smeared with the icing of the cinnamon roll I had brought. Now she wore business casual with a badge clipped to her pocket and a stun gun clipped to her hip.

"Hi, Stacey. Sorry about this. Poche, it's time to return to the lab," she said, and held up her hand as if for a hi-five. They placed their hand over hers, and I realized the hi-five was a symbolic gesture.

"The one called Stacey says they learn here," they said. "I cannot stay?"

"Can't he?" Anya asked me.

I wished I could say yes. What did he want to learn? What was he like? Could he singot with us? "You should ask the school

board first. I have to get back to class. I can give you their contact
— ”

Anya interrupted. "Time is of the essence. Poche, if you really want to go, we can go."

"Yes," they said immediately.

"What? No!" I retorted. I felt irritated that she wasn't listening to me, though I was curious to know why time was of the essence. Yet I couldn't in good conscience let him around the children until I knew it was safe. Poche's ear twisted again. "We have policies around letting strangers into the school. If something happened and somebody got hurt, we would never forgive ourselves."

Anya replied, "The federal government has agreed to allow Sinmai to go wherever they want in Golden to learn about us, so long as they abide by our rules."

"Then please abide by ours, and get permission. I'm not the one who can give it."

Anya said earnestly, "If he can visit just for today, it could mean we learn something that benefits both the Sinmai and humanity."

I wanted to let him in. I wanted to see what he could learn from us. I wanted to teach him, share with him what we did. In my more romantic moments, I thought of my job as teaching children how to be human. Pick up after yourself, wait your turn; if you see something wrong, say something; be kind to everyone... and it killed me that Poche's first lesson on how-to-be-human was to be cautious of strangers.

Reluctantly, I said. "I'm sorry, Anya. The children have to come first."

I returned to class on my own, kicking myself. An extraterrestrial wandering through the streets would be unusual anywhere else in America, but this was Golden, Oklahoma. The speed-bump-sized town made the national news for getting its first stop light in 2015. Ten years later, the Sinmai ship's landing rockets had flattened the stop light. The military moved in and the town had doubled and doubled and doubled. Yet, the first time I had heard of singot was when I met Anya. She had told me, through hiccups and tears on our apartment balcony, that she was the Director of Xenologic Studies at the Interplanetary Institute.

"Oh, wow!" I had said, "What's that like? Did you get to meet the Sinmai? Can they really read minds?"

"Yes and no. We're not sure what's going on. When they align the pads on their fingers and palms, they share information as pure experience. They call it *singot*. A moment where they share what it's like to be them. For example, if I wanted to singot — ” she pressed her hands together " — what I did with you with my colleagues, I would pass on the sensory memory of your voice, the taste of the cinnamon roll, what I felt, what we said... We think it's a perfect transmission of information.

"But singot only works in person. Their technology can't support the volume of information needed to replicate singot or even substitute for it. Also, they must singot to stay healthy, and they need many Sinmai to singot with." Anya wiped her tears away with the heel of her hand. "Six is the smallest number of Sinmai who can singot for extensive periods of time without falling physically or mentally ill. They have a spoken language, but with a limited vocabulary. They think their language evolved so they can signal to each other that they want to singot. They want to learn language as an alternative to singot so they can explore the galaxy farther than they have before."

"I wish I could singot," I said fervently. "That would be amazing."

"That's why we're helping them. We're studying their behavior and anatomy to understand how they do it. In fact, they killed a crew member and gave us their body." My stomach lurched as she went on. "In this case, the one they killed had gone insane. They wouldn't singot with the rest of the crew," she answered my question before I asked it.

"That's..."

"They think of individuality differently than we do," she said, wiping her face. "Why do you want to singot?"

"Why wouldn't I?"

The question was both rhetorical and not. Sometimes I felt like I was hatched from a locker. Born to teach and nothing else. If I could compare my inner life to someone else's, I could understand why I felt different.

✍

Questions pelted me when I slipped back into class.

"Where did the alien go? Is he here? Can we see him?"

Trevor jumped in. "Why don't we start our activity? Paint your favorite memory."

They groaned, but they pulled on their smocks and got busy smearing paint over their paper. If Sinmai were to study pictures drawn by children and took them to be an accurate picture of human life, they would be very, very wrong. Jeanne painted something that could be a dog or a cat or a cow — it had four legs and black and white spots and a bottle-brush tail. I wondered if Poche knew what those animals were.

Trevor gasped. Behind the window of the classroom door, Poche's big golden head loomed. Anya came in, followed by the men, Poche, and the superintendent. The kids gaped. Some ducked behind their canvas.

"We got permission," Anya told me, a little smugly.

The superintendent motioned me closer and said in an undertone, "I said he could watch and participate, but he can't touch the children or be alone with them. And one of the teachers has to be with him at all times."

I forced myself to take steadying breaths and to think deliberately. My eagerness to see what would happen warred with my conscience. How well did Poche understand human speech? Did he understand what we were asking of him?

I said to Poche, "Do you understand the rules?"

"Yes," he said. "Can't touch. Can't be alone."

"And?"

"And a teacher has to be with me."

Think of him as one of the students, I told myself. I took a breath. "Okay." I addressed the class. "Everyone? Poche will be joining us in class today. Let's give him a big welcome!"

"Hi, Poche!" they chorused. The enthusiasm made his fur flare.

"We are painting our favorite memory," I explained to him. "Do you want to try?"

"Yes."

I tied an apron around Poche's belly, handed him a paintbrush, and stood a blank easel with a big sheet of paper before him. "Jeanne, can you share your paint and water with Poche?"

"Yes." She scooted her easel over, shyly.

"Thank you, that's very nice of you. Could you show Poche how to paint?"

"Yes." Jeanne grabbed her brush, dipped it in water, and scrubbed it against the red paint. She poked her canvas a few times. "Like that."

Poche scrutinized the other paintings for a minute. At last, he swirled his brush in blue, and swept it in a circle over the canvas. Anya took notes while one of the men with her recorded Poche on his phone. Poche filled in the blue with patches of deeper blue, then green.

"Is that Earth?" asked Jeanne.

"Yes." More confidently, he loaded his brush with grey and drew a rectangle around Earth, then painted a yellow and brown figure at the bottom of the rectangle. He switched to red, and dabbed dots in a square outside the rectangle.

"Controls," he said.

"Spaceship!" said a little voice at my hip: Toby. The rest of the children abandoned their easels to ogle as Poche swept color across his canvas.

"Yes." He dabbed buttons in other colors and added squiggles — wires? — and added the ears and tails to the figures.

I asked, "Poche, would you share your memory with the class?"

"The memory is..." His fur slicked down and his eyes dilated, scanning blankly, as if searching the wrinkles of his brain. Other than his eyes, he was as still as a tree. At last, he said, "...not... enough... words."

"That's okay," I said. "That's what we learn in kindergarten. Words, and how we use them with others."

✍

A few hours after he was led out of the school, the paperwork was signed, and the Institute rigged the classroom with cameras and microphones and sensors. Every interaction, every word, would be recorded and catalogued.

The next day, Anya hunched in a chair so small her knees practically hit her chin. Like the other kids, Poche had his own cushion, forest green corduroy to contrast with his flaxen fur. Anya looked around the room with a soft, wistful expression I often see on visiting adults without children.

The kids streamed in. When some saw Poche, they gasped and waved. Davy spotted him and dashed back to his mom, burying his head in her thigh. She unwrapped his arms from her leg.

Before we began class, we explained to the children what was going on and allowed them to pepper Poche with questions. Hands rocketed into the air.

"Why did you come to Earth?"

"What is your home planet called? What is it like?"

"Do you like it when we call you alien? Do you want to be called something else?"

Poche answered each question with an air of polite interest. I kept my hands in my lap, though I had a billion questions myself.

For our first exercise, Trevor and I asked the children about their weekend.

Janice's hand zipped into the air. "I wanna share!"

"Okay, Janice, go ahead," I said.

Janice recited, "I went to the recycling center with Mommy. We recycle everything. We got ice cream after. Daddy wasn't home and I sat in his chair. Angela licked my feet. The end."

"Who's Angela?" I asked.

"My cat."

"Excellent. Who's next?"

More hands. One was Poche's.

I called on him.

He said, "I woke when your side of the planet faced your central star, at the time you call 7:46:36 AM central time, in the mothership, in what humans call my 'bed', from a dreamless, 8.96-hour-long, oxygen-supplemented.... thing we do at night?"

The children giggled.

"Funny?" he asked.

I explained, "You don't have to explain every little detail, Poche."

"But that was the weekend."

"We aren't trying to explain the whole weekend. We are sharing the most memorable things that happened during the weekend. What is the essence of the weekend?"

One of his ears twisted. "All of the weekend."

Anya wrote frantically, tearing the paper of her legal pad in her haste to flip to a new page.

"Homework for you," I said to Poche. The children tittered. "Five sentences. No longer than ten words each."

Both ears twisted and his fur frizzed.

"It's doable, I promise," I said. "You don't have to do it now."

He twisted one ear and replied, "Not enough words."

I pulled a beginner's dictionary from the bookshelf and handed it to him. "This is a dictionary," I said. "It will help you understand where words came from, how they are pronounced, and what they mean."

After that, he carried the dictionary around like a blanket. He only set it down at recess to watch the class shout and play. Anya explained games to him: Red Rover, tag, hide and seek, kickball. Mesmerized, he watched the children with the intense stare of a baby as they weaved, collided, argued, cooperated, and ran back and forth across the grass.

"How do they know how to...?" He trailed off. Then he riffled through the dictionary.

The kids pulled him into their games, but he could only stand, puzzled, as the kickball whanged off his belly. After the first brutal game, Kai ran up to him and hugged him.

"I'm sorry," he said. "I love you."

Poche merely said, "It's okay."

At the end of the day, Anya, Poche, and I stayed behind in the empty classroom to go over the day. I saw him turn to the page defining *love*. Anya had stepped out into the hall to have a phone call about confidential Institute stuff, and he and I were alone.

I said, "I don't think the dictionary will help you understand every word."

"Why not?" he asked.

"Sometimes things need to be experienced to be understood. But," I mused, "not everything can be experienced by everyone. Otherwise, there would be no need to communicate."

"Like *abai*?"

"What's abai?"

"Abai is..." His fur slicked down. After a long moment, he said haltingly, "Abai... is... when you don't singot. It makes one..." Poche flipped through the dictionary again, and he did not finish his sentence.

"Like loneliness," I suggested. "A fatal loneliness."

Poche flipped to both words. His ears wiggled. "Yes!" he said. "Some yes."

"Is there a cure for being abai?"

"Singot."

"Like loneliness," I repeated. "Our species are somewhat alike."

"What is the cure for loneliness?"

"Talking or writing to someone could help," I replied. "If the lonely person is honest. But sometimes they don't know what they need to hear. Or say." I hesitated. "I'm in that situation now."

"You need to singot," Poche said authoritatively.

"Agreed."

"Ergh." Poche drummed his fingers and his ears swirled. He looked like he was winding up for something serious. "You may die soon."

"No, I won't," I said, alarmed. "Humans can die from loneliness, but not that easily. Sometimes it can take years. Decades." *Oh God, decades?* said a little voice in the back of my mind.

Poche relaxed.

Anya returned. Her mouth was pulled tight as she set her phone down on the table to record. "Poche, tell us what you thought about today's events."

"What is love?"

I caught Anya's eye and hummed the famous bars from the song. Anya smirked.

She said, "Love is when you feel deep, tender affection for someone. Like how I loved my girlfriend. But it doesn't mean they will feel the same way."

"There're different kinds of love," I said hastily. "And none are less than others. Love for your partner, your parents, your friends, your children, your country — "

Anya cut in, "But the Sinmai don't have to worry about attraction getting in the way. They're all asexual. They don't experience sexual attraction, whatsoever."

I felt a strange internal fracturing, like an ice cube dropped in water.

Poche asked, "Then what is love for?"

I answered, quietly, "Love, I think, makes up the gap between language and understanding. People misunderstand quite often. Sometimes they don't listen. But, if they love each other, they can trust the other person and assume the best intentions from what is said." As I spoke, the fracturing traveled along my nerves and blood vessels. An odd sensation of horror — and relief. *Asexual.*

Poche flipped through his dictionary to 'misunderstand,' 'trust', and 'intentions.' He curled his hands into fists as he scanned the words.

Anya asked him, "What are you thinking?"

"I think I see now," he said. "Sinmai failed to use language correctly before. Yuche said they went abai on purpose. They said we had to... risk it. To test language." He turned the dictionary's pages to the word *risk*. "We did not believe them. And now there are six of us." He opened his hands. "I am thinking, what did Yuche think? They did not have the words that I have now."

Poche's hands clenched briefly, crumpling the page, and he smoothed the paper.

"If... language... can..." He put his hands together. "Singot. It can also..." He took his hands apart. "Stop abai."

"But you don't need to be abai to singot," Anya said.

"You need to be a little abai to singot," Poche replied. "Otherwise... why singot? That's why, I think, Yuche went abai. We... did not...." His mouth worked for a moment before he managed, "Trust."

My heart clenched for the Sinmai. Poche turned the dictionary to the first page of the 'A' section.

"I will need more words," he said. "I will test language, and go abai."

✍

I passed a park, walking from my kindergarten to my apartment, and a couple relaxing on a picnic blanket under a tree. The woman leaned close to the man, laughing, and I could not ever remember being so radiant. *How are they doing it? What does it mean when she looks at his hands, what does it mean when he rolls up his sleeves, what is he doing to her that makes her beam like that? What does it feel like for both of them?*

Was this how Poche felt living with humanity? I thought, *Singot is better. Why articulate something to somebody else when you can just feel it together?* It made sense why the Sinmai would be asexual.

Yet that thought disturbed me. It couldn't be right.

I shut myself in my apartment and researched asexuality.

As I read articles, forums, papers, I felt myself draining into a deadly swallowing sea without bottom. My past felt empty, even as I questioned the emptiness, hoping something would answer back. I thought I had been in love before. A middle-school friend, a sleepover. The lights going out as if snatched away by the lightning storm that rolled in. As I groped for a light switch, I had found a hand. We screamed, then burst into laughter, grabbed again, and caught each other. We were as close as a pair of socks. I'd felt this time and again with others, believing that the urgent wanting (as I imagined sexual desire would feel) would come sometime for the right person. I wanted a light switch or a hand to hold. I tried to imagine sex, and couldn't.

The websites I found emphasized that asexuality didn't mean that you couldn't give or feel love. Asexuality had little to do with the lack of communication. At least, the kind of communication Poche sought. Yet, asexuality felt important to abai and singot, and I couldn't explain why.

I couldn't wait for humanity to invent something that would allow us to singot. Poche was right; language would have to suffice. But the dictionaries wouldn't be enough, because it wasn't just the lack of words — what words we didn't have could be invented. It was the lack of trust that someone else would understand you and be patient with you while you fumbled to explain yourself. But how could he learn patience when he didn't have the time? How long could a Sinmai be abai until they died?

✎

The following day, when going over vocabulary with Poche, he said, "Yesterday, you reacted to Anya's words."

A pit deepened in my stomach. Anya was taking notes beside us. Her eyebrows quirked.

"Uh, yes." I had sworn that I would be honest with children when they asked me questions, and I counted Poche as one of them. "About love. She accidentally touched on something I had been thinking about for a long time."

"What is it?" he asked.

"I'm still thinking about what it means. How to say it." I asked, "Can I tell you later when I know more about how I feel?"

His lips lifted. His gums were black and set with chisel-like teeth beveled to sharp edges. I imagined the crew mate who had been sacrificed. "Abai, Stacey," he said. "That's abai."

He held up his hand suddenly, and I jumped, as if he had been about to slap me. "You will tell me?"

I put my hand to his. "I promise."

Poche flipped to the word 'promise.' He looked mollified, but still suspicious.

"Very good," Anya said, scrawling notes at light speed. "Very interesting stuff."

As class went on, I thought, *Maybe I should have just told them. Why didn't I want to?* Maybe it was because it seemed pretty hasty to tell people I was asexual so soon after discovering it myself. What if I was wrong? I wanted to be wrong. I was delaying for evidence to the contrary: a leaping heart at another person's appearance, an undeniable feeling between the legs. When I thought of a partner, I pictured myself standing next to a blot, like someone had put their thumb over a camera lens.

But it wasn't just that. I was like Tasha, who always could be found hovering outside play groups, waiting to be invited in. I always stepped in to help her. But now I wondered whether I needed an adult to do that for me with other adults. *But I'm an adult, damnit. I should be able to do it myself.*

We stayed behind after class to go over the day, as usual. Anya had brought a bag of clementines and the sweet lobes glowed in the sunlight. Her hand knocked against mine repeatedly as we reached for them. Each time it was like the tongue of a bell resonating through me. As I put a lobe in my mouth, I forced myself to imagine it was her ear. The smooth, plump crescent, warm, tart, bursting.

And then I thought, *What am I doing?*

Anya caught my eye with her deep brown gaze.

Poche said gravely, "Stacey, you are red. Why?"

"Oh, hush." I was mortified, smiling awkwardly. I hadn't thought he would notice.

"You can't say that to him." Anya smiled with crinkling eyes.

"Noooo, I'm not going to say." I was laughing, even as she grabbed my hands. I was half-serious. She was getting the wrong idea. But the contrarian part of me said, "Yes, yes, yes." Where would this go? *Don't you want to know her more? Even if it starts with a misunderstanding?*

"You have to explain, or he won't know." She beamed like the sun. Nobody had ever looked at me like that before. I wanted to blind myself looking.

Both of his ears twisted.

He asked, "Why will you not tell me?"

"Well..." I couldn't answer. I didn't have an answer, at least, not one that I wanted to say out loud. Anya was listening. *Say it*, I thought. "I'm red because I'm sunburned," I said lamely. *Such a coward*, I thought. Breaking my pledge not to lie to children so I didn't have to confront difficult things. Anya raised an eyebrow.

Poche asked, "Why do you say that?"

Anya said icily, "Sometimes, Poche, people are uncomfortable with same-sex flirting."

"I'm not uncomfortable!" I protested.

"Then why don't you explain?"

"Why don't you explain, Anya?" he asked. "Is this a power struggle?"

"No," Anya and I said together.

He asked, "Is there danger nearby? And redness is camouflage?" I chuckled. Anya blistered me with a look. "Is it a secret? Is it like how Sinmai treat *horkew'e* ceremonies, during which we send a young Sinmai into the *threwd* with *sled*, *vie*, and *wave* — "

"Poche," I said.

But he babbled, " — and we tell them, 'Go. Make yourself abai, see how plants go together, how water unmakes itself from clouds, and when you return, singot, and you will know Sinmai and know nothing and they will go out and grow abai with only two hands — "

Anya had pulled out her phone and dialed frantically. Was he going insane? Was this abai? I held up my hands. Fuck my feelings, I'd deal with the fallout with Anya later. But then his fingers wrapped twice around my hand and squeezed. It was like being caught in a machine — flesh bending too far in wrong ways.

I screamed, "I will tell you! Please, let go!"

He yanked his hands away as if he had touched a scorching stove. "I am sorry. Sorry. Sorry."

My heart raced in my throat. My joints cracked, and welts crossed my wrists.

Anya had pulled out her stun gun. When she saw my expression, she shoved it back in its holster.

"Let's end here," she muttered.

Poche's hands flexed and flexed, as did mine. Anya's clenched.

What would have happened if I had been honest? I had been... But I *didn't* know why I had blushed. I thought I was asexual. Right?

Idiot, I told myself. *Language only works if you use it.*

I didn't understand what had happened to me. I thought that if I could just explain what I felt to myself, I would understand. Then I would know what to say to Poche and Anya. I had to know perfectly. Otherwise, it would feel like I was lying to them.

But the contrarian inside me said, *You won't know perfectly. What are you afraid of?*

My answer was meager, pathetic. *I'm afraid they won't believe me.*

And then I felt angry with myself. *How will Poche learn how to trust if I'm not a good role model? I have to tell him soon*, I told myself. *Even if I'm not sure what it is, even if I stammer or stutter. He's trying. Meet him half-way. This I can do for him.*

✍

A storm muscled into the following morning's blue sky. Trevor led the group in a lesson about the water cycle, how clouds form and rain falls. Poche watched the sky with a finger tapping his knee.

The lights flickered.

"It's okay, everyone," said Trevor. "We have our flashlights."

Then thunder shattered the air and the lights went out.

Children screamed. Trevor switched on his flashlight and called for order. The grey-blue disturbed light from the window was all we had, and the flashlights — and Poche, whose hands glowed. A pale blue light emitted from his calluses.

"Poche, how are you doing that?" Anya asked, and held out the recorder.

"The Sinmai evolved to singot," he said. His hands clenched, as if to crush the light. "The ship will be here soon."

The way he sat, the way he looked out the window, the tapping. Something else I couldn't understand.

"Poche?" I said uncertainly.

"Let's go out to the hall," Poche said suddenly, rising.

The hall was dark, except where the storm's light wavered through the windows. The gloom shied away from Poche's upheld hands.

"I have discovered something about the nature of abai," Poche said. In the dark, he looked misshapen, bestial. "Abai is not a disease. It is a stranger-maker, an evolutionary learning mechanism which — " He vibrated. "Which singot overrides." Suddenly, he said, "Do not let the others singot with me, Stacey. Explain to them. I promise I will tell them. I need to stay abai, just for a little while longer — it's the only way to test — "

His words jumbled together.

"Stacey, get away from him," Anya said. She reached for something on her belt, and there was an electric whine.

I said, "Tell me — what's wrong?" I raised my hand.

"Poche, walk in front of us to the lobby," said Anya.

"Anya, wait. I'll take full responsibility."

"For what?" she said tersely.

"Poche, I'll tell you — the thing I didn't want to talk about..." My heart clogged my throat. "The word that I reacted to — what Anya said — about asexuality. I have always felt a little... out of alignment, with people, all my life. When she said that, I realized I was... asexual. And my life made sense." Poche's fur stood on end. "But it scared me, because I didn't know what the rest of my life would look like."

Poche's expression was like none I had ever seen on Earth. He said in a garbled voice, "I don't understand."

I felt like he had reached inside my chest and crushed my heart.

The stormlight dimmed, and so did the slashing of the rain on the windows. Beyond the lobby, over the parking lot, was something that could only be the Sinmai ship. Like a black moon had descended from the sky and blocked the rain. Sirens keened, approaching.

Poche hurried out of the lobby into the rain. From the ship, five Sinmai descended on a platform. The way they glanced around themselves, their gestures, the way they stood — like five fingers on the same hand. Poche approached them and spoke rapidly in Sinmai before they could. He overpowered their attempts to cut in, repeating *abai* and *singot* amidst a torrent of English and Sinmai words. The five exchanged a complicated set of gestures like a secret handshake. Blue sparks danced between their palms like a cloudless summer day, when you can see infinity hinting beyond the sky. Poche shivered. But he stepped away, covered his eyes, and said something in a breaking voice.

The Sinmai lunged for him. They wrestled him down as military vehicles skidded round the corner. Their powerful lights caught the tussling aliens and obliterated individual features. Snarls juddered from Poche's chest. Claws extended from his feet and gouged earth from the lawn. One Sinmai had bit down on his arm with those teeth and another champed his leg, forcing him down.

Tears smeared my vision. I felt divided against myself. *Help him! Leap in, say something! Why don't you do anything? Something!* But what could I say that could replace singot? I had already failed.

The lead Sinmai pinned down Poche's arm, uncurled his clenched hand, and pressed their palm to his.

Light annihilated the schoolyard. When I recall that moment now, it is like a still in a movie, and a bomb has just gone off. It doesn't seem like it happened. I should have felt the blast like a ghostly wall. I know the soldiers who had been running to confront the Sinmai recoiled. I know the Sinmai pile fell apart. I saw one fall to the side, on the road, making an awful scream like an iceberg splitting.

And I saw that Poche lay still. Clearest of all was a black asterisk of soot on the asphalt where his hand should be, and his wrist cuffed with flames.

✍

Next week, kindergarten resumed. I told the class that Poche might not come back. We all cried for a while. I put his painting on the wall so parents and children could see it with the rest of the class. We didn't know if he would come back, but we had to keep going like he would. We set out his floor cushion and put it away at the end of each day. I felt like an extra chamber had been carved out of my heart and my blood had leaked away, and I was only still moving because I was too numb to realize I had died. If only I had had better words and put them in a better order. If only I had told him sooner, he would be alive.

But then he returned.

Certainly, it was a Sinmai, toddling down the sidewalk on the other side of the fence, the stub of an arm bandaged. Children screamed and ran towards him, and Trevor and I ran to call them back. Trevor called, at least — I just ran. Poche waded into the children and they glommed onto him. Anya and the guards who followed him stepped away. Anya looked tense, expectant.

"Good morning," Poche said to me. "I'm sorry."

"We're all just glad you're okay," I said through a tight throat.

"No," he said emphatically. "*I'm* sorry. Poche has died. This body is now Oche."

The children quieted. *Poche has died. This body is now Oche.* These words did not go together with what I saw. They stood straighter. Their speech was clearer. They had Poche's body. Yet, I was looking at a stranger.

To me, Oche held up his hand. With trepidation, I placed mine over it.

"When we singot," he said carefully. "We pour ourselves together and redistribute equally among our bodies. We five Sinmai on Earth are all now Oche. Poche is within us all."

They had killed Poche, as easily as wiping words off a whiteboard. I couldn't believe I had wanted to singot. If perfect understanding with others meant self-destruction, I didn't want it.

Oche's ears were twisted as he watched me. This, I realized, was what Poche realized about singot.

"Humans don't die when they share themselves with others," I said. "We become people through other people, just like you. Only, we do it a little at a time."

He asked. "Then why wouldn't you tell me? What were you scared about?"

"I felt like I had become a stranger to myself. And to other people. I thought that nobody would understand who I was, and I wouldn't understand others either. And then I would be abai forever."

His ears wiggled. "Yes!"

The Sinmai had to leave soon. They had realized that there were too few Sinmai to stay safely on Earth. Before they left, I begged the school to give them the dictionaries, and helped the children write their names in the flyleaves. Anya invited me to watch them leave. One by one they put their hands to mine and disappeared into their ship. Gouts of fire billowed beneath it as it launched, punched through the clouds, and joined the moon in the sky.

I still miss Poche, the instance of individuality that wove into Oche. By now his name must have changed again. Does the whole planet share one name? Was there ever a difference between one of him and all of them? There must have been. And there must be now. Nobody can travel to another world and return unchanged. When the crew returns home, they will greet their citizens as strangers. There will be so much for them to know about Earth. I hope their hands won't explode.

The human body limits us. We can't understand everything all at the same time. We barely understand ourselves, let alone others. But the cool thing about language is that if communication fails, you can try again. I've been talking to Anya. I told her how I thought I was asexual. And she got it! I feel embarrassed for thinking she wouldn't. Things have softened between us, started to flow onward. We're not together, not really. But we're looking in the same direction. Towards the Sinmai home world.

I've started a new career at the Institute. Being a certified friend of Sinmai helped my application jump to the top of the pile. I'll be studying Oche's language now, so I can tell him, "I know why you painted the moment you saw Earth. You were curious to know whether you were alone in the universe. And then you discovered you weren't." The Sinmai trusted that humanity was worth discovering. To live, I must too. And I can't imagine a better life than spending it with people I'll never really know, who will forever surprise me with new aspects to love, unfolding forever together.

✍ ✍ ✍

Initial feedback

I liked the concept and ending. The piece runs substantially (perhaps as much as 50%) longer than it needs to, but there are also some elements that need context or clarification, and I'd have liked to see the characters more developed. I didn't see a strong reason for using 2nd person. The asexuality aspect could also do with more exploration; it didn't feel like an organic, core element as is. I expected Stacey's desire to singot to play a larger role.

Author's intent

What do you think the story's about?
What emotions are you trying to evoke?

To me, the story revolves around this phrase: "I still don't know if I can love. But I can't imagine a better definition of love than spending it with someone who I'll never really know, but who continues to surprise me with new aspects to love, unfolding forever together. Whoever it is."

When I started writing the story, it heavily based on this NPR program (https://www.npr.org/programs/invisibilia/530718193/emotions) about anthropologists believing they had discovered a new emotion. The story also started from a Tumblr screenshot about how kindergarten teachers are actually the perfect teachers for teaching how to be human (see attachment). The idea that you could discover a new emotion gripped me. I had recently realized I was asexual, and I didn't like it *at all*. I wanted to feel something for another person; I wanted to excavate that missing piece. I felt messed up, but ached to share, and wanted not just be seen, but found and spoken to. And most importantly, to be understood. Specifically, I wanted to understand others and be understood perfectly. Hence, *singot*. But if given the chance to *singot*, I'm not sure I would take it. When thinking back over my life and wonder, *God, how I did I miss that I was asexual?* I usually answer, because I was happy as I was. I love learning about the world and the people who walk on it. Why introspect when there's a zillion things to learn? And if we understand immediately, perfectly, does that mean we lose learning? I wanted to explore what we lose by understanding perfectly or imperfectly, using a strong chain of causal and emotional logic, and find an answer I could live by.

Themes:

- Learning/discovery
- Asexuality/identity
- Language/understanding

Emotions:

- Excitement/joy in discovery/learning
- Loneliness
- Fear, confusion

Author's note

The top two comments I get from my writing group and from editors are:

1. I don't get it.
2. The relationships in [insert story here] need work.

These also sum up my life among humanity. Is it any surprise that I wrote a story about effortless understanding?

But the editing process for that story, "Singot", didn't just teach me how readers understand a story. Through revising I came to understand that *understanding itself* can be a deliberate act.

I have a writing group, so I imagined revisions with *Metaphorosis* would be similar to our workshops: line edits, impressions on the story, what worked and what didn't, etc. I didn't anticipate how much the story could be refined. But I had sunk over 80 hours into writing and revising "Singot". I began submitting it to magazines when I could not think of how to make it better. I had an inkling that it was too long. But by how much? I did not have the energy to fathom.

But then I was accepted to *Metaphorosis* — contingent on rewrites. And of course the first thing Morris suggested was that "Singot" was way too long. Possibly, he suggested, it could be cut by 50% or 60%. I thought, *Jesus Fried Christ. Where do I start?*

The only thing I thought I could do was print out the whole story, take up a pen, and cut anything I didn't like. Character not interesting? Slash. Dialogue too superficial? Gone. Can't explain why, but just don't like this part? Bye.

In cutting or combining characters, the ones left got more room to be themselves. Not that it didn't hurt. I cut extra side-scenes with kindergarteners and Poche. Those cuties need a side-story all their own! Maybe I'll write one. But I wasn't sorry to combine two of the main characters. Anya was originally two characters, an arrogant scientist and his sweet, whip-smart assistant. Conjoining them meant suturing together parts that, at first glance, contradicted each other.

But contradiction made the resulting character *realer*. Then, because of her, I thought more critically about the protagonist's contradictory yearning for connection and fear of sharing herself. I could then play them off each other and Poche.

I first thought in cutting that I would lose interesting characters. Who, in my mind (and in hindsight, nowhere on the page), would be a great loss to the story. But in cutting extras, I loved my resulting characters much more, because I had to get to know them more specifically and show that in the writing. The editing process humbled me again and again.

I also gained confidence in my editing chops. I had a bad habit of thinking, "Well, this section is a little dry," or, "this description — would a reader understand it?" and not realizing, or trusting, that my instincts were right and I needed to fix it. I'd like to think it was mostly just weariness or anxiety. Or worse, laziness, or not knowing how to get better. What surprised me about getting editor comments was that how many of them were *not* surprising — I had thought so too. To hear my thoughts stated explicitly from someone whose knowledge I trusted felt empowering.

As we worked through the subsequent drafts, revision clarified "Singot"'s last lines: "I still don't know if I can love. But I can't imagine a better definition of love than spending it with someone who I'll never really know, but who continues to surprise me with new aspects to love, unfolding forever together. Whoever it is." These lines didn't change much between the first and last drafts. But by changing what came before, they became better.

To finish "Singot", I had to realize that if *singot* is the effortless understanding of everything about a person, we'd lose the pleasure of getting to know them.

And what's a story? My working definition is that a story is about someone struggling to do something and how they changed inside as a result of that struggle. The discovery of *singot's* true nature wasn't the story. "Singot" was Stacey's story. Revising "Singot" was mine. We both learned that understanding people must be practiced; that our understandings must be revised constantly as we learn more — and there is always more to learn, and always more to revise. Especially, sometimes disconcertingly, sometimes joyfully, about yourself.

Editor's note

It's not uncommon for me to suggest an author change a story's length. Sometimes I think a story's too short, more often too long, and sometimes just the *wrong* length. In the case of Singot, I thought the original version was substantially too long. As E.C. notes, I suggested it might be as much as 50% too long. That's a heck of a lot, especially when an author has worked so hard to come up with all those words to begin with. Some authors back away from such a request; some don't feel it's justified, and some are unwilling to make such drastic changes. Happily, E.C. is made of tougher stuff, and in the end, "Singot" did lose about 1/3 of its original length. I think it's a clearer, stronger story for it.

All my second readers liked the core of the original story. I and some others didn't like the original's second person approach, we all thought the characters needed some work, and there was a general consensus that the asexuality element could be better incorporated in the story. This latter in particular generated some interesting discussion with E.C., about how people experience asexuality and whether the fact that it can feel tangential necessarily meant it should come across as tangential in the story. Gradually, that element did get woven in more, and I think that helped clarify the story's themes. Doing that also helped to clarify and deepen Stacey's own personality.

One issue that sometimes arises is that, having once identified what the story's principal themes are, it turns out they're not reflected all the way through the story. I felt that was the case here, with E.C.'s themes popping here and there, but not having really consistent threads across the piece. Over a few revisions, and as the story shortened and simplified somewhat, the themes came out more clearly and consistently.

Singot

You scared me when I saw you watching the children play from behind the fence. I thought you were a baseball mascot. Round belly and stumpy legs, noodle arms, and a short muzzle and nubby, teacup ears, lush with wheaten fur. Except you had those long fingers that threaded through the chain link like vines. Even from afar, you had an alertness, a flexibility to your face, not the vacant, manic expression of a mascot. You were the first Sinmai I had seen in person. Immediately, I wanted to know you.

You unwrapped your fingers from the fence and toddled down the sidewalk, still watching. The thirty-two kindergarteners of Zeigler Elementary pointed at you and squealed. A few ran to me. A few more ran to the fence.

I raised my voice. "Get back here, now!"

They stopped. But you rounded the fence and ventured towards us.

And you did not know then, but any stranger that came onto the playground was treated as a threat.

The other teacher on duty, Trevor, blew his recess whistle. His voice rang out. "Everyone, stay behind us."

Toby and Jeanne dawdled between us and you. You had stopped when the whistle cut through the air. Your amiable expression did not change. One ear twisted.

Jeanne whined, "I wanna pet him!"

I snapped my fingers. "Toby, Jeanne, move your butts. Go, or we can go to the office."

They slouched back to the line together. You did not move, merely stared, friendly-looking. I approached you cautiously and used the voice I used on scared children. "Hi there. Can I help you?"

Your voice creaked, as if needing to be oiled. "Can... you?"

"I can help you." I remember thinking, I probably can. "Are you lost?"

"Yes."

"Who are you looking for?"

"Yes. My host, Richard Baum."

Of course it was Richard. "Richard is my neighbor. Why don't we go inside and call him?"

"Why... don't we? Are we?" Your other ear twisted. I realized you understood literally.

"Let us — you and me — go inside — " I pointed at the school. "And call Richard."

Your ears untwisted. "Yes."

I called Trevor, "We're going to the office." Trevor nodded, and herded the kids back inside. You followed me across the grassy yard.

"What is your name?" I asked you.

"Poche," you replied. "And yours?"

"My name is Stacey Ellis."

"What is a neighbor?"

"A neighbor is somebody who lives next to you."

"Where are we?"

"We are in Zeigler Elementary."

"What is a Zeigler Elementary?"

"It's a school. A school is a place where we learn."

The receptionist's eyes popped when we entered the lobby. I explained the situation to her and looked up Richard's number in my phone. I had met him five months previously when he moved into a house adjacent to my apartment. As men maneuvered machines, furniture, and collections of moon rocks through the narrow door, he had plucked my phone out of my hand and thumbed his number in it. "In case of emergencies." He had twitched his eye at me. I thought he had an eye problem. Later I realized he was trying to wink.

I steeled myself and called. Voicemail. "You have reached the personal number of Richard Baum, Director of Xenologic Studies at the Interplanetary Institute. You know what to do."

As I left a message, you inspected the mural in the lobby: a painting of children holding hands on top of Earth and colorful, bubbly words, Welcome to Zeigler! You touched the words and ran your fingers over them.

When I finished, I said, "I have to go back to class. Please wait here. D'Lana will make sure you're okay."

"... Okay."

I slipped into class. Questions pelted me when I stepped inside.

"Where did the alien go? Is he here? Can we see him?"

Trevor jumped in. "Why don't we start our activity? Paint your favorite memory."

They groaned, but they pulled on their yellow smocks and got busy smearing paint over their paper. If the Sinmai studied pictures drawn by children and understood them to be an accurate picture of American life, they would be very, very wrong. Something like a fire or a red tulip. A dog or a cat or a cow — it had four legs akimbo, black and white spots, and a bottle-brush tail. I wondered if you knew what these animals were.

Trevor gasped. Behind the window of the classroom door, your big golden head loomed. I opened the door; you looked innocent; the secretary hurried down the hall.

She said frantically, "I'm sorry, he got away from me. Sweetheart, why don't you come back to the lobby to wait for your host?"

"I want to see," you replied.

"See... the school?"

"See." You gestured at the class. The kids gaped. Many ducked behind their canvas.

"I have not seen... this. I do not have enough words," you finished.

I understood then. You didn't realize that you were breaking social conventions. You were curious.

To the secretary, I asked, "Have you heard back from Richard?" She shook her head. "Let me talk to Trevor."

Trevor and I went to the corner to talk.

"I'm not comfortable with this," he said. "If parents heard an alien walked into class...."

"They'd flip," I finished. "But how many chances will the kids have to meet an alien? Maybe if we set some rules it would be alright."

Trevor pursed his lips. Humanity had heard that the Sinmai were peaceful. You wanted to explore the galaxy, but you needed better long-distance communication. Your audible speech was not enough. So you were hopscotching from planet to planet, looking for information-dense communication technologies and types. Humans languages had the greatest potential, so you stopped on Earth, in five areas: Japan, Mongolia, Belgium, Chile, and here, the United States.

So you told us two years ago.

After a beat, Trevor said, "Just until his host gets here."

I felt an explosion in the pit of my stomach. We returned to you and the secretary. "You can watch and learn, but only if you don't touch the children or be alone with them. Trevor or I have to be with you at all times. And this is only until Richard picks you up. Okay?"

You nodded. What were you thinking?

I addressed the class. "Everyone? Poche will be joining us in class today while he waits for his friend to pick him up. Let's give him a big welcome!"

"Hi Poche!" they chorused. The enthusiasm made your fur flare.

"We are painting our favorite memory," I explained to you. "Do you want to try?"

"Yes."

I tied an apron around your belly, handed you a paintbrush, and stood a blank easel with a big sheet of paper before you. "Jeanne, can you share your paint and water with Poche?"

"Yes." She scooted her easel over, shyly.

"Thank you, that's very nice of you. Could you show Poche how to paint?"

"Yes." Jeanne grabbed her brush, dipped it in water, and scrubbed it against the red paint. She poked her canvas a few times. "Like that."

You held the paintbrush like a stake and stabbed it straight through the canvas. The kids shrieked with laughter. I hid my smile.

I said, "Not like that! Dab, not stab. Look how Jeanne does it." Jeanne daintily dotted her brush over her painting. "Yes... gently...." While I cut a new sheet of paper for your canvas, I asked Jeanne. "What memory are you drawing?"

"Eating barbeque with Pop Pop. This is the sauce."

You asked me, "What is a memory?"

At the time, I wondered: did Sinmai not have memories? I know now you have nearly a perfect memory. Or humanity thinks it's perfect. But of course, you didn't have the vocabulary when you first entered the classroom.

"A memory is an experience you remember," I said.

"What is remember?"

"Remembering is the act of thinking back to something in the past."

"Thinking?"

"Uh-oh." Trevor caught my eye and smiled. You and the kindergartners have never-ending questions in common.

Jeanne explained, "Thinking is talking to yourself in your head."

You said, "Oooo, I understand." I wanted to laugh and cry. Were we dooming Earth? You added, "What is favorite?"

"Favorite is... the thing you like the most. You can have a favorite food, or a favorite chair, or a favorite person...."

"And we are painting the experience we like the most."

"Yes," I said, relieved.

You scrutinized the other paintings for a minute. At last, you swirled your brush in blue, and swept it in a circle over the canvas. You filled in the blue with patches of deeper blue, then green.

"Is that Earth?" asked Jeanne.

"Yes." More confidently, you loaded your brush with grey and drew a rectangle around Earth, then painted a yellow and brown figure at the bottom of the rectangle. You switched to red, and dabbed dots in a square outside the rectangle.

"Controls," you said.

"Spaceship!" said a little voice at my hip: Toby. The rest of the children abandoned their easels to ogle as you swept color across your canvas.

"Yes." You dabbed buttons in other colors and added squiggles — wires? And added the ears and tails to the figures.

I asked, "Poche, would you share your memory with the class?"

Then you did something odd. You met my eyes and raised your free hand, as if offering a solemn high five. The back of your hand was furred, and the fur was silky and dense. The palm was naked, pale brown, and rough, and the meaty parts of your palm and fingertips had raised pads like gold calluses or metallic blisters.

"Singot," you said emphatically and wiggled your fingers. I had no idea what you meant, but I knew what you wanted. I put the tips of my fingers on yours and spread them out. The pads were cooler than the rest of your hand.

But nothing happened.

"But what was the memory?" Toby insisted.

You dropped your hand. You explained, "The memory is me finding Earth."

We heard rapid footsteps approaching the classroom. Richard, a woman with a badge clipped to her sweater, and three large men in white clothes entered the classroom, followed by our secretary. Guns and batons were clipped to their hips. My heart throbbed in my throat. I thought, oh God, why did I let you in? Trevor and I ushered the children to the wall as the newcomers surrounded you.

The woman said in a friendly voice, "Hey Poche, why did you leave the lab?" Richard thrust a recorder between them.

"Hello Anya. I left the lab to go to the store." You stated this as if it was a perfectly good answer.

Anya tried again, "But why did you leave the lab to go to the store?"

"I left the lab to go to the store because I wanted to see the store."

There was an old lady who swallowed a fly. Don't ask me why, I thought. The way you answered questions sounded like the nursery rhyme. Anya caught my eye and gave me a look of good-humored exasperation.

"It's time to return to the lab," she said, holding up her hand as if for a high-five. You placed yours over hers in the same gesture you had done with me.

"I cannot stay?" you asked.

I said, "I'm sorry, Poche. We would love for you to stay and learn with us, but I should have asked the administrators first. We have policies around letting strangers into the schools. If something happened and somebody got hurt, we would never forgive ourselves."

You asked, "What is administrator?"

Richard interrupted me, "An administrator is someone who manages organizations from the top down, implementing — "

You reached over and placed three fingers over Richard's mouth. Richard stuttered and fell silent.

You said, "I want Stacey to explain."

The whole class huddled behind me. The men watched you, alert, hands on their batons.

I took a deep breath. "In school, an administrator is someone who makes decisions for everyone."

"Can they decide to let me stay?" you asked.

"Possibly."

"Can you ask them if I can stay?"

Richard took Poche's fingers off his lips. "Why do you want to attend kindergarten?"

You said clumsily, "I have understood here."

Emotions swept through me like wind — astonishment, exhilaration, joy — and I could not remember the last time I had felt so suddenly strongly about anything or anyone before. Therefore, it pained me to say, "We would be happy to have you attend kindergarten with us, Poche. We'll ask permission first." I wished I could have said, "You absolutely can."

The men and Richard escorted you out. Richard gave me a new business card for an emergency line. The principal and secretary waited out in the hall. Together, we soothed the children, called parents to pick them up, and promised the parents and children that we would keep them up to date. I got a tongue-lashing from everyone involved, but the Institute stepped in. They explained that they were allowing you as much freedom as possible. That you liked me was enough for them to overrule the hesitation of some of the parents and the school board.

This would be unusual anywhere else in America, but this was in Golden, Oklahoma. The speed-bump-sized town made the national news for getting its first stop light in 2015. Ten years later, your ship's landing rockets flattened the stop light. The military moved in and the town doubled and doubled and doubled. The federal government offered moving stipends to professionals to study you and serve other professionals. The children's parents likely worked at the Institute. I heard later that we received at least one call from a parent who wanted their child to attend class with you.

A few hours after you were led out of the school, the paperwork was signed, and the Institute rigged the classroom with cameras and microphones and sensors. Every interaction, every word, would be recorded and catalogued. The school board allowed me to drop to part-time so I could work with you one-on-one. Starting Monday morning we'd have kindergarten. In the afternoon, we'd go over what you learned. Richard gave me a recorder and a microphone and several thick notebooks. The pages were divided into sections like a planner, except, instead of the sections being labeled with the days of the week, they read Date, Time, Context. I was to write two thousand words a day on things I observed.

According to the papers the Institute had given me about your background, you had been selected from the Sinmai population to join the crew to find Earth. I knew that human spaceships would take decades to leave the solar system and asked Richard how you had traveled from so far away. Richard erased the flowers off the classroom whiteboard to draw trajectories, diagrams, formulas, and a picture of a "quote-unquote wormhole." The painting of your favorite memory surfaced in my mind throughout the day. What did finding Earth mean to you? What was singot?

In a meeting at a coffee shop on Sunday, Richard explained the singot problem.

"Singot happens when two or more Sinmai align the pads on their fingers and palms and share information with each other through bioelectrical waves. The process allows them to share a snapshot of an experience. A moment where they share what it's like to be them in a given period. For example, if I wanted to singot what I did with you with my supervisor, I would pass on the sensory memory of meeting you at a coffee shop and talking to you. The coffee's taste and smell, customers talking, the way you look...."

I asked, "So why come to us? What can speech or writing do that singot can't?"

"Singot doesn't work if it's not in person. Their technology can't support the volume of information needed to replicate singot, or even substitute it. Also, they must singot to stay healthy, and they need many Sinmai to singot with. Seven is the smallest number of Sinmai who can singot for extensive periods of time without falling mentally and physically ill. They hope we can replicate singot with our technology or learn language well enough that they can go without singotting for longer periods. And of course we want to help them, because then we would be able to singot, too."

I imagined a telephone for brains. The thought that I might be able to singot one day was heady.

He said, "Humanity already knows why we must communicate: we need other people. Not just for physical needs like clean water, regular food, and shelter, but for emotional needs, like wanting to be seen or loved. Think of the ways humans communicate. Facial expressions. Gestures. The way we stand. Talking, writing, singing... sex."

I kept my face aggressively bland. When I didn't react, he went on. "The Sinmai language lacks many words for abstract things. The Sinmai hypothesize that their speech is for communicating the need to get closer to each other so they can singot. They think we're impossible creatures for being able to communicate to such an extent vocally or physically. They told us that muteness is common among them. Violence is rare and limited to fights against predators. Much of the population is asexual — you know, doesn't experience sexual attraction."

I felt a strange internal fracturing, like an ice cube dropped in water. Asexual. The word I had been unknowingly searching for my whole life. Were you asexual? Was I? Did it mean something important? I needed to know more.

I began to ask another question — something about asexuality's importance to the Sinmai and what it had to do with singot, when Richard said, "They gave up a crew member so we can autopsy them."

He said this so casually that I felt like my mind had stuttered.

I said, "I'm sorry, what?"

"They killed a crew member and gave us their body. They aren't as individual as humans are, so it doesn't matter if they kill one or two." My stomach lurched as he went on, "In this case, the one they killed had gone insane. They wouldn't singot with the crew," he answered my question before I had asked. "They gave us a body and asked us to tell them what we would find."

"Can we allow Poche in class if he killed a crew mate?" I asked. Even as I felt the urge to know more about you, you might not understand how precious each child is, might kill one, the way ants would sacrifice themselves.

Richard waved his hand. "We agreed to allow them to learn about us so long as they don't hurt us."

"How well can they understand us?" I asked.

"Sorry?"

"You can tell somebody not to do something, but do they understand what 'not hurting humans' means? Do they understand how fragile children are?"

Richard chuckled. "Well, that's what we're studying. Comprehension without singot."

"I can't agree to help if Poche doesn't at least understand what it means to hurt someone." He looked taken aback. I pressed on, "I know this is important for humanity, but shouldn't Sinmai understand this first? It's one thing for consenting adults to be involved with this project, but children who don't understand the risks and parents who are told something that may not be true... it's not right."

Richard unfolded his fingers and refolded them. I had rattled him.

He said at last, "Like I said, violence is rare between the Sinmai — "

"Between the Sinmai. We don't know how rare it is between Sinmai and humans," I replied. He grimaced. The prospect of dead children didn't bother him so much as me bringing up something he hadn't thought about.

I said, "Think about what will happen if kids are hurt. Will the rest of the world feel safe with the Sinmai?"

Richard said harshly, "This is the only way we'll know. We must take advantage of the interest Poche has shown in the classroom. We'll have orderlies in case of the worst."

I felt like a spring about to snap. I was curious about you, but I did not trust you.

"Now," he continued. "Part of your role will be to help him understand English. So it is partially your responsibility to make sure he understands."

When I didn't reply, Richard relaxed.

He said, "Let's continue our talks here. We can meet after class and brief each other on what we noticed during the day... and other things."

"Let's keep it professional," I said. I made an excuse and left a disgruntled Richard in the café. I was a little glad I couldn't singot with Richard. With language I could choose what I say, keep private what I thought. Not that Richard would take seriously the thoughts of a Stacey.

Back at my apartment, I researched asexuality. Events in my life that once stood out white-hot and disparate as stars linked together, constellating. Thinking I was a late bloomer. Thinking I haven't met the right person. Wondering what I was missing in love songs. I felt simultaneously childish for not understanding and aloof for not caring. I cared insofar as my parents would make comments, like, "You know, your cousin Mary got engaged the other day." I entered parties lonely and left lonelier. Intense friendships culminated with my friends asking me if I was gay, and that they would support me no matter what, and I would feel taken aback and upset, because I had considered that semi-consciously (as if you can consider it and it's not self-evident), but to hear it out loud and consequently rejecting the idea... And then the shame for feeling that rejection, and the lost feeling. Because I don't know what I am.

Imagine you never had pads on your hands. You could only speak, a learned tool you can never fully master. The thing that makes you essentially Sinmai, gone.

Only, I didn't know what I didn't have. But then, like the North Star had descended into my hand, I had the word.

And of course the word was used for aliens. I thought singotting would allow the pure transmission of the self between two people, and that comparing myself to someone else would let me understand them. I had operated on faith that light roiled inside everyone on Earth, of desires, fears, joy, rage. People are like stars. Children are brilliant in my eyes. Their light is just under their skin, shining through their pores. Adults should be stars. I know they must be, because they were children once, and as open, curious, and happy as most are. But their lights seem to me pinpricks with social distance, hidden — or worse — dimmed or extinguished. I had thought, through a relationship, I would be able to draw close enough to someone to see that light. Discovering asexuality was like being shut in the dark.

Singot would save me, I had thought. I thought singotting would allow the pure transmission of the self between two people, and that comparing myself to someone else would let me understand that difference.

✍

By your first official day in kindergarten, I had devoured all the literature Richard had handed me. I reread everything twice.

Richard and Anya hunched in chairs so small their knees practically hit their chins. Richard readjusted his legs constantly to write comfortably on his clipboard. You had your own cushion, an extra teacher's cushion we had in the supply closet. Anya looked around the room with a soft, wistful expression I often see on visiting adults without children. Humans were all this small once. Sometimes we forget.

The kids streamed in. When some saw you, they squealed and waved. Toby spotted you and dashed back to his mom, burying his head in her thigh. She unwrapped his arms from her leg.

"He's scared of the alien," she said apologetically. "After what happened."

"I'll make sure he's okay. Toby? You don't have to say hi if you don't feel like it." I took him by his hand and led him to his cubbyhole. You watched us with the intense stare of a baby. His mom waved goodbye and his face crumpled. "It'll be okay. I promise."

Before we began class, we explained to the children what was going on and allowed them to pepper you with questions. "Have you been to the moon? Why is the moon in outer space? If you're on the moon, are you still in outer space? Because if you're on Earth, you're not in outer space, but if you're on the moon, you are."

You observed as you always did, with an air of polite interest. The children were wild to help you when you asked questions. The security sent by the Institute, four guards standing by the door, watched intently. I felt unbalanced. You weren't an animal, nor a child. But I couldn't see you as an adult. I know you were an autonomous intelligent being with diplomatic privileges, but the Institute treated you like a mental patient who needs to be monitored.

For our first exercise, Trevor and I asked the children about their weekend.

Janice's hand zipped into the air. "I wanna share!"

"Okay, Janice, go ahead."

Janice recited, "I went to the recycling center with Mommy. We recycle everything. We got ice cream after. Daddy wasn't home and I sat in his chair. Angela licked my feet. The end."

"Who's Angela?" I asked.

"My cat."

"Excellent. Who's next?"

More hands. One was yours.

I called on you.

You said, "I woke when your side of the planet faced your central star, at the time you call 7:46:36 AM central time, in the mothership, in what humans call my 'bed', from a dreamless, 8.96 hour-long, oxygen-supplemented.... thing we do at night? Die."

The children giggled.

"Funny?" you asked.

I explained, "You don't have to explain every little detail, Poche."

"But that was the weekend."

"We aren't trying to explain the whole weekend. We are sharing the most memorable things that happened during the weekend. What is the essence of the weekend?"

One of your ears twisted. "All of the weekend."

Richard wrote frantically, tearing the paper of his legal pad in his haste to flip to a new page. Did the Sinmai not make distinctions of importance?

"Homework for you," I said. The children tittered. "Five sentences. No longer than ten words each."

Both ears twisted and your fur frizzed.

"It's doable, I promise," I said. "You don't have to do it now."

"No," you said. "I have sentences." The classroom quieted again. Giggles erupted from a corner, and Trevor put his hands on the offenders' shoulders.

You said, "First sentence. I experienced a cat named Sweetpea."

The classroom exploded with laughter. After Trevor and I got them under control, I said, "Experienced? Why do you say experienced?"

"The cat did many things and I could not describe them into ten words that would make a sentence. Second sentence. I discovered the word, 'mood,' and it was compelling."

"Why was it compelling?" Trevor asked.

"It was... unspoken atmosphere around humans when they feel... I learned it when Anya was..." You looked to her. She flushed.

Anya explained, "My girlfriend broke up with me over the phone while I was working. Poche picked up on my anger."

"Your face changed, like so." You pulled your lips back. Deep snarl lines wrinkled your formerly innocent face. Your gums were black and set with chisel-like teeth beveled to sharp edges. I imagined the crew mate who had been sacrificed.

"Third sentence," you said to the shocked class. "I met Mr. Churches and Mrs. Churches. Fourth sentence. They met me."

"What did they say when they met you?" I asked.

"Get out of our garden," you replied. The class tittered again. Then you said suddenly, "Why did they make me leave? They said I wasn't allowed on their property. What is property?"

Trevor said, "Property is a thing that belongs to somebody. Somebody owns something."

"Ah," you said. "Things... do not... belong... to one body on Minde."

"But why?" Janelle asked.

Your ear spun, like a satellite dish picking up signals from another planet. Eventually you said, "I do not know."

Toby raised his hand. "What is your last sentence?"

"I surveyed human hi-fives for meaningful communication."

"What did you learn?" I asked.

"Human communication is complex. I will continue my survey."

We gave you a big round of applause and continued with the rest of the class.

Afterwards, recess. You asked me question after question as Richard recorded and took notes: "What are these structures? What are they doing? What is play? What is it for?" A small crowd gathered around you, listening and asking questions.

A pair of girls began playing a clapping game and you stared, rapt. Other kids tugged on your arms, yet you fixated on the girls' hands, which blurred with speed.

"What are they doing? Hi-fives?" you asked me.

"Playing Miss Mary Mack. Neesha, Katy, will you let Poche play?"

"Yes!" said Neesha.

Neesha positioned herself across from you with her hands up. Katy showed you how to hold out your hands facing up. Neesha's hands slammed down and there was a crack.

You shrieked. Your fur spiked as Neesha screamed, and you curled inwards, falling. You writhed, the woodchips of the playground sticking to your bristling fur. Richard knelt, whitening.

Neesha sobbed, "I'm sorry, I'm sorry...."

Trevor and I urged the children to give you room, shooing them back. Richard helped you stand. Every hair on your body quivered on end; you held your hands tenderly.

You croaked, "I am fine."

Nobody believed you. Richard and Anya whisked you away. I fought my rising nausea as I herded the kindergarteners inside. I knew from my own playground days how my hands stung and reddened when someone slapped too hard. The pads on your hands must be super sensitive so you could singot. Getting slapped must have been like getting hit in the testicles. But shouldn't you have known that playing the game would hurt?

You returned to class ten minutes after we started.

Quiet yays rose over the classroom. The children had begged me if you were going to be okay. Seol scooted back her seat and ran over, holding out an ice pack, the kind you put in your lunchbox.

"For your hands," she said.

You uncurled your fingers and took the ice pack. You inhaled sharply. The pack slipped from your fingers, but you caught it.

"Thanks to you?" you said hesitantly.

I corrected, "Thank you, Seol."

Seol beamed.

You held the ice pack pressed gingerly between your palms. Your fur smoothed down. I heard you whisper to Richard, "What is this?" I relaxed.

At the end of the day, Richard, Anya, you, and I stayed behind in the empty classroom to go over the day.

Richard set his phone down on the table to record. "Tell us what you thought about today's events."

You twisted one ear. After a moment, you said. "Sorry is a singot word and an abai word at the same time."

Richard asked, "What does abai mean?"

"Abai... is... single being."

We waited, but you didn't go on.

"I don't understand," Richard said. "Please try again."

"Singot is...." You pressed your hands together. "Abai is...." You separated your hands.

We chewed this over. Was it the antonym of singot? No. Was it a hand-to-hand thing like singot? No. We asked other questions, but explanations didn't make any sense.

You were quiet for a moment before you replied, "I do not have enough words."

I pulled a beginner's dictionary from the bookshelf and handed it to him. "This is a dictionary," I said. "A list of words. It will help you understand where words came from, how they are pronounced, and what they mean."

You paged through it and stopped in the 's' section. You found the definition for sorry, and your ears wiggled.

Since then, you carried your dictionary around like a blanket. You only set it down at recess to watch the class shout and play. Richard explained games to you: Red Rover, tag, hide and seek, kickball. Mesmerized, your gaze followed the children as they weaved, collided, argued, cooperated, and ran back and forth across the grass.

"How do they know how to...." You trailed off. Then you riffled through the dictionary. Richard said that you read it like a novel.

At recess, kids would pull you into their games, but you didn't know how to play. You could only stand, puzzled, as the kickball whanged off your belly. After the first brutal game, Kai ran up to you and hugged you.

"I'm sorry," he said. "I love you."

You merely said, "It's okay." Later, during our lunchbreak, I saw you turn to the page defining love. Richard and Anya had stepped out into the hall to talk about confidential Institute stuff, and you and I were alone.

I said, "I don't think the dictionary will help you understand every word."

"Why not?" you asked.

"Sometimes things need to be experienced to be understood. Like the cat."

"Ahh...." You held the dictionary in your hands. "Abai."

"I think abai is one of those things too."

Your eyes widened. "Yes."

"But not everything can be experienced by everyone," I mused aloud. "Otherwise... there would be no need to communicate."

"Very yes."

I laughed a little. "Poche, will you tell me about Minde?"

"Why?"

"The dossier was... lacking. I want to hear it from you, what you think about it."

Your fur slicked down. Your eyes dilated, scanning blankly, as if searching the wrinkles of your brain. Other than your eyes, you stood as still as a tree.

After a time, I said, "Sorry. It's probably impossible to describe a whole planet with a few sentences."

You relaxed, agreed, "Impossible."

We had hit the limit of what we could do with language at the time. I had asked for too much. When I went home, I reread the dossier, searched for articles on the internet about Minde and the Sinmai, and even plumbed journal articles about you. That there was so little about you was offensive.

That evening, I heard sirens drawing near. Nosy neighbor that I am, I peeked out through my curtains. A ship hovered over the neighborhood. Streetlights gleamed off its black, pocked surface, as silent as a cloud, as weightless, ovoid. Beyond the houses, red and blue lights flickered.

I walked out of my apartment and stood on the steps in my house socks. Richard also came out of his house, wrapping himself in a bathrobe, gawking at the ship. A coin of light appeared on the underside of the ship. A levitating box descended to the street. Six Sinmai stepped out, the colors of chocolate, silver, peaches, snow, and straw. Plus you: wheat.

All six of you toddled towards my apartment. Richard bolted across the lawn, his skinny legs flashing through his bathrobe. He reached my porch before they did and said to me urgently, "Did you call them?"

"No!" I said in astonishment. "I don't know how they know where I live."

You separated from the pack and approached me on your own.

You asked me, "Stacey, do you have more dictionaries? I need as many words as possible. I want to singot through words only."

I replied, "Human communication depends on more than words."

Richard interrupted, "It also depends on the order in which they are used. Who says them. When they are said. Where. Devices of language, like analogy. Emphasis on certain words when speaking, and tone. How someone stands or acts while they speak. You'll need to study language itself."

"I will."

The silver Sinmai, the largest, offered her hands to the two others. They aligned their pads and pressed them together. A spark darted between the pads. You trembled. Maybe I was anthropomorphizing you, but you looked hungry.

"Abai-ye," she said to you.

Your fur had risen, and we could see the effort it took to calm yourself.

As the black cars of the Institute skidded round the corner and approached, the Sinmai returned to the ship. Without you.

"Poche, what was that?" Richard had taken out his recorder as usual. He looked ecstatic, frightened, as if he had seen something beyond his imagination. "Why didn't you return to the ship?"

"I will test the possibility of words," he said. "And singot no more."

My chest tightened as I brought out the dictionaries, plus thesauruses. Hadn't one of your crew already died from not singotting? Were you putting the rest of your crew in danger? Did you understand that you risked self-destruction for understanding? Or were you already succumbing to disease?

✍

You returned to kindergarten as usual the following day, as placid as a cow. Anya took me aside and told me that the Sinmai had given you permission to stay abai. You had been given a room in the Institute to keep you separate from the other Sinmai.

"He can't singot until the end of the experiment. We'll be prioritizing vocabulary and socialization starting now," she whispered during a break. "We're going to the park after kindergarten to do field work. You should come."

I agreed, curious to know what field work meant. I didn't understand why I had been invited until later. I assumed I was brought along because I was good at talking to you.

The park was a long rectangle of manicured grass and trees. In its center was a fountain, spewing water, which sheeted down the sides of a sculpture of Earth. Children, held by their parents, leaned in to put their hands on the surface. When we arrived, you made a beeline for the fountain and spread your hands over the surface too.

"Does this do something?" you asked me. Anya leaned in. She had a Go-Pro strapped to her hat.

"It looks nice, and it feels good," I replied.

You dried your hands on your fur and wandered. People filtered through the park. They lifted their sunglasses to stare at you, raised their phones to take pictures.

We watched you get in line for the ice cream truck. The woman gave him one for free with a flourish. "Aliens eat free!" You put the whole bar in your mouth and scraped it off the stick with your teeth. You groaned, clutching your head.

"Brain freeze!" I laughed. Intrigued, you returned to the back of the line for another.

Anya said quietly, "He's not a child, you know."

Stung, I said, "I know." She raised her eyebrow at me, making me stammer, "I mean, I thought he wasn't. But he seems like one to me. The curiosity," I explained. "The way he approaches new things."

"If this fails, they all might die."

I felt like I had missed stepping off a curb. I had known this. I remembered that seven Sinmai were the least amount of Sinmai you needed to singot for long times without falling ill. And one was already gone.

You had walked a little ways ahead of us. You watched a little girl find a bee crawling over zinnias and put out her finger to let it climb on. Her mother snatched her hand away and spoke sharply. The girl's face crumpled. A ripple ran through your fur, and you leafed through the dictionary.

"I know," I said.

Anya flushed suddenly. "Sorry — there's a lot riding on this. If Poche dies, the Sinmai will leave. They may not make it back with only five."

"No worries. I needed to remember. I feel like I'm a little kid sometimes — always forgetting that I have to be an adult." We walked for a minute before I asked, "If he felt sick, how would we know? And how would we know if it worked?"

Anya took a long breath. "Nobody knows."

I felt oddly elated. "This might be the wrong way to take this... but I'm excited to see if it works."

Anya grinned. "Me too. It's incredible, being the first person in the world to know something." Then, she added, "Have you thought about being an intern with the Institute? You're really good with Poche, and the other Sinmai like you too."

"They do?" I was touched. "But I only saw them once before — over the weekend!"

"Poche's told them all about you."

At the look on my face, Anya laughed. "Dude, I'm not surprised the aliens like you. You know kindergarten is the perfect laboratory for studying how to be human, right? As we grow and change, we're constantly readjusting how to be ourselves with other people. We learn the basics of how to be with each other in kindergarten. Pick up after yourself, wait your turn, if you see something wrong, say something, be kind to everyone... And your entire job is to teach children how to be human."

"Awwww..." I fizzed with giddiness. "I've never thought about it like that before. Thank you."

"Yeah! My whole job is to teach humans how to be aliens. I learn about Sinmai social norms and teach them to potential astronauts so we can be polite when we eventually go to Minde. We have mirrored roles."

"Okay, so how do I be an alien?"

"Well, we greet each other first with a gentle hi-five...."

Anya and I walked close together. Her hand knocked against mine. Each time it was like the tongue of a bell, resonating through me. We bought a bag of cuties and the sweet lobes in the sunlight glowed. As I put one in my mouth, I imagined it was her ear. The smooth, plump crescent, warm, tart, bursting.

And that struck me as not right. I'm supposed to be asexual, I thought. But I couldn't unthink what I thought. So why now? Why haven't I wanted anybody before?

Anya caught my eye with her deep brown gaze.

You said gravely, "Stacey, you are red. Why?"

"Oh, hush."

"You can't say that to him." Anya smiled with crinkling eyes.

"No, no, no." I was laughing, even as she grabbed my hands.

"You have to explain, or he won't know." She beamed like the sun. I wanted to blind myself looking.

Both of your ears twisted.

You asked, "Why will you not tell me?"

"Well..." I couldn't answer. I didn't have an answer. Anya was listening. "I'm red because I'm sunburned," I said lamely. Anya raised an eyebrow. We both knew a sunburn's redness does not flare and fade so easily.

"Why do you say that? Is it a secret?"

"Uh, no, but...." I resisted the urge to squirm.

Anya said icily, "Sometimes, Poche, people are uncomfortable with same-sex flirting."

"I'm not uncomfortable!" I protested.

"Then why don't you explain?"

"Why don't you explain, Anya?" you asked. I secretly cheered until you said, "Is this a power struggle?"

"No," Anya and I said together.

You asked, "Is there danger nearby? And redness is camouflage?" I chuckled. Anya blistered me with a look. A ripple ran through your fur, as it had when you saw the girl with the bee. "Is it a secret? Is it a species thing? Can you tell me? I can treat this situation the same way Sinmai treat horkew'e ceremonies, during which we send a young Sinmai into the threwd with sled, vie, and wave — "

"Poche," I said.

But you couldn't seem to stop.

" — and we tell them, 'Go. Make yourself abai, see how plants go together, how water unmakes itself from clouds, and when you return, singot, and you will know Sinmai and know nothing and they will go out and grow abai with only two hands — "

Your voice slurred and grew louder. People around us craned their heads. Their ice cream dribbled over their knuckles. Phones came out and faced you.

"Poche!" I said sharply. You sputtered, but then picked up again.

"Is it like that? What is the word for the feeling of being alone and unable to share and dying from it? Is it sunburn? Will you be okay? I am sorry, I am sorry, I am sorry — "

Anya had pulled out her phone and dialed frantically. Was it already happening?

"It's okay Poche," I said soothingly. Then, I had an idea. "Give me your hands."

You continued to whisper as we aligned hands. It sounded almost like a prayer. I knew placing our hands together wouldn't be singot. But I thought, if we did it, and if I explained myself as well as possible, then you would ken my meaning. Then, your body would recognize a sort of psuedo-singot.

I said clearly and carefully, "I can't tell you why I turned red, because the reason I blushed is something I'm unsure of myself. Can I tell you later?"

Your fingers wrapped twice around my hand. "You will tell me soon?"

"Yes. I promise."

"What is a promise?"

"A promise is a — " I gasped as you squeezed my hands. It was like being caught in a machine — flesh bending too far in wrong ways, snapping. "I will tell you in the future! Please, let go!"

You yanked your hands away as if you had touched a scorching stove and backed away. "I am sorry. Sorry. Sorry." You gazed around. "Ice pack?"

"I'm okay," I said. I flexed my hands to get the feeling back. "I don't need an ice pack." My heart raced in my throat. I hadn't been able to pull away. My joints cracked, and welts crossed my wrists.

Anya had pulled out a stun gun when I wasn't looking. When she saw my expression, she shoved it in a holster that had been hidden by her oversized sweater. She would have stunned us both, I thought. Which didn't make sense. I wasn't thinking about how you had gripped my hands. At the time, I didn't think Anya would see that as possible violence.

We walked home in silence. The failed attempt at singot mortified me. Why did I think that would work? Yet, it felt right to try. Could you ache for something you could never physically do?

Like feeling a phantom limb for an appendage you never had? Your hands flexed and flexed, as did mine. Anya's were clenched.

I'm sorry. If I had known what I wanted, maybe it would have worked. Anya was probably angry because I'm an adult. I should know by now who I am and what I feel. But I've always felt like a child, dawdling behind the rest of my peers. Sometimes, people don't know what they want. If they want.

Asexual still feels right. But less right than before. I wondered whether I had truly never experienced attraction before, or ignored or misinterpreted attraction. I wanted to know Anya. I don't know whether that's different from wanting her. Sometimes, when people find out what it is they want, they recoil from it, shocked by the unfamiliar sensation.

For how long did we think our bodies would leave us alone?

✍

It was midnight when you pounded on my door. You had a stack of dictionaries and several legal pads. You on the porch, spot lit by the yellow light. Your fur spiked. Your mild eyes had a rim of white, like a horse's.

Your voice cracked. "Stacey. I have made a crucial discovery about the nature of abai, which will transform Sinmai understanding of singot." Where was the ship? Where had you come from? I said your name, but you plowed on. "Abai is a strange-making-ness which can be fatal if not corrected. It derives from the Sinmai spoken word for stranger and singular and has connotations of sickness. I hypothesize that abai is an evolutionary learning mechanism which — which — "

This is from the camera recording. At the time, I could not understand what you were saying, only the sick feeling that it was too soon. Your words jumbled together as you struggled to get them out of you. Your voice rose like a kettle's scream.

"Which singot obliterates!"

Richard's porchlight flicked on. He ran across the lawn. Richard carried a silver stick, which he raised and looked down its length towards you.

I screamed, "No!"

You stopped. Richard too. The crickets silenced. I felt a beat of embarrassment, which evaporated when you began to quiver.

I said, "Richard...put the gun down."

Richard replied, "He's showing symptoms."

"Let's slow down." I quelled the tremble in my voice. You croaked as if to say something. I asked you. "What do we do when we don't know what we feel?"

Your nostrils flared. You said haltingly, "We name our feelings."

"That's right. What do you feel?"

A tremor ran through you. "Abai."

That word.

"Why do you feel abai?"

"I feel abai because.... I sense — sense with eyes, ears, nose, mouth — that there is infinity within each of you. And you cannot share. And I cannot receive."

Familiarity pierced my heart. I said, "Yes. I understand."

Much of the tension escaped your body like a balloon releasing air.

I asked, "Everything okay now?"

"Yes. No. More okay than before. I am abai. I am sorry."

"And you're happy?"

Your ears wiggled. "Very much."

"Good," I said. Richard did not lower his gun as he spoke into a phone. I caught the words emergency, Poche, and abai. "Do you need to singot?"

"No. Yes. Ergh. I have understood again, and I want to again and again and again and — "

"Hey Poche, can you stand away from Stacey?" Richard asked him.

I said, "Please wait just a little — "

Richard cut me off. "I order you to get away from him."

Your lips rolled back, exposing your teeth. You raised your hand to me suddenly, and I flinched. You froze. I froze. I know you weren't going to hurt me. But human instinct is a cursed reaction.

"I'm sorry, Poche," I said.

My throat was tight as I stepped back, to stand beside Richard. Poche stood still. The dictionary warped as his hands closed, its spine breaking, pages splaying. Richard immediately stepped in front of me, still with that goddamn gun raised. My skin crawled when he glanced at me with a crumpled face, as if to say, I know. But that was a guess, like all my life has been guessing what people think and feel, myself most of all.

Lights arced in the sky like meteors in formation. The Sinmai mothership sailed like a great black moon over the rooftops. Sirens keened, approaching. The five Sinmai descended in their elevator, and they approached, as they had before. You spoke rapidly in Sinmai before they could. You overpowered their attempts to cut in, your voice rushing abai and singot amidst a torrent of other words. The five exchanged a complicated set of gestures like a secret handshake. Blue sparks — blue like a cloudless summer day, when you can see infinity hinting beyond the sky in the vibrant depth — danced between their palms. You shivered, and your eyes expanded. But you stepped away, covered your eyes, and said something in a breaking voice that nobody understood.

The Sinmai lunged for you. They wrestled you down as the military vehicles skidded round the corner. Their powerful lights caught the tussling aliens and obliterated individual features. Snarls juddering from your chest. Claws extended from your feet and gouged earth from the lawn. Your wheaten fur flashed through the tangle of limbs. One Sinmai had bit down on your arm with those tombstone teeth and another champed your leg, forcing you down.

You shouted, "Abai-ye! Abai-ye! Stop, I am so close — please! Please!" Tears smeared my vision. My body would not obey my mind's shouted commands. Move, bitch! Help him! Leap in, say something! Why don't you do anything? Something! But what power did saying have that could overcome the fatal need to singot?

The lead Sinmai pinned down your arm, uncurled your clenched hand, and pressed their palm to yours.

Light annihilated the neighborhood. When I recall that moment now, it is like a still in a movie, and a bomb has just gone off. It doesn't seem like it happened. I should have felt the blast like a ghostly wall. I know the soldiers who had been running to confront the Sinmai recoiled. I know the Sinmai pile fell apart. I saw your leader fall to the side, on the road, making an awful scream like an iceberg splitting.

And I saw you lay still. Clearest of all was a black asterisk of soot on the asphalt where your hand should be, and your wrist cuffed with flames.

A soldier gave me first aid for shock. Numb, I gave a statement of events to the commander of the unit, starting when you rang my doorbell. The commander explained that humanity has been forbidden to interfere with disputes among the Sinmai crew.

"We can't impose our values on them," she said as she ended the meeting. "You did the right thing."

I did not believe her. I went back to kindergarten. I told your classmates that you might not come back. Being hugged by fifteen tiny humans who mean it when they hug is the best cure for heartbreak on planet Earth. I couldn't help but bawl. We all cried for a while. I put your painting on the wall so parents and children could see it with the rest of the class. We didn't know if you would come back, but we had to keep going like you would. We set out your floor cushion and put it away at the end of each day. I felt like an extra chamber had been carved out of my heart and my blood had leaked away, and I was only still moving because I was too dumb to realize I had died.

But of course, you did come back, just when we had nearly run out of hope. At least, we thought you meant Poche.

Certainly, it was one Sinmai, toddling down the sidewalk on the other side of the fence, the stub of an arm bandaged. Children screamed and ran towards you, and Trevor and I ran to call them back. Trevor did, at least — I just ran. You waded into the children and they glommed onto you. Richard and Anya stepped away. They looked tense, expectant.

"Good morning," you said to me. "I'm sorry."

"We're all just glad you're okay, Poche," I said through a tight throat.

"No," you said emphatically. "I'm sorry. Poche has dissolved. This body is now Oche."

The children quieted. Poche has dissolved. This body is now Oche. These words did not go together with what I saw. You stood straighter. Your speech was clearer. You had Poche's body. Yet, I was looking at a stranger.

Richard spoke, "We learned that when Sinmai singot — "

You looked to Richard and shook your head. Richard stopped speaking. To me, you held up your hand. With trepidation, I placed mine over it.

"When we singot," you said carefully. "We pour ourselves together and redistribute equally among our bodies. We five Sinmai on Earth are all now Oche. Poche is within us all."

They killed Poche, as easily as wiping words off a whiteboard. I couldn't believe I had wanted to singot. If perfect understanding with others meant self-destruction, I didn't want it.

After a time, I pulled myself together, like pulling the great weight of a tide against the moon.

"Did you find what you were looking for on Earth?" I asked.

"Yes. We — the prior five who became Oche — found pieces of knowledge everywhere. We were each afraid to become Oche after knowing ourselves." You sighed. "But we are so relieved. We have understood."

"Why did you — Poche — fight so hard to stay abai?" I asked. "If it was so painful?"

"We liked being Poche. And we were afraid we wouldn't like who we would become. And that you wouldn't like us anymore."

I pressed my hand to yours and said vehemently, "I will love you however you are."

But of course, you know this. I wrote this down for you because I want you to understand the essence of how I saw our weeks together. After you left, I found a Zulu saying I wanted to share with you: We become people through other people. I still miss Poche, the instance of individuality that wove into Oche. By now your name must have changed again. Does the whole planet share one name? Was there ever a difference between one of you and all of you? I hope it's clear now that when I say you, I mean all of you.

The human body limits us. We just can't understand everything all at the same time. We barely understand ourselves, let alone others. But now I can't imagine a better life than spending it with people who I'll never really know, who will forever surprise me with new aspects to love, unfolding forever together. And I would be happy if they were you.

I've started a new career at the Institute. Back to being an intern. Being a certified friend of Sinmai helped my application jump to the top of the pile. I'll be studying your language now, so I can talk to you. The cool thing about language is that if communication fails, you can try again. I've been talking to Anya. Things have softened between us, started to flow onward. We're not together, not really, but we're looking in the same direction. Towards you. I've started training so I might one day pass the astronaut exam. We have so much to tell you.

Homework: Demonstrate to me that you understand what I've written. Five thousand words. More if you need them. Due next month, when the next signal is broadcast. I can't wait to know what you think.

≋ ≋ ≋

Sorry, Sorry, Sorry, and I Love You

—

L'Erin Ogle

Sorry, Sorry, Sorry, and I Love You

The cave sits in a hillside, with its mouth yawed wide open. It is the kind of cave suited for raising the dead. Shadows move across dark spaces as the witch drags the shattered spines of small trees across the entrance. She stacks them high, leaving a small space to wedge herself through. Soon a fire is lit, its dull glow chasing away the lingering shadows. The fire flickers, and smoke curls in ribbons towards the night sky, pulsing out in breaths.

The witch has an old cauldron, rusted at the bottom, with sharp flakes of metal peeling from the sides. She loosens the drawstring of a cotton sack and reaches inside. The handful of bones are smooth against her fingers, and she carefully places them at the bottom of her cauldron. The bones are all she has left of her son. There are no more silky wisps of golden curls, no milk teeth, no fingernail clippings. All these have been eaten by the cauldron before. She has been casting this spell for so long nothing else exists to her. Her son was the sun that illuminated the whole wide world. He is gone and now her vision has buttoned up tight around the bitter taste of loss and the spell she casts over and over again.

There is a small, silent bundle beside the cauldron that she doesn't look at as she prepares the ceremony. She cannot. She still has a ghost of the heart she was born with, a heart so large she had to carry it outside of her body. As time went, as people carved slivers from her heart, the tissue thickened and twisted, as sometimes happens. Her heart of hearts, the one protected by her own skeleton, that one became wound up with her son's, more enmeshed with every laugh, every coo, every step. Their hearts beat as one, their breaths inhaled and exhaled together.

Most of her heart he took with him to the beyond.

✍

Many years have passed since she woke to find his cold body still bundled in his bed. Her ears dulled at the crack of his ribs under the press of her hands, her lips are cold and numb since she blew her own breath into his mouth, even though there was a small quiet voice in her head that whispered 'too late.' But she didn't give up until her arms shook from the effort, until they gave way and she collapsed on top of him.

Raising the dead requires sacrifice. It always has. She knew that from the moment she was born and from when she left the castle with the spell clutched in her hand. It was all she took with her from that place.

Perry needs to cast her spell and make it last for a moment. She does not wish this world upon her son. Perry herself was raised from this cauldron. She had no parents, no sisters or brothers, and she has had a long, lonely, and desperate life. No, she does not want her son forced to endure the same kind of existence she has. All she requires is a moment long enough to feel his body solid and warm in her arms, to look in his eyes, to whisper she's sorry. There is always too much to apologize for when it's too late to do so. She needs to say sorry she made him sleep in his own bed that night, that if she had cradled him in hers, maybe, just maybe, she would have woken to breathe for him. Sorry for all the times she grew impatient and shouted, sorry for the time he bit her while nursing and she slapped his cheek.

Sorry, sorry, sorry, and I love you. Then, he'll know. Understand the magnitude of her love.

When they began to lower the wooden box into his grave, she tried to throw herself in with his body and tell him one last time. To warm his body against the cold ground. They restrained her. They meant well, but what if she'd been able to say it? Would she be here?

If she wanted to be understood, she would say that when her son was born, her heart came with him, that she watched it learn to crawl and walk and live outside her body. That his life so short left a long, desolate road ahead for her. That living was just another form of torture.

✍

Twenty-five years ago, Perry opened her eyes for the first time. This spell, the same one she holds now, was cast by a desperate witch, for a rich man, over a pile of bones the man brought. The spell was cast, the old witch went into the pot and out came Perry.

The paper the spell is written on gives its ingredients and the proper way to cast it. It does not tell you that what rises from the cauldron is not quite the same person as the bones within. The marrow in the bones is the same, the appearance the same, the winding strands of genes climbing the same ladder. But there is the sacrifice, whose essence is absorbed, and then there is the Beyond. All dark magic comes from the Beyond, from another world that is full of darkness stretching an unimaginable distance. And when magic comes from the Beyond, something comes with it.

When Perry was created, made of bones and magic, she opened her eyes and saw fire, felt it shimmy along her bones, liquid inside her. She stepped from the cauldron a young woman. She was fed and clothed and given shelter. From the bones came love for the man who raised her, faint but a flame nonetheless. The old witch's essence is where Perry's magic came from. From the Beyond came a spot of pure darkness, the blackest sort of magic. But Perry was happy then and the darkness found no room to grow, with Perry's big heart taking up so much space. It wound itself into a tight little knot and dug itself deep into her core, waiting for the time it found a hollow to crawl into and blossom. That is the thing about darkness — it is very patient.

For the first six months of her life, Perry lived hidden away in the rich man's home, knowing she was an awful secret but not why. She did not much care. She was happy with her small existence, with the quickening in her belly that soon would become a bright beaming light to lead her.

The rich man's wife found out, as they always do, and Perry was deposited outside the gates with nothing but the spell that raised her, that ancient parchment, clutched in her hand. Inside her swollen belly, her son grew, and feeling his movements inside her, she forced her heavy, aching body to move west, to knock on doors and ask for work, work of any kind. It was the beginning of a long journey.

✍

She has a box of memories. It's a box she built inside herself, where she put the memories when they washed over her and left her chest aching and her breath coming in blasts of pain. She clings to the box, but she can't open it. Even as the loss cuts away more of her each day, she cannot open the box. The memories come anyway, at odd moments. Sunny days dipping their feet into ponds, a small hand on hers. The tug at her breast. His feet curled in her hand. The look in his eyes at the discovery of every new thing. The smell of his hair, soft and clean. A person cannot take reliving this kind of moment. It would the undoing of anyone.

Loss can define a person, can be vast and heavy, can spread black wings of grief across all that's left. She was hollow when he died. To live, she had hold on to something. For some it's a mother, a father, a sister, a brother. For Perry, it was the spell.

✍

It was the same spell she smoothed out and memorized seven days after the funeral. The paper it was inked on was thin and translucent and bits of it clung to her fingers when she touched it. Perry had never learned to read. But magic is magic, and the language on the parchment came off the page and whispered right into her ear.

There was no other witch that Perry could turn to, to learn the rules of witchcraft. No one to warn her that the little dark knot of the Beyond was gaining power, free to balloon into the hollow space inside her. Perhaps if she had had a teacher...

The what if! Oh, how it sticks in your side sometime, sharp and double edged with regret and hindsight.

Perry just wants to see her boy again. To speak to him one more time. She always knew the spell demanded a life for a life, but she could not, would not cast another into the cauldron. She would not bring her boy back to abandon him, the way she had been abandoned. And though she could not read or write, Perry was smart. She thought she could find a way around the live sacrifice the spell required. A body, newly dead, must still have a glimmer of life in it. She thought that since she did not need to make a new life — she merely needed a small window of time — a fresh corpse would work.

It was hard digging up the first grave. The smell rose up and slapped her face, while the blue skinned girl stared out of empty eye sockets. A worm sat up, looked at her, this strange, wild haired woman, weeping bloody tears.

There weren't enough recent deaths in any town for what she needed. She packed her cauldron and a small bag and travelled from graveyard to graveyard. She learned things, as people do when they do the same thing over and over. She went further south, where the ground was softer. She camped in forests and hid herself away during the day. She had to remain separate and move unseen. The cost was immense. All the dead bodies she carried left marks on her soul. Even though it was born from ugliness, her soul came pure and white and unmarked, as all souls do. It was the world that left dirty prints all over it.

If her soul were detached from her body and held up to the light, where each stain could be pointed out, the tale behind it told, maybe there would be a different story. A different understanding, at least. But that's not how this story goes.

⚖

They will come. They always do. Just as before, she will hear the heavy tread of boots ringing out over the words she chants. There will be the dull flickering light of torches, the sound of a club slapping a thigh. She knows they will come with a heavy burlap sack, a noose of thick rope, the accoutrements necessary to bind and kill a witch.

Each time before, when she cast the final word, the smoke would thin and drift away, the bones of her boy still scattered and motionless in the cauldron. The sound of angry men would be so close so she had to pick up the cauldron and run with the handles blistering the tips of her fingers as she fled men and failure alike. The pattern took its own payment, in the form of her own life ebbing away. It was a little life, a lonely life, but still a life. Years not yet lived were drawn away, leaving a withered old woman with a rust spotted cauldron and a grief-stained box of memories.

The roots of bitterness grow inside her core and flesh out through her body. This is a requirement of black magic. Grief is not enough. There must be something more, a streak of hatred or rage or the like, something that digs in early and festers and sprouts. Inside, her grief is wound up with something more complicated, something black and red and humming.

This is why she crouches by the fire and heats a cauldron of bones and gathers her energy, drawing from the shadows of the cave, from the energy of the fire, from every living thing and object she can. It is time to bring him back from the beyond.

⚖

The walls swell from the pressure building in the cave. You might not see it, but it is happening all the same. The air is heavy and difficult to breathe, and burning embers float in the air.

Perry begins to mutter. Words drop from her lips and land in fat sizzling drops where the boy's bones float. Steam rises and hisses, and the witch prepares to knit the bones. This part has become easy — the round ends of the humerus bones fitting themselves into the circles made by the scapula and clavicle. She knows how to form tendons and ligaments and lay muscled sinew over the top of it. She has done this all before.

The cave is sweltering. It takes effort for the witch to draw a breath as she sweats out what little water her body holds. Strands of her hair drift up to the ceiling. She looks mad, and of course she is, but Perry has never had it easy. The years have been relentless and awful and endless, like a machine whose sole purpose was to grind her down.

Does the bundle whimper before it meets the cauldron?

Does it matter?

It doesn't, for the record. This is the first time the witch, who used to be a good witch named Perry, has prepared to give something living to the cauldron. She plucked the babe from its crib only because it was near death. Whether it was a boy or a girl, she never looked. All she saw was the sunken plates of the soft spots, the blue tinged lips, the glassy eyes. Another babe starving while they held feasts in grand houses, in palaces, while she and others not born with fists of gold went cold and hungry and full of impotent fury.

Never underestimate the power of bitterness.

She doesn't look at the babe, but she cradles it against her chest for a moment, feeling its cold skin. Perhaps she could be satisfied with another's child. Perhaps this child could soothe her torn heart. But then the babe exhales a ragged half breath, and she knows this babe cannot be saved either.

The babe goes into the cauldron, and the rooms breathes. There is something faintly beating, as soft as the wings of a hawk gliding down to snatch his prey.

Inside the cauldron, a liquid sheet rises up and draws itself over the skeleton.

Perry cries, but even she doesn't know what for. For her son, for the babe she just let go of, for who she once was paling in the face of who she's become, for the loneliness and the hollowness and for that shred of hope, the hope of all hopes. Her weeping shakes the walls of the cave, and the men below the mouth of the cave hesitate, but of course they still move forward. This was always going to be how the story ended.

✍

Perry weeps as she watches the skin-covered skeleton rise. There is little time. The men are arriving at cave's entrance. They are shouting about something, but she only hears a muffled roar. She feels the cave falling away from her. She reaches out with trembling fingers, to touch the boy, but it isn't her boy.

He's too tall. Her boy was just past a year, just tottering around on fat baby legs, just saying "Mama, mama."

Do they grow in the Beyond?

Perry touches rough sandpaper skin, nothing like the soft smoothness of her boy. When she removes her hand, the body crumples back into the cauldron, accordion-folding itself back to where it came from.

"No, no, no," she wails. She has gone and done the thing, the thing the spell demanded, that she didn't want to do, for nothing. It was all for nothing. She has been dog paddling her way through this darkness and now she stops swimming, now it swallows her whole. Down and down she goes, where not even the sound of trees being dragged from the entrance can reach her.

She steps to the cauldron, her bones cracking, and peers in it. A person might say she could not fit inside, but only a person who does not understand that the world is vast and does not care to be understood.

The men move the logs. The little space Perry wriggled through is growing wider, almost large enough to fit a man's shoulders. There are shouts and grunts and Perry hears none of it. She steps onto the rim of the cauldron, her old, wrinkled toes gripping the side. "I love you," she says. "I love you, I always loved you. I do still, always."

The first man into the cave sees the old woman tottering above a black pot of fire and shouts for her to stop. She turns to him, eyes full of broken things. Then something happens to her face, something breathing the fire of life across it, a shared moment.

"I'm sorry," she says and lets herself fall backwards into the cauldron. She makes no sound. The cauldron burns hotter and hotter, until it holds no bones, just dust and ashes

✍ ✍ ✍

Initial feedback

I like the prose and concept. The heart metaphor could be sharper. The end was a bit overwrought. The piece runs long, and it feels like there's a lot of repetition. Aspects (esp. Evan & Perry) aren't clear. What the spell actually accomplishes is unclear for some time. Why does she sacrifice others rather than herself? The shift to direct narrative on about p5 is jarring.

Author's intent

What do you think the story's about?
What emotions are you trying to evoke?

The story's about the lengths people would go to to speak to a lost loved one. Child loss is a little different in my opinion/experience. Emotionally, I wanted to express the magnitude of grief of that loss, as well as the isolation that follows, particularly for someone without a family.

She doesn't sacrifice herself because she suffers guilt from not being good enough — she has to see him/apologize.

Its quite a personal story for me — I really wanted to convey a type of grief that had equal measures of grief, isolation, and anger.

Author's note

I've been very lucky to undergo the revise and rewrite option offered by *Metaphorosis* five times, and "Sorry, Sorry, Sorry, And I Love You" is probably the story that underwent the most extensive number of changes, for which I am grateful. The story is about the profound changes that occur in a bereaved mother trying to cope with the sudden loss of her child. The draft I initially delivered was very disorganized, more of a collection of feelings and scenes than an actual story. Part of the reason for that is that it's a very personal story, as my son died just before his third birthday. It was hard to view the main character and story objectively, which is why all those scenes and emotions I spat out made sense to me, but as the story underwent revisions, it was clear that to a reader, it *didn't* quite make sense and didn't flow well. The story's original message/journey/outcome didn't change, but the changes that were made helped the story flow and become more readable. I'd also say it became more cohesive as a whole.

The revisions that were hardest to make was the elimination of some lines that were really things that I was saying, that didn't fit with the story or the main character, because there were additional things I wanted to say, but I wasn't the main character. The story was much better off by cutting those out on the last rounds. I've always enjoyed the revision process, because I've found that in my experience the edits and suggestions made always made the story better. It can be a hard pill to swallow to cut out something you love, but at the end of the day the story was always the important thing. It's just asking the question if an edit will make a stronger story and if the answer is yes, then do it!

One of the most helpful things for me, and something I've utilized much more, was writing down each individual scene and then organizing them in how they appear. Which is very helpful for me, since I don't ever plot or do more than a vague outline, because I usually don't know where I'm going to end up. I enjoyed this revision process quite a bit and really felt like the story became much more streamlined and easier to follow. In the end, the important part of the story, the struggle with grief and the lengths one would undertake to have a loved one back, shone through.

Editor's note

L'Erin Ogle has been published in *Metaphorosis* more often than anyone but me (I publish one of my own stories every year). I know that submitters sometimes think editors have 'favorites', but since I read blind, I can say with confidence that L'Erin's style just works for me. That doesn't mean I just accept her stories as they are, though. "Sorry, Sorry, Sorry, and I Love You" was the third story I bought from L'Erin, and, as with the others, it went through several revisions — this story more than others. I liked the prose and the concept, but felt the story was too long, somewhat repetitive, and needed clarity in some areas. However, as with Pauline Yates, I knew that L'Erin was willing to put in the work, and that if we stuck to it, the result would be great.

There's no knowing what's behind a story when it first comes in. Some authors are deeply invested personally in their stories, and it's easy to poke a delicate area without knowing it. In describing her intent for the story, L'Erin mentioned that it was quite personal to her, something I thought I'd picked up hints of on her social media. That made the revision process even trickier, and made it more important that L'Erin and I had an existing relationship and I knew she had thick skin. I try to be sensitive, but I'm aware that my editorial comments sometimes come across as brusque, and I try to mitigate that. (In a different context, I once met someone who'd received my editorial comments on a professional matter. Her reaction when she learned my name taught me a lesson: "That's *you*? But you're so nice! And on paper, you're ..." [I filled in 'such a jerk' and left the gathering enlightened]). We all want to end up with a strong story, but the last thing I want is to trample across someone's memories to get there.

It's important to know that revision isn't always an entirely linear process. Often, an author will propose an approach, and if it makes sense to me, I agree that they should try it out. Sometimes, the new approach doesn't work and is abandoned. That happened in this story — L'Erin proposed a dark fairy tale approach, and I thought it was a failure. I'm always sorry to say that — I know how much work it can be to write — but there's no sense in building on a weak foundation. L'Erin dropped that attempt and went back to the original style, but with cuts and polish, and it worked better. But we'd never have known if she hadn't been willing to experiment.

I think one of L'Erin's strengths is her use of metaphor (possibly why her style works for me; see name of magazine), and I felt that was true here as well — the metaphors were strong and interesting. However, I didn't feel they were clear. I and my second readers had trouble following the original story, and I felt the metaphors were in part to blame. There can be too much of a good thing, and much as I love metaphor, I suggested L'Erin trim some of hers back to let the narrative come through more clearly.

There were more rounds of clarification and cutting. It's an iterative process. I focus on larger things first, then smaller, so it can seem we're treading the same ground sometimes when looking at the same portion of the story, but I'm looking for different things at different times, and it's just not practical to list all possible weaknesses all at once — plus, it would be incredibly daunting to try to address everything in one go. So, stamina can be important to the process, and happily L'Erin has plenty. She kept going, and I thought the final result was great.

Sorry, Sorry, Sorry and I Love You

There is a witch casting a spell in a small cave. The cave sits with a mouth yawed wide open in a hillside. Before she entered the cave, the witch dragged fallen trees with shattered spines across the entrance. She stacked them high, leaving only a small space to wedge herself through at the top. From this irregular little hole light flickers and smoke curls. It pulses in and out, breathing, gathering strength.

In the cauldron, the witch stacked her son's bones. This is all she has left. No wisps of golden curls, no milk teeth, no fingernail clippings. All these have been used up. She has been casting the spell for so long nothing else exists anymore. All the world has drawn tight and buttoned up around a boy who had curls soft as silk, a smile that lit up the sky.

Loss defines the witch. She knows nothing but the bitter taste of hollow spaces spread across the whole of her.

She doesn't look at the bundle beside the cauldron as she prepares the ceremony. She can't. For the witch was born with a heart sized so large she had to carry it outside of her body. As time passed, people carved slivers from her heart, and the tissue grew thick and twisted, but the part hidden inside beat on. The moment her son drew his first breath, she bestowed her heart upon him, the whole wide world that grew inside her laid at his lap.

He carried most of that in his chubby little boy hands to the beyond.

The pieces that are left cannot look at what she must do, what is required of her.

She only wants a moment. A moment to touch him again, to whisper she's sorry she wasn't a better mother. To say she's sorry she made him sleep in his own bed that night, that if she had cradled him in hers perhaps she would have woken to breathe for him. Sorry, for the times she grew impatient and shouted, sorry for the time he bit her while nursing and she slapped his cheek without thinking.

Sorry, sorry, sorry, and I love you. She needs to say it again, over and over, until she knows he knows. Understands, the magnitude of her love that dwarves cities and towers and the night sky. At the burial, she tried to throw herself in the grave with his cold blue body and tell him one last time. They restrained her. They meant well, but what if she'd been able to say it? Would we be here?

Understand, that her heart was given to him at birth, that it crawled and walked around outside her body.

Just one moment, to know him in her arms again.

✍

The witch was raised from the dead from the very same cauldron she carries. There was a man, Ethan, who wished to raise the spirit of a lover, someone he had loved ten years before. He had never been able to let go of her, even as the memory of her death (murder) fell away, as he married a wife who was barren, even as he grew older and into power, he was haunted by the ghost peeking around the corners of his mind.

The what if. Oh, how it sticks in your side, sometimes.

The witch who raised the witch from the dead had children and a dead husband. There were too many mouths to feed. Her children had hollow cheeks and skin so thin a firm grasp split it. Ethan came to her, to escape his life for a moment. She was his favorite. Ethan always did have a fondness for damsels in distress. He asked her about her husband. He told her about the ghost living inside his head.

The first witch wanted to shake her head, at the foolishness of men. Of people. It was the people who had no starving children, no dead husband, that clung to a sliver of the past as if it was a life boat. The girl was just a girl, she wanted to tell him. It's you who has made her someone else in your mind. It is your knuckles white from holding on so tightly. But the children were hungry.

Ethan liked to look through her books. He liked the feel of old pages against his skin, the promises they made. Things money couldn't buy, unless one of your ladies of the night was a witch.

He read the page titled, 'There is another life beyond this one.'

He had questions.

No one raises the dead anymore, the first witch told him. It comes with a price no one can pay.

Ethan didn't care about cost.

He offered riches. She refused.

Raising the dead always ends in blood. How could it not?

The first witch's oldest was of age to care for the others. The first witch bargained a small shop for the price of herself, accounts of a reasonable amount for each of her children. She ensured everything was in place. Then she allowed herself to say goodbye.

It was not an easy thing, to fling herself into the boiling cauldron with a dead girl's bones. She had to picture her children's chests, skin spread taut over ribs, their hollow dark eyes. She heard them whispering 'hungry, Momma.'

In she went.

Out came the second witch.

✍

They will come. They always do. It happens over and over, the heavy tread of boots, the flickering of torches, the sound of a club slapping a thigh. There will be a heavy burlap sack, a noose of thick rope, the necessary accoutrements to bind and kill a witch.

When the smoke thins and drifts away, the bones of her boy still scattered and motionless in the cauldron, she will run with her sack of bones and her cauldron, blistering the tips of her fingers as she flees men and failure alike. To undertake a raising of the dead, to command the bones of your only child to raise and to draw skin over a skeleton, to love again, requires commitment. It demands all of what is left of it, it draws years you haven't lived yet over your body and soul, leaves a withered old woman with a rust spotted black cauldron, alone with the ruins of what was.

She was young once, too. She had marvelous red hair that hung to her hips, heavy and luminous. She had long arms and legs, strong and roped with muscle and tendons, that lifted and carried and lived. Years passed and her yarn of hair grew skeins of gray, then white. It thinned and shortened, as her spine rounded and her hands grew calloused and discolored.

Each time she cast the spell, more of her own life ebbed away, a little life, a lonely life, but still a life.

Bitterness grew roots inside her core and fleshed out through her body. The things raising the dead demanded her to do, the deadening of her spirit, it required this.

Raising her dead child called for a sacrifice. It was not her sacrifice to make but she had no say in her boy's end, either. She cannot justify what she does, but her own loss is hollow and swallows her whole.

The walls swell from the pressure building in the room, imperceptible to the naked eye, but happening all the same. The air is heavy and difficult to breathe, embers floating in the air.

The witch begins to mutter faster, words dropping from her lips to land in fat sizzling drops in the round black cauldron where the boy's bones float. Steam rises and hisses and the witch prepares to knit the bones, the round ends of the humerus bones fitting themselves into the circles made by the scapula and clavicle, waiting to be joined by tendon and ligament, by muscled sinew —

✍

When the second witch rose, she was not the first witch, nor the woman whose bones she came from, but both of them and some other essence. What comes from the beyond, the beyond decides what comes with it.

But the brand-new witch, her heart bloomed and beat until Ethan's ears pulsed with it. He opened the door to the little room and saw the one he could never forget standing silken in the dull light of flickering candles. "It's you," he whispered.

Raising the dead is birthing a human. Not a baby, but the commitment is the same. Someone is all alone in this world by your doing. The witch who has no name, Ethan calls Perry. It's not her name, it's the name of a dead girl, but we'll call her that anyway. It's as good as any.

You know what happens next. Perry is bound to Ethan as Ethan is not bound to her. Ethan cannot be bound, he is bound to another. Even the life he deposits inside Perry will not bind him.

Perry makes it six months, hidden away in rooms with no windows, knowing only Ethan and his hands and quick mouth, before Ethan's queen discovers exactly why her husband has been humming a tune under his breath. She always did envy the dead girl. She was the one who pushed her off the ledge of the quarry, of course. These things happen. Hell hath no fury, or something like that.

Perry is lucky to have her head. Ethan turned away from her but he forbade the queen from killing her.

Imagine how angry that made her.

Perry left with her belly heavy with child, escorted by guards and deposited outside the city gates.

Inside his loneliness, Ethan bit his fingers and inside his skin, he howled with fury at his impotence.

✍

It was hard digging up a dead child. The first time, the smell rose up and slapped her face, while the blue skinned girl stared out of empty eye sockets. A worm sat up, looked at her, this strange, wild haired woman, weeping bloody tears.

She didn't like doing any of this. She had to crouch down on her haunches that first time, shut her eyes, murmur her boy's name over and over until she could see his face, his mop of gold, his big toothless smile. Only then could she wrap a blanket around the body, lift it into her arms, and set it down to refill the grave. Only then could she trudge home with her burden and cast her spell.

It failed. The spell calls for a sacrifice. It doesn't come out and say living — these things never do — but she knew what it meant. Still, it didn't declare itself as a hard and fast rule. The first girl was a week gone, according to the tombstone. There was just a whisper of power that time, the skeleton moving into place, but no tissue to attach it.

There weren't enough deaths in any town for what she needed. She packed her cauldron and a small bag and travelled from graveyard to graveyard. She learned things, as people do when they perform the same duty over and over. She went further south, where the ground was softer. She camped in forests and hid herself away during the day. She had to remain separate and move unseen. The cost of this I cannot tell you. You must come to that yourself.

All the dead bodies she's carried leave marks on her soul. Even though it was born from ugliness, it came as all souls do, pure and white and unmarked. It is the world that leaves dirty prints all over it.

If her soul were detached from her body and held up to the light, where each stain could be pointed out, the tale behind it told, maybe there would be a different story. A different understanding, at least. But that's not how this story goes.

✍

Does the bundle whimper before it meets the cauldron?

Does it matter?

It doesn't, for the record. This is the first time the witch, who used to be a good witch named Perry, plucked the babe from its crib only because it was near death. Whether it was a boy or a girl, she never looks. All she saw was the sunken plates of the soft spots, the blue tinged lips, the glassy eyes. Another babe starving while they feasted in the palace.

Never underestimate the power of bitterness.

She doesn't look at the babe, but she cradles it against her chest for a moment, feeling its cold skin. Perhaps she could be satisfied with another's child. Perhaps this child could soothe her torn heart. But then the babe exhales a ragged half breath, and she knows this babe cannot be saved either.

The babe goes into the cauldron, and the rooms breathes. There is something faintly beating, as soft as the wings of a predator.

Inside the cauldron, a liquid sheet rises up and draws itself over the skeleton.

The witch weeps, but even she knows not for what. For her son, for the babe she just let go of, for who she once was paling in the face of she's become, for the loneliness and the hollowness and for that goddamn shred of hope, the hope of all hopes. The weeping shakes the walls of the cave, and the men below the mouth of the cave, they hesitate. Yet they still move forward.

✍

Inside the witch's heart, there is a box full Sof memories. She clings to the box but she can't open it. Even as the loss cuts away more of her each day, opening the box — she cannot do that. The memories will come. Sunny days dipping their feet into ponds, a small hand on hers. The tug at the breast. His feet curled in her hand. The look in his eyes at the discovery of every new thing. A person cannot take that. It would the undoing of any of us.

✍

A person could wonder what happened to Ethan and the queen, the ones who caused all this mess. Did the queen ever feel guilty? Was she punished in any way for her reprehensible deeds? Did Ethan still long for Perry? Did he ever think of her, does he think of her now, as she squats dead hearted in a cave trying to raise their son? Did he think of her when she had a live boy, carried him on her back as she cleaned homes far richer than the small shack she and the boy shared? Ethan was warned that the raising of the dead had rules and consequences.

Ethan and the queen's part of this story is finished. It is the nature of stories, that chapters end and minor characters leave without a goodbye. Good riddance, some might say.

✍

The weeping witch watches the skin covered skeleton rise. She feels the cave falling away from her. She reaches out with trembling fingers, to touch the boy, but it isn't her boy.

He's too tall. Her boy was just past a year, just saying Mama, and this is a young man.

Do they grow in the beyond?

The witch touches rough sandpaper skin, nothing like the soft smoothness of her boy. When she removes her hand, the body crumples back into the cauldron, accordion folding itself back to where it came from.

"No, no, no," the witch wails. She tears what's remaining of her hair by the roots. Her mind shatters, pieces ricocheting around in her head. They cut her to pieces. She has been drowning in grief and now it swallows her whole. Down and down she goes, no thought of escaping this time. All was lost, all had always been lost, since the beginning.

She was always damned from the beginning.

She steps to the cauldron, her bones creaking from being still, and peers in it. A person would say she could not fit inside, but only a person who does not understand the world is vast and does not care to be understood.

The men move the logs. There are shouts and grunts and the witch hear none of it. She steps onto the rim of the cauldron, her old, wrinkled toes gripping the side. "I love you," she says. "I love you, I always loved you, always from the first moment, I'm so sorry I wasn't better, I'm so sorry, my love."

The first man into the cave sees the old woman tottering above a black pot of fire and shouts for her to stop. She turns to him, eyes full of broken things. Then something happens to her face, something breathing the fire of life across it, a shared moment.

"You have his eyes," she whispers, and lets herself fall backwards into the fire. She makes no sound, as she turns to ash.

Cale, nineteen years old, raised by a woman who was deposited outside the same palace gates heavy with child, bows his head and says a silent prayer.

This is the end of the story as it is known.

✍ ✍ ✍

RENEWAL

—

MICHAEL GARDNER

Renewal

John waited for Holly, continually clenching and then unclenching clammy hands. He sat on the edge of the bed, his stomach roiling, his feet tapping the floor incessantly. It never got easier. He always dreaded the confirmation. It was inevitable and yet most of him wanted to delay. *Another month,* he thought, *just one more. I'll be better prepared then.*

There was a soft click from the ensuite door, and then it was opening. John swallowed. He attempted to convey a neutral expression behind which he could hide his growing dismay. Holly emerged from the bathroom, beautiful in her pink nightie. She flicked auburn hair from her smiling blue eyes and, as she held aloft the pregnancy test with the telling blue cross, her face lit up.

John absorbed the jolt to his guts as best he could, but it was hard to give nothing away when he knew he'd be dead before his son was born.

"So, what do you think?" Holly asked expectantly, her smile beginning to falter.

He forced a grin, hoping it didn't look like a grimace. His mouth felt thick and dry, but he made it move.

"That's amazing," he said. And when she squealed and threw herself at him, he almost believed his words. He drew Holly close and rested his head on her shoulder, inhaling her scent of soap and lavender. God, he'd miss this.

"I've been wanting this for so long," she whispered in his ear. "And you're going to be such a great Dad."

The dread remained, poking at the base of his stomach, but for the moment he allowed her joy to seep in and settle on top, almost disguising it.

"And you're going to be an amazing Mum," he said, and he knew it to be true.

✍

Staring up into the blanket of darkness hovering over the bed, John imagined it consuming him. Holly was snoring softly next to him but, despite her proximity, he felt alone.

They'd talked for a long time before bed. Baby names, plans for renovations, cots, prams, and clothes. Her enthusiasm was infectious and, for a short time, he'd immersed himself in the fantasy of fatherhood.

But that seemed long ago. Now, he was focused on bitter reality. There was so much he needed to do before the end.

He'd have to see his lawyers, and soon. They'd tell Holly about the life insurance policy after he was gone. But he also needed to update his ledger and add it to the package they were already holding for his unborn son. He'd need to recommend a replacement for himself at the University. Change the car into Holly's name. Clean his things out of the back room.

After cycling through his list several times he found his thoughts shifting to the inevitable and imminent pain. His, and his family's.

He sighed, and rolled onto his side, the pillow hot against his ear.

He'd have to warn Julie, he realised. He knew Holly wouldn't want his Mum to be first to know about the baby. The two women had never been close, and Julie was to blame for that. But he had to tell her. Maybe if he'd never shared his secret with Julie he could have waited. But what was done was done.

His thoughts began repeating. As they did, he refined his plan here, added something new to his list there. Eventually, he fell into a restless and uneasy sleep.

✍

He was back in Scotland, shivering at the top of Heaval hill overlooking the bay. Icy water lapped at Kisimul Castle, a squat building of grey stone on an island off the coast of the village of Castlebay.

Ellie's labour screams carried on the wind up from the castle. They were laced with anger, which was his fault. He'd promised to give up the drinking and the women that came with it. But he hadn't. Even after she'd fallen pregnant. Deep down, he'd always assumed that Ellie needed him more than he needed her. She'd had to kick him out for him to realise his mistake. How stupid he'd been. Risking long-term happiness for short-term gratification.

The headaches had begun soon after his expulsion from the castle. A pain that pulsed at the back of his eyes, like needles jabbing him from the inside. The first had lasted for days, and he'd known then that something was wrong. That had been four months ago.

The sun sank in the sky behind him, his thin shadow elongating, stretching down the hill towards the bay. The sharp wind whipped his green and blue kilt and stung his skinny legs. Once, those legs had been planks, but the sickness had eaten away at him, leaving him withered and unable to defy the cold.

Was the sickness divine punishment? Or just bad luck?

As he stood on the hill listening to the birth of his first child, his bones aching, his head throbbing, tears streaming down his cheeks, he was ashamed of the selfish existence he'd led. *My whole life has been a waste.*

God, what he wouldn't give to do it all over, and better. He could have made so much more of what he'd been given if only he'd understood the things he did now.

Ellie delivered an extended shriek and, soon after, a great pain exploded in his head. The dewy grass, the rocky crags, the bay and the castle, all of it became white light. He screamed, and then everything was black.

Black.

And black.

But then illumination came from an orange glow and he found himself confined and wet, enclosed in a tight, fleshy cage. He couldn't control his limbs. They were not his own. Small, slimy, and jerky.

On impulse, he twisted towards the orange light. At the same time he was suddenly pushed from behind by a strong, contracting muscle. His prison squeezed and pushed until light filled his eyes, until cool air caressed his head, until he was out, and cold, and blinded, and scared. Several hard blinks cleared his eyes and there, looking down on him, larger than he ever remembered her, was Ellie. The angry expression of the last few months had melted.

"I think," she whispered to him, "I'll name you Johne MacNeil."

He tried to speak, but the only sound that emerged was a gurgle.

✍

The tears had dried, but Julie's eyes remained red. She sat, hunched at her kitchen table, nursing a cup of tea. John sipped his own tea, waiting for her to speak.

"I guess this means I need to make good with her?" she finally said.

"Mum, you don't have to do anything you don't want to. But I'd definitely appreciate it if you could make amends before ... my transition."

"Hmm," Julie said. She raised the cup to her mouth and took a long, loud slurp. She placed her cup back on the table with a clink.

John watched her closely.

"I'll need her permission to see you when you became my grandson, so I kind of have to make more of an effort, don't I?"

"I'm sure Holly would appreciate that."

Julie gave a short, sharp, "ha", like she didn't believe him.

"Does she know about you, like I do?"

John paused, and then looked down at the table.

"No. I've never told anyone but you."

"Well, that's wrong. You should tell her."

John's eyes widened in surprise.

"But — "

"Just because we don't always get along doesn't mean I want her to suffer. Telling me helped me cope. And God knows she'll need something to help her cope when you start getting sick."

John opened his mouth, then shut it quickly and turned away. He nearly blurted out that telling Julie was a mistake. It might have made her feel better, but it had also led to her jealousy of Holly. But he learned from his mistakes. *Make each life better than the next.* That was the aim. Better job, less pain, happier families. And no more jealousy.

"Do you remember when we met?" Julie asked, her tone softer.

He returned his gaze to Julie, then smiled.

"Of course."

He saw her again as he had that first day. The tight blue jumper, the white miniskirt. Beautiful, confident, comfortable in her own skin.

"Have I changed much?" Julie asked, breaking his reverie.

"You're my mother now."

"I know that," Julie snapped, "and you're my son. But you know what I mean."

John chuckled, shaking his head.

"No. Not much. The spark I remember, the fight, it's all still there. And you still know how to order me around."

She smiled. The first since he'd given her the news.

"Speaking of which, you can help me take some garden waste to the tip."

John took Julie's empty cup from her and placed it along with his in the sink.

"She will forgive me, won't she?" Julie asked, staring out across the table towards the backyard. "I mean, I realise I've been petty at times. Even nasty on occasion. I couldn't help it, you know. Seeing you with her ..."

John was shocked by the fear he heard in his mother's voice. But then, he realised, if she couldn't reconcile with Holly, there was a chance she'd lose him for good and she'd have no one to blame but herself.

"Yes, Mum. She will if you're genuine. Holly's not the type to hold grudges."

Julie sat there for a time, staring off into space. Finally, she sighed and rose to her feet. She took John's hands in hers and looked up at him, determined.

"Ok," she said. "I'll make this right. You just watch."

<hr/>

John sat at the breakfast bar watching Holly mix cake batter. The small, tight bump that was her belly pushed against her shirt.

He hit call on his phone and raised it to his ear. There was a soft click, and then Julie's voice.

"Hello."

"Hi, Mum, it's me." Holly turned and checked the oven, but John could tell she was listening.

"Hi, honey. What's up?"

"Just ringing to give you some good news," John said, "Holly's pregnant."

"So you're finally telling people. That took long enough. So when can I visit and sort this mess out?"

"Oh, I'm so glad you're excited," John replied. He watched Holly straighten and tilt her head slightly. "And we're both really happy."

"Maybe I should talk to her now. Actually, that's a good idea. Put her on."

"No," John shot back quickly. Holly was hovering over the bowl, but she wasn't mixing. She was looking at John. He forced a smile to his lips. "No, not much morning sickness. Holly is really well. Glowing actually," he said, regretting doing so instantly. It didn't sound like him. Holly's smirk said as much.

"Well, bad luck. I will talk to her. And if you don't put her on now, I'll just call her phone."

Jesus, Mum. God, she was a stubborn woman.

"Ha, yes. Good one. I guess I can do that."

"Good. But before you go — how are you, honey? Are you feeling ok?"

John paused. The headaches had already started.

"Yep, fine," he lied.

Julie sighed. He wondered if she knew he was lying. Probably. But she didn't say anything.

"Ok, pass me to Holly."

John covered the mouth piece with his hand.

"She wants to speak to you," John said, offering the phone to Holly.

Holly's eyes widened in surprise.

"Really?" she mouthed silently, looking dubious.

John shrugged, then nodded.

"She's going to be a grandmother. She's excited."

Holly hesitated for a moment, then reached out and took the phone. She turned her back on John and walked from the kitchen towards the hall.

"Hi, Julie. How are you?"

A pause. John stood up, took a glass from the cupboard and filled it with water.

"Thanks, Julie. We're happy too."

There was a long pause. John watched Holly's face intently. He could hear the buzz of Julie's voice from far away, but he couldn't make out what she was saying. Holly's face softened.

"Oh, thanks. Yes, me too. Look ... no, fair enough."

Another long pause.

Holly was nodding now. She looked at John and raised her eyebrows, then turned and disappeared down the hall. John drank his water and then sat at the bench again. It was best to wait. He shouldn't eavesdrop.

A couple of minutes later Holly returned and gave him his phone. Without saying a word, she returned to stirring the batter.

"Well?" John asked.

"Did you put her up to that?"

"I honestly have no idea what you talked about. What did she say?"

Holly stared at him, examining his face for a lie. But he saw that she found none. Her gaze softened.

"I never thought the old girl would surprise me. She apologised. She wants to fix things between us. She said she wants to be a good grandmother and a decent mother-in-law."

John smiled. This was good. It'd make things easier, for them and him.

"And you need to put some sheets on the spare bed. She's coming to visit on the weekend."

"Oh. And you're ok with that?"

Holly looked up from the batter.

"I don't know. But I think we have to give it a shot, right? For our little girl or boy."

✍

John awoke in darkness with the coppery tang of blood at the back of his throat. He put a hand to his face and it came away slick. Shit. He turned and saw that Holly was still asleep. He sniffed hard, rose from the bed and then shuffled into the ensuite. He closed the door and turned on the light. Looking back at him in the mirror was something from a horror movie. Blood streamed from his nose, down over his mouth and neck and out across his pyjama top. Shit, shit, shit, John thought. He wrenched toilet paper from the roll and balled it up and held it to his nose. How the hell was he going to clean this up before Holly woke?

Then Holly screamed.

John threw the door open and found Holly shaking, pointing at the bloody sheets.

"It's ok, honey, its ok," John mumbled. "I'm ok. Just a bleeding nose."

"That's not just a fucking bleeding nose, John. I thought you'd been murdered. Look at the blood. Look at it."

John looked into her wide eyes. He saw the shock, fear and panic, and he suddenly felt guilty. *This is going to hurt her as much as me.* But what could he do about it? This was his life now. And hers, he realised.

"I'll clean it up. I just need a minute to stop the flow," he said softly.

Holly rose from the bed and took a deep, shuddering breath.

"I'll wet a cloth," she said, taking a tentative step towards him. She reached out with a trembling hand and took hold of his arm. Her short nightie clung to the bulge of her stomach.

"Tomorrow, I'm booking you in to see Doctor Rouch."

"Honestly, I'm fine."

"No you're not, John. This is not normal and I'm taking you to see my doctor. Understand?"

John smiled beneath the ball of crimson toilet paper. He loved her for wanting to look out for him better than he did himself. And despite knowing what the diagnosis would be, his heart clenched at Holly's concern.

"Ok."

"Good. Now, let's clean you up."

John watched the steam rising from his coffee. He wondered where the time had gone since Holly had first taken him to the doctor. As with previous transitions, life had become disjointed. Jumping forward and then slowing when he least expected. Sometimes, he wished he could just skip to the end.

"Sorry?" he inquired, looking up at Julie, who sat across the table from him.

"I *said,*" she repeated, "what did the specialist say?"

"Same thing they said thirty six years ago. Cancer."

"Oh, come on. Medicine has advanced a hell of a lot since the eighties. What options do you have?"

John rolled his eyes.

"Chemotherapy, and then maybe surgery. But you and I know better."

John inhaled the earthy aroma of his coffee. He lifted the cup to his lips, sipping slowly, deliberately, as Julie pushed her chair back from the table with a screech and stood.

"So you're not even going to try?" She stomped to the kitchen sink where she dropped her cup with a clang.

"I don't know. Holly wants me to — "

"But you know better, right?"

John remained silent as he watched Julie return to the table and plant both hands on it, leaning over him.

"You selfish child. Holly wants you to live. I want you to live. But you, you're already thinking about the next life. How to make it better. How to get a better job. A better wife. Don't you think I know Holly is my upgrade?"

"Oh, come on."

"I know and you know. Everything is about what you can improve. Have you ever stopped to think that what you already have might be damn perfect? And if not perfect, then close enough?"

John sighed. He didn't need this now.

"Mum, I'm going to die. It's inevitable. But you know I'll be back. And you'll both still have me."

"But maybe you don't have to die, damn it," Julie hissed, tears in her eyes. "I don't know why I even bother. It was the same last time. You don't fight, you don't try to hold on. You don't even have the courtesy to let us comfort you or grieve with you. You just bloody disappear into yourself."

"I'm going for a walk." He stood up and moved towards the front door.

"Just try the chemo. Show Holly and me you're not completely selfish, ok?"

He paused at the door and turned back. Behind her angry posturing, John saw anguish in Julie's eyes. Was he as bad as she said? He hadn't meant to hurt her last time and he didn't want to hurt her now. He loved her and Holly more than they could possibly know. But chemo couldn't stop the transition. But then, maybe that wasn't the point. If seeing him try relieved a little of Julie's and Holly's pain, then maybe a little extra suffering on his part could be worthwhile.

"I'll think about it," he responded. He pulled the door open and slipped outside.

✍

Time was a hundred kilogram weight attached to John's mind. He battled his heavy eyelids as the second hand on the clock on the wall made one painful jerk after another. His hospital gown itched and his arm was cold as poison dripped from a transparent bag into a tube, down to his left wrist where it entered his vein through the cannula. The room had the faint scent of chlorine. The liquid would make him sick later, he knew. But now it dripped, like the second hand, slowly. He was trapped in a moment that he'd like to move past.

Time was becoming more inconsistent as he neared the end. He dreaded the long pauses. He nearly had everything prepared for a successful transition and yet, here he was, treading water, watching the second hand, tick, tick, tick. Why did time barely move when he was by himself?

A pang of bitterness assaulted him as he cursed Holly for abandoning him today. But just as quickly he pushed his selfish thought away. *It's me who should have been with her.* A twenty week scan and he wasn't there to see Holly's face when she found out they were having a boy. God, he was a shit.

He suddenly longed for home. To talk to her. To see her joy. To hold onto that moment.

The clock tick, tick, ticked.

✍

John was frozen mid-heave, unable to breathe, unable to move, long after the last of the liquid had been expelled from his stomach and splattered against the bowl. Still, his diaphragm lurched and squeezed. His face ached, his mouth locked open until, finally, the spasm relented and he sucked in air.

Cold beads of sweat ran into his eyes. All John could do was stare at an area of clean porcelain at the back of the bowl, somehow untouched by his assault. His pallid hands clung to the toilet and shook.

Finally, certain he had nothing more to give, he slumped to the cool tiled floor, exhausted and empty. He hated this. This nothing right now. And the one before that, and before that.

But he knew his life wasn't just a series of empty moments. There was substance in between. He tried hard to recall the details of his trip with Holly to the coast last weekend, but nothing stood out.

Why? Why was right now so clear and last weekend — when he knew he felt good — a haze? Was it him, or the sickness?

✍

He woke up screaming. Holly turned and held him for a glorious moment, with her plump belly pushed into his trembling back. Then she was gone, asleep, and he was alone in the dark as time ticked wearily on. One more moment, alone, cold.

But that wasn't right, was it? He thought hard. And then he realised that she had held him for at least an hour. She would have held him longer, he was sure, but he had pushed her away and asked her to sleep.

It was him who'd sought solitude, not her.

✍

John was hunched over a box of his old journals. He picked out the most recent one and began to peruse it, surprised to find that it had been years since he'd made an entry. That was odd. He hadn't intentionally decided to stop, he just had. And yet he'd been religious about keeping these journals for generations. He'd relied upon them to help him clarify the life lessons that he'd record in his ledger. He returned the book to the box and picked out another at random and began to read.

He didn't hear Holly come in, so he gave a little start when she squeezed him from behind, her large belly pushed into his bony back.

"Oh," he said, turning, "you're here."

"I'm always here".

Holly was kneeling on the carpet, smiling. He looked her over for what felt like the first time in months. Her belly was round and tight, her hair thick and shiny. She looked so fresh, so clear. It was like he'd just surfaced from a deep ocean dive — strange to be above the water's surface, but wonderful to be breathing real air.

"Hey," he said, admiring her. How had he missed all of this?

"Hey yourself. What are you doing?"

"I was feeling all right, so I decided to clean my junk out of the back room."

Holly's smile faltered. John saw the discomfort in her eyes. She knows I'm cleaning up for when I'm gone, he thought.

"We need to make room for the baby, right?" John lied. He forced a smile to his lips. "But I got distracted. Do you remember I used to keep journals?"

Holly hesitated, but then smiled again.

"Yes, of course. Did you find anything good?"

John furrowed his brow.

"I was just reading about our first trip to the coast."

"Broulee?"

"Yes. It was supposed to be a surprise, remember? But it ended up a disaster."

"I don't know if I'd use the word disaster," Holly said. She shifted position, moving until she sat alongside John. He felt her warmth and breathed her in. She took the journal from him and started running her finger down the page.

"We got stuck in traffic in the mountains, so the three hour trip took five. And when we got there, we couldn't find anywhere decent to stay because I hadn't booked ahead — so we ended up in that terrible caravan park."

"Rings a bell," Holly said, flipping through the pages of the journal. "But what about the rest?"

"What do you mean?" He picked up another of his books.

"What about the walk along the beach we took the day after we arrived? That storm came in and we found a quiet place on the sand and sat there, just watching the lightning off the coast. Sitting there in your arms, that was perfect for me. Well worth the couple of inconveniences we faced to get to that moment, don't you think?"

John looked at Holly, confused.

"You're serious, aren't you? You don't remember how dull that drive was, how shitty the accommodation?"

Holly chuckled, shaking her head. She dropped the journal, leaned over and kissed him.

"When you find something good, come get me. I'm putting dinner on."

Holly rose to her feet and left the room.

John flipped through more journals. They read like a checklist of what had gone wrong in his life. An essay he could have written better at university. A wooden table he tried to make that was never level. An anniversary dinner he burnt. Holly was right. None of this was important.

He realised that he'd taken the same outlook into the last six months. Ignore the good, focus on the moments that should have been better, the things that he might improve next time. He forced himself to remember. Not the chemo, not throwing up — the real moments. The memories hit him hard. Holly holding him in the night. Holly forcing him to eat when he didn't feel like it. Holly laughing with Julie.

He sat there, stunned. He understood now why he'd stopped keeping the journals. There was nothing that he could learn from them that would help him find anyone better than Holly in his next life.

When he finally moved again, it was to bundle up all of his journals in his arms and take them out to the bin. Then he went into the kitchen, walked up to Holly who was mixing dough, and turned her and kissed her before she could say a word. After her initial surprise, her lips softened and she responded warmly.

John pulled back.

"Forget that, let's go out tonight. I'm feeling hungry for once."

Holly's eyes glistened.

"I'd like that."

✍

John awoke to the sound of Holly crying, and he noticed that his right side was damp.

"John, something's wrong. I think the baby's coming early."

John's heart lurched.

"It's ok. Everything will be fine. I'll call the hospital," John said, jumping up and grabbing his phone. What was happening?

He wasn't sick enough yet. He always knew when time was up. He felt it in his bones. A brittleness and a sickness that was all consuming. But he still felt very much here. This had never happened before. Was it the chemo?

The midwife on the phone reassured him and asked him to get Holly to the hospital as quickly as possible. After the midwife hung up, he phoned Julie.

"I'll be there as soon as I can," she said, hanging up abruptly.

Then he helped Holly to the car, comforting her as best he could, knowing he might not be with her much longer.

✍

John held Holly's hand tightly while Doctors Roberts and England talked quietly in the corner of the room. The midwife, Sally, examined Holly, who lay on her side, pillows propped under her left hip. John fought the urge to vomit, and ignored the weakness in his legs. He didn't know how long he could continue standing, but he'd let Holly squeeze his hand while he could. Because he wanted to be here, damn it, to share this experience with her.

Just then, he heard Julie loudly remonstrating outside the birth suite doors.

"What do you mean I can't go in? They're my family and I want to see them."

"You can let her in," Holly said, panting between contractions. "I'd like her in here. Please."

The doctors looked at John. John nodded, and soon Julie was standing next to him dabbing Holly's face with a warm cloth.

"Nice to see you're still here," Julie directed to John as Holly squeezed his hand and moaned as another contraction took hold. John leaned against the bed for support, easing the strain on his tiring legs.

The two doctors separated. Doctor Roberts began to set up a radiant warmer nearby. Doctor England consulted briefly with Sally, and then moved towards Holly's feet.

"Ok, Holly," Doctor England said, "I know we've been saying to resist the urge to push, but on the next contraction, it's time to push."

"Oh, thank God," Holly panted. And soon she was groaning loudly, her face screwed up tight as pain hit again.

"Ok, that's great," the doctor said. Sally, who was to John's left, pulled Holly's leg further towards her. "I can see the baby's head."

John rose up a little to get a better view and, holy shit, he could see it too. Just the top of some wet, dark hair, but it was amazing. He tried to hold himself erect to keep his eyes on his son, but then his legs wobbled and he suddenly felt dizzy.

He reached out, trying to grasp at the bed, but his eyes fluttered and, from somewhere distant, he heard a thud and a clatter.

The world was black, but with an orange glow. He was cosy and warm and yet encompassed by a deep, aching sadness he had never experienced before. Julie would never chastise him again as his mother and Holly would cease to be his wife. He would lose so much. There would be no more of Holly's smile — the special one she reserved for when he pleased her. No more watching her brush her hair as she hummed softly to herself. No more cakes. He felt it all wash past and over him, slipping through his fingers. It would soon be replaced with that look of sadness he always saw in his new mother.

He was squeezed and pushed. Time was nearly up. John panicked and bucked and kicked. For once, he was not excited about the prospect of a new life. He was happy now, here. And wasn't that all that mattered? He hated to admit it, but Julie was right. Some people never came close to having all he did and he'd been letting it all go.

So he scrambled, trying to hold onto his life. He pushed aside the pain and the minutiae, and sought out the real moments. Holly's laughter. Holly rubbing his back as he fell asleep in a sweat. Julie ordering him around her garden. He held on tightly and ignored the opportunities for improvement ahead. He remembered and focused and saw with clarity the glint in Holly's smiling eyes as she told him he would be a Dad. He saw it and felt it — the new possibilities of his life continuing.

The black withdrew rapidly and was replaced with bright lights.

He felt arms around him, lifting him into a chair.

"No you don't, you selfish bastard," Julie whispered in his ear. "You're staying here and seeing this."

"Yes, Mum," John mumbled. He opened his eyes and saw tears in Julie's. Her face was ashen, but she smiled, relieved. Sally hovered just behind Julie, concern etched across her face. Julie leaned closer again.

"Are you back for good?" she whispered, tears splashing his face.

"I hope so."

"He's ok, love," Julie said to Holly, wiping at her eyes. "He's just a bit dizzy. A quick rest will fix him up."

But Holly didn't respond. She was groaning, panting, crying, straining.

"That's good. Very good, Holly. Just one more and ... done," Doctor England said.

John saw the obstetrician hold up a tiny baby, who opened its mouth and wailed.

"Congratulations. A baby boy."

In a wave of activity, the cord was cut and the baby was passed to Doctor Roberts, who quickly laid it down on the radiant warmer where she checked him over under the heat lamp.

Julie helped John to his feet, his arm around her shoulders. Holly lay on her back, her eyes clenched shut, like she was afraid to open them and confirm that her son was real.

"Hey," John whispered, leaning close to her and kissing her on the cheek. "You did it."

She opened her eyes and looked into his.

"You're ok?"

"I'm fine," he said, smiling.

Doctor Roberts was suddenly standing by the bed and handing Holly her baby. She accepted him, her mouth agape, but no words came out. She just stared at their tiny son, soundlessly, breathlessly, a tiny presence in her loving embrace.

"Being premature, he'll need to spend time in the special care nursery. But everything looks great," Doctor Roberts said.

John ran his hand delicately over his son's slick scalp and he felt an electric pulse through his fingertips as tears welled in his eyes.

"He's beautiful," Julie said, as she shifted under John's weight. And he was, John saw. Because he looked like Holly.

✍

"Now, you're sure?" Holly asked. She stood just inside the front door, her eyes flitting from John, to Daniel cradled in his arms, and then back to John.

"Yes, I told you, go. We'll be fine."

"But you're still recovering. You've — "

"I've been in remission for a month. I'm fine. You've spent enough time caring for the two of us. It's time to spend a little time on you."

John gently ushered Holly out the door. She stepped outside reluctantly, her brow furrowed, her mouth a frown.

"Call me if anything goes wrong, ok?" she said. "I'm just down the road at the hairdressers, so I can be back in five minutes."

"Will you get going?" John said, laughing. "We're fine."

She hesitated, then leaned forward and kissed John and then Daniel. After one last look at both of them, she finally turned and walked away from the house.

John shook his head, and then stepped back inside, closing the door behind him. He glanced down at his son to find him in the middle of a big, gummy yawn, and he was suddenly struck by a recollection of what it had been like, beginning life again. He didn't miss it. He'd done it so often that it had become a well-rehearsed play. Yet since Daniel's birth he'd been assaulted by a kaleidoscope of emotions — protectiveness, pride, worry, doubt, and sheer, unbridled joy. After such a long time on this earth, it was amazing to be completely uncertain about what he was doing because he was experiencing something new.

John inhaled deeply, and smiled down at his son who was looking up at him with big, curious eyes.

"Ok, little man. Time for bed," he said. He laid Daniel down in his basinet and then stood nearby, watching as Daniel's eyelids drooped, sprung open, and then slowly closed. This was one glorious moment worth holding on to.

✍ ✍ ✍

Initial feedback

I like the concept and the latter part of the execution. The piece opened slowly, and it took a while before I found it interesting; the introduction of the concept could have been smoother, and we never get much hint of the trigger, other than being a bad partner. The piece runs a bit long. The end could use some polish. I'm not a fan of the title.

Author's intent

What do you think the story's about?
What emotions are you trying to evoke?

Regarding your questions on meaning and emotions, I wrote this story thinking of those times in my life when I've focused too much on the past. I get stuck in my own head sometimes and spend a lot of times reliving things I've done wrong, considering how I might do them better if I had the chance again, etc. Which got me to thinking, what if you could keep reliving your life, trying to make it better, fix the wrongs of the past, learn from your mistakes? Would that lead to a perfect life? Or would striving for perfection lead to an obsession that meant you missed out on the here and now? Would the constant promise of another go at perfection blind you to how good you might have things?

John's character is very much a representative of this thinking. He lives each life trying to improve, particularly influenced by the regret he feels for his first life. But when John also knows he is dying, he has a tendency to lose sight of what he has got as he becomes consumed with self pity and as he begins thinking about the future.

Julie, though, is the character that calls John out. She has already seen how he disappears into himself at the end. I wanted her to radiate the frustration I hope the reader feels watching John impotently accept his future.

Through the middle of the story, I want to convey John's withdrawal and Julie's frustration. From the scene where Holly catches John reading old diaries, I want the story to become uplifting. I want Holly to show how perceptions can be very different. He obsesses on the small failures, she remembers the good experiences. And from that realisation, I want him to change his view and begin to fight for the life he has — the good points, the mediocrity, the low times, all of it.

Author's note

"Renewal" was the third story I ever sold. *Metaphorosis* was a relatively new magazine at the time, and it promised feedback on stories, and comprehensive editing if Morris saw potential. As a relatively new writer, both offers appealed.

When I submitted "Renewal", I received a reply from Morris that indicated he saw potential in the story and wanted to work with me on it. However, he was clear up front that he considered the story needed work if he was to publish it.

Morris suggested cutting several distracting scenes to bring the true story to the fore. He also provided suggestions to tighten the prose and clarify the narrative. Oh, and a new title. He hated my original title, which in hindsight, I'm embarrassed by. It felt like I'd reverted to my teenage years and was trying to be too clever.

It can be confronting to hear your story is good, but without significant work, would be unlikely to pass a slush pile. Personally, I got over that quickly. I soaked up Morris' advice. I craved it.

At that stage, I wasn't part of a writing community where I could seek critiques for my stories. While I roped in friends as first readers, that was more about high-level reactions to the narrative, characters, ideas, rather than detailed structural edits. So yes, there is a moment where you feel the gut punch of the initial critique. But it's only a moment. A beat later you push that aside, peruse the comments carefully and realise they're helpful. The key for me was that I quickly saw that Morris understood the story I was trying to tell, and that his comments were directed at helping me tell it more clearly.

The key edits for "Renewal" were a new beginning, and the removal of a repeated dream sequence. I'd initially started the story too early. Morris' suggested changes to the beginning helped start the story in the middle of the action. And the dream sequence, well, I thought it was an interesting, surreal, prophetic sequence. Morris helped me see that it didn't progress the narrative. Which meant it was a distraction.

Morris promised me it would hurt to remove so much content. And it did. Briefly. But like removing a splinter, there's a little pain, then you feel better. The changes I made sharpened the story, made it more direct, and helped better highlight the dilemma that John faced.

All in all, I cut around 1,500 words.

I don't have any negatives to share about the editing process. I thought Morris was polite, direct, insightful, and helpful.

I've now had four stories published in *Metaphorosis* magazine, and another two stories published in Metaphorosis anthologies. Each has gone through a thorough editorial process. And each has been improved by it.

Editor's note

Sometimes I come across a story that I think has real potential, but that needs a fair amount of work. In those cases, I try to emphasize to authors (especially those new to the magazine) how much is required — especially if that work involves cutting. I don't subscribe to the 'kill your darlings' philosophy, but they're also not *my* darlings, so when I see the need to cut, I say so. It's always a bit of a toss up whether authors will be open to that, especially once the process starts and they see that I'm serious. To his credit, Michael put in all the hard work, and cut with good will.

I felt the original version started slowly and didn't introduce its concept or trigger clearly enough. I also felt it was too long. There was a surrealist/dream sequence that I didn't think was working, and I suggested cutting much of the beginning entirely. Michael didn't flinch, and I thought the story worked better for it.

Beyond the length and setup issues, I thought that the protagonist's motivations and purpose needed some clarification. The husband, John, was clearly trying to do better and be better, but I felt that purpose could be introduced more clearly, and the realization that he'd been focused on the wrong thing entirely could come more gradually.

No one really likes to cut prose they've worked hard on, but I think "Renewal" is evidence of how even painful cuts can help the story emerge. When I first offered Michael the rewrite, knowing how much I thought was required, I didn't know him and wasn't sure how it would go. I knew I wasn't prepared to publish the original version. Would the author be flexible enough to make changes, or would we go our separate ways? As it happens, he was, and I'm glad for it, not just for "Renewal" but for the many other stories of Michael's I've published since then (I believe he's now about to catch up with L'Erin Ogle for number of pieces in *Metaphorosis*).

Ouroboros

John stood in the desert, shielding his eyes from incandescent sunlight. A breeze stirred white sand around his ankles and cooled the sweat that trickled down his back. His stomach flipped and turned, filled with dread.

John turned. A bare magnolia tree grew impossibly from the parched earth. On a branch, nearest him, a bud emerged and opened, displaying a large, purple flower. Black clouds clawed their way up over the horizon and then raced across the sky, casting shadows across the land. The sky grew dark. A single drop of rain fell and landed on one petal of the flower, turning it to dust. The air vibrated.

I still don't understand, thought John. It has to mean something, right?

John awoke in darkness with a shrill ringing in his ears. He felt alone, despite the proximity of his wife. He knew in his gut that Holly had conceived and that he would die before his son was born.

The pillow was hot against his ear, so he rolled onto his back. After a few seconds, his eyes began to decipher shapes in the dark. Holly snored softly as the tinnitus in his ears receded. An owl screeched outside the bedroom window.

His lids were heavy. His pulse raced and his stomach churned. Nine months left at most, he thought. But this time would be different. This time, against his better judgement, he had shared his secret and he worried how she would cope. He'd have to warn her, he thought.

John closed his eyes. Flashes of light snaked across the back of his lids. He waited, ignoring the doubts that assaulted him, pushing thoughts and imagined future scenarios from his mind until, eventually, his body responded to his will and fell into the comforting blackness of sleep.

✍

The radio woke John. He opened his eyes and found Holly already awake and smiling at him. Amber hair slid across her blue eyes. She was beautiful, he thought. Then he remembered his dream.

"Hey gorgeous, you sleep well?" Holly asked. She licked her thick red lips and sighed.

John forced a smile, hoping it did not look like a grimace.

"Sure."

"Weren't we sleeping in today?" Holly mumbled as she closed her eyes again.

"Yeah, sorry. I accidently left the alarm on."

"Ok. Well, we're up now. What's the plan? You want to go out for breakfast?"

"Ah, actually, I forgot to mention, I need to duck up and see Mum."

Holly's eyes sprang open and she glared at John.

"You forgot. Really?"

"Look, I'm sorry. But I promised I'd help her move some furniture …"

"John, we've talked about this. You don't need permission to see her, but it would be nice to have some notice when you go. I could have planned something."

"I'm sorry," John apologised, a little tersely. "It's not like I'm asking you to come with me."

"Don't give me that shit. You know I'm right."

John said nothing.

Holly sat up, turned from John and swung her legs over the edge of the bed. He felt guilty. Why did he always get so defensive? He should apologise, but he didn't.

"Just go."

"I'll be back by lunch tomorrow."

Holly stood and then glided from the room.

John packed quickly and lightly. When he left the bedroom, he spied Holly out on the back deck, sipping a coffee and playing with her phone. He took a step towards the garage, then stopped and sighed. He dropped his bag and withdrew his phone from his pocket, then dialled. He watched Holly through the back window as she shook her head and raised her phone to her ear.

"Yep," Holly answered. "I didn't know you had left yet."

"I haven't."

Holly turned and John waved. She shook her head.

"So, is there a point to this childish call?"

"Yeah, I'm calling to say I love you, I take you for granted and I'm sorry I didn't tell you about visiting Mum."

There was a pause. Holly turned her back on John again.

"Really, is that all?" Holly asked. But her tone had changed and John knew she was smiling.

"No, one more thing. I also meant to tell you that clearly, due to my behaviour, I owe you a gift."

"Hmm, really. Well it better not just be crappy chocolates."

"Damn it," John replied, a smile dancing on his lips. "I guess I better get some flowers as well as a Crunchie from the servo."

Holly laughed — a deep, throaty guffaw that betrayed her slight build. John loved her laugh. He opened the back door and walked out onto the deck.

"You clown. Travel safe, ok? I'll see you tomorrow."

"Will do. Love you," John said. As he hung up the phone, Holly turned and embraced him. He kissed her forehead, then released her.

"Ok, I better get going."

There was no worse feeling then dying, hated by those you loved, he thought, as he walked to the garage. He had learnt that five hundred and sixty five years ago.

Angus sat on dewy grass at the top of Heaval hill, overlooking the bay. Icy water lapped at Kisimul Castle, a squat building of grey stone perched on an island off the coast of the village of Castlebay.

The screams of a woman in labour carried from the Castle to the top of the hill. The screams were laced with anger, and that was his fault. Ellie had left him four months ago, after she had found out about the other women. He had been lucky that her father had not killed him. Not long after, the nose bleeds began. And time had raced forward, lurching towards an end point that filled him with dread.

The sun sank in the sky behind Angus and a sharp wind whipped his green and blue kilt — ice daggers in his skinny legs. Once, those legs had been planks, but over the last few months a sickness had eaten away at the muscle and left a withered body that could no longer defy the cold.

Was the sickness divine punishment? Or was it just bad luck? There was nothing he could do to atone now, but he was struck with the thought that his whole life had been a waste. And now, his bones aching, his head pounding, listening to the birth of his first child, tears streaming down his cheeks, he was ashamed of the selfish existence he had led.

Ellie delivered an extended shriek which floated from the Castle up the rocky outcrop and to Angus. A great pain exploded in his head. He squeezed his eyes shut against the pain and cried out. Then, just as suddenly, the pain was gone and the world faded to black.

Black.

And black.

Then a light.

An orange light. Angus was confined and wet. He could not move his limbs. They were not his own. Small, slimy and jerky. His mind told him to head for the light. So he did. Behind him he was pushed by a strong, contracting muscle. His confined space squeezed him and pushed his head towards the light until he was out and blinded. Several hard blinks cleared his eyes and there, looking down on him, larger than he ever remembered her, was Ellie. The angry expression of the last few months had melted. She was tired and pleased.

"I think," she whispered to him, "I'll name you Johne MacNeil."

Angus tried to speak, but the only sound that emerged was a gurgle.

✍

A black Audi A8 hummed past John as he took his foot off the accelerator and coasted into Bowral. The road was lined with ivy covered stone walls. The car slowed and the drone of tyres on asphalt was momentarily replaced by the soft 'tick, tick, tick' of the indicator as John eased into a gravel driveway. He drove slowly up to his mother's home. As he cut the engine, the French doors swung open and his Mum — Julie — stepped onto the deck and waved.

Her once black hair was grey, and she had tight lines around the corners of her eyes and mouth. Signs of a lifetime of smiling. She was still pretty, even in her late fifties.

John emerged from the car and the gravel crunched under his feet. A magpie warbled from a nearby elm tree.

"Well, this is a nice treat," Julie said, flicking hair from her eyes. She stepped down from the deck and began walking towards him. "To what do I owe the pleasure?"

"Hi Mum," John said, but he did not return her smile. He hated giving bad news. "Holly's pregnant."

Julie stopped and her lips quivered. Then her legs gave way.

John raced forward and caught her under her arms before she collapsed to the ground. She began to wail and her body shook with sobs.

The tears had dried, but Julie's eyes remained red. She sat, hunched at the kitchen table, nursing a cup of tea. John sipped his own tea, waiting for Julie to speak. He knew there was no point forcing her to converse before she was ready.

"I guess this means I need to make up with her?" she finally said.

"If you'd like. I mean, it would make things easier."

"Hmm," Julie said. She raised the cup to her mouth and took a long, loud slurp. She placed her cup back on the table with a 'clink'. "I wouldn't like. I find her uppity and difficult ..."

"Mum, let's not do this again."

"But," Julie said, ignoring John, "I want you in my life and I'll need her permission to see you when you became my grandchild."

"Ok. I'm sure Holly is ready to fix this as well."

"Does she know?"

"She wouldn't know she is pregnant yet. It's too early."

"I didn't mean that. Does she know about you, like I do?"

John paused and then looked down at the table.

"No. I've never told anyone but you."

"Well, I think that's wrong. You should tell her."

John's eyes widened in surprise.

"But ..."

"Just because we don't get along doesn't mean I want her to suffer. Telling me helped me cope. And God knows she'll need something to help her cope when you start getting sick."

John opened his mouth, then shut it quickly and looked away. He nearly blurted out that telling Julie was a mistake. It might have made her feel better, but it had also led to her jealousy of Holly. But he learned from his mistakes. Make each life better than the next, he thought. That was the aim. Better job, less pain, happier families. And no more jealousy.

"Do you remember when we met?" Julie asked, her tone softer.

He stared at Julie for a moment, then smiled.

"Of course."

The door groaned as John entered the empty lecture theatre. He was early. He walked to the front and placed his briefcase on the table next to the lectern. He inhaled deeply. He liked the smell of universities. A mix of muskiness and bodies in close proximity.

John was nervous, but excited. Damn, it was good to finally be here, he thought. After five centuries labouring and doing other menial work to get by, he had finally learned that a job could be about more than money.

John unlocked his briefcase and removed his notes. He turned the projector on, which whirred to life and emitted a faint scent of burnt plastic.

The first of his students strolled into the room, talking, oblivious to his presence. And then more and more followed. When the room was half full, he rapped the lectern with his knuckles.

"Ok, people, if we can take a seat and begin," he projected, pleased with how his voice carried across the theatre. Huh, he thought to himself as the class quietened, they actually listened.

"Ok, this is European history 1010. And I'm Doctor Neil. Given no one has stood up and left, I'll assume you are all in the right place, or too embarrassed to admit you're in the wrong room."

A soft chuckle from the room. John relaxed. He opened his mouth to begin his lecture when the door swung open and banged against the wall. Standing in the doorway was a dark haired girl wearing a tight blue jumper and white mini skirt.

"Oh, shit. Sorry," the girl said.

"Please, Miss. Take a seat."

The girl ambled up to the front row and then sat down directly in front of John. She smiled at him and then began rummaging in her bag.

John recommenced his lecture. But he was soon interrupted by a 'thump' as the girl threw her bag to the ground.

"Excuse me."

John stopped, surprised.

"Yes, Miss."

"It's Julie."

"Ok, Julie. Can I help you?"

"Yes. Do you have a pen I can borrow?"

The classroom murmured and giggled.

Who was this woman? John thought. She was so confident and brash. She was also attractive. He pulled a pen from his pocket and offered it to the girl, who accepted it with a smile.

"Anyone else need a pen, a note pad, a snack maybe?" he asked, drawing a laugh from the group. Julie laughed hardest of all. She leant back and crossed her legs, causing her skirt to ride high on her thighs. They were muscular and smooth.

John swallowed and began again. This time, he progressed without interruption.

At the end of the lecture, feeling good, he began packing his briefcase as his students rushed from the theatre. When he had finished, he looked up to find Julie still sitting in front of him, chewing on the pen.

"Hi," she said, removing the gnawed pen from her mouth.

"Hi."

She offered the mangled pen to John, who shook his head.

"No. Please, keep it," he said. He picked up his briefcase and took a step from the lectern, when Julie stopped him with a question.

"Do you want to grab a drink later?"

John cleared his throat. Who was this woman? He knew he couldn't go out with her. She was a student.

"Sure," he responded, surprising himself.

"Great. I'll meet you at your office at 6.30."

Julie rose quickly and skipped out of the theatre. She hadn't even waited to check that John was free at 6.30.

✍

Julie chuckled as John finished retelling the story. The first grin he had seen since he had shared his news.

"Have I changed much?" she asked.

"Yes, you're my mother now."

"I know that," Julie snapped, "and you're my son. But you know what I mean."

John sighed.

"No. Not much. A little older, but the fight is still there. And you still know how to order me around."

"Speaking of, I've got some garden waste I need taken to the tip. But first, do you think I should give Holly a call? You know, start the reconciliation before she knows that I know she's pregnant."

"No," John replied. "Trust me, she will be more receptive if she sees an obvious reason for your change of behaviour. If you start being nice out of the blue, she'll be suspicious."

"Hmm. She's an odd one."

"Mum ..."

"Yes, yes. Ok. I'll leave it for now."

John chuckled to himself. Had Julie changed — barely? She was always a woman of action. If John had left proposing any longer, he was certain Julie would have done it for him. He shook his head and stood up.

"Ok, let's get that rubbish," John said, taking Julie's cup from her and placing it in the sink.

"Do you think she will forgive me?" Julie asked. John was shocked at the fear in his mother's voice. But then, he realised, if this did not work she would lose him, and she would have no one to blame but herself.

"Yes, Mum. If you're genuine. Holly doesn't hold grudges."

Julie rose to her feet and took John's arm in hers.

"Ok. Enough of this. To work."

And with that, she led John to the backyard.

✑

John sat at the breakfast bar watching Holly mix cake batter. He hit call on his phone and raised it to his ear. The hallway clock ticked softly, just audible over the hum of the oven.

There was a soft click and then Julie's voice.

"Hello."

"Hi Mum, it's me." Holly turned and checked the oven, but John could tell she was listening.

"Hi honey, what's up?"

"Just ringing to give you some good news," John said, "Holly's pregnant."

"So you're finally telling people. That took long enough. So when can I visit and sort this mess out?"

"Oh, I'm so glad you're excited," John replied. He watched Holly straighten and tilt her head slightly. "And we're both really happy."

"Maybe I should talk to her now. Actually, that's a good idea. Put her on."

"No," John shot back quickly. Holly was hovering over the bowl, but she wasn't mixing. She was looking at John. He forced a smile to his lips. "No, not much morning sickness. Holly is really well. Glowing actually," he said, regretting doing so instantly. It did not sound like him. Holly's smirk said as much.

"Well, bad luck. I will talk to her. And if you don't put her on now, I'll just call her phone."

Jesus, Mum, John thought. God she was a stubborn woman.

"Ha, yes. Good one. I guess I can do that."

"Good. But before you go — how are you honey? Are you feeling ok?"

John paused. The headaches had started and he had already had one nose bleed.

"Yep, fine," he lied.

Julie sighed. He wondered if she knew he was lying. Probably. But she did not say anything.

"Ok, pass me to Holly."

John covered the mouth piece with his hand.

"She wants to speak to you," John said, offering the phone to Holly.

Holly's face crinkled and she shook her head.

John continued to hold the phone.

"She's going to be a grandmother. She's excited."

Holly sighed and took the phone. She turned her back on John and walked from the kitchen to the hall.

"Hi Julie, how are you?"

A pause. John stood up, took a glass from the cupboard and filled it with water.

"Thanks, Julie. We're happy too."

There was a long pause. John watched Holly's face intently. He could hear the buzz of Julie's voice from far away, but could not make out what she was saying. Holly's face softened. She appeared surprised.

"Oh, thanks. Yes, me too. Look ... no, fair enough."

Another long pause.

Holly was nodding now. She looked at John and raised her eyebrows, then turned and walked down the hall. John drank his water and then sat again. It was best to wait. He shouldn't eavesdrop.

A couple of minutes later Holly returned and gave him his phone. Without saying a word, she returned to stirring the batter.

"Well?" John asked.

"Did you put her up to that?"

"I honestly have no idea what you talked about. What did she say?"

Holly stared at him, examining his face for a lie. But he saw that she found none. Her gaze softened.

"Well, I never thought that old girl would surprise me. She apologised. She wants to fix things. She said she wants to be a good grandmother and a decent mother-in-law."

John chuckled.

"And you need to put some sheets on the spare bed. She's coming to visit on the weekend."

"Oh. And you're ok with that?"

Holly looked up from the batter.

"I don't know. But I think we have to give it a shot, right? For our little girl or boy."

John stood, crossed the kitchen and gave Holly a kiss on the cheek.

"I love you, honey," he said. Then he wandered off to put sheets on the bed as instructed.

✍

John stood in the desert. Underfoot, a lizard scurried across the sand towards the magnolia tree, which was covered in purple flowers. The tree shimmered in the heat.

A zephyr lifted sand around his feet and, overhead, dark clouds filled the sky. The zephyr intensified. Became a breeze. Then a wind. Then a gale. The bright purple flowers held on gamely to the branches of the magnolia as the gale battered it. And then, on the edge of the brewing storm, John heard something. Something he had never heard, or at least noticed, before. Whispering.

"... ole .... ownnnnnn ..."

What the hell was that, John thought. At first he thought it was the wind, but maybe not. Maybe it was coming from the tree itself. Or the ground beneath.

"... ole .... owwwwwwn ..."

John dropped to the ground and put his ear to the sand. Grains of sand vibrated against his face. It was the tree, he was sure. Deep down in its roots it was trying to speak to him.

He felt the first drops of rain on the side of his face.

No, not now, he thought.

He looked up to see the flowers of the magnolia disintegrate into dust as the rain fell heavily on the tree.

John awoke in darkness with tinnitus in his ears and the coppery tang of blood at the back of his throat. He put a hand to his face and it came away slick. Shit. He turned and saw that Holly was still asleep. He sniffed hard, rose from the bed and tip toed into the ensuite where he closed the door and turned on the light. Looking back at him in the mirror was something from a horror movie. Blood streamed from his nose, down over his mouth and neck and out across his pyjama top. Shit, shit, shit, John thought. He wrenched toilet paper from the roll and balled it up and held it to his nose. How the hell was he going to clean this up before Holly woke, he thought? Then Holly screamed.

John opened the door and found Holly shaking, pointing at the bloody sheets.

"It's ok, honey, its ok," John mumbled. "I'm ok. Just a bleeding nose."

Holly began to cry. John saw the fear in Holly's eyes and, belatedly as always, he remembered that his demise affected others as well as him.

"That's not just a fucking bleeding nose, John. I thought you'd been murdered. Look at the blood. Look at it."

"I'll clean it up. I just need a minute to stop the flow."

Holly rose from the bed and took a deep breath.

"I'll wet a cloth," she said, taking a tentative step towards John. She reached out with a trembling hand and took hold of his arm. Her short nighty clung to her stomach, which now formed a noticeable bump.

"Tomorrow I'm booking you in to see Doctor Rouch."

"Honestly, I'm fine."

"No you're not, John. That is not normal and I'm taking you to see my Doctor tomorrow. Understand."

John smiled beneath the ball of crimson toilet paper. He loved her for wanting to look out for him better than he did himself. And despite knowing exactly what the diagnosis would be, his heart clenched at Holly's concern.

"Ok."

"Good. Now let's clean you up."

Holly let go of his arm and walked into the bathroom to run a cloth under cold water.

✍

John stared at the steam rising from his coffee. He wondered where the time had gone since Holly had first taken him to the Doctor. As with the previous times he had grown sick, life had become disjointed. Jumping forward and then slowing when he least expected. He had little time to ponder what it all meant.

"Sorry?" he inquired, looking up from his coffee. Julie sat across the kitchen table from him.

"I said," she replied, emphasising the 'said', "what did the specialist say?"

"Same thing as the doctors you took me to see thirty six years ago. Cancer."

"Oh, come on. Medicine has advanced a hell of a lot since the seventies. What options do you have?"

John rolled his eyes.

"Chemotherapy and then surgery. But you and I know better."

John blew steam from his coffee and lifted the cup to his lips, sipping slowly and deliberately. Julie pushed her chair back from the table with a screech and stood abruptly.

"So you're not even going to try?" Julie asked, turning from the table and stomping to the sink where she dropped her cup with a 'clang.'

"I don't know? Holly wants me to …"

"But you know better, right?"

John remained silent.

"You selfish child," Julie said. She returned to the table and leant over John. "Holly wants you to live. I want you to live. But you, you're already thinking about the next life. How to make it better. How to get a better job. A better wife. Don't you think I know Holly is my upgrade?"

"Oh, come on, Julie."

"Don't give me that. I know and you know. Everything is about what you can improve. Have you ever stopped to think that what you already have might be damn perfect? And if not perfect, then close enough?"

John sighed. He needed to take a walk.

"Mum. Julie. I will die. You know I will die. But I will be back. And you will both still have me."

"But maybe you don't have to die, damn it," Julie hissed, tears in her eyes. "I don't know why I even bother. It was the same last time. You get the news and then you bloody disappear into yourself. You don't even have the courtesy to let us comfort you or grieve with you."

"I'm going for a walk." John stood and walked towards the door.

"Just try the chemo," Julie said as John passed her. "Show Holly and me you're not completely selfish. Ok?"

"I'll think about it," he responded as he opened the door and left the house. But he knew he would relent.

Time was a hundred kilogram weight attached to John's mind. He battled his heavy eyelids as the second hand on the clock on the wall made one painful jerk after another. His hospital gown itched and his arm was cold as poison dripped from a transparent bag into a tube, down to his left wrist where it entered his vein through the cannula. The room had the faint scent of chlorine. The liquid would make him sick later, he knew. But now it dripped, like the second hand, slowly. He was trapped in a moment that he'd like to move past.

Time was becoming more inconsistent as he neared the end. He dreaded the pauses and lurches. He had trouble holding on to the good moments. One minute he was smiling at Holly across the table eating dinner, the next he was here, watching the second hand 'tick, tick, tick'. Why did time barely move when he sat by himself, watching poison pumped into his veins?

A pang of bitterness assaulted him as he cursed Holly for not being with him today. But just as quickly he pushed his selfish thought away. It's me who should have been with her, he thought. A twenty week scan and he wasn't there to see Holly's face when she found out they were having a boy. God he was a shit.

He suddenly longed for home. To talk to her. To see her joy. To hold onto that moment of joy.

The clock 'tick, tick, ticked'.

✍

John was frozen, mid-heave, unable to breath, unable to move, long after the last of the liquid had been expelled from his stomach and splattered against the bowl. Still his diaphragm lurched and squeezed. His face ached, his mouth was locked open until, finally, the spasm relented and he sucked in air.

Cold beads of sweat ran into his eyes. All John could do was stare at a rare clean piece of porcelain at the back of the bowl, somehow untouched by his assault. His pallid hands clung to the toilet and shook. John slumped to the cool floor and sat, feeling glorious nothing. The nausea was temporarily gone, the coolness was nice, and he was left holding onto another nothing. Life paused amongst the mundane and the shit. And yet his trip with Holly to the coast last weekend was over soon after he had fallen asleep in the car, waking, to arrive home, late Sunday, memories of beach and cold water a blur. Why did this happen at the end? Was it him, or the sickness?

✍

He woke up screaming and didn't know why. Holly turned and held him for a glorious moment with her plump belly pushed into his trembling back. Then she was gone, asleep, and he was alone in the dark as time ticked wearily on. One more moment, alone, cold.

But that wasn't right, was it? He thought hard. He knew she had held him for at least an hour. She would have held him longer.

It was him that had pushed her away and asked her to sleep. How could he keep taking her love for granted like that?

✍

He was hunched over the box of old journals when Holly squeezed him from behind, her large belly pushed into his bony back.

"Oh," he said, "you're here."

"I'm always here".

John turned and stared at her. He saw Holly clearly. John felt like he had just crawled out of a fast running stream and relief washed over him.

"Hey," he said, smiling as he took her in for what felt like the first time in six months. Her belly was round and tight and her hair was thick and shiny. Where had he been? John thought. How did he miss all of this?

"Hey yourself. What are you doing?"

"I was feeling all right, so I decided to clean my junk out of the back room."

Holly's smile faltered. John saw the discomfort in her eyes. She knows I'm cleaning up for when I'm gone, he thought.

"We need to make room for the baby, right?" John lied. He forced a smile to his lips. "But I got distracted. Do you remember I used to keep journals when we first met?"

Holly hesitated, and then returned his smile.

"Yes, you were religious about them. Did you find anything good?"

John furrowed his brow.

"I just finished reading about our first trip to the coast."

"Broulee?"

"Yes. It was supposed to be a surprise, remember? But it ended up a disaster."

"Disaster? What do you mean?" Holly asked. She walked into the room and sat next to John. He felt her warmth and breathed her in. She took the journal from his hand and started running her finger down the page.

"Remember, we got stuck in traffic in the mountains, so the three hour trip took five. And when we got there, we couldn't find anywhere decent to stay because I hadn't booked ahead — so we ended up in that crappy caravan park."

"I don't recall much of that," Holly said, flipping through the pages of the journal.

"Well, it's all in there," John said, motioning to the journal as he picked up another of his books.

"I can see that, but it's missing so much."

"Like what?"

"I don't remember half of the stuff you've written down here. What I remember is walking along the beach at dusk the day after we arrived, then sitting in the sand holding each other as a storm off the coast lit up the sea with lightning. Sitting there, in your arms, you resting your chin on my head — I think that was when I first knew I loved you."

John looked at Holly, confused.

"You're serious, aren't you? You don't remember how dull that trip was, how shitty the accommodation?"

Holly laughed.

"I remember the good moments, John. I mean, when you eat one of my cakes, do you really care whether I broke the eggs perfectly. All I care about is whether it tastes good."

"You're a strange woman, Holly," John said, smiling.

"And you're a strange man."

Holly dropped the journal, leaned over and kissed John.

"When you find something good, come get me. I'm putting dinner on."

Holly rose to her feet and left the room.

John flipped through more journals. They read like a checklist of what went wrong in his life. An essay he could have written better at university. A wooden table he tried to make that was never level. An anniversary dinner he burnt. Holly was right. None of this was important. So why did he feel compelled to record it?

He suddenly realised that he'd taken the same outlook into the last six months. Ignore the good, focus on the negative. He forced himself to remember. Not the chemo, not throwing up — the real moments. The memories hit him hard. Holly holding him in the night. Holly forcing him to eat when he didn't feel like it. Holly laughing with Julie. And, as he remembered, he realised he had barely inquired about how Holly was doing. Pregnant, reconciling with a woman she didn't like, and caring for a self-absorbed, ungrateful prick of a man who was dying without a fight.

John was disgusted with himself. He bundled up all of his journals in his arms and took them to the bin. Then he went into the kitchen, walked up to Holly who was mixing dough, and turned her and kissed her before she could say a word. After her initial surprise, her lips softened and she responded warmly.

John pulled back and looked at her.

"Forget that, let's go out tonight. I'm feeling hungry for once."

Holly's eyes glistened.

"I'd like that."

The magnolia was in full bloom and the flowers smelled sickly sweet. It was dark. Black clouds blotted out the sun and a strong wind whipped up flurries of sand that assaulted his legs. It felt like hundreds of mosquitos attacking him.

A guttural voice moaned. John knew this time it was coming from the ground. Not just the ground, but from under the tree.

Lightning snaked silently across the black clouds, lighting the scene in spectacular white for a brief moment.

"... old ... ownnn ..." the ground growled.

John fell to his hands and knees, crawled through the sand eddies towards the base of the magnolia and began to dig with his hands. The guttural voice grew louder.

"... OLD ... ONNNN."

It was coming from the roots of the tree. He still could not decipher the message, but he was getting closer. Just a few more handfuls of sand, he thought. The wind increased in intensity and a crack of thunder left his ears ringing. He dragged out a final scoop of earth and then surveyed the hole. The exposed roots were vibrating. But with the howling wind, he still could not understand their message. So he thrust his head into the hole and pressed his ear to the roots. Finally, over the roar of the wind and sand and thunder, he heard clearly.

"Hold on," the tree whispered.

John awoke in a lather of sweat, his ears ringing. Holly was crying and his side was wet.

"John, something's wrong. I think the baby's coming early."

John's heart ached.

"It's ok. Just take deep breaths and I'll call the hospital," John said, jumping up and grabbing his phone. What was happening? He wasn't sick enough yet. He always knew when time was up. He felt it in his bones. A brittleness and a sickness that was all consuming. But he still felt very much here. This had never happened before. Was it the chemo? Something else?

The midwife on the phone reassured him and asked him to get Holly to the hospital as quickly as possible. After the midwife hung up, he phoned Julie.

"I'll be there as soon as I can," she said, hanging up abruptly.

Then he helped Holly to the car, comforting her as best he could, knowing he may not be with her much longer.

John held Holly's hand tightly. Two doctors talked amongst themselves as a midwife examined Holly. John fought the urge to vomit and ignored the weakness in his legs. He did not know how long he could continue standing, but he would let Holly squeeze his hand while he could.

Just then, he heard Julie loudly remonstrating outside the birth suite doors with a midwife.

"What do you mean I can't go in? They're my family and I want to see them."

"You can let her in," Holly said, panting between contractions. "I'd like her in here. Please."

The doctors looked at John. John nodded, and soon Julie was standing next to him dabbing Holly's face with a damp cloth.

"Nice to see you're still here," Julie said to John, as Holly squeezed his hand and moaned as another contraction took hold.

The two doctors separated. One began to set up a heated crib, and the other moved towards Holly.

"Ok, Holly," the obstetrician said, "I know we've been saying to resist the urge to push, but on the next contraction, it's time to push."

"Oh, thank God."

Holly groaned loudly.

"Ok, that's great," the doctor said. The midwife on John's left pulled Holly's leg further towards her. "I can see the baby's head."

John looked down and, holy shit, he could see it too. Just the top of some wet, dark hair. He felt faint. His eyes fluttered. His legs wobbled. He heard a distant clatter as he collapsed.

The world was black, but with an orange glow. He was cosy and warm and yet encompassed by a deep, aching sadness he had never experienced before. Julie would never chastise him again as his mother and Holly would cease to be his wife. He would lose so much. There would be no more of Holly's smile — the special one reserved for when he pleased her. It would soon be replaced with that look of sadness he always saw in his new mother. No more watching her brush her hair as she hummed softly to herself. No more cakes. No more lounging on the couch watching movies with her. No more missing the end of the movie as they made love. He felt it all wash past and over him, slipping through his fingers.

Jesus, he thought, as he watched it all go. He would really miss this. What could be better than Holly? A better job? More money? Another woman? He suddenly scrambled, trying to hold onto life, but it was like trying to catch water.

He was squeezed and pushed. Time was nearly up. John panicked and bucked and kicked. For all the possibilities before him, for once, he was not excited. He was happy now, here. And wasn't that all that mattered? Jesus Christ he hated to admit it, but Julie was right. Some people never came close to having all he did.

The dream. What did the tree say? "Hold on."

So he did. Not the pain and the minutia, but the real moments. Holly's laugh. Holly rubbing his back as he fell asleep in a sweat. Julie ordering him around her garden. He held on tightly and ignored the possibilities ahead. He remembered and focussed and saw with clarity the glint in Holly's smiling eyes as she told him he would be a Dad. He saw it and felt it — the new possibilities of his life continuing.

The black withdrew rapidly and was replaced with bright lights.

He felt arms around him, lifting him onto a chair.

"No you don't, you selfish bastard," Julie whispered in his ear. "You're staying here and seeing this."

"Yes, Mum," John mumbled. He opened his eyes and saw tears in Julie's. Her face was ashen, but she smiled, relieved. Julie leaned in close.

"Are you back for good?" she whispered, tears splashing his face.

"I hope so."

"He's ok, love," Julie said to Holly, wiping her eyes. "He just needs a rest."

Holly was crying and straining and moaning at once.

"That's it, that's it and ... all done," the obstetrician said. John looked up from the floor to see the obstetrician hold up a tiny baby. "A baby boy."

The midwife cut the cord and then passed it quickly to the second doctor who took the baby away to the heated crib. Julie helped John to his feet.

"Given the baby is a premmie, he'll need to spend some time in the special care nursery. But everything looks great. He's a real beaut," the midwife said to Holly.

John leaned on Julie and shuffled to the crib and watched the paediatrician wrap the baby in a blanket. John held a hand to his mouth and tears welled in his eyes. The baby looked just like Holly.

The paediatrician picked the baby up and took it to Holly and placed it on her chest. John followed and took Holly's hand as she wrapped her other arm around their son. Julie was soon pushing him into a chair next to the bed.

"Just a couple of minutes, ok?" the paediatrician said. Then we have to take him to the special care nursery, but you'll be able to see him again very shortly.

Holly looked at John.

"We did it," she said. "Now we just have to get you right."

✍

John was tired, but in a good way. It had been two days since he had received the news that his cancer was in remission. John lay on the couch watching footy. Holly was napping on the other couch and Daniel was in his basinet sleeping, making little grunts and involuntary movements.

John closed his eyes, content, and drifted to sleep.

The desert was still and the magnolia was in bloom. Black clouds opened and rain began to fall. As the drops hit the flowers, they disintegrated into ash and fluttered to the sand below.

Panic rose in John. What did this mean? What was happening? The wind grew and the rain intensified, assaulting the now empty branches. John was confused. Wasn't it over? Hadn't he moved on?

The rain eased, the wind died, and the clouds began to dissipate. The sun emerged and the air became sticky and warm. Then John saw it. New leaves burst from the lower branches of the magnolia. Then more and more until a flurry of growth covered the branches of the tree with fresh green leaves.

The magnolia stood in the desert still, but very much altered. No flowers, but the old tree was fresh and green for the first time.

✍ ✍ ✍

FREE HUGS

—

JENNIFER SHELBY

Free Hugs

Beware: Hugbot ahead, warned a scrawl of white paint across a brick wall. Cyndl paused in her journey through the dead city and stared at the words while a complicated blend of grief and hope blossomed inside of her.

She defied the graffiti and kept moving until the alley opened into a treed square. The Hugbot gleamed in the center, caught in a halo of sunlight and memory. Its body was vaguely humanoid: a metal torso with arms, a short vertical indentation to suggest legs, and tracks instead of feet. Its head was a silver egg with eyes and a mouth. Cyndl had heard that the original prototypes had been sleek, sophisticated, and more human-like, only to be scrapped when people used them for something more than innocent hugging.

The foam latex along the bot's inner arms, chest, and neck, once offering a pillowed embrace, now hung in ragged ribbons. Its pressure sensors would still be in good shape; the engineers had taken special care with those to prevent crushed customers and their associated lawsuits.

A thick chain around its left track tethered the robot to a link hammered into the concrete. A ring around this anchor had been grooved into the cement by the bot's desperate, hopeless circling. Cyndl curled her lip in disgust. "That kind of cruelty is never necessary," she muttered to herself.

The bot's ocular receptors were dark, and a dusty cobweb drifted lazily over the mesh speaker that was its mouth. Cyndl wiped it away, her hand lingering on the familiar oval of the metal face. A whisper of tears prickled at her eyes.

Someone had tied a filthy sheet around the neck of the bot, covering the solar panel. This had likely been meant as a kindness; a temporary means to keep the bot powered down. The rotten fabric fell apart under Cyndl's fingers as she untied it, and the sheet whooshed to the ground in a plume of disintegrated fibres.

The solar matrix beneath the sheet appeared to be in good condition. 'No wonder these things survived the Climate Wars,' Cyndl thought.

She knelt to detach the chain from the Hugbot's foot track. The links were strong, but she had a hacksaw in the patched pack that never left her side. She pushed dirty strands of silvered hair behind her sunburnt, peeling ear, set her jaw, and began to work.

Sweat soaked through her shirt by the time she'd finished and kicked the chain away. The bot had yet to wake up. It usually took a few hours for the solar batteries to charge.

✍

Six-year-old Cyndl forced herself to walk. Her cheeks burned with the salt of dried tears. The wind whipping over the city stung her face, but if she turned away, she'd see the tower, and she did not want to see the tower.

Cyndl wasn't supposed to be alone in the ravaged world. She was supposed to be in the digital realm with the Technicians who'd built the tower, but they had flopped and soiled themselves as the electricity uploaded them to the realms. Her fear had overpowered her faith and she'd pulled out her upload cable.

Cyndl collapsed into a puddle, taking long drinks that tasted of earth and filled her mouth with silt. A glint of metal shifted in the space between her and the edges of the city, a reflected light that drew closer until a machine materialized.

The robot's shadow fell over her and it lifted her with gentle arms, cradling her body as it carried her away from the tower. She slipped in and out of consciousness. Each time she awoke anew, the bot's lights blinked. "Would you like a hug?" it asked her.

✍

Cyndl shook her head to ground herself in the present. The Hugbot would be charged soon. She pulled a crab apple from an overgrown ornamental and sat on the ledge of a dry fountain, taking a bite and watching the city for movement. The crab apple tasted tart, but it was wet and fresh, and she relished the treat.

Wild animals had claimed the rotting city, birds flying from broken windows and raccoons skulking through open doorways. The old Tech Cults had been the last hangers-on to sedentary lifestyles, but people still marked their travels by these ruined cities. A Technician tower loomed at the edge of the western skyline. There was a tower for every dead city, but Cyndl didn't like to acknowledge them.

The first lights flickered on the bot's control panel. It opened its eyes and turned its head to her. "Would you like a hug?"

Cyndl closed her eyes for a moment, overcome by the emotional weight of the familiar, tinny voice. "Hey, Hugbot."

"I am Unit 2201. I was created to provide safe physical contact." The bot projected a hologram of a nondescript individual in a suit into the air between them. Cyndl had dubbed this person Hugbob when she was little. "Here at Lovelace Robotics, we know how hard it is to refrain from hugging your loved ones as we do our duty to defeat the virus. That is why Lovelace Robotics created the Safe Family Avatar. Now you can send Grandma what she really wants for her birthday: a hug from her grandchildren."

In the grainy hologram, an elderly woman wept into the robot's neck as it embraced her. "The Safe Family Avatar's upper body is made of soft, padded latex for the feel of a real hug. Using our patent-pending, non-invasive technology, our Safe Family Avatars scan the levels of oxytocin, the human happiness hormone, in your hug recipient's bloodstream. This enables us to ensure the optimal hormone levels for best mental health benefits have been achieved. Following each embrace, the Safe Family Avatar engages Disinfect Protocol, designed to destroy any germs that may have been transferred during physical contact."

The hologram shut down. "Free hugs," said the bot.

Tears tracked down Cyndl's cheeks, but a small smile waited on her lips. "The Hugbot who raised me played that hologram for me whenever I had nightmares." She cocked her head. "They found me after I escaped from the Tech Cults and they taught me how to survive. And, of course, I hugged them whenever their programming told them they needed one."

The Hugbot didn't say anything and Cyndl giggled nervously. "Sorry if I'm talking too much. It's been a while since I've had a Hugbot to talk to." She gave an awkward shrug. "I'm on my own a lot. I've tried to join traveling groups, but I never last long. The nightmares come back." She considered the crab apple core in her hand. Its pink flesh had oxidized to a rusty brown.

"Travelers do not like hugs," said the Hugbot.

"No." She tossed the core onto the ground.

"People are afraid of Unit 2201," said the Hugbot.

"That's not your fault." Cyndl gestured in the direction of the tower. "After the Tech Cults, people got superstitious of machines. You bots are the black cats of the modern world."

"Safe Family Avatars are not cats," said the Hugbot.

"It means they think crossing your path brings bad luck." Cyndl eyed the bot to gauge its reaction, but the robot did nothing. "It's not your fault that your programming tortures you when you have no one to hug, either. Your programmers just wanted you to work hard; they didn't expect this." She held up an end of the chain she'd cut away from its track.

"Would you like a hug?" asked the Hugbot.

"How long has it been since someone hugged you?" asked Cyndl.

"Thirty-two years, eight months, seven days."

Cyndl winced. "That's a long time, Hugbot. When your Disinfectant Protocol goes off after that long without use, it's probably going to kill you. I've seen it happen a few times with other Hugbots. But if it doesn't..." Cyndl tried to push down a surge of hope with a gulping breath. "We could travel together. I lost my Hugbot a long time ago."

✍

A sob burst out of Cyndl as she lunged the wagon forward, stepping into the shadow of a Technician tower for the first time since she'd failed to upload. The Hugbot in the wagon listed severely to the right, its bottom half and track assembly melted into a blob of silvery metals. "FREE HUGS FREE HUGS FREE HUGS!"

Tiny lights inside the tower winked red and green; it still had power. An upload cable waited inside. Cyndl swallowed hard, her hand unwilling to reach out and grab the thing. The robot's voice burst through the memory that threatened to surface. "HUGS FREE FREE." And then the cord was in her hand and she was wrapping the Hugbot's metal fingers around it.

"Once I turn the power on, the current will fry your circuits. It'll be just like the Hugbot we saw that got hit by lightning. You'll be dead."

"FREE FREE FREE."

Cyndl nodded, swiped at her tears, and dashed into the tower. The breaker panel swung open beneath her fingertips and someone had written UPLOAD in red marker with an arrow pointing to a black plastic switch. The Hugbot still screamed, but a softness fell over the world. Her thumb and forefinger pulled the breaker to the opposite side with a heavy click. The blinking lights inside the tower pulsed, dimmed, and the Hugbot outside fell silent. For a moment, there was peace. Until the grief came.

✍

The Hugbot in the square rocked on its tracks as if it were deliberating. A dried leaf wedged beneath its tracks pulled free and a breeze sent it tumbling across the square, then out of sight. "Free hugs," the bot said at last. "Would you like a hug?"

Cyndl got to her feet. "I would love one."

The robot's arms were rough as they wrapped around her slowly, double-checking their safety sensors to avoid crushing her. It had been too long since Cyndl had felt the gentle crush of a robotic hug. She let her longing for the old companionship expand and her tears slip free.

The Hugbot beeped to signal optimal hormone levels had been reached and released Cyndl from its embrace. "You're a good bot." Cyndl told them.

"Thank you," said the Hugbot. "Please stand back while I engage Disinfectant Protocol."

Cyndl walked away, giving the robot space. Protocol required the Hugbot to heat their surfaces to a minimum of five hundred degrees Celsius to kill off any germs. She waited for the pop before she turned to watch the contained explosion as the protocol malfunctioned. Smoke poured from the Hugbot's seams. "Free hugs," it slurred as its light dimmed for the last time.

Cyndl watched black smoke billow from the Hugbot until it faded to a noxious wisp. Only then did she pull a hand-drawn canvas map from her pocket, marked with Hugbot locations she'd gleaned from travelers eager to avoid the machines. With a sorrowful glance at the ruined bot, she crossed out an H.

The nearest city plotted to the east displayed multiple H's and Cyndl had heard rumors that it housed an old Hugbot factory. Maybe this would be her last journey alone. Her heart fluttered with hope as she put her things away, shouldered her pack, and headed east.

✍ ✍ ✍

Initial feedback

I like the concept and elements presented, but overall, the story feels a bit thin, and the arc flatter than I'd like. The backstory is somewhat awkwardly presented, and it would be good to have a better, clearer understanding of Cyndl's past with Hugbots — you may want to restructure the story to focus more on that.

Author's intent

What do you think the story's about?
What emotions are you trying to evoke?

I think this story is about compassion and longing for something lost.

In my imagined version of her past, Cyndl escaped a post-doomsday tech cult and her Hugbot helped her survive. Her experiences with a different form of programming help her see past the Hugbot's tattered appearance and better understand the torture the Hugbots endure. I have a few ideas of what may have happened to Cyndl's Hugbot that has set her on her current path that require more time to develop but they should help 'thicken' the story.

Author's note

When I submitted "Free Hugs" to *Metaphorosis*, I knew I'd be in for a lot of back-and-forth as we edited the story. However, this wasn't my first story in *Metaphorosis*, so I'd already learned to trust B Morris Allen's instincts. I knew if I pushed past any initial resistance I might have, I'd learn a great deal and my story would be better for his suggestions.

Before "Free Hugs", I'd always had this thought that 'flashbacks are bad' and had never written them into a story before. B Morris Allen didn't deliberately tell me to add flashbacks, he told me that I needed to get rid of the infodumps and this was the only way forward that made sense to me in rewrites. The flashbacks gave me the chance to deepen the dynamic between Cyndl and the Hugbot who raised her, which heightens the emotional impact of the story hundredfold.

Looking back, I think that not only did I learn to avoid blanket statements of what is good and bad in writing, I also learned how to use the flashback as a tool.

One of the big changes we made to Free Hugs was the ending, deepening Cyndl's character from someone who happened to come across a Hugbot like the one that had raised her, to someone who was actively searching for Hugbots. Someone who recognizes that she isn't going to fit in with regular society, is okay with that, yet wants to rebuild her lost family the only way she can. It's not an entirely selfish endeavor on her part either, as most of the Hugbots she finds are malfunctioning and she can end their pain. This change took Cyndl's character from something of a vague drifter into someone with purpose, intent, and meaning.

When B. Morris Allen asked me what I thought "Free Hugs" was about, I had thought about it before, but there is something about writing the intent down that clarified the way I perceived that intent in the story. Asking myself this question and writing out my answer is something I picked up from this process that I use in self-editing my stories now. It's amazing what you can learn from the editing process if you're open to it.

Editor's note

All my second readers and I agreed that while the concept of "Free Hugs" was strong in the original version, the backstory could be more smoothly handled, which Jennifer's revised flashbacks accomplished admirably.

While smoothing the backstory, the readers and I agreed that it would be nice to see a little more of the protagonist's history with hugbots, making the story a little more personal. Reinforcing that, I felt that the original piece had some extraneous elements that took away from the main story — details about the cults and the microscopics that had brought the situation about. While it was interesting in itself, I felt that it tried to fit too much into a short story. The extra worldbuilding raised questions that couldn't be answered in the small space of the story and weren't really essential to it. It's always tempting to include all the things you've figured out about the world you've created, but if they don't match the story you're actually telling, they may not help. There's no reason you can't use all that detail for another story, though. Similarly, sometimes the revision process allows a writer to reuse bits that had been tossed out earlier. Here, I thought Jennifer had a nice, compact, poignant story about Cyndl and hugbots that worked best with a tight focus, and she was able to reuse parts of an ending that hadn't worked in her original composition. Never throw anything away!

Free Hugs

A Hugbot stood before her in the abandoned city square. Cyndl froze when she saw it, an old grief reawakening inside of her. It had been almost a decade since she'd last seen a Hugbot, and this one was in rough condition.

The robot's body was vaguely human-shaped; a blob of metal torso with an indentation to suggest legs and tracks instead of feet. Its head was a silver egg with eyes and a mouth. Cyndl had heard that the original prototypes were sleek, sophisticated, and more human-like, only to be scrapped when people used them for something more than innocent hugging.

The silicone along the bot's inner arms, chest, and neck, once creating a pillowed embrace, now hung in ragged ribbons. Its pressure sensors would still be in good shape; the engineers took special care with those to prevent crushed customers and their associated lawsuits.

A thick chain around its left track tethered the robot to a link hammered into the concrete. A ring around this anchor had been grooved into the cement by the bot's desperate, hopeless circling. Cyndl curled her lip in disgust. "Come on now, that kind of cruelty is never necessary."

The bot's ocular receptors were not lit up and a dusty cobweb drifted lazily over the mesh speaker that was its mouth. Cyndl wiped it away, her hand lingering on the familiar oval of the metal face.

Someone had tied a filthy blanket around the neck of the bot, covering the solar panel on its back. This was likely meant as a kindness; a temporary means to keep the bot powered down. The rotten fabric fell apart under Cyndl's fingers as she untied it, the blanket whooshing to the ground in a plume of disintegrated fibres that stung at her eyes and she didn't dare breathe in.

The solar matrix beneath the blanket appeared to be in good condition save a telltale stain of rust. *No wonder these things survived the war*, Cyndl thought, not for the first time. The rust leaked down from a seam where the silicone once attached to the bot's backplate. She'd never seen a Hugbot without this same staining.

Cyndl knelt to detach the chain from the Hugbot's foot track. The links were strong, but she had a hacksaw in the patched pack that never left her side. She pushed dirty strands of besilvered hair behind her sunburnt, peeling ear, set her jaw, and began to saw.

Sweat soaked through her shirt by the time she'd finished and kicked the chain away. The bot had yet to wake up. It usually took a few hours for the solar batteries to charge.

While she waited, Cyndl pulled a crab apple from an overgrown ornamental and sat on the ledge of a dry fountain, taking a bite and watching the city for movement. The crab apple tasted tart, but it was wet, fresh, and she relished the treat.

She'd come through here before, after the war. Wild animals had since claimed the rotting city, birds flying from broken windows and raccoons skulking through open doorways. Few humans lived sedentary lives anymore; the unpredictable weather of the world's wrecked climate made it safer to keep moving, chasing warmth, though they marked their travels by these ruined cities.

The first lights flickered on the bot's control panel. It opened its eyes and raised its head to her. "Would you like a hug?" it asked in a tinny voice.

Cyndl closed her eyes, unprepared for the emotional punch the words would have. "Will you tell me your story, Hugbot?" she asked, buying herself a few moments to collect herself.

"I am Safe Family Avatar Unit 2201. I was created to provide safe physical contact."

Cyndl nodded. It had been a long time since humanity fought the Microscopics, a deadly, invisible enemy that invaded the world through human contact. The same enemy that led to the creation of the Hugbots.

The bot projected the usual advertisement into the air between them. "Here at Lovelace Robotics, we know how hard it is to refrain from hugging your loved ones as we do our duty to defeat the Microscopics," said a nondescript individual in a suit. "That is why Lovelace Robotics created the Safe Family Avatar. Now you can send Grandma what she really wants for her birthday: a hug from her grandchildren."

In the grainy hologram, a gray-haired woman wept into the robot's neck as it embraced her. "The Safe Family Avatar's upper body is made of soft, padded silicone for the feel of a real hug. Using our patent-pending, non-invasive technology, our Safe Family Avatars scan the levels of oxytocin, the human happiness hormone, in your hug recipient's bloodstream. This enables us to ensure the optimal hormone levels for best mental health benefits have been achieved. Following each embrace, the Safe Family Avatar engages Disinfect Protocol, designed to destroy any Microscopics that may have been transferred during physical contact."

The hologram shut down. "Free hugs," said the bot.

"I've met a lot of bots like you." Cyndl reached for another crab apple. "I think I've got the story down now, so please, stop me if yours is any different."

The Hugbot's ocular devices pivoted to see her better. The whir of its focusing mechanism told her she'd captured the bot's full attention.

"You were abandoned after we defeated the Microscopics, but before the war. Your clients often cried into your shoulder and over time the salt in their tears corroded the wiring behind the seam in your neck panels. Neither you nor any of your peers reported this malfunction because it effectively hotwired an addiction into your hardware."

A light blinked below the bot's left ocular device. It was recording her.

"And that addiction is to the oxytocin hormone released when you hug humans, right?"

The bot didn't answer right away. When it did, it asked her, in its ever-unwavering voice, "Would you like a hug?"

"And it worked out okay for a few years because people remembered you with fondness and nostalgia. Then the war came, and everything changed. Bandits tried to steal your solar panels, but Lovelace Robotics had seen that coming. Your defensive protocol ruined your reputation. Exposure to the sun disintegrated the silicone that softened your hugs. It shrank and wrinkled, falling into tatters which got caught in your tracks. People didn't like hugging you anymore, did they? They started calling you creepy. First, they got nervous and then they got mean." Cyndl gestured to the newly broken chain with her half-eaten crab apple. "All you wanted was a hug, but no one would hug you anymore."

"Free hugs," said the Hugbot.

"And you're trapped, because you can't overcome an addiction that's hard-wired into your physical systems and you don't have a purpose beyond hugging. You just wander the world, looking for someone to hug."

"Would you like a hug?" asked the Hugbot.

"How long has it been since someone hugged you?" asked Cyndl.

"Thirty-two years, eight months, seven days."

Cyndl winced. "That's a long time, Hugbot. You do realize that when your disinfectant protocol goes off after that long in disuse, it will probably kill you?"

The bot rocked on its tracks as if it were deliberating. A tattered plastic bag wedged beneath its tracks pulled free and a breeze sent it tumbling across the square, then out of sight. "Free hugs," the bot said at last. "Would you like a hug?"

Cyndl got to her feet and tossed the apple core away. "I would love one."

The robot's arms were rough as they wrapped around her slowly, double-checking their safety sensors to avoid crushing her. Cyndl leaned her cheek against the telltale rust spot on its neck. It felt good to be hugged again.

She closed her eyes, remembering the Hugbot who had raised her in its strange way, feeding her and protecting her in return for hugs. They'd needed each other: the Hugbot, to end its torture; Cyndl, to stay alive in an increasingly inhospitable world. It may have been a robot, but her Hugbot had always been kind to her. Cyndl tried to offer a similar kindness to those she met in her travels.

Tears slipped from her eyes. It was good to remember her old savior.

The Hugbot beeped to signal optimal hormone levels had been reached and released Cyndl from its embrace. She wiped the tears from her face and nodded. "You're a good bot."

"Thank you," said the Hugbot. "Please stand back while I engage Disinfectant Protocol."

Cyndl walked away, giving the robot extra space. Protocol required the Hugbot to heat their surfaces to a minimum of five hundred degrees Celsius to kill off any Microscopics. She waited for the expected pop before she turned to watch the contained explosion as the protocol malfunctioned. Smoke poured from its seams. "Free hugs," it slurred as its light dimmed for the last time.

"I hope you find some peace now," Cyndl whispered to the flames. She shouldered her pack and turned away, moving through the ruined city.

✍ ✍ ✍

GOING HOME

—

MARTIN WESTLAKE

Going Home

The eerie howl of the Ekranoplan's jet engines echoed around the city's early morning streets. Dimitriy's stomach lurched involuntarily. A ground effect craft, they called it, designed to be a troop carrier, now recycled as a passenger craft, plying the route between Derbent and Astrakhan. The relic, all stubby wings and a massive, V-shaped tail, howled there and back three times a day. He loathed it, but it was the only way he could get to the laboratory in Astra.

Every Monday morning for over a year, Dimitriy had suffered the same torment of emotions. Anastasia said nothing anymore as they kissed. "Think of the children," she had said in the old days, before she'd realised entreaties were useless. "They need their father." He missed the whole school week. Sasha, the younger, still greeted him with affection on Saturday mornings, but Andrei, now in his teens, had become increasingly sullen. Dimitriy wanted to tell him how sorry he felt, but the truth was that he didn't. Guilty, yes; sad, yes, in a bittersweet sort of way; but not sorry.

Then there was the Ekranoplan. Anastasia had been unable to leave Derbent when Dimitriy had taken on the Astrakhan job and he had accepted that. The car trip took ten hours in the summer and in the winter the roads were frequently impassable. No, the only viable means of getting there was the Ekranoplan. He would never get used to it, though. Whenever there was the slightest hint of a breeze, his heart dropped, for the monstrous thing could only take off facing into the wind, and that meant riding the incoming waves, like a ship. Once it was up in the air the ride was smooth, but how he hated the take off! The only thing that made the mixture of sadness, guilt and fear worthwhile every Monday morning was a euphoric sense of anticipation; the knowledge that he would soon once again be where he most desired to be.

✍

His path through the sleepy streets to the Ekranoport took him past his old workplace, the Caspian Gates Secondary School, reminding him of the day it had all begun. He'd stayed behind to help a group of fifteen-year-olds, then hurried home. A tall, thin, grey-suited, sallow-faced man was waiting for him outside the main entrance to their block of flats. A cigarette bobbed on his lower lip as he spoke. He seemed oblivious to the February cold, though both men's breath clouded about them.

"Semenov?" he said.

Dimitriy nodded.

"Could we talk?" said the man, gesturing towards a bar.

There was something about him — not furtive, but a sense of secrecy all the same. The man bought two vodkas and they sat at a scuffed table.

"To your health," he said, raising his glass. He stubbed out his cigarette in an old dented aluminium ashtray and lit another. "Ivanov," he said. "Rear Admiral Anatoly Ivanov, Caspian Flotilla, Astrakhan."

"There's been a mistake," said Dimitriy.

Ivanov shook his head. He gestured to a passing waiter and ordered two more vodkas.

"I shouldn't stay," said Dimitriy.

"Tell me, Dimitriy Semenov," Ivanov said; "how much do you earn?"

"Enough," said Dimitriy.

"Why are you a teacher?" Ivanov leaned forward over the table. "You are a brilliant physicist with a top doctoral thesis in Biology and Materials Sciences from Moscow State University and yet you hide yourself away at the Caspian Gates Secondary School teaching low-grade mathematics to misfits."

"My wife...," Dimitriy began.

"We know all about your wife," Ivanov said.

"It's time I left," Dimitriy said.

"Sit down," said the Admiral, gesturing with his half-empty vodka glass. "What I mean is that we know she has all her family here. That's why you're here, isn't it?"

Dimitriy said nothing.

Ivanov leaned over the table again. "The motherland calls, comrade."

Motherland! Comrade! Dimitriy knew immediately that the job had to be some sort of secret military work.

"It's not what you think, Semenov," the Admiral continued. "If I told you now, you wouldn't believe me."

Dimitriy inadvertently looked into his empty glass. Ivanov flagged the waiter down and ordered two more vodkas.

"No!" said Dimitriy.

"For the road."

The Admiral toyed with his cigarette lighter, an old-fashioned metal model with a flip top and a thick wick. Then he looked up at Dimitry. "Interested?" he asked. "We'll pay you four times what you are getting at that dump of a school."

"The catch?" said Dimitriy.

Ivanov drank off the remainder of his vodka and placed the glass down gently on the tabletop.

"You'd have to come to Astra, Monday to Friday. We'd cover your board and lodging."

"How would I...?"

As if to anticipate his question, the unmistakable howl of the evening return Ekranoplan came to them through the thin glass window.

Ivanov reached into his pocket, drew out an envelope and placed it on the table.

"Your ticket's in there. This coming Monday. The seven-thirty departure. When you get to Astra, make your way to the Moskva Hotel. A room has been booked in your name. I'll join you there for lunch. It's half-term. The school won't miss you."

Back home, after the children had gone to bed, sitting in the low light at the melamine kitchen table, he and Anastasia had discussed the offer in earnest whispers. He had doubts, but she was logical and reassuring. The money was important. With the kids growing, it would be good if they could rent somewhere larger. If he didn't like the work, whatever it was, he could always return to his teaching. What did they have to lose?

✑

Dimitriy had been travelling to Astra for just over two months when Anastasia first put the question to him. He had known it must come. She had nodded and accepted so mildly when he'd first explained that he couldn't talk about his work, but who could blame her, now that the yearning had started? She chose a Saturday evening. The children were in bed. The classical music radio channel was on, and she'd put a cloth and a candle on the dinner table. They talked about Sasha and Andrei, and then about her family. At the end of the meal, Anastasia took Dimitriy's hands across the table. *Here it comes*, he thought. But she simply looked into his eyes and asked if he felt all right. She'd told him he seemed preoccupied, as if his mind were elsewhere.

He'd laughed. "I'm fine," he'd said.

How could he tell her? Even if he had told her, she wouldn't have believed him.

The second time, Anastasia had been more direct. Dimitriy had just returned.

"Did you miss us?" she asked.

"Of course!"

"Really?"

She went back to the kitchen. There was no cloth and no candle on the table. Over the meal, her replies were monosyllabic. Afterwards, he went to help her with the washing up, but she insisted on doing it alone. He sat on the sofa and waited until she emerged, drying her hands on a tea towel.

"Dima," she said, "are you sure you're not having a relationship of some sort in Astra?"

✍

Astrakhan was on a broad river, not a sea. Its waterways gave the impression the city was floating. Unlike Derbent, there were no hills behind, and no citadel looming over the city. Rather, the great Trinity Cathedral soared upwards, with its gold-capped green domes. Astrakhan was flat and expansive. Being there gave Dimitry a sense of a new beginning. He hadn't realised, until he first set foot in the place, how oppressed he'd felt back home. That first Monday, still wobbly from the flight, he'd walked easily to the Moskva Hotel, a great block of fake chrome and smoked glass. A room had been booked, as Ivanov had promised. The clerk told him a table had been reserved in the restaurant for twelve o'clock. Dimitriy went to his room, unpacked the few belongings he had brought, then turned on the television and watched a programme without really following it. What was Ivanov going to offer him, he wondered?

The Admiral was sitting at their table when Dimitriy came down, a vodka in front of him and a cigarette on his lower lip. He nodded curtly.

"Welcome to Astra," he said. "A drink?"

"Thank you," said Dimitriy, "but I don't drink at lunchtime."

Ivanov beckoned a waiter over.

"Today, you'll make an exception."

When the waiter had brought their drinks, Ivanov raised his glass. He had ordered caviar, brought by another waiter on a bed of ice. "Eat," he insisted gruffly.

"Thank you," said Dimitriy.

"Thank Mother Russia," said Ivanov, stubbing out his cigarette.

They started to eat, digging out the glutinous eggs with small mother-of-pearl teaspoons.

"What do you know about Tunguska?" the Admiral asked.

"Siberia? The beginning of the last century?"

Ivanov nodded. "30 June 1908," he said.

"I remember the pictures," said Dimitriy. "All those felled trees. A meteor, right?"

"Da, da," said Ivanov. "That's what people think."

"Think? What was it, then?"

"We don't know." He lit another cigarette. "I've brought a file for you to read, but before that, I want you to sign this."

Ivanov tugged an envelope from his jacket pocket and drew out a folded sheet of paper. "Official Secrets Act," said the Admiral, unfolding the sheet. "I will only tell you more if you sign. To be clear, if you sign the declaration and do not respect it, you could be tried and imprisoned. Not even your wife. Got it?"

Dimitriy read the declaration, his hand trembling. He would have liked to talk to Anastasia. Suddenly, she seemed very far away. He read it again.

"I need to think about it," he said. "I need to talk to my wife."

Ivanov shook his head grimly. "It's now or never," he said.

Dimitriy sighed and thought about the money. With such a salary they could easily rent a three-bedroom apartment. He was sure Anastasia would have agreed. She would surely have wanted to know what work the Admiral was offering. He signed and dated the paper and handed it back.

"Good," said Ivanov, putting it back in his pocket. He gestured to a waiter to clear their table and ordered two more vodkas.

"The Tunguska region wasn't as sparsely populated as people think," said the Admiral. "Quite a few people heard and saw something." He lit a cigarette. "It started with noises from the sky."

"Noises?"

"Da. You'll read the transcripts. Some of the witnesses said it was like trumpets."

"Heavenly trumpets?" said Dimitriy ironically.

Ivanov sneered.

"The noises went on for about a week," he continued.

"Then?" asked Dimitriy.

"There was some sort of *conflict*, in the sky," said Ivanov. "Some sort of *celestial* conflict."

"'Celestial'? You seem to be choosing your words with care, Admiral."

Ivanov stubbed out his cigarette.

"You'll read the file and see for yourself. As good scientists, we try always to keep open minds."

"The word 'conflict'," said Dimitriy, "suggests that more than one body or object might have been involved, right? And the word 'celestial' suggests this was high up?"

"There are drawings in the file," the Admiral said, "based on contemporary eyewitness accounts. The locals, the Evenki, were convinced they'd seen their god, Ogdy, in a fight."

"Fascinating," said Dimitriy, "but I am not sure why this should bring me to the Volga Basin and the Official Secrets Act."

Ivanov lit another cigarette.

"Leonid Kulik," he said. "A mineralogist. He came to Tunguska several times, starting in 1921. That was already thirteen years after the event. There was no crater — that puzzled him. How could there have been a meteorite impact if there were no crater, and if there were no fragments? He realised the fragments might have blasted out craters that had then got filled in. So, he kept digging holes to try and find filled-in craters with remains of one sort or another at the bottom — something, anything. No joy. Until 1938. His last expedition. One of his men found something, deep down, in a pit. Whatever it was, it blinded the man. He complained of an intense, searing light, then he lost his sight. Kulik's workers mutinied. For them it was proof they were messing with Ogdy. They dragged the man out and refused to get into the pit. Kulik had to shovel most of the earth back in himself. He measured the location as accurately as he could, and then returned to the Mineralogical Museum in Leningrad. He planned to return with his own men, but the Germans invaded in 1941 and he joined the fighting. The next year he died of typhus in a POW camp."

Ivanov drank some vodka.

"Whatever they found," he continued, "remained lost in the archives. For a long time, as you know, the motherland had more important things to think about than primitive superstitions. But in 2007 a group of archivists started going through Kulik's papers. When they got to the file about the 1938 incident, the team had the good idea of involving us."

"Us?" said Dimitriy.

"The security services," Ivanov said. "If another expedition to Tunguska were to be launched, they knew they'd need state resources. They dressed it up as being about some potentially weaponizable force. They weren't entirely wrong. Kulik's coordinates were accurate. They used a remote-controlled digger. Once they'd reached the depth Kulik recorded, they lowered animals down to the bottom. All came back blind. So, they were at the right place. A remote camera relayed images of glittering metallic fragments. They sent down instruments, but the instruments measured nothing. A volunteer discovered that *reflections* of the fragments could be observed in a mirror. Using remote cameras and mirrors, the fragments were dug out of the pit bottom. It was all hit-and-miss. Somebody thought of lead, being a heavy metal, so they fashioned a lead-lined steel box and used a remote-controlled robotic arm to shepherd the fragments towards the box and seal the lid."

"Shepherd?"

"You'll learn about that," Ivanov said; "*if* you take the job." He stubbed out his cigarette, drank off his vodka, and continued. "The fragments were then brought to a ..." (he coughed) "... *facility* here in Astrakhan. The box was opened and the fragments were housed in a specially-constructed room. That, Dimitriy Semenov, is where you come in. We want to analyse the fragments. Test their qualities." He leaned over the table as if to share a confidence. "And perhaps," he said, "replicate them."

Dimitriy felt the thrill of scientific discovery and the repulsion of a lifelong pacifist. But curiosity gripped him strongest. If only he could tell Anastasia! He was sure she would have been just as fascinated.

The Admiral got to his feet.

"I will be waiting outside tomorrow morning at seven," he said, "and will take you to the facility."

Dimitriy watched as Ivanov threaded his way steadily through the tables. That word, *comrade*, again. When he had gone, Dimitriy picked up the file and hurried to his room.

✍

The Admiral was waiting for him on the hotel's esplanade in a sleek black chauffeur-driven limousine. He was in his uniform, his gold brocaded cap on the seat beside him.

"Is this a Zil?" Dimitriy asked, getting into the tobacco-fugged interior.

"The 4104," said the Admiral. "The Navy is determined to keep them going until they fall to pieces."

He lit a cigarette. "You read the file?" he asked.

"Of course. Do you want me to believe that the Evenki saw angels?"

"*You* saw the drawings," said Ivanov. "*I* don't want you to believe anything."

"Yes," said Dimitriy, "I *saw* the drawings."

The Admiral gazed through the smoked glass window.

"Do you believe in angels, Dimitriy Semenov?"

"No," said Dimitriy, "I don't. But what else can be made of those drawings? And those sounds; if not something like trumpets, then what?"

Ivanov shook his head.

"I told you; we are trying to keep open minds. You have to remember in 1908 the Evenki were a primitive, superstitious people. When something they didn't understand happened, they naturally ascribed it to their god, Ogdy."

"You don't think there was a conflict?"

"Imagine if you were a primitive people and something massive exploded overhead," said Ivanov. "Wouldn't you extrapolate from what you knew? Battle, noise?"

"And those trumpeting noises *before*?" asked Dimitriy.

Ivanov chuckled.

"*You* called them 'heavenly trumpets', Dimitriy Semenov, but you don't believe in such things, do you?"

"Of course not, Admiral. But what are the alternative explanations?"

Ivanov tutted. "You are a scientist, aren't you? Because we don't know the answer doesn't mean there isn't one. We just don't know it yet — perhaps we'll never know it. What we *do* know is that we have seven fragments of an unknown powerful material that *may* have fallen from the sky about the time of the Tunguska event. We can, and must, try to know as much about those fragments as possible, using scientific methods, and not basing our judgements on superstition and hearsay and eye-witness accounts from long ago."

"Of course," said Dimitriy, chastened. "It's those pictures in the file. My imagination ran away with me."

The Admiral stubbed out his cigarette.

"We have arrived," he said.

✍

Some five months after Dimitriy started the job, Anastasia stopped making dinner on Friday evenings. The first time, she told him she'd been feeling unwell, and he accepted the explanation unthinkingly. He ate alone in the kitchen. The next Friday, though, the new practice had been rationalised; she said it was too late in the evening to eat a full-blown meal — better that he snacked or had a bowl of soup or a salad. He again accepted the explanation. Then, one Friday, when he came to bed, he found her weeping.

"What's the matter, Ana?"

She rolled over and he saw that her eyes were puffed up.

"I just wish you'd tell me," she said. "About her, whoever she is."

"There is no her," Dimitriy insisted.

"You can't hide it from me," Anastasia said. "I see the way you look as though you have been torn away from someone."

"There is no other woman, Anastasia."

"Is it a man? I'd understand."

"There's nobody else, I swear!"

"You think I'm stupid? You can't wait to get back on Monday mornings."

She rolled away and wept herself to sleep. He stared up at the ceiling. She was right, of course. The weekends back home in Derbent had become a torment.

✍

"Welcome to Astrakhan State Technology University," said Ivanov, checking his cap's position in the glass of the chauffeur's partition.

The Admiral led him through the glass-fronted entrance. Students milled about, seemingly unfazed at the image of a uniformed Admiral threading a path through the crowd.

"Where are we going?"

"The Institute of Oil and Gas." Ivanov led the way across the leafy campus to a nondescript red brick construction. They went through rotating doors and stopped before a block of lifts. When the lift came, the Admiral pushed the button for –2, but he kept his finger on the button a long time. Ivanov turned to face a small camera in one corner of the roof of the lift and gave a salute.

"Forgive the cloak-and-dagger stuff," he said. "Until the Union collapsed, the Caspian Flotilla was based in Baku, but a lot of the command structure was kept safely within Russia itself, including here, in Astra. The Americans knew that, of course. This place was just as much of a target, so special underground facilities were built for the command structures. That's where we are going now."

By then, the lift should have reached –2 level, but felt as though it were still in motion. After several minutes of slow movement, the lift stopped, and the doors slid open. In front of them stood two armed, uniformed guards. Behind them was a vast, brightly lit space. Ivanov produced papers and explained about Dimitriy. Once the papers had been stamped, the soldiers stood aside and let them pass.

"It's quite a hike," said the Admiral.

The vast space was devoid of human activity, but all around them stood massive columns of plastic-wrapped material.

"Thousands of men could live down here for years," said Ivanov.

On the far side of the bunker, Ivanov led Dimitriy into a complex of smaller spaces. Each entrance was a double-doored air-pressurized port. Finally, they came to a twin set of grey-painted heavy steel doors that had been swung open.

"Here we are," said the Admiral. "The playroom; the laboratory."

They were greeted by the head of the scientific team, Fyodor Babikov, a beanpole of a man wearing large tinted spectacles. Ivanov left them together, promising to return at the end of the day. Babikov showed Dimitriy to the changing room. There were sinks, lockers and benches. They scrubbed up together, then dressed in classic surgical gear. Afterwards, Babikov led Dimitriy into a small meeting room. The walls were lined with large drawings showing distinctive geometrical structures. Babikov gestured for him to sit down at a table and sat opposite.

"What has Admiral Ivanov told you?" he asked.

"The basic story," said Dimitriy. "And I've read the file."

"Did he tell you about their effects?"

"The blindness?"

"Well, there *is* that," said Babikov. "But you don't need to worry. The lab is rigged so that you simply cannot look directly at the fragments. You can only see them indirectly by using the mirrors we've installed, or by using the camera. But did Ivanov not talk about anything else?"

"Nothing," said Dimitriy.

"Mmm... He was probably afraid he'd scare you off."

"Why would I be scared?"

"They seem to have an addictively euphoric effect on some people."

"Some?"

"It seems to depend. There's nothing chemical about it."

"How do you know this?"

"You're not the first expert drafted in. In fact, you are the third."

"The others?"

Babikov shook his head.

"They didn't last very long. The first was here for just over a year. The second lasted almost two years."

"Where are they now?"

"Locked away," said Babikov.

"And you?"

"Nothing," said Babikov. "But, then, I don't spend hours in the viewing room."

"All right," Dimitriy said. "What else did Ivanov *not* tell me?"

"There isn't a whole lot more to know."

"How long have the fragments been here?"

"Since 2008."

"And you have honestly learned nothing?"

Babikov grinned.

"Honestly, very little. I'll tell you everything we know, but it won't take long."

Dimitriy leaned back in his chair.

"Tell me," he said.

"We know they have properties, and powers. The power to blind people, for example."

"Are we sure of that?"

"You mean?"

"Well," said Dimitriy, "we've only had that one example, of the man down the pit, back in 1938. It could have been a stroke, couldn't it?"

"You're forgetting the animals," Babikov said. "Anyway, there have been quite a few unfortunate episodes since."

"Here?" asked Dimitriy.

"Yes," said Babikov. "People who didn't listen. People who didn't believe. An accident. A drunk."

"How many?"

"Enough for us to know that the fragments, if looked at directly, cause blindness in humans, as in animals. Even welding masks didn't help."

"You've tried reptiles?"

"Oh, yes," said Babikov. "We've tried reptiles *and* squid and octopus *and* insects. We've tried everything," he said. "The fragments have the same effect on any sort of eye known to us."

"Your instruments?"

"Show nothing. Whatever this effect is, it is produced in an undetectable way."

"What else?" Dimitriy asked.

"Oh, the euphoria business."

"Can you be sure of that?"

"Scientifically, no. But there must be a strong presumption."

"Two cases only? You can't presume anything from that."

"You are right," Babikov said, smiling ruefully. "Let me just call it a *hunch*, then. Two highly intelligent, balanced, reasonable scientists, both following a similar pattern of obsessiveness and increasingly frequent episodes of manic euphoria, culminating in madness and confinement in clinics. I agree with you, Dimitriy Semenov. It could be sheer coincidence, but I think not."

"All right," said Dimitriy. "What else?"

"We have found a way to manipulate the fragments," said Babikov. "Only one metal may touch them — gold. All others melt away as they get near. Once we realised that, we had special gold implements made up that could be attached to the arms of the robots — that is the main way in which you will be working with the fragments, if you need to manipulate them."

"But it is curious," said Dimitriy, "gold being so malleable — like the lead in which they were encased."

"In retrospect, the lead-lined box was a crazy risk," said Babikov. "Who knows what might have happened if they had melted their way out during the trip?"

"What else?"

Babikov shook his head in sudden exhaustion.

"We know next to nothing, and that is all we know."

"Now you are talking in riddles."

Babikov looked at Dimitriy for a few moments, as though brought back from a reverie.

"We cannot record images. Nothing works; film, X-rays, electro-magnetic resonance imaging, transmission electron tomography... Whatever sort of imaging we have tried to use, nothing shows up. They are definitely there; we can see their reflection, but we can't capture them as images, and that means that we can only study the fragments themselves."

"What about microscopes?" asked Dimitriy.

"Lenses work," said Babikov. "But you cannot record what you are seeing."

"You can't draw them?"

"No, no," said Babikov. "They can be drawn, at least — hence all of these..." he waved at the drawings hanging on the walls around them. "Your predecessors' masterpieces."

"May I?" Dimitriy asked.

Babikov nodded.

Dimitriy studied the drawings for a while.

"I have an idea," he said. "But I'll wait until you've finished."

"Second," Babikov continued, "they are constantly levitating."

Dimitriy raised his eyebrows.

"They always hover, never touching any surface."

"Some sort of energy, then?"

"I think so, but we can detect nothing. We thought of magnetism or light but it's neither of those." Babikov smiled and shook his head. "Believe me, Dimitriy Semenov, we have tried and tested many ideas — all fruitlessly — so far."

"I understand what Ivanov was getting at now."

"Getting at?" said Babikov.

"We were talking about scientific method. He said we don't know the answer yet, and perhaps we never will."

✍

That very first time Dimitriy came back from Astrakhan she'd known already, he realised — or, rather, she'd suspected already. Something had happened. He couldn't entirely hide it from her. For a start, there was the fait accompli of his decision. He had taken the job without first discussing the offer with her. It was so generous, he said, that he had decided on the spot. That wasn't the whole truth, of course. She asked about the work. He told her how he'd had to sign a declaration and was now bound by the Official Secrets Act. He saw her recoil.

"It isn't what you think," he'd said.

"What is it, then?" she'd asked.

"Something unimaginable," he'd replied.

She'd wrinkled her nose. "Can't you give me a clue?"

He'd laughed. "I promise you it's nothing sinister."

"I can see you are enthusiastic about it."

"Come with me to Astrakhan, Ana," he'd urged. "Bring the children. We can make it work."

"We discussed all that," she'd said, shaking her head. "My job, my family, the children's schools..."

He'd nodded his head slowly. Already, his thoughts were drifting back...

"Dimitriy?"

"I'm sorry, my love," he said. "I was daydreaming."

✍

He'd listened patiently as Babikov listed the other properties his team had so far noted. The seven fragments were identical in appearance. Each was a convex oblong, about nine centimetres long by five centimetres wide. From a distance, they seemed to be golden in colour but, the stronger the magnification, the less colour there was. From very close up they seemed neither transparent nor invisible, and completely colourless yet iridescent. The fragments' default position was to hover vertically in an overlapping formation, like the defensive *testudo* Roman legionaries had sometimes adopted with their shields. If the fragments were separated, they immediately moved back to the *testudo* formation. Once again, Dimitriy studied the drawings on the walls.

"So, what's this big idea of yours?" said Babikov.

"*Lepidoptera*," said Dimitriy.

"Butterflies?" said Babikov, momentarily confused. "We'd thought of fish scales, but *lepidoptera*?"

"In appearance they seem similar to fish scales, it is true, but butterfly scales have three-dimensional lattices that cause iridescence, and I just wonder whether some similar effect is not at work with these scales — and they *are* scales, Babikov, aren't they? They're not just fragments."

Babikov blushed. He took off his glasses and polished the lenses.

"Ivanov doesn't like such talk. I think he's right. We shouldn't leap ahead of ourselves."

"But are we?" said Dimitriy. "We know — or we assume — that these fragments fell to earth in June 1908, right?"

Babikov shook his head.

"No," he said. "We know only that they were found in the area where that event occurred."

"Ivanov gave me to understand there was a probability."

"So there may be," said Babikov. "But he doesn't want us to start wandering off into anthropomorphism and zoomorphism and all the rest of it. We know only what we know. The rest is speculation. If the Admiral hadn't given you the file, you wouldn't have started thinking along these lines."

Dimitriy smiled.

"What lines, Fyodor Babikov? What lines are those?"

Babikov remained silent.

"All right," said Dimitriy. "I'm sure you have similar thoughts. These so-called fragments are themselves a fragment that fell off something much larger, probably during that 'event' of 1908 — off a wing, maybe?"

"Enough!" said Babikov, waving his hands in front of him.

But somehow, Dimitriy *knew*; the fragments *belonged* to something.

✍

In February, just over a year after his first visit to Astrakhan, Anastasia put the ultimatum to him. He couldn't blame her. The Christmas period had been disastrous. Derbent was bitterly cold and the streets were littered with filthy snow and slush where the gritters had passed. The morning, midday, and evening howls of the Ekranoplan as it departed and returned punctuated Derbent's days just as accurately and regularly as a clock tower bell. He couldn't wait to get back to Astra. He was constantly irritable with the children and mostly morosely silent with her. He felt dreadful. He needed to be back, to be back with *them*, in their presence. When the holidays were finally over, and he had been leaving for the Ekranoplan, she had said, "I can't say I'm sorry to see you go, Dimitriy. You have to get a grip on yourself. Whatever is going on in Astrakhan, you have to put a stop to it. It is ruining you and us."

That had been January. He had got worse over the following month. Then, one Friday evening in late February, she took the final initiative. Part of him felt she was absolutely right — he felt sorry for her and for Andrei and Sasha. But another part of him just didn't care. Or, rather, it only cared about *them*, the angelic fragments (which was what he called them now), and about being with them.

The children were in bed. The classical music radio channel was on. She'd even put a lit candle on the laid dinner table. It was the first time in a long time that she had cooked a meal for his return. At the end of the meal, Anastasia took his hands across the table.

"I am so very sorry, Dima," she said, "but I can't take this anymore."

"What do you mean?" he blustered.

She smiled and put a finger to his lips to hush him.

"You know what I mean. I have spoken to you so many times."

She was right.

"So, now what?" he asked.

"I'd like you to resign from your job in Astrakhan."

"But how would we..." he began, blustering again.

She shook her head and smiled wistfully.

"We were fine before. We'll be fine again."

"But my work is important."

"I'm sure it is, Dimitriy but, please, let somebody else do it."

He burst into tears.

"I can't," he wept. "I just can't."

"What do you mean? What is it that has such a hold over you? If it is not a mistress, then what is it? Drugs? Is that it? You can tell me. Please."

"It's none of those," he blurted. "But I can't tell you."

"Of course you can!"

"I have signed the Official Secrets Act, Ana."

"I promise I won't tell anybody else. Who could I tell, anyway?"

Dimitriy shook his head.

"If you won't tell me," said Anastasia, her tone hardening, "that's it."

"What do you mean?"

"I'll leave you, Dimitriy."

His shoulders sagged.

"All right, I'll tell you," he said finally.

He told her about his second meeting with Ivanov, and the file about the 1908 Tunguska event and Kulik's 1938 discovery. He told her about his first entry into the thick-walled, steel-shuttered underground space where the plate glass and mirrors had been set up to enable scientists to gaze indirectly on the fragments. He told her about his indescribable feelings of ecstasy, of euphoria, when he was in the presence of the angelic scales, and how the obsessive feeling had grown until it had now overwhelmed all other considerations. He told her about the steel shutter inside the space housing the scales which Babikov had to operate every day so that Dimitriy could at least no longer gaze upon the angelic fragments, and the way he, Dimitriy, had to be dragged out of the space by orderlies and given sedation before he could be convinced to return to his hotel room in the evenings.

Anastasia sat patiently through his explanation.

"All right," she said when he had finished. "Suppose everything you've told me is true. Where do you think this will all end?"

"I have to finish my work," he said. "Nobody understands the fragments better than I do. I have a *feeling* for them, don't you see? I understand them; their need to return. You see?"

She looked at him with sad eyes. "Of course I do, Dima," she said, "but you need to take a break. You're working yourself crazy."

"I can't take a break, don't you understand? I *must* continue."

"Nobody would blame you for taking a break," she said.

"But the *work*," Dimitriy insisted. "I *must* be there."

She shook her head. "No," she said. "You must stop this nonsense. You *can* stop it, you know. Let somebody else do it."

"NO!" he shouted, startling himself as much as Anastasia. "I can't let someone else come in. *I* must be with them. You can't stop me now." He broke off and wept. "Don't you see?" he said. "It's stronger than me."

Anastasia shook her head once more.

"You must choose," she said softly.

"No!" Dimitriy sobbed. "Please don't make me choose."

"If you go back to Astrakhan on Monday, then we will move out."

"But the children need their father!" Dimitriy blurted.

"Don't be a fool," Anastasia snapped. "The children haven't had a father for over a year now."

He nodded and hung his head. "All right,' he said. "Where will you go? Your parents?"

She nodded.

Good, thought Dimitriy, with a sense of wonderment at his own callousness. *Now I can go back to the fragments.*

✍

Anastasia didn't come to the doorstep with him. He'd kissed her on the head as she lay in bed. She didn't move, though he sensed she was awake.

"Goodbye, Ana," he said. "I still love you, you know. And I'm sorry. I just have to be there."

He closed the door and walked through the slushy remains of the snow to the Ekranoport. He was petrified of the take-off, as usual, but his heart had already filled with joyful anticipation. As the Caspian Queen approached Astra, the sea became agitated and the sky darkened. A strong wind blew up and Dimitriy could feel that the pilot was struggling with the controls. He was relieved when the craft slowed down and started its long taxi up the relative calm of the Reka Bakhtemir channel. Ivanov was waiting for him on the quayside.

"Something's going on," he said. "We've been hearing noises in the sky."

"Heavenly trumpets?" said Dimitriy.

"Noises in the sky," Ivanov repeated. "But, yes, not unlike the descriptions the Evenki gave in 1908."

"Could it be?" asked Dimitriy.

"Be what?" said Ivanov, drawing on his cigarette. The sky flashed. A long roll of thunder sounded. "And we've been having strange weather. Look at those clouds."

Dimitry looked up at the dark, corrugated formation hanging heavy and low over the city. Thunder reverberated above and around them.

"And the fragments," Ivanov continued, "have started to oscillate."

"Oscillate?"

"All right," said the Admiral, flicking away his cigarette and blowing out smoke. "They seem to have become agitated."

"I can't wait to see them."

Ivanov gave him a sour stare then lit another cigarette and leaned against the Zil.

"I'm not sure that's a good idea, Dimitriy Semenov. They are no longer stable."

"What do you mean? I've got to see them. You know that."

"Pull yourself together," said the Admiral.

"It's just that I've *got* to see them. Surely you have understood that by now?"

The sky flashed and flickered. Ivanov looked up and waited for the roll of thunder.

"This is not normal," he said. "Something is going on."

"There's a connection?"

"I don't know, but I have a sense there might be. It's almost as though the scales are trying to escape."

"Ah! Escape?"

"Babikov says they have already melted through the gold lining on the roof of the cell."

"No!" said Dimitriy. "Then we must hurry. They are going back. I knew it!"

"Back?" Ivanov drew deeply on his cigarette. "Take my advice," he said. "Return to Derbent. The Ekranoplan will be leaving very soon. Go back to your wife and children. Maybe it's nothing. We'll see. Come again tomorrow."

"There's no point," said Dimitriy. "They've left me."

"Because of this?" Ivanov asked. "Because of your..."

"Yes," said Dimitriy.

Ivanov nodded slowly and drew again on his cigarette. They heard the distinctive whine as the Caspian Queen's jet engines started up.

"Go!" he urged.

"I can't!" Dimitriy sobbed. "I must see *them* again."

They leaned on a railing and watched as the gangplanks were drawn away and the aft and forward doors closed. The sky flashed vividly. A dockworker cast off the mooring ropes. When they had been entirely wound back on board, the jet engines roared, and the Caspian Queen sailed slowly out into the Volga. They heard the familiar howl as the captain increased the power and taxied the strange vessel down towards the sea channel.

Ivanov flicked away his cigarette, then opened the door of the Zil.

"We'd better hurry," he said.

✍

"Ana," called her mother. "Come quickly."

Anastasia pulled the plug in the kitchen sink, wiped her hands on her apron and joined her parents in the living room. They were watching a Russian television channel and the news bulletin had just started. Sasha was playing on the floor. The newsreader was halfway through the headlines. A train had crashed just outside Vladivostok. The President had visited a new LPG facility at the port of Murmansk...

"What is it, mama?"

"Ssshhh," said her mother, "you'll see in a moment."

The newsreader finished the headlines. Anastasia's mother turned the volume up.

"And now we go back to our main news item this evening. Reports are coming in of a massive explosion on the northern outskirts of the city of Astrakhan, at the premises of the State Technology University. The explosion is said to have occurred in an underground research facility situated beneath the University's parkland.

"As can be seen from these helicopter images, several buildings have collapsed and the police and the fire services are searching the rubble. Among those missing are the director of the Caspian Flotilla's scientific outreach programme, Rear Admiral Anatoly Ivanov, and the head of the Astrakhan State Technology University's Oil and Gas Institute research programme, Fyodor Babikov. An acclaimed Moscow State University materials scientist, Dimitriy Semenov, who joined the research team from Derbent, is also missing."

Pictures of the three men flashed up on the screen for a few moments.

"That's Daddy," said Sasha.

Anastasia nodded tearfully.

"Yes, darling," she said.

✍

"Babikov!" Dimitriy cried. He staggered out into the remains of the room where he had first met the scientist. He could hear flames flickering. The air was heavy with smoke. A long, low groan sounded out. "Babikov!" he said, "Is that you?" Dimitry staggered over to where he thought Babikov's office had once been. He heard the groan again. "Babikov?"

"Dimitriy Semenov," whispered the scientist. "What has happened to your eyes, man?"

Dimitriy smiled, the charred skin wrinkling where his eyes had once been.

"The fragments have gone back to their rightful place," he said. "I'm going home now."

✍ ✍ ✍

Initial feedback

I liked the setting and characters. It was never quite clear what a 'ekranoplan' is, since the word doesn't suggest any form of aircraft. I was distracted, trying to figure out what the 'ekran' (screen) element of it was. The characters are good, but the tone is dry, and the piece moves slowly and could do with a fair amount of cutting/compression. The piece doesn't do as much with its concept as it might. There isn't much of a resolution to the piece, and it felt a little more like the setup for a longer piece than a complete story.

Why are they so certain that molten lead won't harm anything? Dimitriy does seem very quick to jump to angels. What is Bologna working with, since they seem to have no artifacts? What blocks the effect, and why? Why is there a crater this time, since it was important that there was not one last time?

Author's intent

What do you think the story's about?
What emotions are you trying to evoke?

The basic theme is that ecstasy, religious or otherwise, can help overcome great fear but also do great harm. Having just re-read the story again, I would agree with you that the story could do better at conveying that. To work!

I was interested by what you wrote about it feeling like a set-up for a longer piece. It is true that as I initially wrote the piece I wondered whether the story would not be more suitable for a novella that would enable me to flesh out the characters and their locations but, on reflection, I decided it would work better in a more compressed form (which, clearly, needs to be compressed still further).

Author's note

My relationship with *Metaphorosis* and with Morris began with a constructive rejection — an invitation to re-write, but with no guarantee of subsequent publication. Like many SF short stories, I imagine, "Ekranoplan" — the original title of "Going Home" — was a combination of several ideas: the further reaches of Soviet Cold War technology; the 1908 Tunguska event in Siberia; and a Russian scientist who not only comes to believe in angels but becomes addicted to the ecstasy close proximity to them brings — at the cost of all that is dear to him in life. Morris wrote encouragingly that the story had great potential, but he accurately put his finger on a number of shortcomings. For a short story, it was overlong. Perhaps it could have worked as a novella, but that would have involved a degree of investment I couldn't make. I had concentrated on the science and technology to the detriment of the interrelationships between the story's characters. And there was insufficient resolution at the end. Above all, though, Morris asked me to tell him what the story was really about and what emotions I was trying to evoke. The theme, I realised, was not about technology or angels but, rather, about how ecstasy — religious or otherwise — can help overcome great fear but also do great harm. Thereafter, I pruned the story back considerably, threw out a lot of the science and technology cleverness, brought the scientist's tortured relationship with his wife and children much more into focus, gave the story a more satisfactory resolution and changed the title. I forget how many revisions the story went through subsequently — four or five? — but the key editorial moment, from my point of view, was the realisation about what I really wanted to show.

In retrospect, all of that editorial questioning was the best thing that could have happened to the story; it has since been selected for the annual anthology, *The Best of British Science Fiction 2021*. Without Morris's persistence, and support, that simply wouldn't have happened.

Editor's note

As with some other pieces in this anthology, I was wrong about aspects of Martin's story. In particular, the title — originally, "Ekranoplan". It happens that I speak some Russian and live with a native speaker. I couldn't make sense of *ekranoplan*, which to me translated as 'screen-plan' or maybe 'plane-plane', and which I found distracting. Martin later shared with me links to the historical ekranoplan, whose name clearly made sense to the Soviets who designed it. A little knowledge is a dangerous thing.

On a broader note, the story isn't really about the vehicle at all, but about the people and the effects of the scales on them, so I still felt the new title worked better. My other, more substantive concerns were about the tone of the piece, some of the mechanics of the scales and their containment, and the length of the story.

The original version was about 9,500 words, and struck me as awkward. The piece then felt like the introduction to a much longer story — not really resolved or complete as it stood. I suggested that either it should expand to a novella to dig more deeply into the issues (but noted that we didn't then publish novellas) or condense to a shorter story that focused more closely on the relatively small cast of characters. I thought either could work effectively, and happily for *Metaphorosis*, Martin chose to focus the story, with the final being about 7,300 words. Cutting is painful for many writers, but Martin took on the task with a will, and very effectively.

It's not always easy to say what a story is actually about. Writers don't always set out to write about a particular theme, but there is one there, nonetheless. Every story is about something, whether intentionally or not. To me, an important part of this story was about the characters. Religious ecstasy, as Martin noted, was certainly an important aspect of the narrative, but for me, the central element was the relationship between Dimitriy and Anastasia. I'd found the tone of the original version on the dry side for that core story. By the final version, however, I thought that Martin had brought out the tension in the relationship (caused by Dimitriy's obsession with the scales) very successfully.

There are stories in which the mechanics of what happens don't really matter — we're content to accept some magical realism without much explanation. More often, though, the mechanics and logistics do need to make sense, and the ramifications of some aspects of magic or science don't become clear until closely examined. Here, I had questions about the initial handling of the scales — why had they been treated as they were? To answer that requires knowing both something about what the scales were in the story, and how they were initially perceived. While it's important not to let questions like these derail the primary narrative, it's also important that underlying mechanics not distract from it. In this case, Martin cleared up some of the technicalities in a way that allowed the focus to stay on the characters, despite the intriguing mystery of the scales.

Ekranoplan

Every Monday morning for over a year Dimitriy suffered the same torment of emotions. Anastasia didn't say anything anymore as they kissed on the doorstep, but she didn't need to. He knew what she was thinking, and she was not wrong. He could easily find work elsewhere that maybe would not pay as well but would not impose the same five-day-long absences upon their relationship and their family. "Think of Andrei," she would say in the old days, before she realised entreaties were useless. "Think of Sasha. They need their father." She was right about that as well, he was sure. The kids were in bed by the time he got back on Fridays, so he missed the whole school week. Sasha, the younger, still greeted him with unconditional delight and affection on Saturday mornings, but Andrei, now into his teens, had become increasingly sullen. There was an unspoken reproach in his bearing. Dimitriy wanted to tell his son how terribly sorry he felt, but the truth was that he didn't, despite it all. Guilty, yes; sad, yes; but not sorry.

And then there was the Ekranoplan. Anastasia had refused to leave Derbent when Dimitriy had taken on the Astrakhan job and he accepted that. Her family had lived in the city for a long time. Her parents, brothers, sisters and various aunts and uncles still lived there. They were, frankly, essential infrastructure for the weeks when she had to work the night shift at the hospital. In any case, as an Azerbaijani she wouldn't have felt at home in Astrakhan, even assuming she could have got a similar job there. She would never have settled at so great a distance from her loved ones. In a car, the trip took ten hours in the summer and in the winter, with ice patches and snow drifts, the roads were frequently impassable. The nearest airport was Uytash, a hundred kilometres away, and from there Dagestan Airlines provided just one flight to Astrakhan, in the middle of the week. The only viable means of getting there and back was the Ekranoplan, which covered the distance in a little over ninety minutes. He would never get used to it, though. Whenever there was the slightest hint of a breeze his heart dropped, for the monstrous thing could only take off facing into the wind, and that meant riding the incoming waves. Once it was up in the air it was fine and the ride was smooth, even when it glided over the ice floes in the winter, but how he hated the take off! The only thing that made the sadness, guilt and fear every Monday morning was the joyful anticipation; the knowledge that he would soon once again be in the company of the angelic fragments. ...

✍

Not even the school kids were up yet, Dimitriy thought, as he walked through the still sleepy morning streets to the Ekranoport. His path took him across his old route to work in his former life at the Caspian Gates Secondary School. That fateful day, he'd stayed behind, as he did most afternoons, to help a group of fifteen-year-olds with their mathematics. The next week was the half-term break and he wanted to be sure that they wouldn't forget everything by the time he saw them again. When he jumped off the trolley bus, not far from the block of flats where he and Anastasia lived, Ivanov was waiting for him; a tall, thin, grey-suited, sallow-faced man with a cigarette that bobbed on his lower lip as he spoke. He seemed oblivious to the February cold, though both men's breath clouded about them.

"Semenov?" he said.

Dimitriy nodded.

"Could we talk a moment?" said the man, nodding towards a seedy bar embedded into the ground floor of the block of flats.

"What's this about?" asked Dimitriy.

"Please," said the man. "You'll come?"

There was something about him – not furtive, but a sense of secrecy all the same. The man bought two vodkas at the bar and they sat at a scuffed table.

"To your health," the man said, raising his glass.

"Your health," said Dimitriy, and the two men drank.

The man stubbed out his cigarette in an old dented aluminium ashtray and lit another.

"Ivanov," he said. "Anatoly Ivanov. Rear Admiral Anatoly Ivanov, Caspian Flotilla, Astrakahn."

"There must be some mistake," said Dimitriy.

Ivanov drew heavily on his cigarette and shook his head.

"No," he said. "No mistake." He gestured to a passing waiter and ordered two more vodkas.

"I shouldn't stay long," said Dimitriy.

"I won't keep you too long," said Ivanov. He stubbed out his cigarette in the ashtray, but he didn't light another. "Tell me, Dimitriy Semenov," he said, "how much do you earn?"

"Enough," said Dimitriy, sullenly.

"Why are you a teacher?" Ivanov asked, leaning forward over the table. "You are a brilliant physicist with a top doctoral thesis in Biology and Materials Sciences from Moscow State University and yet you hide yourself away at the Caspian Gates Secondary School teaching low-grade maths to misfits..."

"My wife...," Dimitriy began.

"We know all about your wife," Ivanov said.

Dimitriy got up.

"It's time I left," he said, "I don't like this conversation, Admiral Ivanov."

"Sit down," said the Admiral, gesturing with his half-empty vodka glass.

Dimitriy sat down.

"What I mean is that we know she has all of her family here. That's why you're here, isn't it?"

Dimitriy said nothing.

"I've come to invite you to work for the motherland, Dimitriy Semenov." Ivanov lit another cigarette and leaned over the table again. The motherland calls, comrade."

Comrade! Dimitriy knew immediately that the job would be some sort of secret military work.

"It's not what you think, Semenov," the Admiral continued. "If I told you now, you wouldn't believe me."

Dimitriy looked into his empty glass. Ivanov flagged the waiter down and ordered two more vodkas.

"No!" said Dimitriy.

"For the road," said Ivanov.

"All right, for the road."

The Admiral toyed with his cigarette lighter, an old-fashioned metal model with a flip top and a thick wick, for a few moments. And then he looked up at Dimitry and said, "Interested?"

Dimitriy nodded his head slowly.

"Maybe."

"We'll pay you four times what you are getting at that dump of a school."

"The catch?"

Ivanov drank off the remainder of his vodka and placed the glass down gently on the tabletop.

"You'd have to come to Astra, Monday to Friday. We'd cover your board and lodging."

"How would I…"

As if to anticipate his question, the unmistakable howl of the evening return Ekranoplan came to them through the thin glass window.

Ivanov reached into his pocket and drew out an envelope. He placed it on the table.

"There's a ticket in there. This coming Monday. The seven-thirty departure. When you get to Astra, make your way to the Admiral Hotel, and I'll join you there for lunch. A room has been booked in your name. It's half-term. The school won't miss you. See you at the Admiral Hotel?"

"Is this a joke?" Dimitriy asked.

Ivanov stubbed out another cigarette.

"What do you think?" he said. "It's easy to remember, though, isn't it?"

✍

Dimitriy had been travelling to Astra for just over two months when Anastasia first started to voice concern. It was a Saturday evening. The children were in bed. The classical music radio channel was on, and she'd put a lit candle on the laid dinner table. Thinking about it later, he realised that she had first couched it as concern for him. She'd made a deliciously tender lamb hinkal with cheap mutton, tenderised on the balcony with the rolling pin, and a delicate Pakhlava, washed down with a bottle of Georgian wine he had brought back with him. Over the meal, they talked about Sasha and Andrei, and then about her family, and then the weather. At the end of the meal, Anastasia took Dimitriy's hands across the table.

"My love," she said, "please don't take this the wrong way, but I just wondered; are you all right?"

Dimitriy frowned. "What do you mean?" he asked.

"It's difficult to explain," she said, "but you seem sort-of preoccupied."

"Preoccupied?"

"Yes. As though your mind is elsewhere."

He saw she was serious. He smiled. "I promise you, I'm fine," he said.

"Is everything all right with your job?" she asked.

"The job is *wonderful*," he said. "I am enjoying it *so* much."

"Are you sure, Dimitriy?"

He smiled at her and squeezed her hands, and then he began to laugh.

"The music," he said.

She looked puzzled.

"The music on the radio. It's Scriabin. The Poem of Ecstasy."

"So?"

How could he tell her? He was sworn to secrecy, but even if he had been able to tell her, he thought, she wouldn't have believed him.

✍

He would never forget that first time. He had told Anastasia about Ivanov's strange appearance and his enigmatic proposal, and they had discussed it. They had decided he should go. What did he have to lose? School was off for a week. The money was not to be sniffed at. With the kids growing, it would be good if they could rent somewhere larger. In any case, if he didn't like the work, whatever it was, he could always turn it down and return to his teaching.

So, that Monday morning he put on his good suit and walked down to the Ekranoport with Ivanov's ticket in his pocket. He was, he realised, like somebody who lived near to an airport but had never had any reason to take a flight. The morning and evening howls of the Ekranoplan as it departed and returned punctuated their days just as accurately and regularly as a clock tower bell. And now he was going to take it.

The thing was huge. Its strange, v-shaped tail towered over the terminus building. He presented his ticket and took his boarding pass, went through security, then waited with everybody else in the lounge. The windows let out over the thing's matt grey hull which, he was frightened to see, was rusting in places. When the boarding call came, he must have looked out of place for one of the stewards approached him and asked if it were his first time. Dimitriy said that it was. They must, he thought, have been trained to recognise the novices.

"There's nothing to worry about," said the steward. "It will probably feel a little strange at the beginning. Remember, though; it is a boat that will become a plane. Once the pilot has sufficient altitude, she'll lower the nose and accelerate and then the rest is just plain sailing. You'll see – very smooth."

"Thank you," said Dimitriy. "I'm sure I'll be all right."

"Don't forget your headphones," said the steward, handing him a pair from a rack on the wall.

"Headphones?"

The steward smiled and invited Dimitriy over to a window. "Look," he said. "Do you see?"

"I see," said Dimitriy. It was obvious, when he thought about it. Jutting out from the front of the fuselage, in front of the passenger cabin, were four massive jet engines, placed side-by-side. Dimitriy remembered that they could be seen from afar. Together with the four on the other side, they looked from a distance like mini wings.

"We wouldn't fly without the downward pressure from those," said the steward, "but they are a little bit loud! The plug is in the armrest."

Dimitriy sat in his seat, fastened his seat belt, put on the headphones and plugged them in..

"Welcome to the Caspian Queen," he heard a soothing voice say. "This is your captain speaking..."

The woman's voice exuded calm and authority. Dimitriy felt his pulse rate slow a little.

"It's a fine day and visibility is excellent," the captain's voice continued. "There's a westerly wind and it's going to be a little choppy before we take off, but then we'll have a great ride. We will be taxiing out in a few minutes. If you haven't put your headphones on, please do it now!"

Dimitriy closed his eyes and tried to think of pleasanter things. He tried to picture Anastasia and the children. The headphones were no good. He could hear the terrible howl of the engines as they were turned up to full power. The Ekranoplan juddered and shuddered and rocked sickeningly to one side and then the other. The howl grew in intensity and he felt himself being pushed back into his seat, and then they seemed to be bouncing off the waves and, suddenly, all became smooth for a few seconds, and then the captain turned the nose down to horizontal and he dared to open his eyes and look out of the window. The citadel glowered, as it had done for centuries, above the city of the forty heroes and then a flash of spray obscured the view and by the time the water had dribbled down the window, Derbent was far behind them. Ice-floes flashed by beneath.

"This is the captain again," came the lady's voice. "I'm sorry if the take-off was a little bit bumpy. We're now cruising above the sea at our maximum speed and we expect to arrive at Astrakhan on time. In the meanwhile, our stewards and hostesses..."

What had he done for the remainder of the trip? He had only hazy recollections. The headphones gave a strange sense of detachment. Perhaps he had dozed? In any case, he remembered the brief moment of excitement when the Ekranoplan began to fly over the frozen lake, the lurching feeling when the Ekranoplan became a ship again, where the icebreakers had cleared a route, and then the long, slow taxi, the jets moaning, up the Reka Bakhtemir channel to the mighty Volga itself and along to the city of Astrakhan.

✍

The second time she voiced concern, Anastasia was more direct. Dimitriy had just got back.

"Did you miss us?" she asked.

"Of course I did!" he said.

"Really?" she said.

"What does that mean?" he asked. But deep down, he knew. Anastasia had gone back to the kitchen. The table was laid for two but, he noted, there was no cloth and there was no candle. He turned on the radio and tuned it to the classical music channel. She put her head around the kitchen door.

"Do we have to have that on?" she asked.

"No," he replied. "Of course not."

Over the meal, he asked about the children and her family. Her replies were sullenly monosyllabic. At the end, he went to help her with the washing up as he always did, but she shooed him out of the kitchen and insisted on doing it alone. He sat on the sofa and waited. She emerged, drying her hands on a tea towel.

"You've changed," she said. "Are you sure you're not seeing someone?"

Dimitriy snorted.

"Seeing someone?" he repeated.

"Yes, Dimitriy. I mean are you having a relationship of some sort?"

"Of course not, my love. Of course not!"

There were tears in her eyes.

✍

Astrakhan exuded a very different atmosphere. For a start, it was on a broad river, not a sea, and the old bridge over the Volga gave a sense of space that was missing in Derbent. And then there were the various tributaries and canals and ports that gave the impression that the city was almost floating. There were no hills behind, no citadel looming over the city but, rather, the great Trinity Cathedral soaring upwards, with its gold-capped green domes. Derbent's historical tactical role as a military pinch point was emphasised by the way it huddled between the hills and the sea – not for nothing was it called the Gate of Gates. Astrakhan, on the other hand, was flat and expansive. Simply being there gave Dimitry a sense of a new beginning. He easily found the Admiral Hotel, a great block of fake chrome and smoked glass. A room had been booked, as Ivanov had promised, and the clerk told him that a table had been reserved in the restaurant for twelve o'clock. Dimitriy went to his room, unpacked the few belongings he had brought, then turned on the television and watched a programme without really following it. What was Ivanov going to offer him, he wondered?

The Admiral Ivanov was already sitting at their table when Dimitriy came down, a vodka in front of him and a cigarette on his lower lip. He nodded curtly but didn't get up.

"Welcome to Astra," he said. "A drink?"

"Thank you," said Dimitriy, "but I don't drink at lunchtime."

Ivanov beckoned a waiter over and ordered a vodka.

"Today, you'll make an exception," he said.

The Admiral had ordered caviar, brought by another waiter on a bed of ice.

"Thank you," said Dimitriy, who had only once before eaten the delicacy.

"Thank Mother Russia," said Ivanov, stubbing out his cigarette.

Once the blinis arrived, they started to eat, digging out the glutinous eggs with small mother-of-pearl teaspoons.

"And now," said the Admiral. "To work."

"I'm ready," said Dimitriy.

"What do you know about Tunguska?"

"Siberia? The beginning of the last century, wasn't it?"

Ivanov lit a cigarette, then nodded.

"30 June 1908," he said.

"I've seen the pictures," said Dimitriy. "All those trees. Wasn't it a meteor or a comet or something?"

"Da, da," said Ivanov. That's what people think."

"Think? What was it, then?"

"We don't know." He lit another cigarette. "I've brought a file for you to read, but before that, I want you to sign this."

He drew an envelope out from his jacket pocket. That pocket was like a magician's hat, Dimitriy thought. Ivanov opened the envelope and unfolded a sheet of paper.

"What is it?" asked Dimitriy.

"It's a declaration," said the Admiral. "Official Secrets Act. Everything I have to tell you from now on is secret. I will only tell you anything more if you sign the declaration. To be clear, if you sign the declaration, and you do not respect it, you could be tried and imprisoned. Understood? Not even your wife. Got it?"

Dimitriy read the declaration, his hand trembling a little, then nodded. Ivanov handed him a pen and he signed and dated the paper and handed it back.

"Good," said Ivanov. He folded the declaration, put it in its envelope and then placed the envelope back in his pocket. He gestured to a waiter to clear their table and ordered two more vodkas.

"Tunguska," Dimitriy prompted him. "You were saying…"

"The region wasn't as sparsely populated as people think," said the Admiral. Quite a few people heard and saw something of what happened." He lit a cigarette. "It started with noises from the sky."

"Noises?"

"Some of the witnesses said it was like rutting stags roaring, only louder. Others said it was like somebody moving furniture overhead." He drew on his cigarette. "Still others said it was like trumpets sounding single notes."

"And they saw nothing?"

"Not at first. The noises went on for about a week. There's a much fuller account in the file."

"And then?" asked Dimitriy.

"And then there was some sort of conflict in the sky."

"Conflict?" asked Dimitriy, his attention caught by the strange word.

"Yes," said Ivanov. "Some sort of celestial conflict."

"Celestial?" Dimitriy repeated. "You are choosing your words with care, Admiral."

Ivanov nodded and stubbed out his cigarette.

"I am indeed," said Ivanov. "You will read the file and see for yourself. As good scientists, we try always to keep open minds."

"The word 'conflict'," said Dimitriy, "suggests that more than one body or object might have been involved, right?" Ivanov nodded. "And the word 'celestial' suggests this was high up in the atmosphere?"

Ivanov nodded again. "You'll see," he said. "There are some drawings, based on eyewitness accounts at the time. The locals, the Evenki, were all convinced they'd seen their god, Ogdy, in a fight."

"How extraordinary," said Dimitriy. "I am truly fascinated, dear Admiral, but I confess I am not sure why any of this should lead you to bring me to the Volga Basin, a great pleasure though it is."

Ivanov lit another cigarette.

"Kulik," he said. "Leonid Kulik. A mineralogist. He came to Tunguska several times. There was no crater – that's what puzzled everybody. How could there have been a meteorite impact if there was no crater, and if there were no fragments? He kept digging holes to try and find some sort of mineral remains – something, anything. No joy. Until 1938. His last expedition. One of his men found something, deep down, in a pit. Whatever it was, it blinded the man. He complained of an intense, searing light, and then he lost his sight. Kulik's workers mutinied. For them it was proof that they were messing with Ogdy. They refused to get into the pit. Kulik had to shovel the earth back in himself. He measured the location as accurately as he could, and then returned to the Mineralogical Museum in Leningrad. He planned to return again with his own men, but the Germans invaded in 1941. He joined the fighting and the next year died of typhus in a POW camp."

Ivanov stopped and finished off his vodka.

"Another?" he asked.

"Exceptionally," said Dimitriy. He would, he thought, sleep it off before he started reading the file.

The Admiral lit another cigarette.

"Whatever they found," he continued, "remained buried in the archives. For a long time, as you know, the motherland had more important things to think about than primitive superstitions. But in 2007 a group of archivists started going through Kulik's papers. When they got to the file about the 1938 incident, one of the team had the good idea of involving us."

"Us?" said Dimitriy.

Ivanov coughed.

"The State," he said. "The security services. The armed forces. If another expedition to Tunguska were going to be launched, they would need state resources. They cleverly dressed it up as being about some potentially weaponizable force, and they weren't entirely wrong. You can read the whole story in the file. It was a major operation. They dug the pit using a remote-controlled digger. Once the fragments were re-discovered, they lowered various animals down to the bottom. All came back blind. They sent down instruments to take measurements, but the instruments measured nothing – I mean, as though there were nothing to be measured. A soldier volunteer, realising that nothing seemed to happen with a camera and a screen, discovered that the fragments could be observed through a mirror. Using cameras and mirrors, the fragments were dug out. Molten lead was poured around them and allowed to cool, and then the fragments were removed, inside the lead."

Ivanov stubbed out his cigarette, drank off his vodka, and continued.

"The fragments were brought to a..." (he coughed) ... "a special naval facility here in Astrakhan. The lead was melted off and the fragments revealed again. And that, Dimitriy Semenov, is where you come in. We want to analyse the fragments. Find out what they are made of. Test their qualities." Then he leaned over the table as if to share a confidence. "And perhaps," he said, "replicate those qualities."

Dimitriy felt simultaneously the thrill of scientific discovery and the repulsion of a lifelong pacifist. But curiosity got the better of him.

When he had rapidly gulped down one last vodka, the Admiral got to his feet.

"You'll see in the file. There's a bunch of Italian scientists, at Bologna University, who think they're onto something. But what they think they have found doesn't contradict what we have got. I will be waiting outside tomorrow morning at seven o'clock and will take you to the facility. Until tomorrow, comrade."

Dimitriy sat and watched as Ivanov threaded his way through the tables without any hint of drunkenness. That word, "comrade", again. When he was sure that the Admiral had gone, he picked up the file and hurried to his room.

✍

Ivanov was waiting for him on the hotel's esplanade in a long, low, sleek black limousine, complete with chauffeur. The Admiral was in his uniform, his gold brocaded cap on the seat beside him.

"Is this a Zil?" Dimitriy asked, as he got into the tobacco-fugged interior.

"The 4104," said the Admiral. "Including special triple-laminated glass protection against radiation. They should be collectors' items now, but they were built to last and the Navy is determined to keep its pool going until they start to fall to pieces."

He lit a cigarette.

"Did you read the file?"

"Of course I did, Admiral."

"And?"

"Did the Evenki see angels?"

"You saw the drawings," said Ivanov.

"I saw the drawings and they look to me like two angels fighting in the sky."

The Admiral looked through the smoked glass window for a few seconds.

"Do you believe in angels, Dimitriy Semenov?" he asked.

"No," said Dimitriy, "I don't. But what else can be made of those drawings? And the sounds; were they heavenly trumpets?"

"As I told you yesterday, we are trying to keep open minds," Ivanov said. "You have to remember that back in those times the Evenki were a primitive, superstitious people. When something they didn't understand happened, they ascribed it to their God, Ogdy."

"You don't think there was a conflict, then?"

"I don't know," said Ivanov. "Imagine if you were a primitive people and something massive exploded overhead, with a great flash of light and a boom, most probably, as the thing, whatever it was, broke the sound barrier. Wouldn't you extrapolate from what you knew? Battle, and noise?"

"And the heavenly trumpets?" asked Dimitriy.

Ivanov chuckled.

"That's what you call them, Dimitriy Semenov, but do you believe in heavenly trumpets?"

"Again, Admiral, my answer is no, of course. But what is the alternative explanation for those noises?"

Ivanov tutted.

"You are a scientist, aren't you? Because we don't know the answer doesn't mean that there isn't an answer. We just don't know it yet – and perhaps we'll never know it. What we do know is that we have three fragments of an unknown powerful material that seem to have fallen from the sky about the time of the Tunguska event. We can, and must, try to know as much about those fragments as possible, using science and scientific methods, and not basing our judgements on superstition and hearsay and eye-witness accounts from long ago."

"Of course," said Dimitriy, feeling suitably chastened.

The Admiral stubbed out his cigarette.

"We have arrived," he said.

✍

About five months after Dimitriy had started the job in Astra, Anastasia stopped making dinner for his return on Friday evenings. The first time she invented a diplomatic excuse. She told him she'd been feeling unwell all day, and he accepted the explanation unthinkingly. He made an omelette and ate alone in the kitchen, while Anastasia went off to bed. The following Friday, though, the new practice had been rationalised; she had realised, she said, that it was too late in the evening to eat a full-blown meal – better that he snacked or had a bowl of soup or a salad. Again, he accepted the explanation unthinkingly until, one Friday, when he came to bed, he found her weeping.

"What's up, my love? What's the matter?"

She rolled over to look at him and he saw that her eyes were puffed up.

"I just wished you'd tell me, that's all," she said.

"Tell you what?"

"About her, whoever she is."

"But there is no her," Dimitriy insisted.

Anastasia snorted.

"You can't hide it from me," she said. "I see the way you arrive back in Derbent saddened, as though you had been torn away from someone."

"It's just not true, Anastasia. There is no other woman."

"Is it a man, is that it? I'd understand, you know. I just wish you'd tell me."

"There's nothing to tell you, I swear!"

"Come on! Do you think I'm stupid? I see the way you can't wait to get back on Monday mornings."

"There's nobody, Anastasia, do you hear me? There's nobody!"

She rolled over and wept herself to sleep. He stared up at the ceiling for a long time, listening to her sobs as they slowly softened to sniffles and then to normal breathing. She was right, of course, about the symptoms. He was becoming steadily more obsessed. The weekends back home in Derbent were becoming a torment. But there was nobody else – that was where she was wrong.

✍

"Where are we?" Dimitriy asked.

"Astrakhan State Technology University," said Ivanov, putting on his cap and checking its position in the glass of the chauffeur's partition. "Come."

The Admiral led him through the low, glass-fronted entrance. Students milled about them like in any university. They seemed unfazed at the image of a uniformed Admiral threading a path through the crowd.

"Where are we going?"

"The Institute of Oil and Gas," said Ivanov. He led the way through the main administrative building and across the leafy campus to a nondescript red brick five-storey construction. They went in through rotating doors at the entrance and Ivanov led the way to a block of lifts. Dimitriy wondered if the fragments were kept in one of the Institute's laboratories but, if so, security seemed to be extraordinarily lax. When the lift came, they got in and the Admiral pushed the button for –2, but he kept his finger on the button a long time. There was a small camera in one corner of the roof of the lift. Ivanov turned to face it and gave a salute.

"What's up?" asked Dimitriy.

"Please forgive the cloak-and-dagger stuff," said the Admiral. "Until the Union collapsed, the Caspian Flotilla was based in Baku, but a lot of the command structure was kept within Russia itself, including here, in Astra. The Americans knew that, of course. Astra was just as much of a target as Baku. So, special facilities were built for the command structures, and that's where we are going now."

By then, the lift ought to have reached –2 level, but it felt as though it were still in motion. After several minutes of slow movement, the lift stopped, and the doors slid slowly open. In front of them were two armed guards. Behind the guards was a vast, brightly lit room. Though they clearly recognised him, Ivanov presented the guards with papers. Once these had been stamped, the soldiers stood aside and let them pass.

"It's quite a hike from here," said the Admiral.

"I admire your fortitude," said Dimitriy.

"Fortitude?"

"Your last cigarette was in the Zil, Admiral."

Ivanov stopped and stared at Dimitriy.

"Where did you do your military service, Dimitriy Semenov?" he asked.

Dimitriy blushed.

"I did military education whilst I was at university, Admiral. I only did six months' service after that."

Ivanov scowled.

"In a uniform?"

"No, Admiral. In a laboratory, mostly."

Ivanov nodded slowly.

"I thought so," he said. He sniffed scornfully, turned and began walking again.

The vast space was devoid of human activity but all around them were massive columns of material.

"Stockpiles?" asked Dimitriy.

"Thousands of men could live down here for years," said the Admiral. He snorted. "Thousands of years, probably."

On the far side of the underground hanger Ivanov led Dimitriy into a complex of smaller spaces. Each entrance was a double-doored air-pressurized port. Finally, they came to a double set of grey painted heavy steel doors that had been swung open.

"This is it," said the Admiral. "Your playroom; the laboratory."

They were greeted enthusiastically at the doors by the head of the scientific team, Fyodor Babikov, a beaming beanpole of a man wearing large tinted glasses. Ivanov left them together, promising to return at the end of the day. Babikov showed Dimitriy to the changing room. There were lockers, but no locks, and benches in the middle, with coat pegs above them. They scrubbed up together and then dressed up in classic surgical gear. When that was done, Babikov led Dimitriy into a small meeting room. The walls were lined with large blown-up photographs showing microscopic structures. Babikov gestured for him to sit down at a table and sat on the opposite side.

"What has Admiral Ivanov told you?" he asked.

"The basic story," said Dimitriy. "And I have read the file."

Babikov nodded.

"Good, good," he said. "And did he tell you about their effects?"

"About the blindness? Oh, yes."

"Well, there is that," said Babikov. "You know what they say, "Only the eagle may look into the sun." But you don't need to worry about that. We've rigged the lab in such a way that you simply cannot look directly at the fragments. They are housed in a recess facing away from the viewing window and you can only see them indirectly, either by using the mirrors we've installed, or by using the camera. Did Ivanov talk about any other effects?"

Dimitriy shook his head.

"No," he said. "Nothing else."

"I suppose he was afraid he might scare you off. The thing is, they seem to have a euphoric effect on some people, and that euphoria can become addictive."

"Euphoria, you say?"

"Yes, it depends on the person and for the time being is, like everything else, completely inexplicable and unmeasurable. There's nothing chemical about it and scans show nothing."

"How do you know this?"

"You are not the first expert we have drafted in, Dimitriy Semenov."

"Ah?"

"In fact, you are the third."

"The others?"

Babikov shook his head.

"They didn't last very long, I'm afraid. The first was here for just over a year. The second lasted almost three years."

"And where are they now?"

"Locked away," said Babikov.

"And you?" said Dimitriy.

"Nothing," said Babikov. "I have been here from the beginning. But, then, I don't spend hours in the viewing room."

Dimitriy nodded.

"All right," he said, curtly. "What else didn't Ivanov tell me?"

"Well," said Babikov, "there isn't a whole lot more to know."

"What do you mean?"

"We know very little."

"How long have the fragments been here?"

"Since 2008."

"And you have learned nothing? Honestly?"

Babikov grinned nervously.

"Honestly, very little." He stood up and pointed at the large blow-ups on the wall. "I'll tell you everything we know, but it won't take very long."

Dimitriy leaned back in his chair.

"Tell me," he said.

"We know they have properties, and powers. They have some sort of power to blind people, for example."

"Are we sure of that?"

"What do you mean?" asked Babikov.

"Well," said Dimitriy, "we've only had the one example, of the man down the pit, back in 1938. It could have been a stroke, couldn't it?"

Babikov shook his head and smiled ruefully.

"Unfortunately, there have been a few episodes since," he said.

"Here?" asked Dimitriy.

"Well, yes, "said Babikov. "People who didn't listen. People who didn't believe. An accident. A drunk."

"How many?"

"Enough for us to know that the fragments, if looked at directly, cause blindness in most animals."

"Reptiles? You've tried reptiles?"

Babikov nodded.

"And octopoda?"

"Oh, yes," said Babikov. "We've tried squid and octopus, if that's what you mean."

"Insects?"

Babikov sighed.

"We tried everything," he said. "They have the same effect on any sort of eye."

"All right," said Dimitriy. "Let's assume that these effects exist."

"But they do, I assure you, Dimitriy Semenov."

Dimitriy nodded.

"Then what do your instruments show?"

"Nothing. Absolutely nothing. Whatever this effect is, it is produced in a way undetectable to us and, please, don't ask whether we've checked our instruments. Of course we have. All of them! Whatever these powers are, they work on a spectrum unknown to us."

Dimitriy nodded again.

"What else?" he asked.

"The euphoria business."

"Can you be sure of that?"

"Scientifically, empirically," said Babikov, "no. Statistically, there must be a strong presumption."

"Two cases only? That's a tiny number. You can't presume anything from that."

Babikov smiled ruefully again.

"You are right, of course," he said. "Let me call it a hunch, then. Nothing more."

"Just two cases!"

"Two highly intelligent, balanced, reasonable scientists, both following a similar pattern of obsessiveness and then increasing episodes of manic euphoria, culminating in madness and confinement in clinics. I agree with you, Dimitriy Semenov. It could be sheer coincidence, but I think not."

Dimitriy nodded.

"What else?" he asked.

"We have found a way to manipulate them," said Babikov. "Only one metal may touch them – gold."

"Ah-ha!" said Dimitriy. "An extra-terrestrial element."

"Well," said Babikov. "That's only one theory about accessible gold on the earth's surface, as you know full well."

"I'm sorry, Babikov It was a poor attempt at a joke."

"Whatever, the point is that the only mineral that can touch the fragments is gold. All others melt away as they get near. Once we realised that, we had special gold implements made up that could be attached to the arms of the robots – that is the main way in which you will be working directly with the fragments."

"I understand," said Dimitriy. "But it is curious – gold being so malleable – like the lead in which they were encased."

"Everything about the fragments is curious," said Babikov. "Everything."

"What else do we know?"

Babikov shook his head in sudden exhaustion.

"The truth is, as I told you before, that nothing we know is really knowledge. It is, rather, knowledgeable ignorance. We know next to nothing, and that is all we know."

"Now you are beginning to talk in riddles. What I mean is, have you discovered other properties or powers?"

Babikov looked at Dimitriy for a few moments, as though he had been brought back from a reverie.

"I shall tell you," he said, "and then you'll understand. First, we cannot record any images of them. Nothing works; film, X-rays, electro-magnetic resonance imaging, transmission electron tomography... Whatever sort of imaging we have tried to use, nothing shows up. They are definitely there; we can see their reflection, but we can't capture them as images, and that means that we can only study the fragments themselves."

"What about microscopes?" asked Dimitriy.

"Lenses work," said Babikov. "But you cannot record what you are seeing."

"You mean you cannot draw them?"

"No, no," said Babikov. "They can be drawn, at least – hence all of these..." he waved at the drawings hanging on the walls around them. "Your predecessors' masterpieces."

"May I?" Dimitriy asked.

Babikov nodded.

Dimitriy stood up and walked around the room, studying the drawings.

"What sort of magnification are these? I mean, roughly."

"They vary," said Babikov, "but around five. Why?"

"I have an idea," said Dimitriy, "but I'll let you finish first."

He sat down again.

"Second," Babikov continued, "they are constantly levitating."

Dimitriy raised his eyebrows.

"Constantly?"

Babikov nodded.

"You'll see," he said. "They are always hovering, never touching any surface."

"Then they have access to some sort of energy?"

"Well," I think so, "but we can detect nothing."

"What about when they were brought here?"

"In the solidified lead, you mean?" said Babikov.

Dimitriy nodded.

"That was well before my time. I don't think the Army realised what it had taken on at that point. I suppose the fragments might somehow have created a space for themselves in the lead. But I don't know. There were no notes about that."

"Magnetism?"

Babikov shook his head.

"We thought of that, of course. But, no..."

"Light?"

Babikov smiled and shook his head.

"Believe me, Dimitriy Semenov, we have tried and tested many ideas – all fruitlessly, so far."

"I understand what Admiral Ivanov was getting at now."

"Getting at?" said Babikov.

"We were talking about scientific method. He said we don't know the answer yet, and perhaps we'll never know it."

✍

That very first time Dimitriy came back from Astrakhan she knew already, he realised – or, rather, she suspected already. Something had happened. He couldn't entirely hide it from her. For a start, his decision was a fait accompli. He hadn't asked her before deciding; he couldn't. She asked about the work. He told her he had signed a declaration and was now bound by the Official Secrets Act but, he insisted, as he saw her recoil, it wasn't what she thought.

"What is it, then?" she asked.

"Something unimaginable," he replied.

"I thought we were going to decide together," she said.

"For reasons I cannot reveal, my dearest, I had to decide on the spot. Believe me," he continued, "I took the decision in our best interests; you, me, Andrei, Sasha..."

That was a lie, a knowing lie. He watched with a sort of inner fascination as she first processed what he had said, and then accepted it, nodding her head slowly.

"Of course," she said. "You must have done."

"Come with me to Astrakhan, Anastasia," he said, knowing full well what the answer had to be.

"I can't, Dimitriy. You know I can't. My job, my family, the children's schools..."

And he, in his turn, nodded his head slowly, faking the slow dawn of comprehension. Of course, she couldn't come to Astrakhan with him; he had always known that – but he had to go. He just had to.

✍

Dimitriy listened patiently as Babikov listed the other properties his scientific team had so far noted. The seven fragments were identical in their appearance. Each was a convex oblong, about nine centimetres long by five centimetres wide. From a distance, they seemed to be golden in colour but, the stronger the magnification, the less colour there was. From very close up they seemed neither transparent nor invisible, but completely colourless yet somehow iridescent. The fragments' default position was to hover vertically in an overlapping formation, like the defensive *testudo* Roman legionaries had sometimes adopted with their shields. If the fragments were separated, they immediately moved back to the *testudo* formation. Once again, Dimitriy studied the drawings on the walls.

"So, what's this big idea of yours?" said Babikov.

"*Lepidoptra*," said Dimitriy.

"Butterflies?" said Babikov, momentarily confused. "We'd thought of fish scales, but *lepidoptra*?"

"In appearance they seem also similar to fish scales, it is true, but what makes me think of the *lepidoptra* scales is their photonic architecture. I studied them for my degree in Moscow – that's why I know. Butterfly scales have complex three-dimensional periodic lattices that cause the iridescence, and I just wonder whether some similar effect is not at work with these scales – and they are scales, Babikov, aren't they? They're not just fragments."

Babikov blushed. He took off his glasses and polished the lenses to win himself some time.

"Rear Admiral Ivanov doesn't like such talk, and I think he's right. We shouldn't leap ahead of ourselves."

"But are we?" said Dimitriy. "We know – or we assume – that these fragments fell to earth in June 1908, right?"

Babikov shook his head.

"No, no," he said. "We know only that they were found in the area where that event occurred."

"But even Ivanov himself gave me to understand he thought there was a connection."

"And so there may be," said Babikov. "But he doesn't want us to start wandering off into anthropomorphism, zoomorphism and personification. We know only what we know. The rest is idle speculation. If the Admiral hadn't given you the file, you wouldn't have started thinking along these lines."

Dimitriy smiled.

"What lines, Fyodor Babikov? "What lines are those?"

Babikov remained silent.

"All right," said Dimitriy. "I'm sure you have similar thoughts. These so-called fragments are themselves a fragment that fell off something much larger, probably during that 'event' of 1908 – a wing, maybe?"

"Enough!" said Babikov, waving his hands in front of him. "It is time you saw them for yourself. Are you ready?"

✍

It was in February, just over a year after his first visit to Astrakhan, that Anastasia put the ultimatum to him. He couldn't blame her. The Christmas period had been disastrous. Derbent was bitterly cold and the streets were littered with filthy snow and slush where the gritters had passed. He couldn't wait to get back to Astra. He was constantly irritable with the children and mostly morosely silent with her. He felt dreadful. He needed to be back, to be back with *them*, in their presence. When the holidays were finally over, and he had been leaving for the Ekranoplan, she had said, "I can't say I'm sorry to see you go, Dimitriy. You have to get a grip of yourself. Whatever is going in in Astrakhan, you have to put a stop to it. It is ruining you and us."

That had been January. If anything, his behaviour had got worse over the following month. Then, one Friday evening in late February, she took a final initiative. Part of him felt that she was absolutely right. That part of him felt so sorry for her and for Andrei and Sasha. But another part of him just didn't care. Or, rather, it only cared about *them*, the scales, and being with them.

There was, he saw, a deliberate symmetry in the situation. The children were in bed. The classical music radio channel was on, and she'd even put a lit candle on the laid dinner table. It was the first time in a long time that she had cooked a meal for his return, but there was no wine; he hadn't thought to bring a bottle from Astra. Why would he have done? Over the meal, they talked about Sasha and Andrei, and about her family, and the weather. And then, at the end of the meal, Anastasia took Dimitriy's hands across the table.

"Dimitriy," she said, "I am so very sorry, but I just can't take this anymore."

"What do you mean?" he blustered.

She smiled and put a finger to her lips to hush him.

"You know what I mean, Dimitriy. I have spoken to you so many times."

He nodded. She was right.

"So, now what?" he asked.

"I'd like you to resign from your job in Astrakhan."

"But how would we..." he began, blustering again.

She shook her head and smiled wistfully.

"We were fine before, Dimitriy. We'll be fine again."

"But my work is important."

She smiled again.

"I'm sure it is, Dimitriy but, please, let somebody else do it."

He burst into tears.

"I can't, dear Anastasia," he wept. "I just can't."

"But what do you mean, Dimitriy? What is it that is exercising such a hold over you? If it is not a mistress, then what is it? Drugs? Is that it? You can tell me, Dimitry. Please."

"It's none of those," he blurted. "But I can't tell you. I just can't tell you."

"Of course you can tell me! I promise I won't tell anybody else."

"I have signed the Official Secrets Act, Anastasia. I can't!"

"I promise I won't tell anybody else. Who could I tell, anyway?"

Dimitriy shook his head.

"All right," said Anastasia, her tone hardening. "If you won't tell me, that's it."

"What do you mean?"

"I'll leave you, Dimitriy. This simply cannot continue."

He sniffed and rubbed his eyes on the backs of his hands. His shoulders sagged.

"All right," he said finally. "I'll tell you."

So, he told her. He told her about his second meeting with Ivanov, and the file about the 1908 Tunguska event and Kulik's 1938 discovery. He told her about his first entry into the thick-walled, steel-shuttered underground space where the plate glass and mirrors had been set up to enable scientists to gaze indirectly on the fragments. And he told her about his indescribable feelings of ecstasy, of joy, when he was in the presence of the angelic scales, and how the obsessive feeling had grown until it had now overwhelmed all other considerations. He told her about the steel shutter inside the space housing the scales which Babikov had to operate every day so that Dimitriy could at least no longer gaze upon the angelic fragments, and the way he, Dimitriy, had to be dragged out of the space by orderlies and given sedation before he could be convinced to return to his hotel room in the evenings.

Anastasia sat patiently through his explanation.

"All right," she said when he had finished. "Let's just suppose everything you've told me is true. Where do you think this will all end?"

"I don't know," said Dimitriy. "All I know is that I must be there."

She shook her head.

"No, Dimitriy," she said. "You must stop this nonsense. You can stop it, you know."

Dimitriy wept again.

"I can't," he said. "It's just stronger than me."

Anastasia shook her head once more.

"If you go back to Astrakhan on Monday, then I will be moving out – with Andrei and Sasha."

"But you can't!" Dimitriy blurted. "The children need their father."

"Don't be a fool," snapped Anastasia. "The children haven't had their father for over a year now."

"Where will you go? Your parents?"

Anastasia nodded.

Good, thought Dimitriy, with a sense of wonder at his own callousness.

✍

Anastasia didn't come to the doorstep with him. He'd kissed her on the head as she lay in bed, but she didn't move, though he sensed she was awake.

"Goodbye, Anastasia," he said. "I still love you, you know. And I'm sorry."

He locked the front door and walked through the slushy remains of the snow to the Ekranoport. As the Caspian Queen approached Astra the sea became agitated and the sky darkened. A strong wind blew up and Dimitriy could feel that the pilot was struggling with the controls. He was relieved when the craft slowed down and started its long taxi up the relative calm of the Reka Bakhtemir channel. The Admiral was waiting for him as he got off.

"What's up, Admiral?" he asked.

"Something's going on," said Ivanov. "We've been hearing noises in the sky."

"Heavenly trumpets?" said Dimitriy.

"Noises in the sky," Ivanov repeated

"What did those noises sound like?" asked Dimitriy.

"Da, da," said the Admiral. "Like the descriptions the Evenki natives gave in 1908."

"Could it be?" asked Dimitriy. "Could it be?"

"Be what?" said Ivanov, drawing on his cigarette. The sky flashed and a long roll of thunder sounded. "And we've been having strange weather. Just look at those clouds."

Dimitry looked up at the dark, corrugated formation hanging heavy and low over the city. Thunder rolled and reverberated above and around them.

"And the fragments," Ivanov continued, "have started to oscillate."

"Oscillate?" said Dimitriy.

"All right," said the Admiral, flicking away his cigarette and blowing out smoke. "They seem to have become agitated."

"Agitated? I can't wait to look."

Ivanov lit another cigarette and leaned against the Zil.

"I'm not sure that's a good idea, Dimitriy Semenov. They are no longer stable."

"What do you mean? I've got to see them. You know that."

"Pull yourself together," said the Admiral.

"It's just that I've got to see them. Surely you have understood that?"

Ivanov lit another cigarette. The sky flashed and flickered. He looked up and waiting for the roll of thunder.

"This is not normal, Dimitriy Semenov," he said. "Something is going on."

"You think this weather is related somehow?"

"I don't know. But the scales have become potentially dangerous. It's almost as though they are trying to escape."

"Escape?"

"Barikov tells me they have melted through the gold lining on the roof of the cell."

"No!" said Semenov. "We must hurry."

Ivanov drew deeply on his cigarette.

"Take my advice, Dimitriy Semenov," he said. "Go back to Derbent. The return Ekranoplan will be leaving very soon. Go back to your wife and children. Maybe it's nothing. We'll see. Come back tomorrow."

"There's no point," said Dimitriy. "They've left me."

Ivanov nodded.

"Because of this?" he asked. "Because of your..."

"Yes," said Dimitriy. "Because of the..."

Ivanov nodded and drew on his cigarette. They heard the distinctive whine as the Caspian Queen's jet engines started slowly to turn.

"Go back," he urged.

"I can't!" Dimitriy sobbed. "I must see them."

They watched as the gang planks were drawn away and the aft and forward doors closed. The sky flashed again as an orange-clad dockworker cast off the mooring ropes. When the ropes had been entirely wound back on board the Ekranoplan, the jet engines began to roar, and the Caspian Queen sailed slowly out into the Volga. Then they heard the familiar howl as the captain increased the power and taxied the ship away down towards the sea channel.

Ivanov flicked away his cigarette, then opened the door of the Zil.

"Come," he said, "we'd better go to the Institute."

✍

"Anastasia," called her mother. "Come. Come quickly."

Anastasia pulled the plug in the kitchen sink, wiped her hands on her apron and joined her parents in the living room. They were watching a Russian television channel and the news bulletin had just started. Sasha was playing on the floor. The newsreader was halfway through the headlines. A train had crashed just outside Vladivostok. The President had visited a new LPG facility at the port of Murmansk...

"What is it, mama?"

"Ssshhh," said her mother, "you'll see in a moment."

The newsreader finished the headlines. Anastasia's mother turned the volume up.

"And now we go back to our main news item this evening. Reports are coming in of a massive explosion on the northern outskirts of the city of Astrakhan, at the premises of the State Technology University. The explosion is said to have occurred in an underground research facility situated beneath the University's parkland. As can be seen from these helicopter images, the explosion has created a deep crater, and the blast wave has flattened trees and buildings in all directions. Astrakhan's hospitals are already overflowing with burns victims, many of them students, and many of them reportedly blinded by the extremely bright light. The police and the fire service are searching for victims in the collapsed buildings. Among those already confirmed as being among the dead are the director of the Caspian Flotilla's scientific outreach programme, Rear Admiral Anatoly Ivanov, and the head of the Astrakhan State Technology University's Oil and Gas Institute research programme, Fyodor Babikov. An acclaimed Moscow State University materials scientist, Dimitriy Semenov, who had joined the research team from Derbent, is missing, presumed dead."

Pictures of the three men flashed up on the screen for a few moments.

"That's Daddy," said Sasha.

Anastasia nodded tearfully.

"Yes, darling," she said.

"We're now heading over to our Astrakhan Oblast correspondent, Igor Davidov," the newsreader continued. "Good evening, Igor. What can you tell us?"

"Well, good evening, Viktor, and good evening to all our viewers. The situation here in Astrakhan is still very confused, but we're gradually getting a clearer picture. According to a Russian Federation Navy spokesman, the Institute's research team was at work on a new form of energy generation when the explosion occurred. Eyewitness accounts speak of a column of fire and smoke rising high up into the air. But others report that some sort of winged craft was seen at the top of the column, raising concerns that this may have been an aerial aggression of some sort."

"Can you tell us anything more about that, Igor?"

"The Navy are denying it. They say it was an accident and that the blast was underground and did not come from a bomb or any other sort of attack. But some eyewitnesses seem to contradict that account. I spoke a few minutes ago to one of those eyewitnesses, Irina Yeshevsky."

The image showed an older lady, her head wrapped in a scarf. Her glasses were dirty, and she wore a grim expression.

"Could you tell us what happened?" asked the reporter.

"There were these noises," said the woman.

"Noises?"

She nodded.

"Like trumpets," she said. "And the weather was playing up. You must have seen them clouds, no? Then there was a huge flash and a short while later a big roar and I saw a lot of smoke and fire rushing upwards to the north of the city, upwards into the sky. Very bright, it was."

"And then?"

"And then I saw something high up above, like a huge plane, and the fire and the cloud seemed to meet up with it."

"Meet up with it?"

"Yes."

"And what did this plane look like?"

"Well, it was flashing gold in the sun, and it had big wings and ..."

She hesitated.

"Go on."

"Well, they seemed to flap."

"To flap? Can you be sure of that?"

"Yes, yes. I'm not making it up, you know."

"And what do you think it was."

"Well," said the old lady, scowling with thought. "If I didn't know better, I'd say it was an angel..."

Through the thin glass of the living room window, Anastasia Sementova and her family heard the unmistakeable howl of the evening Ekroplan, back from Astrakhan, back to the City of the Forty Heroes, the Gate of Gates.

✍ ✍ ✍

Satyajit Ray's Beard or the Lack Thereof
—
Abhijato Sensarma

Satyajit Ray's Beard or the Lack Thereof

"And why would there be multiple Earths in the same universe?" the counsellor asks me. She's not *my* counsellor — and this isn't my world. But she still has the same pair of spectacles resting on the bridge of her nose, and she peers through them to look at me. She must have been confused at the start of today's discourse. Usually, we talk about my marriage being in the wrong place, not my body being on the wrong planet.

I slip forward on the sofa. The woman sitting beside me looks at me with concern — but now that she's out of my line of sight, I can think better. It took me some time to accept the fact that she's my wife in this world. She has a shaved head here, but what truly took me by surprise was the fact that we were sleeping in the same bed when we woke up. And when I told her I shouldn't be there, she looked at me with an expression of love for me which I did not know she still allowed herself to reveal.

When I first came here, I did not know what to expect — in many ways, I still don't. But my professional life's turned out to be the same as it's always been. I'm still a quantum engineering professor. I'm still working on teleportation. And I still *feel* like myself — I'm a resident of my own mind, at the very least. But there're two big differences in this world that set it apart from mine.

"If the shape of the universe is flat enough, as evidence seems to suggest, then it's constantly expanding." My hands spread outwards in front of me as I start my monologue. It's a habit I have. "And if molecules are allowed to arrange themselves in every way they can over infinite space, they'll eventually run out of unique combinations. Patterns will start repeating — and the same worlds will arise in different parts of the universe."

The counsellor nods again. She steals the slightest of glances at my wife between looking up from her notebook and looking at me — "Have you considered the possibility ... that this may be a reaction to your wife having cancer?"

I bend my head sideways, confused. Couples therapy has never been my favourite part of the weekend, but neither has the counsellor ever been this wrong. She thinks I'm going crazy.

My wife's bald head steals my attention more than her eyes. But oh, her eyes do read of pity. I don't want any.

"*My* wife isn't dying from cancer." I say it with an emphasis on my baritone. It sounds harsh, almost dismissive. *You're in denial*, the counsellor seems to think. But once again, she doesn't say anything. She simply brings up her arms to the handrest on her seat and leans on it, thinking of how to approach this case.

Just then, the alarm clock in her room goes off. She snaps her fingers and mutters "*Turn est.*" A switch moves by itself, and the alarm stops ringing. "Time's up, so that will be all for today. I think we're making real progress here so far. Same time, next week?"

She smiles at me, but I retain my nonchalance. I stare at the portrait of Satyajit Ray in the background — he's the most revered filmmaker in Bengali cinema. But here, he has a beard akin to a Tagore, whereas Ray was famously clean-shaven in my own world. This isn't my home. And this isn't the Ray whose films I've grown up watching.

The portrait shouldn't even be there — in my world, the counsellor hung her framed diploma on this wall, so that it would be facing us during the session. But in the strange new place I find myself in, the diploma's on the other side of the wall, where Ray's portrait should have been. It's a reversal which doesn't say much, except that this isn't my world to inhabit.

I look at the woman who claims to be my wife. As a way of compensation for my harshness, she says to the counsellor, "Thank you, Doctor." Then, she mutters something under her breath. I don't catch the spell this time around. She's intentionally using the tone she always does when she's cross with me. And before I can do anything about it, a white beam of energy envelops her. By the time the energy dissipates, so does she. I'll find her at home again.

"Umm," I say, looking around the room. I run my fingers over the leather on the sofa with my left hand, and run the other hand across my hair. "I guess ... I'll just walk back home."

I nod awkwardly at the counsellor and pat my thighs before getting up. She looks at me with concern that brims over to amusement. She doesn't say anything, of course — but she's only human.

The counsellor's the least of my concerns as I walk down the stairs and make my way onto the road. The *autorickshaws* and taxis converge in the middle of the four-way intersection, pausing for a moment when the signal opens for the other side. Soon, their turn comes as well. I stand and stare at them for a while, until all the vehicles I tried to keep track of have disappeared out of sight. There isn't too much of a difference between the public transportation of the Kolkata I know and the one I'm in right now, except for the fact that all vehicles hover above the ground here. They have no wheels, but they do have drivers and an automated gear shift technique that does not require the assistance of hands.

I've learned about it on the Internet, which is no less fascinating or abusive than the one I know from my own planet. I'm a product from before the World Wide Web's time, but the evolution of science seems to have followed a less stringent path on this world, where magical spells do a lot of what science and maths account for in mine. I don't like this place.

It's been less than twenty-four hours since I found myself in this world, but in that time, I've come to understand that the most commonly used spell is the one which helps in transportation. People don't use it all the time, and prefer using public vehicles when they can — it's akin to not taking a helicopter every time you want to cross the street, I guess. But the spells used here are strange, as spells have always been. They're spelled in Latin, as well. What *is* the one for transportation, though?

I try saying it out loud. "Trans — transvec — *transvectio* — "

And just as I pronounce the spell — it's the correct one, it seems — I find myself disintegrating. It's a strange sensation, and I would think about it more if not for the fact that my mental facilities seem to be incapacitated. When I feel complete again, with my senses and my cognitive abilities returning, the first thought I have is — "What on Earth?"

It's an ironic choice of words considering my situation. I find myself looking straight at Satyajit Ray's bearded portrait again. According to the *Basic Dictionary of Magic* — whose online website I accessed yesterday — one's always transported to the place they're thinking about at the time of saying the spell. Using this spell effectively is an acquired habit.

I look down, and there is the counsellor again, peering over her spectacles and straining her neck with curiosity no longer censored by the hours she's being paid for. I see a notepad on her lap. She's probably filing away the minutes of today's session with us before the next client arrives.

"Hello ... What may I do for you?" She tries to wear a smile on her face, but her lips twitch back to a more neutral position.

I chuck my head to the right and smile, embarrassed at this intrusion of mine. "I've just transported myself to the wrong place when I intended to go back home. You see, I was thinking about your place instead of mine, and I'm new to this magic business, so I didn't realise what would happen if I said *transvectio* — "

And just then, I can't feel my toes again. I realise what's going to happen next — *I've spoken the spell, haven't I?* But before I can think too much about the nuances of transporting for the second time in as many minutes, I'm no longer able to feel my thoughts either. It's serene, almost meditative, to not carry the worries of these worlds on my shoulders.

But when my feet touch the ground again, I throw up. It's on a familiar rug — the one I brought back home after spending a year in Switzerland working on the effects of extreme altitudes on my teleportation machine. The machine never worked. And in this world, it doesn't need to.

"Hey," I hear the familiar voice say. It's my wife's, even if it's mellowed down now. Probably because of the cancer. And also, because her husband seems to have gone crazy.

I look up at her. She's in her robes, getting ready for a bath. But before I can tell her anything — or apologise as a way of coming to terms with the place that is going to be my home for the rest of my life — I feel my eyes closing. I didn't even say a spell this time. *Where am I going now?*

But before I can take in my new surroundings, my face hits the floor. The first — and last — thought I have here is that my nose is going to hurt like hell when I wake up again.

✍

On opening my eyes, I see the roof above my head. I can still hear the public vehicles making their way past our home on this main road of the city. I never liked this place, even though the apartment itself is fine. Furnished at the time of purchase too. It's just that the commotion of the bazaar and the cars have never been to my liking. On the other hand, my wife thought the familiar sirens and rhythmic honks which compose this room's overtones would give me comfort when I came back home after the uncertainty of conducting experiments at my laboratory. I didn't think it would help, but over time, the sounds of the street have indeed turned meditative for me.

I find a reflection of my life in the taxis which pick up their passengers below at inflated rates. You can bargain, you can curse, and you can go anywhere you want — but at the end of the day, the taxi always drops you off at home. You've seen the sights of the city, yet there's the same old bed you need to sleep on. Beside a woman you loved once, but now can't bear to touch.

She realises I'm awake, though, and moves into my field of vision. I still don't want to touch her, because she isn't mine to have, and she isn't mine to love. But even if she were, would I want to? I feel uncomfortable about the realisation that she's a mortal — in both this world, and the one I've come from.

Before I can grasp at the finer ends of this chain of thought, I'm brought back to reality by a sudden pang of physical discomfort. My eyes look down, and I can see the bridge of my nose — it's certainly not where it should be. It's bent way too much towards my right. It's on the verge of being numb, but isn't, which makes the pain intolerable now that my senses are fully returning.

This wife moves her fingers and says a spell which does not penetrate the ringing sound in my ears. But the sound eventually dissipates, and as it does so, I feel my nose align itself properly. It almost twitches — no, it *jumps* back into its place.

I want to move away from her, for no fault of her own. She reminds me of my own wife too much — the one with whom disagreements have turned into silent nights. But even now, when she seems as foreign to me as she's ever been, I cannot stop admiring her. She always was the more tenacious of us. During separation or a bout with cancer, how does she remain the pleasant one?

She looks at me now with a love in her eyes I did not know I'd been missing. A love which is unconditional and comes out in moments of solidarity that have not yet turned into gestures born out of obligation.

But I cannot allow myself to reciprocate the feeling, even if I feel a tinge of heartache. For, as much as I want to reach out now, and brush my hands against her hardened cheeks, she still isn't mine to love. So, I push my arms against the surface I'm lying on, attempting to get back up.

"No, you must rest. Have you forgotten about that time we went to Darjeeling and you transported twice in a minute?" The voice lets out a laugh, but she doesn't see it through. I've seen her do this before, but I realise now why she does it. We've hurt each other too much, you see, and expressing ourselves has become a luxury. A laugh about the good old times has long been replaced by a few more moments of silence in my world.

"What happened to me? Am I a serial fainter in this world?" The weather's always been oppressive in this part of the country during the summers.

"You've got the Paralysis Syndrome, or have you forgotten that as well?" she asks. I shoot her a look. *I never knew*, I would like to tell her, but it wouldn't help.

Her head bows down as a way of resignation. "Your heredity means you can't teleport yourself like the rest of us can. You can only do it twice a day. You get quite tired otherwise. You pass out, like you did today."

I try to nod, but my head doesn't seem to be able to lift itself from the pillow for now. However, I do seem to recollect a stray line from the *Dictionary of Magic*'s entry about the subject. Something about people being born with a rare variation of the 24th pair of chromosomes, the ones that grant humans their ability to interact with magic. A pair which — in my world — is considered to lead to deformities and death rather than magical abilities.

"I … I really might not be who you think I am."

She places a hand on her temple and looks away. "The mosquitoes are going to start entering the room again — let me shut the windows. *Prope.*" And on cue, the windows move inwards, as if they're intoxicated by a breeze blowing out of the room. The illusion of normalcy is shattered when the latches attached to the bottoms of the windows pick themselves up and lock them into their positions on the windowsills. Estranged or not, my wife remains cool across realms.

And right then, the first lines of Rabindra Sangeet burst through our closed windows, drowning out the noise of the receding vehicles as the last strains of sunlight drain away and the artificial lights take over. *"Ami chini go chini tomake, ogo bideshini." I know you, oh, I do, foreigner.*

Ah yes, I do. She's going to be my life now — there's no escape from it, and somewhere deep inside, I don't want there to be any. It will take time to learn this world's spells, perhaps, and it will take time to convince the counsellor that I was truly having a nervous breakdown about my wife's cancer today. But things aren't as bad with my wife here as they are back home. Our time together will be curtailed, but maybe I can learn to love her again all the same.

"Did I ever stop loving you?" I ask her, as a way of enquiring about the work I would need to put in to have a better relationship with her.

She shoots me another look. But I've always been this way, asking questions about love and existence while lying on the bed with a broken nose, if only figuratively. So, she answers, "No. As a matter of fact, ever since my diagnosis, you've loved me more than you ever have."

I try to nod, but it ends up looking like an awkward twitch of the head. She understands, though, and she laughs. For the first time in months, I'm able to smile with her. Oh, how I've missed that feeling of having someone there for me. The baggage of death takes precedence over marital discontent, I realise.

"Why does my nose ... feel normal?"

"I fixed it. It's the first spell you ever taught me. Transportation helped us get away from either of our parents if they saw us when they weren't supposed to. You always landed on your nose whenever you fell unconscious. And I was always there for you. To fix your nose. Or just fix your hair."

So, in this world, I did find a way of escaping her parents. A less painful way than jumping out of her window from the first floor and breaking a bone in my leg that one time, for sure.

"Does this help you remember anything?" she asks.

"It does," I reply, remembering the exuberance of her youth — and mine — with a fondness I didn't think my marriage would still entail. "But then ... it doesn't." She sighs.

I've never believed in karma. Neither did I ever believe in magic before I saw it with my eyes. Perhaps this mystical experience of love I don't deserve is karma repaying itself for things I've done in lives I cannot remember. I would like to confess my sins to her, tell her how I've mistreated her.

But before I can, my wife rests her hands on my forehead. "You've become very tired because of this ordeal. Sleep now, and I'll sleep alongside you. Hopefully, you'll be in your senses when we wake up tomorrow. *Somnus.*"

And I feel myself drifting away again. I slip into oblivion, akin to how I've felt while teleporting before. But this time, I'm not reappearing to a different part of the world. My mind merely guides me to a world of my own. I feel a comfort I haven't felt for a long time now — the comfort of falling asleep next to someone you love.

✑

"So, you believe you're from another dimension?" the doctor asks. I nod and look around the room. I see laminated certificates hanging where Satyajit Ray's portrait should be hanging. The portrait occupies the space on the wall right behind me. If I didn't know better, I would have thought the counsellor had just exchanged our seats as a way of giving the two of us a 'new perspective'.

But when I turn around to look at the portrait, Mr. Ray's likeness hangs up there without a beard on the man's face, as if it's a joke. His beard's the most iconic part of his appearance — and this world doesn't even have that. Alongside the fact that it believes magic exists only in escapist novels and ancient scriptures.

"Umm, yes, I do." I don't put in too much effort into my assertion, because I'm truly not interested in this session. This counsellor isn't the one I've been intimate with about my Paralysis Syndrome. And this wife isn't the one I've grown so close to because of her terminal cancer. She looks much younger sitting beside me now, untouched by fate or fear.

She loves me in this world as well. But she doesn't have terminal cancer — yet — and this makes her more placid, less lively, than my wife. The man who's actually married to her was the one who filed for divorce. On the other hand, my affection for her has turned platonic with the changing of worlds. I would like to embrace her, and apologise for the sins of another man, but I love her only as my confidant from a different life. It wouldn't be fair to love her any more than that.

She brought me in for an emergency counselling session today. She checked my temperature and cooked me a good meal first, even though I've become the one to do that in my own marriage back home. She cares for me, yes, she does — yet, as much as I care for this woman too, I can't seem to love her.

"Have you considered that this could be related to the fact that the two of you want a divorce?"

"Ah," I say. "It's the farthest thing from what I want, though."

My wife shoots me a look. "You're the one who wanted it the most."

I get up from my place, and throw out my hands — it's a sign of desperation in this world too, I hope. "I'm sorry, but this is all too much for me. Transvectio." I stand in my place, but nothing happens.

I'd forgotten. I don't have the chromosomes I need to perform magic in this world.

The counsellor bends her eyebrow at me. "I've been learning a bit of Latin to cope with all this stress," I inform her. It's a trick I picked up at school, whenever anyone caught me practicing spells in an empty classroom or in a corner of the playground — I've never been good at magic. The excuse usually failed to protect me from the ridicule of my classmates when I was younger, but now, it helps me slip out of my unsuccessful attempt at teleportation.

I look around this familiar room set up in an alien manner for what I hope is the last time. "I think I need a break. I'm unable to cope with the pressure, and I'd appreciate some space rather than being dragged down for therapy to this office. My apologies, I'll have to get going now." I do my best impression of storming out of the room and down the stairs of the large hospital. Theatrics, it turns out, will always convince others to leave an upset man alone, whether it has something to do with magical civilisations or not.

Some use the elevator, of course, but it's a relief to see most others walking beside me on the stairs. In my world, the presence of magic means people teleport themselves to the other end of a long journey in a matter of minutes. Everyone except for people like me, that is. On the other hand, everyone here needs to sit down and let a good old engine — and a decent driver — do the work instead.

As jarring as this reality has been to me so far, including the experiences with my very own wife, the biggest incentive for staying in this world has been the respect engineers are given here. In the society I've grown up in, engineering as a career has always been treated akin to a punchline. The electricity plants that power most of the world, the equipment that makes surgeries easier for Medical Wizards, and of course, the transportation that helps the less biologically gifted ones among us — they're only possible with the help of scientists like us. But it's the Wizards who are at the helm of affairs. They're the most influential politicians and academics. They get to decide what others are known as. Many books have called the people of my profession an 'afterthought', replaceable tools only there to help the Wizards accomplish their goals. But society wouldn't be able to hold itself together if our kind disappeared overnight.

This world, on the other hand, designs its fervour around supernatural elements of a different kind. I see the people praying in makeshift temples and on the rickshaws that carry models of their deities wherever they go. Not being treated as a dispensable labourer comforts me in a way I've never felt about my professional identity before. I wouldn't mind staying here — but I can't.

I've fought for a semblance of respect towards my profession for the longest time. It's the reason I started experimenting with manufacturing a teleportation device using scientific apparatus rather than relying on the genetic predispositions of the population. I've found what I've sought for all my life — but this isn't earned.

So, I make my way to the most familiar place I know after my home — the University I work at. The only difference being that here, the campus isn't guarded by magical sharks floating in the air.

Rather, the University's guarded solely by the same people I've become good acquaintances with back in my realm. It is closed off to students at this time of the evening, but when I flash my ID at one of the guards — a card which surprisingly does not morph itself into a miniature replica of its holder in this world — he lets me in. "Welcome, Professor," the man says, and steps aside.

I make my way up to the second floor. Room 616. *Here it is. I stand in front of the door for a moment, then another, and then another. It's on the last beat that I have to remind myself once more of the nature of human existence here. You've got to turn your own door handles in this world.*

I enter the room and switch on the lights. Here lies the machine. It looks the same. It's cylindrical, with a hollow, secured chamber in the middle of it large enough to fit a human — the place where the person must enter if they're to teleport. This machine remains in its prototype stage, just like mine.

The most essential discovery I've made exists here too, in the form of a neutrino battery on top of the machine, powered by an alloy of platinum and plutonium. A 'radiation cover' ensures the battery is shielded and the machine can be dealt with in normal clothing. As a matter of abundant precaution, I slip on the gloves lying on the counter.

I proceed to open the chamber and look at the controls when I realise these gloves are not infused with any magical spells. This means that they aren't really protecting me from any radiation-related accidents. But I carry on. A preliminary inspection should not take long.

The machine looks the same on the exterior as mine. The keypad has an extensive entry system which allows for transportation to different parts of the Universe, even though this is an ambitious addition to the machine's infrastructure. It's purely theoretical, because it cannot function. Mine didn't, at least.

I pick up a screwdriver and unshackle the interior of the machine. Another cursory glance reveals what I've been suspecting ever since I entered this lab. The prototype, it turns out, is indeed a bit different looking here — on the inside! *I shift my focus away from the similarities and study the differences between my device and the one this Earth's version of me has created.*

I put on my protection kit and start with my work. I note down observations in my favourite notebook — this world's version of it, anyway. Blueprints lie all around my corner of the lab, and my suspicions are confirmed.

He's created one half of the machine, with his work delivering solutions to the long-drawn questions I've asked myself over the years during its construction. His configurations reveal things like how the neutrino battery should be wired to the quantum transportation engine, and whether I should add a circuit breaker before or after the feed from the electronic transmitted attached to the keypad is integrated into the CPU (before, of course, but only with a special modification to the industry model to make it compatible with my work). His notebook combines with my knowledge to show me the full picture, and thus, I can now complete this Teleporter to make it a functional one.

The switch must have happened yesterday, under the improbable conditions across both ends of the Universe where similar worlds created two polar opposites of machines which also had perfect compatibility with each other. The alignment of similar cellular structures did the rest, and the ambiguity in the positions of supercharged, hyperactive atoms altered the probabilities of their positions. This simultaneously attempted operation of compatible halves led to some sort of superimposition of the machine and its contents before the eventual separation. During this time, our consciousnesses must have switched — because while my body feels the same, it's lost the power to perform magic here — so it's likely his body. My counterpart probably has my former abilities, under this hypothesis.

But again, it's just that — a hypothesis. I can't remember for the life of me how I ended up tucked in bed on this world. I was a mess when I woke up in the morning. Maybe it's just the machine that does it. All I know is that the rest of my life seems perfectly stored in my mental faculties.

Such a freak accident probably won't occur again — neither the transportation, nor the memory loss — but it doesn't need to. I now know how to configure this machine, and make it work from a single location. If I do manage to work things out soon, I can go home again, and help my other self out too.

Let's see how I go about rescuing both versions of myself now — and inventing intra-dimensional teleportation along the way.

✍

When I open my eyes, I expect to feel her palm on my forehead again, ready to put me to sleep if I haven't come around to what she thinks are my regular senses. Sunlight is peering in through the windows, which are open again, and carrying in the familiar hum of the vehicles during office hour.

I slide up in my bed and feel the sour taste in my mouth. I'll need to brush my teeth. What was the spell for doing that, again? *"Puriter lavit dentes." Have clean teeth.* It's the wordiest phrase I learned yesterday, but also the most convenient one of them all. I would also love to learn the spell which lets me floss, even though I've never done that as a regular human being before.

The brush should've been floating towards me with the perfect amount of paste on it, a proportion which no human hands could ever conjure. But it doesn't. I say the words louder. "*Puriter lavit dentes.*"

"Have you really been taking your Latin classes so seriously?" my wife asks. She'd been asleep, beside me. "I didn't realise you were taking any at all."

I turn towards her. Yes, I'm seeing *my* wife, because she has her long hair again. She's also got the beautiful smile and that radiance which comes from being optimistic about what life plans for you next.

And then, the memories come back to me in bits and pieces. I recollect the strange feeling with which I was greeted when I met another part of myself in a world which seems too distant to exist now.

He told me the theory he'd postulated, and introduced me to his machine — it was incomplete, yet revealed all I needed to know to get home. We worked on completing it overnight, and now, here I am, before the break of dawn. I can't recollect all the details, but I remember enough. He said he's noted down all that I would need in my notebook to construct another machine. I want to rush down to the University's laboratory to check if the memories I've retained aren't betraying me. And if there already is a fully functional Teleporter in my lab.

I remember his parting words as well. *Love your wife as much as you can, for as long as you can. Some of us don't have her for much longer — but then, neither will you, if you stop loving her.*

She still wears a look of confusion on her face, though, as she should. This is the first time in months that we've shared the same bed — I must have slipped in while she was asleep. She would have no way of knowing I've changed overnight, once again.

"Are you ... wearing a wig?" I ask.

Now, she shoots me the familiar look which indicates her confusion has been superseded by amusement. "I'm going to call the counsellor again. You could do with some medication — I didn't realise our divorce would get to you so much ..."

"You don't need to do that," I say.

Questions of science can wait — it's the ones of my heart that need to be answered first. In this world, *my* world, I realise that the two of us still have time. My wife's concerned. She's been concerned for the longest time, hasn't she? There's a tinge of sorrow which hides beneath her façade as well, but it's not of the inevitable kind. We can make things better between us.

"I've got another question," I say.

"What's it this time?"

"Did Satyajit Ray ever have a beard?"

"No, he was an indie filmmaker — not a crazy loon."

I break out into a smile. "I've been feeling like one myself up until now."

She tilts her head to the left.

I reach forward to caress her hair, and then I hug her for the first time in months — I didn't want to before, but now that I can, I wouldn't be having this any other way. She tries to move away at first, but then, she embraces me too.

We need to work on our relationship — a lot. But I'm in my own world again, in the arms of my own wife, and with an enriched Latin vocabulary. It isn't going to be easy. But the time to try isn't a luxury everyone has, unlike us.

I break away from our embrace for a moment. "I want things to be better. I want us to be happy again. And I don't want to leave you," I say.

"Neither do I."

"We can try again, can't we?"

She nods. Amidst the moments of silence yet to retreat from our relationship, I reach forward and embrace her once more. She's never stopped loving me, and now, I realise that neither have I.

✍ ✍ ✍

Initial feedback

I liked the tone, concept, and the novel twist of having each develop one half of the machine. However, the characters feel underdeveloped — especially the changes of heart of the original narrator and his wife — how and why do they reconcile so easily? The technology of it all could use a little expansion as well, especially in clarifying how the two halves of the machine worked together, and where they go from here.

The piece feels a bit on the fence as to whether it's a neat idea story or a character story. It could work as either, though I think the character side has more promise. The closing was a bit of a downturn for me, as it suggests perhaps it was all a dream.

Author's intent

What do you think the story's about?
What emotions are you trying to evoke?

The themes I'm going for are as follows:

1. *Importance of profession*: In India, being an engineer is akin to being a man of indisputable repute within the middle class buble. What I'd aimed to show was how in another world, engineers are treated like artists and performers in this world — as dispensable parts of society, even though their importance is embedded within the functioning of our people. In the process, maybe I could reflect how interchangeable — and irreplaceable — the reputations of these professions actually are.

2. *Love and marriage*: The character motivations need to be more fleshed out, I agree. What I was striving to portray was the indifference which creeps into the middle phase of so many marriages because of monotony. In the first world, the lives of the couple have been shaken up because of the wife's terminal illness. This means they are spending their precious time together, and reconciling over their differences to create as many 'happy memories' as they can.

On the other hand, the world in which the wife is perfectly healthy is also the one in which the couple's on the verge of a divorce, because of the aforementioned monotony creating conflict. The protagonist's visit to a world where he sees his wife being vulnerable and loving makes him do the same when he returns to his own spouse. The terminal illness might not be there — but the love has certainly been carried over to his original home at the end of the story.

3. *The consequence of circumstances*: This theme carries itself over from the previous one. The machine, in many ways, is a symbol of the two protagonists' contrasting marriages. They're the same people, and their 'structure' is the same — but the circumstances of life have led them down two very different paths, which on being interlinked, has allowed them to 'solve' their problems. (For the Second Protagonist it could be earning self-belief while working his ridiculed profession).

Also, a brief note about the ending. Maybe my execution was off, but what I strived to do was show how it *could* have been a dream, but it isn't. Because his wife does make the remark about him 'learning Latin' — something which proves there is continuity with what we've just witnessed (in the therapy room where the second version of the protagonist tries to transform himself). I'm on the fence about the ending myself. I thought I could either modify this version in the rewrite, or end the story with an optimistic open ending in the second world itself. I prefer the former, especially because I wasn't too keen to make the two characters interact directly on the page. It would seem a tad bit preachy, I felt. Modifying the original ending would also allow for the husband's rediscovered love to be evident to the reader.

Author's note

The revision process of "Satyajit Ray's Beard or the Lack Thereof" was a daunting one. I had only worked on professional edits with an editor once before — and it was for a flash fiction piece. On the other hand, the *Metaphorosis* website guidelines emphasised the importance it gave to the revision process for refining any piece they accepted.

After reading my submission, Morris asked me for a rewrite. My initial drafts had been on the fence between being a plot-aligned story and a character one. I chose to go with the latter as I moved through the revision process. Morris' inputs about the same helped me gain clarity about this matter and many others, which were as useful as all the times I spent away from my laptop screen in between the different edits.

The structural changes to a story have always been the hardest for me to make, since they require the entire narrative to be updated at a logistical level every time one portion of it sees some essential aspect updated. Now that I look back at it — as is the case with most published works an author puts out — there are some changes I still want to make. But by the time we had reached our fifth round of edits, the narrative was in a much better place, especially in terms of the primary themes I wanted to convey through it. The biggest benefit I gained from the revision process was thus the clarity my story achieved.

This also came at times through the removal of phrases — especially those that spoke with a more 'dream-like ambience' than the rest of the prose. While I was initially reluctant to go through with some of Morris' edits because of my attachment to the initial draft, hindsight gives me the satisfaction of knowing the story achieves what I wanted it to without using stylistically focused paragraphs which hindered the flow of the narrative.

Working with Morris has taught me a lesson that has become clearer to me as I've worked with editors all over the world in the time since then. The fresh pair of eyes they provide to a story allows for them to see the contrast between the vision of the author writing the piece and what the actual story achieves on its own. Though there is subjectivity involved in this process, an empathetic conversation between the editor and the writer is sometimes all it takes for them to bridge this gap as much as possible.

In my case, the revision process particularly helped in correcting the lack of resolution for several character arcs in the story. My protagonist had achieved redemption in my mind, but I could not accurately reflect it in the story itself. Similarly, his wife was a bit too accepting of his apology towards the end of the narrative. Going through the piece with Morris helped me replace the shaky ambiguity of this resolution with a more grounded one. The threads of the story too now connected well enough to give me the confidence I needed to leave the marital future of my characters relatively more up in the air.

The differences between my initial submission and the one published on the website are reflective of any revision process' two biggest aims: they helped me fix the structure of the narrative, as well as improve the stylistic nuances of my prose. Seeking to preserve the original vision for a story about to undergo revision is a useful guideline to follow — but as long as the writer and the editor are in respectful communication, the revision process can flower in ways it might not have otherwise in either of their isolated imaginations.

Editor's note

There are often many, equally valid ways a story can go forward — as in the length of Martin Westlake's story. Here, I felt the original version of Abhijato's story could work either as a technical, concept-focused story or as a character story. I generally prefer character stories, but that's not the only choice. In this case, as Abhijato notes, he decided to focus on character, and I felt that was the best choice for the themes he said he wanted to highlight (e.g., love and marriage). With that established, I was able to suggest that the protagonist's change needed more foundation. Often, a reader can presume that a character acts in particular way because we're familiar with the underlying trope, but I feel most successful stories give their characters independent grounding. Here, I thought the wife was too accepting, and we didn't see the husband's turnaround. Once those characters and their motivations came more clearly into focus, the story felt more convincing.

While having decided on a character-based story, the concept and gadgets didn't fall entirely by the wayside, of course. There was a certain amount of adjustment needed to make sure the concept made sense and had its own internal logic. I liked the twist that both halves of the machine had been developed independently, but there was a little work in marrying them up properly.

I did suggest that Abhijato make some other changes to the story. There was a dream framing in the original piece that I felt detracted from the interesting concept. It's also not uncommon for a story to have multiple possible ending points. Sometimes that's intentional and effective. Sometimes, it's a bit misleading, and prepping the reader for an ending only to have the story continue can wear them out. Abhijato smoothed out a few such possible endings to focus on just one that resolved and highlighted the themes most effectively.

Satyajit Ray's Beard or the Lack Thereof

I drift as I dream. Yet, I haven't been truly asleep — or awake — for the longest time now.

I feel at odds with this world. I feel at odds with my wife. And I feel at odds with this room I sit in with her, facing the counsellor whom I've known for many years. I can't seem to recognise her now.

"So, you believe you're from another dimension?" the doctor asks. She's still got the spectacles which rest on the tip of her nose. She peers through them to look at us.

"Well, no," I say. I stutter — I'm not unsure of what I want to say, but I'm unsure of how it'll be received. "I'm from another *world*."

The counsellor nods at this statement. I know that nod. She doesn't agree with what I say — it isn't her place to pass judgement, after all. But she does understand. To empathise with the place I'm coming from a bit better — metaphorically, that is — she asks, "What's the difference according to you?"

"Another dimension means ... another universe." I look at the wall behind her to gather my thoughts. There's a painting of Satyajit Ray in the background — the most revered filmmaker in Bengali cinema. But here, he has a beard akin to a Tagore, whereas the former was famously clean-shaven in my own world. This isn't my home. And this isn't the Ray whose films I've grown up watching. "Another world means it's in the same universe — just far away from this galaxy."

"And why would there be multiple Earths in the same universe?"

I reach forward in my sofa. When I first arrived in this world — beside my wife who had a shaved head all of a sudden — I didn't know what my life was like here. But it's turned out to be the same as it's always been. I'm still a quantum engineering professor. I'm still working on teleportation. And I still *feel* like myself — this is my own body. But there's just the two big differences in this world which set it apart from mine ...

"If the shape of the universe is flat enough, as evidence seems to suggest, then it's constantly expanding." My hands are in front of me, accompanying my explanation by forming its own gestures and spreading outwards. It's a habit I have. "And if molecules are allowed to arrange themselves in every way they can over infinite space, they'll eventually run out of unique combinations. Patterns will start repeating — and the same worlds will arise in different parts of the universe."

The counsellor nods again. She steals the slightest of glances at my wife in between looking up from her notebook and looking at me – "Have you considered the possibility … that this may be a reaction to your wife having cancer?"

I bend my head sideways, confused. Couple therapy has never been my favourite part of the weekend, but neither has the counsellor ever been this wrong. She thinks I'm going crazy, even though it's not me who's dying from cancer in this world.

My wife's bald head steals my attention more than her eyes. But oh, her eyes do read of pity. I don't want any.

"*My* wife isn't dying from cancer." I say it with an emphasis on my baritone. It sounds harsh, almost dismissive. *You're in denial*, the counsellor seems to think. But she doesn't say anything. She simply brings up her arms to the hand rest on her seat and leans on it, thinking of how to approach this case.

But just then, the alarm clock in her room goes off. She snaps her fingers and mutters *"Turn est."* A switch moves by itself, and the alarm stops ringing. "I'm sorry, but that will be all for today. I think we're making real progress here so far. Same time, next week?"

She smiles at me, but I retain my nonchalance. I stare at the portrait of Satyajit Ray in the background — my counsellor preferred keeping her doctorates on this wall. They're on the opposite one in this world, laminated and hung behind us.

I look at the woman who claims to be my wife. Almost as a way of compensation, she says to the counsellor, "Thank you, Doctor." Then, she mutters something under her breath too. I do not catch the 'spell' this time around — she's intentionally carrying the tone she always does when she's cross with me. And before I can do anything about it, a white beam of energy envelops her. By the time the energy dissipates, so does she. I'll find her at home again.

"Umm," I say, looking around the room as I drag myself to the edge of my end of the sofa we've been sitting on. I run my fingers over its leather with my left hand, and run the other hand across my hair. "I guess … I'll just walk back home."

I awkwardly nod at the counsellor and pat my thighs before getting up. She looks at me with concern which brims over to amusement. She doesn't say anything, of course — but she's only human.

The counsellor's the least of my concerns as I exit the room, walk down the stairs and make my way onto the road. The *autorickshaws* and taxis converge in the middle of the four-way street, before diverging to their respective routes once the signal has opened again. There isn't too much of a difference between the public transportation of the Kolkata I know and the one I'm in right now, except for the fact that all vehicles hover above the ground here. They have no wheels, but they do have drivers and an automated gear shift technique which does not require the assistance of hands.

I've learned about it on the Internet, which is no less fascinating or less abusive than the one I've known from my own planet. I'm a product before the World Wide Web's time, but the evolution of science seems to have followed a less stringent path on this world, where magical spells do a lot of what science and maths account for in my one. I don't like this place.

I should have seen that coming. It's been less than twenty-four hours since I've found myself in this world, but in that time, I've come to understand that the most commonly-used spell is the one which helps in transportation. What is it, though?

I try and say it out loud. "Trans — transvec — *transvectio* — "

And just as I pronounce the spell — I do manage to recollect the correct one, it seems — I find myself disintegrating. It's a strange sensation, and I would think about it more if not for the fact that my mental facilities seem to be incapacitated. When I feel complete again, with my senses and my cognitive abilities returning, the first thought I have is – "What on Earth?"

It's an ironic choice of words considering my situation. I find myself looking straight at Satyajit Ray's bearded picture again. Ah why, I've landed up in the very place I was thinking about while saying the transportation spell. According to the *Basic Dictionary of Magic* — whose online website I accessed yesterday — one's always transported to the place they're thinking about at the time of saying the spell.

I look down at the counsellor, and there she is, peering over her spectacles and straining her neck with curiosity no longer bound by the hours she's being paid for. I see a notepad on her lap. She's probably filing away the minutes of today's session with us before the next client arrives.

"Hello, sir ... What may I do for you?" She tries to wear a smile on her face, but her lips twitch back to a more neutral position.

I look around the room once again. Yes, it's just as it had been when I left. No reason for it to change, I suppose. "I've just transported myself to the wrong place when I intended to go back home. You see, I was thinking about your place instead of mine, and I'm new to this magic business, so I didn't realise what would happen if I said *transvectio* — "

And just as my eyebrows shoot up on realising what I've done again, I can't feel them anymore. I stop thinking for the second time in as many minutes. It's serene, peaceful, almost meditative, to not be able to think about the worries of these worlds.

But when my feet touch the ground again, I throw up. It's on a familiar rug — the one I brought back home after spending a year in Switzerland working on the effects of extreme altitudes on my teleportation machine. The machine never worked. And in this world, it doesn't need to.

"Hey," I hear the familiar voice say. It's my wife's, even if it's mellowed down now. Probably because of the cancer. And because her husband seems to have gone crazy.

I look up at her. She's in her robes, getting ready for a bath. But before I can tell her anything — or apologise as a way of coming to terms with the place which is going to be my home for the rest of my life — I feel my eyes closing. *I didn't even say a spell this time, where am I going again?*

The last thing I remember is the realisation that at least I'm not *going* anywhere this time around as my face hits the floor. Also, my nose is going to hurt like hell when I wake up again.

✍

On opening my eyes, I see the roof above my head. I can still hear the public vehicles making their way past our home on this main road of the city. My wife always wanted to have a home facing the streetlamps and local markets from a closer proximity I would have liked. And the familiar sirens and rhythmic honks which compose this room's overtones are the very reason I felt the way I did before. But over time, and even now, I've grown to feel a comfort in them.

It carries me through the realisation that my nose is bent way too much towards my right. I didn't know you could feel that, but I certainly do. It's on the verge of being numb but isn't, which makes the pain intolerable now that my senses are returning.

And now, I feel it click back in place. It almost twitches — no, it jumps back into its place. I'm able to move my neck. I push my arms against the surface I'm lying on, attempting to get back up.

"No, you must rest. Have you forgotten about that time we went to Darjeeling and you transported twice in a minute?" The voice lets out a laugh but doesn't see it through — she must have been reminded of the present situation.

"What happened to me? Why did I faint?" My vision aligns itself to reveal the woman sitting in front of me. Again, it's my bald wife.

"You've got the Paralysis Syndrome, have you forgotten that as well?" she asks. I shoot her a look. *I never knew*, I would like to tell her, but it wouldn't help.

Her head bows down as a way of resignation. "Your heredity means you can't teleport yourself like the rest of us can. You can only do it once a day or so. You get quite tired otherwise. Pass out, like on occasions like these."

I try to nod, but my head doesn't seem to be able to lift itself from the pillow for now. However, I do seem to recollect a stray line from the same *Dictionary*'s entry about the subject. Something about people being born with a rare variation of the 24th pair of chromosomes in a person's genes, the one responsible for granting humans their ability to interact with magic. A pair which — in my world — is considered to lead to deformities and death rather than magical abilities.

"Darling, I ... I really might not be who you think I am."

She places a hand on her temple and looks away at the windows. "The mosquitoes are going to start entering the room again — let me shut the windows. *Prope*." And the windows move inwards, as if they're intoxicated by a breeze blowing out of the room. The illusion of normalcy is shattered when the latches attached to the bottom of the window pick themselves up and lock them into their positions on the windowsills. My wife is cool across realms.

And right then, the first lines of Rabindra Sangeet burst through our closed windows, drowning out the noise of the receding vehicles as the last strains of sunlight drain away and the artificial lights take over. *"Ami chini go chini tomake, ogo bideshini."* *I know you, oh, I do, foreigner.*

Ah yes, I do. This is going to be my life now. The time I get to spend with my life has been curtailed — in this life, at least, if not the next ones. I'll make the most of it, no matter how less that time turns out to be.

"Why does my nose ... feel normal?"

"I fixed it. It's the first spell you ever taught me — transportation helped us get away from either of our parents if they saw us when they weren't supposed to. You always landed on your nose whenever you fell unconscious. And I was always there for you. To fix your nose. Or just fix your hair."

So in this world, I did find a way of escaping her parents. A less painful way than jumping out of her window from the first floor and breaking a bone in my leg that one time, for sure.

"Does this help you remember anything?" she asks.

"It does," I reply, remembering the exuberance of her youth — and mine — with fondness I didn't think a mid-life crisis would entail. "But then ... it doesn't." She sighs.

I've never believed in karma. But neither have I ever believed in magic before I saw it with my eyes. Perhaps, this is karma repaying itself for things I've done in lives I cannot remember. I would like to confess my sins to whoever's listening, though.

Before I can, my wife rests her hands on my forehead. "You've become very tired because of this ordeal. Sleep now, and I'll sleep alongside you. Hopefully, you'll be in your senses when we wake up tomorrow. *Somnus*."

And I feel myself drifting away for a final time today. It feels as serene as it's done in the past. But this time, I'm not drifting away to a different part of the world — my mind merely guides me to one of my own, as a way of comfort and company through my sleep beside these cacophonous streets.

✍

I drift as I dream. Yet, I haven't been truly asleep — or awake — for the longest time now.

I feel at odds with this world. I feel at odds with my wife. And I feel at odds with this room I sit in with her, facing the counsellor whom I've known for many years. I can't seem to recognise her now.

"So, you believe you're from another dimension?" the doctor asks. I nod and look around the room. I see laminated certificates hanging where Satyajit Ray's portrait should be hanging. It does occupy the space on the wall right behind me. If I didn't know better, I would have thought the counsellor had just exchanged our seats as a way of giving the two of us a 'new perspective'.

But when I turn around to look at the portrait, Mr Ray's likeness hangs up there without a beard on the man's face, as if it's a joke. His beard's the most iconic part of his appearance — and this world doesn't even have that. Alongside the fact that it believes magic exists only in escapist novels and ancient scriptures.

"Umm, yes, I do." I'm not interested in this session. This lady isn't the one I've been pouring out my heart to for the past couple of years. And this wife isn't the one I've grown so close to because of her terminal cancer. She looks much younger sitting beside me now, ignorant of her faith in other worlds.

But she doesn't have the glow which comes from being optimistic about your death rather than your life. So far, she has come across as the kind of partner who remains aimless in her middle age, taking the time life's granted her as a commodity rather than a gift with no receipt. I would like to, but I can't seem to stand her.

"Have you considered this could be related to the fact that the two of you want a divorce?"

"Ah," I say, "It's the farthest thing from what I want, though."

My wife shoots me a look. "You're the one who wanted it the most."

I get up from my place, and throw out my hands — it's a sign of desperation in this world too, I hope. "I'm sorry, but this is all too much for me. Transvectio." I stand in my place, but nothing happens.

I'd forgotten. Spells don't work in this world.

The counsellor bends her eyebrow at me. "I've been learning a bit of Latin to cope with all this stress," I inform her.

Then, I look around this familiar room set up in an alien manner for what I hope is the last time. "I seriously find myself unable to cope with the pressure — I'll have to get going now." I do my best impression of storming out of the room and down the stairs of the large hospital. Theatrics will convince humans as long as humanity persists, magical or not.

There are so many others who descend the stairs alongside me. Some still utilise the elevator, of course, but it's such a relief to see other people walking instead of teleporting their way around the world with the ease of a single word and a determined mind, not affected by genetics in a world where all others seem flawless. I've got a limited perception of this place, though. As a result, I'll refrain myself from passing a definitive judgement.

As jarring as this reality has been to me so far — including the experiences with my very own wife — the biggest incentive of staying back in this world has been the respect engineers are given here. Back in my world, we're something of a punchline, despite the stability we've brought to the world over the years as a professional breed. It's because those proficient in magic believe they can survive without the assistance of basic mechanics and science. They're mistaken — but they're also the ones ruling us.

This world designs its fervour around supernatural elements of a different kind. I see the people praying in makeshift temples and on the rickshaws *which carry models of their deities wherever they go. But not being treated as a dispensable labourer comforts me in a way I've never felt about my professional identity before.*

A semblance of respect is what I've been seeking for the longest time. It's the reason why I started experimenting with manufacturing a teleportation device using scientific apparatus rather than relying on the genetic predispositions of the population. I've waited almost twenty-four hours on this world to ensure my experimentation does not make me fall flat on my face in the absence of a reliable confidant.

My University is closed off to students at this time of the evening, but when I flash my ID at a University staff member — a card which does not morph itself into a miniature self in this world — he lets me in. "Welcome, Professor," the man says and steps aside.

I make my way up to the second floor, move around the left side of the aisle, and keep to its left. Room 616. Here it is. I stand in *front of the door for a moment, then another, and then another. It's on the last beat that I have to remind myself once more of the nature of human existence here. You've got to turn your own door handles in this world.*

Once I've replaced the keys in my pocket after using them to unlock the door, I enter the room and switch on the lights. Here lies the machine. It is large enough to fit a human, yet it remains in its prototype stage. It's made out of a metallic chamber coated with aluminium and copper, along with an alloy featuring equal parts of platinum and plutonium responsible for promising discoveries of excitement of neutrons when activated with the hypercharged cells connected to the entire device, lying on top of the structure to maximise its reach.

Ah, but it's a bit different-looking here! *And this is where I begin to shift my focus away from the similarities and start studying the differences between the device I've constructed and the one this Earth's version of me has created.*

I peek out of the corridor. There's no one around in this area. I walk out of the college and only return ten minutes later, carrying with the me the most necessary item required for me to continue my work — a packet of three *samosas which shall accompany me for the rest of the evening.*

I taste just the one before beginning my work. They're as good as they've ever been, whether they've been sunk sufficiently long enough in peacock-influenced flammable oil mid-air or not. I switch off my phone and start noting down the initial observations I need to make in my favourite notebook already being used in this lab. My original suspicions are confirmed.

This machine is a peculiarity compared to the one I've been working on, fulfilling just the basic similarities required to host a human within the apparatus while the transformation mechanism is theoretically supposed to work out. The rest of the parts — and there are lots of them — remain incomplete or ill-judged in their presentation. Just as they'd been in mine.

But wherever I see his results being successful from the logs in the entry journals, I realise the truth behind the matter. He's created one half of the machine, with his answers delivering the solutions to the long-drawn questions I've asked myself over the years. It seems like an ingenious piece of scientific innovation from the perspective of the other half.

The facts of the matter, though, mean that the exact problems he's been stuck on — like me — have already been put in place as functional parts of the machine I've been functioning.

The switch must have happened yesterday, under the improbable conditions across both ends of the Universe where similar worlds created two polar opposites of machines which also had perfect compatibility. The apparatus must have been supercharged by the hyperactive atoms in the engines of the respective devices. Our bodies converged — or at least our respective consciousnesses — and as a result, we were swapped.

That's my hypothesis. I can't remember for the life of me how I ended up tucked in this bed or on this world, but I was a mess when I woke up in the morning. The device must erase the short-term memories of those who use it, even though the rest of my life seems perfectly stored in my mental faculties.

Such a freak accident probably won't occur again — but it doesn't need to. I now know how to configure this machine to replicate mine sufficiently enough for it to be functional in one location, and not across worlds. If I do manage to work things out as soon as I can, I can go home again. Help my other self out too. Considering there is someone who exists like me, who isn't going to try and kill his otherworldly twin at gun point or anything of that sort.

Let's see how I go about rescuing myself now — and well, inventing teleportation along the way in order for that to happen.

✍

When I open my eyes, I expect feeling her palm on my forehead again, ready to put me to sleep if I haven't come around to what she thinks are my regular senses. I'm ready to defend myself, more alert than relaxed after not having to think about the anxiety of being on another world. For long enough, too, considering how the sunlight is peering in through the windows. They're now open.

I slide up in my bed and feel the sore taste in my mouth. I'll need to brush my teeth. What was the spell for doing that, again? *"Puriter lavit dentes." Have clean teeth.* It's the wordiest phrase I learned yesterday, but also the most convenient out of all of them. I would also love to learn about the spell which lets me floss, even though I've never done that as a regular human being before.

The brush should've been floating towards me with the perfect amount of paste on it, a proportion which no human hands could ever conjure. But it doesn't. I say the words out louder. *"Puriter lavit dentes."*

"Have you really been taking your Latin classes so seriously?" my wife asks. She'd been asleep, beside me. "I didn't realise you were taking any at all."

I turn towards her. She looks at me with thde confusion which must have carried itself overnight. But there's something different — something I wouldn't have expected. My wife has her long hair again. The silky hair, the beautiful smile, and the radiance which comes from being optimistic about what life plans for you next.

"Are you ... wearing a wig?" I ask.

Now, she shoots me the familiar look which indicates her confusion has been superseded by amusement. "What have you been going on about since yesterday, darling? I thought it was some sort of a hangover which would pass by now ..."

I bend forward on my elbows to look into her eyes. They aren't filled with regret just yet. They're the eyes of *my* wife, now. "I've got another question."

"What's it this time?"

"Did Satyajit Ray ever have a beard?"

"No, he was an indie filmmaker — not a crazy loon."

I break out into a smile. "I've been feeling like one myself up until now."

She tilts her head to the left again. "Oh, are we going to be alright?"

I reach forward a bit more, and hug her for the first time in months — I didn't want to before, but now that I could, I wouldn't be having this any other way. "Yes," I say, letting her reside in my embrace as long as she wants to stay there. "I love you, and I hope you haven't changed your mind about loving me back while the real me's been away."

I drift as I dream. It's time to wake up now.

✍ ✍ ✍

Wytchen Wood

—

Lori J. Torone

Wytchen Wood

A decade of shavings covered the floor of Lewys's carpentry shop. He didn't bother sweeping any more, although he probably should — wood without magic produces a drab dust that desiccates the throat, shrivels the lungs. He coughed and gulped from his flask, stepping back from his work. Carving the finishing scrollwork on yet another hope chest for the latest bride-to-be in town did nothing to fill his own hollowness.

"Wait for me," she had whispered in the wytchen grove so many years ago, her berry-scented breath caressing his cheek, "I will come back to you." She'd taken magic with her, in the wytchen dust glinting in her sunlit hair as she waved goodbye from the newly-carved wagon. She took his heart as well, but left hope in its place.

Over the years, hope had drained into loneliness, empty and aching, present in the sound of his saw's jagged edge, the taste of his own cough-strained, stale breath, the starkness of his bedroom above the shop. No chance of a bride now, for him, in this small town where he had spurned all coy glances sent his way, waiting for his true love to return.

He wished he hadn't waited.

Still coughing, Lewys threw open the window shutters. He gulped fresh air. Delighted cries of children entered with the breeze.

A pageant wagon creaked into the town square outside his shop, horseless, shedding curls of magic onto the cobblestones from its warped wytchen beams. Children dropped coins into a box attached to the wagon's carriage and scrambled for seats. Eyes widening in shock, Lewys unconsciously dug his fingernails into the windowsill. The wagon's wood was peeling, its stage floor crooked, but it was still the same one. The only one.

As the threadbare curtain opened, more wood peels and sparkling dust showered the stage from the covered wagon's rafters, a natural emission of the enchanted wood, once cut and carved. A princess puppet slumped against a painted forest backdrop. She wore a gown the deep blush of sunset, the falling wytchen dust creating a net of crystals in her golden hair. With the clack of wooden joints, she began a light, graceful dance. A troll, lumbering in from stage right, tore a gasp from the children.

Lewys saw what the audience did not know to look for: The shadow of the puppet master's hands weaving along the stage floor. These puppets had no strings. The wytchen wood itself conjured the play, the magic within the wagon and the carved puppets animating them, their movements directed from above by the puppet master's hands.

After the princess outsmarted the troll, she befriended a dragon, its velvet tongue unfurling like a panting dog. Adults and children alike cheered when she saved a village from a witch.

The curtain closed; the crowd dispersed.

Lewys grabbed his jerkin and dashed outside.

The wagon's damage looked even worse up close. Red rope secured the corners, but it was a temporary bandage for the cracked joints which exposed the wood's inner pith.

The old puppet master emerged from behind the curtain. "Master Lewys, look how well your craft weathered the years. Although, I must admit, some repairs are needed."

"Master Rhodri, you take me for my father," Lewys replied. "He is gone these last ten years. I have his carpentry business as well as his name now."

Hobbling towards him on gnarled joints as the stage boards shifted and groaned, the old man squinted at Lewys. "Aye, I remember you," Rhodri said, beckoning the carpenter to follow him into the narrow living space behind the stage backdrop.

"Is your daughter here?" His lips were dry; his heart constricted with a bare remembrance of hope.

A slow smile deepened the lines on the old man's face. "You remember Roselyn?"

✍

The first time Lewys had seen Roselyn, she was sitting on a stump in the wytchen grove, her hair a curtain over her face and lap. He was passing through on his way further into the forest, hatchet slung over his shoulder. "My lady?" he said, approaching carefully, as he would a hare in a thicket, "Are you well?"

She looked up then, and instead of a face smudged with tears as he expected, he saw one smudged with ink from the parchment and quill in her hands. Her eyes were startled, as blue as an open sky. The sun blinked through the branches and transformed her hair into spun gold.

Lewys caught his breath.

"Indeed, I am very well," she replied. "Do you like stories?"

"What? Uh...yes. Doesn't everyone?" he stammered.

"Good!" She jumped off the stump and pocketed an inkwell that had been lying in the grass. "This one is finished. You can be our practice audience." She grabbed Lewys by the wrist and he let go of his hatchet in surprise, dropping it behind him. He spluttered a weak protest — he was supposed to meet his father for work — but the girl tugged him away, into the stand of birch trees that bordered the road into town.

"Audience for what? You don't even know me!"

"Of course I do. Father!" She shouted as they came upon an old wagon pulled into the grass on the side of the road. "The carpenter's son has agreed to see the new play!"

Lewys recognized the man sitting in the grass in front of a small fire, stirring the contents of a pot hanging from a tripod. He was an itinerant toymaker; every girl in the village had at least one of his wood and cloth dolls. Lewys himself had a painted jester on a stand, cleverly rigged to somersault when a button was pressed. It was still on a shelf above his bed, even though he was too old to play with it now.

Master Rhodri looked from his daughter to Lewys and back again. "Roselyn, are you sure..."

She pulled her father to his feet and thrust the parchment into his hands. "Look, I finished! It's the perfect story for the new puppets! Oh, be careful, it's still wet."

"All right, then," Rhodri said, pulling a handkerchief out of his vest pocket to wipe his fingers, "but only if the young man does not mind."

Lewys did not. Roselyn showed him where to sit in the grass beneath a tree, the gentle push of her hand through his shirt sending thrills along his skin. She was a flurry of activity, her bright hair and patched dress swinging to and fro as she fetched the puppets and whispered to her father as he studied the parchment. The puppets were exquisitely carved, like all the dolls Rhodri made, but these had moveable joints and strings, each attached to a cross of wood. Their hair was tangled yarn and their clothes multi-colored swatches of fabric.

Roselyn and her father climbed into the wagon and lowered the puppets into the grass below. The wooden figures clacked as they began to move, and within minutes Lewys forgot about the strings connected to the pair in the wagon above, their hands moving the crosses gracefully. A curtain lifted in his mind.

The story unfolded, wordless but spoken through the puppets' movements. Within Lewys's eyes, the wagon turned to mountain ranges, the grass to a river ford, so real that he could feel the cold wind in the high cliffs and hear the rush of the river. He was immersed in the hardships the brothers faced as they searched for each other. His heart leapt at their final happy reunion. When the puppets bowed, the story's spell over Lewys's mind broke, and he returned with a jolt to his seat in the grass, cooled by the shade of the tree. Roselyn's pleased face smiled down at him from the wagon. He broke into spontaneous applause.

"That was well done," a voice called from further back in the trees. Lewys turned and sprang to his feet. His father approached with his two apprentices. "No wonder my son has shirked his duty for the day." He held out the hatchet. Lewys took it as his father said more quietly, "I was afraid something happened to you, lad." Lewys's face reddened.

"It's my fault," Roselyn said, as she gathered the puppets up. "I did not give him much choice. Please do not be angry with him."

Rhodri came down from the wagon. The carpenter shook his hand, then looked up at the girl, his eyes squinting against the high sun. "Well," the Master Carpenter said, then turned sharply to Lewys, whose color deepened to scarlet. "I can see the appeal of such a play." The apprentices, a few years older than Lewys, grinned and elbowed each other.

"The puppets," he turned back to the toymaker, "are they a new crafting?"

"Yes. My first two. My daughter has great plans for me to make others. She wants a dragon and a witch in particular. And a girl puppet, of course."

The elder Lewys rubbed his chin, dark with beard. "There was something about that play, something quite powerful. I forgot where I was for a while. And I realize that I am long overdue for letters to my own siblings."

"My daughter wrote the story," Rhodri said proudly. "First I had the puppets in mind as another toy, but it was Roselyn's idea to perform plays with them. Do you truly think others will enjoy such entertainment?"

"Truly, but you need a proper stage — a pageant wagon, perhaps, so you can still travel as you do." The carpenter hesitated, glancing at his apprentices, then looked up at Roselyn again. He seemed to make up his mind, and continued, "There is a special wood that I use only for certain projects. I would like to build a pageant wagon for you with this wood. I never take payment for wytchen," he added quickly, when Rhodri blanched. "As I said, it is only for special creations. And I believe this project, and your work, is worthy of it."

Lewys looked at his father in shock. He vaguely remembered the wizened man, passing through town, who had shown his father how to cut wood from the strange trees that no axe could fell before, how to craft an object — for him, it was a staff — with tools and words.

His father had used the wytchen only one other time, as far as Lewys knew, to build a cradle for their neighbor's infant born two months too soon. It was a gift that his father carved in haste, neither eating nor sleeping, in order to finish it by dawn the day after the birth. Within hours after a peaceful nap in the cradle, the child stopped struggling to nurse, and thrived thereafter.

"Come with your daughter to my workshop tomorrow," the master carpenter continued, waving away Rhodri's stammering gratitude. "I'll draw up the plans and we can talk about them over supper." He gestured to Lewys as he turned, a slight smile on his lips. "Let's go. Enough stories for today. Back to chopping wood, lad."

✍

The aged puppet master did not answer Lewys's question, but he did not have to. There was no sign of his daughter among the clutter of tools, wood, parchment, and ink pots on the table. Clothes spilled out of a trunk, child's dresses with snippets removed. A torn blanket lay rumpled on the floor. Lewys's heart sank.

How foolish he had been to wait.

The puppet princess was sitting upright in a cabinet with the troll, dragon, and witch on a shelf beneath her. A pile of bedraggled puppets lay at the bottom.

"I'd like to commission you for repairs."

Lewys looked at the rafters and walls, sunlight spearing through the gaps. Rhodri added, "I have the coin to pay you, whatever the cost."

"It's not that, sir." He tried to control his tone, but anger still sharpened his words even after all these years. "There are no wytchen trees left." One of the apprentices, addled with mead in the tavern, had broken his oath and spilled the secret of the grove; news that the master carpenter could release the trees' magic had spread like fire afterwards. The townspeople turned on his father when he refused their foolish requests for wedding rings, pendants, furniture, even an entire house made from wytchen. But the final demand, a flagship, had come from the duke himself in his manor on the coast, delivered with a subtle threat on the carpenter's son's life.

The entire grove was consumed. His father had fallen ill during the ship's crafting and died soon after it was completed.

"But surely you can repair the existing wood?"

Lewys regarded the puppet master, with his bent back and knotted bones, and said kindly, "All due respect, Master Rhodri, but perhaps a warm hearth in a home without wheels would serve you better now."

The old man nodded. "It probably would. But," he gestured to the puppets in the cabinet, "I must continue to tell her stories."

The puppet princess was as finely crafted as porcelain, the warm scent of beeswax polish lingering on her milk-white skin of peeled wytchen wood. Lewys slipped his fingers along the gold cascade of her hair, a silken balm over his callused skin. He had touched Roselyn's hair this way, shyly, so many years ago in the wytchen grove, as his father cut and shaped the wood for the pageant wagon. The elder Lewys murmured words under his breath as he worked, words that he whispered in Rhodri's ear when he handed him small blocks of wytchen.

Coaxed by his daughter, Master Rhodri had fashioned them both toy swords out of plain oak. Lewys and Roselyn pretended they were heroes, fighting trolls and witches, befriending dragons, crafting their own fairy tales from shadows at the forest's edge. Lewys was awkward and reluctant at first, feeling as if he were too old for this play, but Roselyn's earnest imagination captivated him. And it was worth the teases of the other apprentices just to sit close to Roselyn afterwards, their heads touching, as she penned their play into stories for the puppets.

Her lips were always stained blush from the wytchen berries they were not supposed to eat, the red berries marked with stars that she hid in her dress pocket. When the pageant wagon was completed, oiled and shining like the moon, Lewys watched as it rolled away from the grove without need of a horse, Roselyn blowing kisses as she peeked out from behind the curtain. When it was gone, he ate the berry she had slipped into his hand with a whispered promise.

It had flooded his mouth with bitterness, the taste surprising him after her sweetly-scented breath.

Lewys finally asked the question he had been dreading. "Roselyn is happily married, then?" He tried not to sound bitter, but her name was no longer sweet in his mouth either.

"No. She is not. I wish..." Rhodri took a deep, shaky breath. "Her heart just...stopped." The words were a hammer blow to Lewys, leaving him cold and numb, his mouth drier than bone. His fingers, still caressing the puppet's hair, froze. "One minute she was reading aloud her new story and the next.... It was soon after we left the grove. I don't know what happened."

The old man paused, wiping his eyes with a grimy handkerchief from his pocket. "My wife had died when Roselyn was an infant. My daughter was all I had. My heart lies in that grave with her. To keep living, to keep going...." His voice cracked, and he cleared his throat. "I wanted to save her, to bring her back to life. Impossible I know, but a father will do anything for his child... at least, like this, she can live on in her stories. The stories that she loved, that she lived to write. Her legacy." He reached out and touched the puppet's hair also. "Roselyn and her mother had the same color hair. It is beautiful, isn't it?"

Lewys snapped his hand away, stumbling over the puppet detritus spilling out from the cabinet's bottom.

"You must understand — I could not let her go! But she grew so cold...her hair was the only thing unchanged. It was the only thing still her." The old man twisted his hands, choking back a sob. "Everything I did, all my carving, was for my daughter. She was the meaning behind my life's work. She still is. And I have to give her what life I can."

Master Rhodri's struggle to contain his grief echoed in Lewys's own hollow chest. After a moment, he said, "I do understand."

Slowly Lewys collected the puppets from the floor, a mess of small swords and fractured oak limbs. All princes. "Can I fix these for you?" he asked.

Composing himself, shaking his head, the puppet master replied, "They were my gifts, to commemorate her birthdays." He cleared his throat again. "She never got the chance to create a story of true love. I thought perhaps I could write one for her. But the words never came, and the princes never worked right. And I'd find them damaged the next day. If they were made of wytchen, perhaps it would be different, but I used all the blocks your father gave me. Nevertheless, I keep trying, every year."

Lewys was silent for a while, his hands cradling the broken princes. Wytchen dust drifted down from the wagon's ceiling, glittering bright as a promise that had not been broken after all.

I will come back to you.

"I will do something for you, Master Rhodri. And for her."

Back in his room he packed a satchel with a flask of water and food from his meager pantry, then secured a hatchet to his belt. Walking through the bare patch that had once been the grove, he glanced behind him, making sure he was alone before entering the thick forest beyond. He had released the apprentices after the flagship was completed; his destination was a secret only he knew, now.

After an hour, the woodland sloped upwards as the pine trees thinned. He came to a ledge where a single tree grew, slanted trunk and low, leafy branches thriving against the crisp sky: The wytchen sapling that Lewys and his dying father had transplanted here, hidden from human greed. It was larger now, although not as thick and full as the ancient ones in the grove had been. Another sapling, perhaps a year or two old, grew in a sunny spot near its parent. Lewys swallowed the sudden lump in his throat.

He poured water on the roots as an offering, giving some to the sapling as well, and tied a red ribbon around a thick branch as he had seen his father do. Then he sat, the trunk pressing into his jerkin, thinking of what could have been, while the sun painted the sky the color of the princess's gown, of Roselyn's lips, which had never touched his. As the sun descended into the dark forest below him, he hefted his hatchet and spoke his request to the tree.

He hoped he was worthy.

When Lewys came back to the wagon Rhodri was snoring in a corner, blanket wrapped around him and tucked under his grizzled chin. He used the old man's tools, peeling and smoothing the small branch the wytchen had granted him, carving a face, body, and limbs, whispering his father's words to the wood for the first and last time. Rummaging through the trunk, he found the remnants of a white shawl which he cut with a pair of silver scissors to make a doll-size tunic and pants, needle and red thread moving as deftly as when he sewed patches into his own clothing. He painted the eyes and mouth.

Lewys took the puppet princess down from her shelf, arranging her carefully on the work table next to the newly carved prince, staring at her for a long time. He touched her hair again. Leaning close, his lips almost touching her cheek, he breathed deeply. As his lungs filled with her wytchen wood scent, his heart returned, brimming with magic and love as when they had been younger. "Roselyn," he murmured, "I kept my promise too. I waited."

With the scissors he cut his own hair off, and stitched the dark locks to a small felt cap. Uncorking a bottle of pine resin, he brushed the thick glue on the cap and attached it to the puppet prince's head.

Wooden hands twitched, clacked against each other.

Lewys's joints buckled and he flopped to the floor.

✍

His name, whispered against his cheek. A whiff of familiar berry.

Lewys opened his eyes. He was sitting in the old wytchen grove under one of the trees, crisscrossing branches spread out above him, and for one disorienting moment he thought the branches were the rafters of the pageant wagon.

Someone was sitting next to him. He turned, and Roselyn's smiling face filled his vision. Reaching out, tentatively, to touch her cheek, he whispered, "Are you real?" His fingers felt strange, stiff.

She laughed. "As real as you," she replied, standing. A pile of berries cascaded from her billowing silk skirts. She pulled him to his feet, and his joints cracked loudly. Lewys pushed the aches in his body aside — Roselyn was here, in front of him, alive and looking more beautiful in a sunset-colored gown than he had ever beheld. Her hair was a curtain of golden strands over her shoulders, a net of crystals holding the strands away from her perfect face.

"I am glad you are finally here, with me, my love," Roselyn whispered, standing so close to him, her eyes sparkling. Lewys folded her into his arms, his heart overflowing, seeking out her lips with his own.

"Not yet," she said, placing her fingers over his mouth. A loud roar sounded from the depths of the forest. Roselyn broke from his grasp. "Father wrote us a story. I don't know all the details, but I know it has a happy ending. We have to work to get there, of course." She gestured to the sword buckled at his hip and, when he stared at it dumbfounded, unsheathed it for him and put it in his hand. The blade was etched with runes. "You're a prince, Lewys."

She pulled a matching sword from a concealed fold in her gown. "I found this one hidden in a wytchen trunk before you came."

Another roar, closer this time, shook the leaves of the trees. Both sword blades began to glow.

"An enchantment! But do you know why?" Prince Lewys asked.

"No," Princess Roselyn said excitedly. "I suppose we will have to figure it out! Remember that friendly dragon? Things aren't always what they seem. We must be clever as well as brave." She smiled up at Lewys, and he had never known such happiness, such excitement.

"We have a new life ahead of us, my love," Roselyn said, and Lewys ached to kiss her. "Are you ready for adventure?"

Magic fell in curls and crystals from the wytchen wood above them. Strange shadows began to move beneath their feet. Lewys took his true love's hand, and together they turned to face the beginning of their story.

✍ ✍ ✍

Initial feedback

I like the prose, concept, and characters. However, I think the story still needs quite a bit of work. This feels like a sketch, in places, and the backstory could do with more depth — for example, the point that she writes stories is submerged in both of them making up stories in their youth. Why does he wait to raise the question of the daughter with the father — why not lead with that? The end is a bit of a jumble, and the shift in perspective makes it stumble.

Author's intent

What do you think the story's about?
What emotions are you trying to evoke?

My original idea for this story was a folkloric tale of star-crossed lovers. I wanted the protagonist's physical transformation to not only be a product of inner change but also a sacrifice, leaving the reader with a bittersweet feeling at the end.

Author's note

"Wytchen Wood" was my first time working with an editor on a story. I didn't quite know what to expect, although as an English teacher I surmised it would be much like my one-on-one conferences with my writing students, and indeed I learned more about story craft and process from Morris than I had up to that point in my writing career.

When I received the revise/resubmit email, it struck me how Morris felt the story still needed to be fleshed out. The version I submitted had been the 6th draft (starting from a flash piece), and I remember feeling a bit out of my element if after that much time and work it still read like a 'sketch' in parts! But I was eager for the wonderful opportunity to revise with a professional.

My original idea for the story was a folkloric tale of star-crossed lovers. I wanted the protagonist's physical transformation to not only be a product of inner change but also a bittersweet sacrifice. I've since learned how useful thinking up a logline for your story is, especially for revision, but I believe what Morris got spot-on in his initial comments was that the characters' backstory needed more depth and the original ending was jumbled with an awkward point of view shift.

These suggestions truly brought out something more in the story that was waiting beneath the surface. I added more to Roselyn's characterization, and, surprisingly to me, Lewys's father decided to make an appearance also. But what excited me most was that a theme developed organically from the backstory: the universal effects that stories have upon those who are touched by them. In this case, it is the oral storytelling tradition creating a peculiar immersive effect on the listeners/viewers, hinted at in Lewys's and his father's reactions to the puppet play. Then I attempted to connect this to the ending, with Lewys and Roselyn alive within a world of story, a very real world to them in which they do not perceive themselves as puppets, but finally have their chance at a happily-ever-after together.

As I revised, I realized I wanted to spark thoughts for my readers about this immersion experience: What causes us to 'lose ourselves' in a story? Is there a real realm of imagination, a tangible collective unconsciousness, the 'cauldron of story', as Tolkien put it? Reader immersion that results in fan fiction or cosplay seems to give characters a life beyond the pages of their original stories. At the resolution, Roselyn tells Lewys she is "as real as you." It's a topic I've thought about often. I always feel like my characters have found me, rather than the other way around, and I am simply the doorway for them to this world.

The ending put me in a bit of a quandary as to how to keep the same point of view if Lewys is a puppet, but the backstory theme set the pieces in place. It is a completely different ending and a more effective one.

After the initial email, the story went through two developmental passes with suggestions from Morris. Besides the two major revisions above, these also included clarifying the magic system and the fact that Rhodri used his deceased daughter's hair to create the puppet, as well as tying the theme even more closely both to the characters' endings and to Roslyn's father through dialogue. After this, there were copy edits with minor tweaking to create the final version.

In my writing circles I have heard that an editor's job is to make both the story and the writer better than they were. For myself this was certainly true, and it is because of Morris's editing process that "Wytchen Wood" went on to be accepted for publication in one of our modern versions of the oral storytelling tradition, the weekly fantasy podcast *Podcastle* (Feb. 2021).

Editor's note

It's not unusual for themes in the story to develop as it goes through revision. Sometimes, the author was wrong (or changes their mind) about what the most important element is. Sometimes, a subsidiary theme takes over the story as other things change. And sometimes a brand new theme emerges, as Lori notes happened to her. That can be a boon, especially if it clarifies other elements of the story or gives new significance to the existing narrative.

I liked a lot about this story going in — prose, concept, characters — but I still felt it needed work. I thought the original skipped too quickly past some elements, that more backstory would give the piece more depth, and that some of the themes (as I saw them) were obscured. There was a change in perspective at the end that I felt distracted from the story.

Lori addressed the backstory and perspective issues immediately, and with good effect. That put the focus more clearly on resolving some of the mechanics of the magic system — how wytchen wood and dust worked. That also came together fairly quickly, and left only minor polishing to do. It's rare that the stages of revision are so nicely contained — usually, each set of changes stretches across a couple of revisions. Here, though, it was an admirably efficient and effective process.

Wytchen Dust

A decade of shavings covered the floor of Lewys's carpentry shop. He didn't bother sweeping any more, although he probably should — wood without magic produces a drab dust that desiccates the throat, shrivels the lungs. He coughed and gulped from his flask, stepping back from his work. Carving the finishing scrollwork on yet another hope chest for the latest bride-to-be in town did nothing to fill his own hollowness.

"Wait for me," she had whispered in the wytchen grove so many years ago, her berry-scented breath caressing his cheek, "I will come back to you." She took magic with her, in the wytchen dust glinting in her sunlit hair as she waved goodbye from the newly-carved wagon. She took his heart as well, but left hope in its place.

Too late now. Over the years hope had drained into loneliness, empty and aching, present in the sound of his saw's jagged edge, the taste of his own cough-strained, stale breath, the starkness of his bedroom above the shop. No chance of a bride now, for him, in this small town where he had spurned all coy glances sent his way, waiting for his true love to return.

He wished he hadn't waited.

Still coughing, Lewys threw open the window shutters. He gulped fresh air. Delighted cries of children entered with the breeze.

A pageant wagon creaked into the town square outside his shop, horseless, shedding curls of magic onto the cobblestones from its warped wytchen beams. Children dropped coins into a box attached to the wagon's carriage and scrambled for seats. Eyes widening in shock, Lewys unconsciously dug his fingernails into the windowsill. The wagon's wood was peeling, its stage floor crooked, but it was still the same one. The only one.

As the threadbare curtain opened more magic showered the stage from the covered wagon's rafters. A puppet slumped against a painted forest backdrop: A princess wearing a gown the deep blush of sunset, the falling wytchen dust creating a net of crystals in her golden hair. With the clack of wooden joints, she began a light, graceful dance. A troll's appearance, lumbering in from stage right, tore a gasp from the children.

Lewys saw what the audience did not know to look for: the shadow of the puppet master's hands weaving along the stage floor. These puppets had no strings. The wytchen wood conjured the play from its dust and the shadow of intention.

After the puppet princess outsmarted the troll, she befriended a dragon, its velvet tongue unfurling like a panting dog. Adults and children alike cheered when she saved a village from a witch.

The curtain closed; the crowd dispersed.

Lewys grabbed his jerkin and dashed outside.

The wagon's damage looked even worse up close. Red rope secured the corners, but it was a temporary bandage for the cracked joints which exposed the wood's inner pith.

"Lewys, look how well your craft weathered the years." The old puppet master emerged from behind the curtain. "But it is long past the time for repairs."

"Master Rhodri, you take me for my father," Lewys replied. "He is gone these last ten years. I have his carpentry business as well as his name now."

Hobbling towards him on gnarled joints as the stage boards shifted and groaned, the old man squinted at Lewys. "Aye, I remember you," Rhodri said, beckoning the carpenter to follow him into the narrow living space behind the backdrop.

Lewys's heart sank. There was no sign of the puppet master's daughter among the clutter of tools, wood, parchment, and ink pots on the table. Clothes spilled out of a trunk, child's dresses with snippets removed. A torn blanket lay rumpled on the floor. Wytchen dust mixed with plain wood shavings on the floor.

How foolish he had been to wait.

The puppet princess was sitting upright in a cabinet with the troll, dragon, and witch on a shelf beneath her. A pile of bedraggled puppets lay at the bottom.

"I'd still like to commission you for repairs."

Lewys looked at the rafters and walls, sunlight spearing through the gaps. Rhodri added, "I have the coin to pay you, whatever the cost."

"It's not that, sir." Lewys sighed. "There are no wytchen trees left." News that his father could release the trees' magic had spread like fire all those years ago. The final demand, a flagship, had come from the duke himself, who would brook no refusal. The entire grove was consumed. His father had fallen ill during the ship's crafting and died soon after it was completed.

"But surely you can repair the existing wood?"

Lewys regarded the puppet master, with his bent back and knotted bones, and said kindly, "All due respect, Master, but perhaps a warm hearth in a home without wheels would serve you better now."

The old man nodded. "It probably would. But," he gestured to the puppets in the cabinet, "I must continue to tell her stories."

The puppet princess was as finely crafted as porcelain, the warm scent of beeswax polish lingering on her milk-white skin of peeled wytchen wood. Lewys slipped a finger along the gold cascade of her hair, a silken balm over his callused skin.

"You do remember my daughter? Roselyn?" the puppet master asked softly.

Lewys remembered the sun blinking through the wytchen branches, chasing after the girl as they played hide-and-seek in the grove, his father cutting and shaping wood for the wagon, murmuring words under his breath, words that he whispered in the puppet master's ear when he handed him blocks of wytchen.

Coaxed by his daughter, Master Rhodri had fashioned them both plain oak swords. Lewys and Roselyn pretended they were heroes, fighting trolls and witches, befriending dragons, crafting their own fairy tales from shadows at the forest's edge.

"Yes, Roselyn," Lewys said, the name sweet in his mouth. Her lips were always stained blush from the wytchen berries they were not supposed to eat, the red berries marked with stars that she hid in her dress pocket. When the pageant wagon was completed, oiled and shining like the moon, Lewys watched as it rolled away from the grove without need of a horse, Roselyn blowing kisses as she peeked out from behind the curtain. When it was gone, he ate the berry she had slipped into his hand after her whispered promise.

It had flooded his mouth with bitterness, the taste surprising him.

"She is happily married, then?"

"No. Her heart just...stopped. Soon after we left the grove. I don't know what happened." Rhodri hesitated as the carpenter's face turn pale. "It was very hard to keep going when I felt like I had buried my own heart with her. I needed something..." His voice cracking, he touched the puppet's hair also. "Something of her to hold on to."

Lewys snapped his hand away, stumbling over the puppet detritus spilling out from the cabinet's bottom.

"You must understand," Rhodri begged. "My daughter was all I had. I carved puppets for her, to give life to her stories." The old man twisted his hands, looked down, blinking.

Master Rhodri's struggle to contain his grief echoed in Lewys's own hollow chest. Slowly he collected the puppets from the floor, a mess of small swords and fractured oak limbs. All princes. "Can I fix these for you?" Lewys asked.

Shaking his head, the puppet master replied, "They were my gifts to her, to remember her birthday, after she...." He cleared his throat. "She never created a story of true love. I thought perhaps I could write one for her. But the words never came, and the puppets never worked right. I always found them damaged when I woke the next day. Nevertheless, I keep trying, every year."

Lewys was silent for a while, his hands cradling the broken princes. Wytchen dust drifted down from the wagon's ceiling, glittering bright as a promise.

I will come back to you.

"I am going to do something for you, Master Rhodri. And for her."

Back in his room he packed a satchel with a flask of water and food from his meager pantry, then secured a hatchet to his belt. Walking through the bare patch that had once been the grove, he glanced behind him, making sure he was alone before entering the thick forest beyond. After an hour the woodland sloped upwards as the pine trees thinned. He came to a ledge where a single tree grew, slanted trunk and low, leafed branches thriving against the crisp sky: The wytchen sapling that Lewys and his dying father had transplanted here, hidden from human greed.

He poured water on the roots, tied a red ribbon around a branch. Then Lewys sat, the trunk pressing into his jerkin, thinking of what could have been while the sun painted the sky the color of the princess's gown, of Roselyn's lips which had never touched his own. As the sun descended into the dark forest below him, he hefted his hatchet and spoke his request to the tree.

When Lewys came back to the wagon Rhodri was snoring in a corner, blanket wrapped around him and tucked under his grizzled chin. He used the old man's tools, peeling and smoothing the small branch the wytchen had granted him, carving a face, body, and limbs, whispering his father's words onto the wood for the first and last time. After rummaging through the trunk, he found the remnants of a white shawl which he cut with a pair of silver scissors to make a doll-size tunic and pants, needle and red thread moving as deftly as when he sewed patches into his own clothing. He painted the eyes and mouth.

Lewys took the puppet princess down from her shelf, arranging her carefully on the work table next to the newly carved prince, staring at her for a long time. He touched her hair again.

Leaning close, his lips almost touching her cheek, he breathed deeply. As his lungs filled with her wytchen wood scent, his heart returned, brimming with magic and love as when they had been children playing in the grove. "Roselyn," he murmured, "I kept my promise too. I waited."

With the scissors he cut his own hair off, every last lock. He stitched them onto a small felt cap. Uncorking a bottle of pine resin, he brushed the thick glue on the cap and attached it to the puppet prince's head.

Wooden hands twitched, clacked against each other.

Lewys's joints buckled and he flopped to the floor.

✍

The old man woke. Wytchen dust trickled down from the pageant wagon rafters, gleaming in slivers of daylight. Rhodri pulled himself up from his bedding and leaned on his work table, yawning and rubbing the dust that had settled on his face overnight away with one hand. He stared once his eyes cleared, his hand over his mouth.

Two puppets sat upright in front of him, blonde hair and dark hair bestrewn with crowns of wytchen dust that sparkled in the clear morning light. "Roselyn?" He reached out to touch the puppet princess's hair, then the smooth wood of the new puppet's skin. "Can it be? Have you found your true love?"

The puppets' hands moved. Their fingers interlocked.

Rhodri was overcome for a few moments by the rapid beating of his heart. "Well, then," he said, and wiped at his wet face as he searched the table for his parchment and ink pot. They had been knocked to the floor, the ink staining a crumpled set of clothes.

The puppet master paused. The jerkin's creases were filled with lines of a mundane, flaky dust.

He bowed to the puppet prince, as low as his gnarled back would allow. "If you will allow me, I will write you a play worthy of your love." Rhodri picked up the ink pot and parchment and found a fresh quill, dipping it into the little ink left.

Magic fell from the wagon beams in curls and crystals, settling upon the puppets and parchment. The words flowed easily this time.

✍ ✍ ✍

THE FUTURE IN A WASH BASIN

—

ERIN KEATING

The Future in a Wash Basin

Co. Cork, 1896

Siobhan O'Keeffe Mahoney had never seen her own reflection. It was not for lack of trying. She would pass the only mirror in the house she shared with her father and brother, then quickly turn around, as though she could surprise it into revealing her image. She would stare so long into the gray waters of Schull Harbor on a windless day that, once, one of the rotten neighborhood boys pushed her in. She'd floated, of course. She would press her nose to the long icicles that formed beside their door in January, hoping for the briefest glimpse of the sea blue eyes and coppery hair she had inherited from her mother. But never once had she seen her own reflection.

Instead, she saw the future.

And from Siobhan's place in the worn armchair by the hearth, the future looked bleak.

Finn MacCotter stood opposite her, wringing his cap in his hands. She had understood all of the words Finn had said individually, but couldn't make sense of them in the order in which he had delivered them.

Siobhan wiped her clammy palms on her skirt. "I'm sorry, Mr. MacCotter. Am I correct that this is a proposal of marriage?"

Finn MacCotter glanced over his shoulder, where Siobhan's father, Cormac Mahoney, stood with his arms crossed.

"I certainly hope you're not sorry to hear it." He let out a wheezy laugh, and his freckled cheeks flushed. "My Da, eh, you know he's not well. He wants to see me, eh, settled. And he and Mr. Mahoney being such good friends and all — "

Siobhan's father cleared his throat. Finn stopped talking.

Siobhan supposed she shouldn't be surprised. She was newly twenty-two and Finn a few years older, but it felt like there were fewer people their age in Schull Harbor by the hour — all packing their bags for America. Siobhan's stomach churned at the mere thought. How could they leave the only home that they knew for a place full of strangers?

Siobhan glanced over Finn's shoulder at the gilded-frame mirror that hung above the hearth. The clear surface of the mirror rippled as she looked at it. Should she marry Finn MacCotter or refuse? Each time she wavered, a misty image bubbled to the surface. That was what she loved most about the future — it was never set. Time ran steadily, like a river, and every decision she made took her down a different route of its forking path.

Siobhan saw herself scrubbing cow dung off Finn MacCotter's boots if she accepted or scrubbing her brother's children's dirty nappies if she refused. She would wash butchered blood from the cracks in Finn's leather gloves, or she would wash the blood from her sister-in-law's bedsheets after another birth. She would stare at the ceiling waiting for Finn to finish laboring over her in bed, or she would stare at the ceiling in the attic, displaced from her room, praying her screaming nieces and nephews would fall asleep.

Siobhan gripped the armchair with white knuckles. Her fingernails sank into the worn fabric. Was this it, then? Was she trapped by two tiresome fates — the obedient wife or the spinster aunt — without anything to call her own?

But then the image shifted to reveal a blonde daughter swaddled in Finn's arms. Siobhan nearly leapt from the armchair, her heart in her throat. If she took this path with Finn, she would have a daughter. Her mother's line would continue.

Siobhan blinked herself back to the present, to this worn armchair. She managed a smile. "Well, Mr. MacCotter, your proposal is certainly as good as any."

"Lovely! Eh, thank you. I'll, eh, go tell my Da." Finn MacCotter placed the wrung-out cap on his head. As soon as the front door closed, her brother and sister-in-law rushed in from the kitchen. They offered their congratulations, her sister-in-law trying awkwardly to embrace Siobhan around her own swollen belly.

Siobhan looked at her father, but he was studying the mirror closely, as he always did when he caught her scrying, wondering what secrets it revealed to his daughter.

✍

That night, after some revelry with the neighbors, Siobhan put on her wool jacket, took an oil lantern from the hook by the door, and headed out into the dark. The late-March air cooled her flushed cheeks, warm with whiskey and the heat of a dozen bodies cramped in their small front room. The oil lantern lit only a small patch of road in front of her. It didn't matter. Her bones knew the way. She trod down Colla Road, away from the yellow, blue, and plum-colored houses of the main street. Between the trees and the shore scrub she could spy the inky water of the harbor and the lone light of a ship.

Soon, she came upon the cemetery. It sat beside the ruins of Saint Mary's Church, a roofless stone structure overgrown with shrubbery and moss. The old gate squeaked as she entered. Two matching headstones on freshly weeded plots sat at the base of the hill, overlooking the harbor. Siobhan settled down in the grass, leaning against her mother's cold stone.

"Ma, Gran, I'm getting married," she whispered.

And somewhere, far away or very near, Bridget O'Keeffe Mahoney and Emer Sullivan O'Keeffe listened. Siobhan felt heat flickering behind her navel — her magic. When she was a girl, she'd felt it strongest in Gran's kitchen, watching the old woman grinding herbs into healing salves. But in the years since Gran's death, it felt strongest here.

This was the land where her mother and her gran had practiced their craft. This was the land where her own daughters would learn their arts. Even though the town seemed to be growing smaller each day, she couldn't bear to leave Schull Harbor and the bones of the women who came before her. This land was her inheritance.

She pressed her fingers to the earth and spoke the Old Irish word for 'water'. It was a tongue lost to nearly all but the wise women, a language she had learned from her gran. The ground yielded to her touch, and soon fresh water bubbled up and pooled at the base of the stones. She would use the water's surface to scry.

She had chosen the path in which she would bear children — even if they were Finn MacCotter's children. Her mother's line would continue. Her daughter would learn magic at her elbow.

Siobhan whispered, "Show me my line."

The surface of the water rippled, revealing the image of a blonde little girl. The child hid behind Finn's legs, his arms stretched out in front of her — shielding her from something. In this vision, Siobhan reached for her daughter, but the girl and Finn both backed away. They looked afraid — afraid of her.

Siobhan sank her fingers into the dirt, felt the comforting hum of her foremother's magic.

"Again," she demanded of the water through gritted teeth.

The next vision had the same blonde girl studying a children's catechism in the MacCotter's large parlor. The view was at a strange angle, but then the vision grew wider until Siobhan saw herself peering through a crack in the doorway. Then Finn appeared, his mouth in a tight line, and closed the door.

"No," Siobhan gasped. She could hardly breathe over the lump forming in her throat. "No, no, no."

She sank her hands into the pool of water, splashing away the vision. "Please, do any of them practice?" she begged. "Do any of them scry?"

The water grew cloudy with mud and when it settled, the image of three copper-haired girls flashed in quick succession.

Then, for the first time in Siobhan's life, she thought she saw her reflection. A sea blue eye stared back at her, too close to the surface of the water.

It blinked.

Siobhan, startled, tumbled backward into the grass. But she crept forward again, and peered into the pool. The face pulled away from the water's surface, revealing the girl's other eye, a pert freckle-dusted nose, and a crooked smile with new teeth growing in awkwardly.

"Hi!" The girl said. Her face rippled as a gentle breeze skirted across the surface of the water. Her voice was strange, an accent with sharp, narrow sounds that grated Siobhan's ears.

"Hello," Siobhan said cautiously. Often, she could hear the scenes that she scried, but she had never been able to communicate with them. Something about this seemed touched with fae magic.

"Do you see funny things in the mirror too?" the girl asked.

"I do," Siobhan answered.

"Have you ever seen yourself?"

"No."

"Me either." The girl shrugged. "What did you ask the mirror to see? Oh, I guess you aren't using a mirror, are you? You're all — wavy."

Siobhan laughed, the sound so loud in the silent night that she scared herself. This girl spoke so many words, and so quickly. The flame in Siobhan's stomach grew hotter, white heat rippling through her body. It was a powerful feeling, a prideful and protective affection. She hadn't expected to feel it this suddenly. Perhaps it was because she knelt on her mother's and gran's graves — a heritage of blood and bones. This was a girl of her line.

"I asked to see my family," Siobhan said.

The girl grinned, lips parting to reveal her lopsided teeth again. "You're Siobhan, aren't you?" Siobhan must have made a surprised face, because the girl laughed. "My mom's told me all about you — you're her great-grandma — I think. I'm Bridget! It's nice to meet you."

Siobhan caught her breath hearing her mother's name spoken in the girl's strange voice.

"Tell me about your mother," Siobhan whispered.

She listened to Bridget tell her about her mother, who was attuned to stones and crystals, who used citrine to manifest enough cash to make ends meet, rose quartz to ease her broken heart after Bridget's father left, amethyst under Bridget's pillow to keep bad dreams away.

Hearing the stories reminded Siobhan of the tales she'd heard of her own mother, who could press her hands to a stone and hear its history.

As the moon rose and set, the water slowly dried up. Siobhan finally said goodbye to Bridget — this scried girl with her mother's name — who stared up at her through the water. When Bridget's image was gone, and Siobhan was alone in the cemetery once more, she whispered a prayer of thanks over the graves. Her line would go on.

But she couldn't shake the image of her blonde daughter's wide blue eyes and trembling mouth. What could make a child look at her mother like that?

✍

The next day, Siobhan and her father donned their Sunday best and walked down the long dirt road toward MacCotter's Farm. The cows in the pasture lumbered up to them, stretching their heads over the low stone walls as though to inspect Siobhan personally. Milk, cheese, butter, and the highest quality meat came out of MacCotter's Farm. At least a dozen men in town were employed there as farmhands — those who did not go to sea every day, as Siobhan's father did.

The morning damp clung to Siobhan's skin. Her cheeks stung with cold when they finally reached the MacCotter's stone house. Finn MacCotter answered the door, smartly dressed, with his curly blond hair parted and beard newly trimmed.

"Welcome, eh, if you'll follow me this way."

"Is that them?" A voice called from the other room.

"Yes, Da!" Finn shouted back.

Finn led them into the foyer. Siobhan had been inside the MacCotters' house before — they held an annual Christmas party for the whole town — but she hadn't expected it to look so splendid on an ordinary day. The dark wooden banisters gleamed. She followed the stairs with her eyes, generations of blond MacCotters looking down on her from oil portraits. To their right was a large formal dining room, where the MacCotters hosted Christmas dinner at a table laden with silver. To their left was a dimly lit parlor that was twice the size of the Mahoney's front room. There Mr. MacCotter sat in a chair by a roaring fire, wrapped in blankets.

Despite the grandeur, a chill shuddered down Siobhan's back. Without the bustle of the Christmas guests, an eerie quiet sat heavily on the house.

"Cormac, welcome! And Miss Mahoney, come here, come here." Siobhan allowed Mr. MacCotter to kiss her hand.

"Finbarr!" Mr. Mahoney boomed, shaking Mr. MacCotter's liver-spotted hand. "All's well with the farm?"

Though they were the same age, Mr. MacCotter seemed decades older than his friend, stooped and hunched with pain no one could cure. Perhaps Gran O'Keeffe could have healed him, had he fallen ill in her time.

"Fine, fine," Mr. MacCotter wheezed. "Except I don't know how I'll keep staffing it. America is stealing all my farmhands' sons. It seems a man can't expect his children to stay in one place anymore. We must be the luckiest men in all of Cork."

Siobhan glanced at Finn, who stood stiffly beside his father, his eyes fixed to a spot on the floor. Had he ever dreamed of leaving for America, like so many others? Or was he like her — proud to be tied to this land and his family's history here?

Mr. MacCotter cleared his throat with a phlegmy rattle in his chest. "Now, Miss Mahoney, let me look at you."

Siobhan wore a dress of carnation red, a fawn-colored wool shawl embroidered with rosebuds, and her coppery hair neatly pinned. Of course, there had been no way for her to see how she looked. But, that morning, as she peered into her wash basin, Bridget's face had appeared.

Bridget was older than she'd been when they'd spoken in the cemetery — now a woman in her sixties with elegant white hair. Bridget had said that Siobhan looked beautiful. That was better than any reflection.

"Turn please," Mr. MacCotter said. Siobhan gave a girlish twirl and Mr. MacCotter let out an annoyed sound like a cow's loam. "No, girl, slowly, please, slowly."

So, Siobhan turned slowly in a full circle, feeling the weight of the men's eyes on her. She tried to make a face to her father, but his arms were crossed, watching Mr. MacCotter closely.

"Very good. Now, if you would please smile," Mr. MacCotter instructed.

Siobhan did her best lady-like smile, demure and closed-lipped. Again, a cow-like sound burst from Mr. MacCotter, sending spittle flying. "No, girl — your teeth. I want to see your teeth."

Siobhan realized that she was not a woman, trying to impress her father-in-law, but a cow being inspected at auction. She bared her teeth, curling her lips as far back as she could manage.

"Siobhan!" her father hissed.

But Mr. MacCotter didn't seem to notice the gesture. "She's looks healthy, and any daughter of yours must have a strong constitution. Her hips — wideset — good for child-bearing. We'd hate to see her go the way of her mother."

A flame sparked in the pit of Siobhan's stomach, equal parts magic and rage.

Siobhan tried to keep her voice level. "There was nothing wrong with my mother."

"Siobhan, now is not the time," her father warned, his voice low.

"Of course, my girl, of course. If your kind father had insisted the doctor be present for the whole labor instead of leaving it up to his addled mother-in-law, perhaps she would have made it," Mr. MacCotter said.

Fire spread through Siobhan's core, heat moving up into her chest. Frost began to spread on the windowpane as she balled her fists. She muttered the Old Irish word for 'breath', trying her gran's old trick for calming a racing heart.

"What was that, girl?" Mr. MacCotter demanded. The word 'girl' chafed at her skin.

The frost grew with a low cracking. Siobhan snapped. "If my father hadn't called for the doctor at the last minute and had let my gran continue her treatment, my mother most certainly would have made it."

Gran O'Keeffe had told her the story. Her father, in his terror, called for the doctor, who had thrown Gran O'Keeffe from the room. She had finished brewing ergot tea — a thimbleful of ergot powder brewed in boiling water — that would make her mother's uterine muscles contract and stop the bleeding. The doctor had knocked the teacup from her hand, convinced ergot was poisonous. He packed Bridget O'Keeffe Mahoney full of cotton, which she bled through, and bled through, and bled through, while the tea that could have saved her seeped into the floorboards. Gran O'Keeffe rocked Siobhan, newly born and wailing, outside the door while her daughter died.

"I said not now, Siobhan!" her father snapped.

The thick ice on the window shone like silver. And in it, Siobhan saw herself in labor, her face red with sweat, screaming in primal pain. When the child arrived in the world, Finn snatched it from her arms, as though Siobhan was diseased.

She squeezed her eyes shut, willing the image away.

"There, there, my girl. I did not mean to upset you. Of course, you miss your mother at a time like this," Mr. MacCotter said.

In truth, Siobhan rarely missed her mother, though she would never dare say that aloud in front of her father. There was no need to miss her; her presence was constant. Every time she felt her magic tug at her stomach, it was like her mother was there beside her. But in this house, with its too-dark and too-quiet rooms, lorded over by Mr. MacCotter and his ever-watchful gaze, could she practice safely here?

Mr. MacCotter squeezed her hand, and Siobhan fought the urge to pull away.

Panic flickered and flared in her chest like a dying candle. These men would snuff her out.

✍

Hours later, Siobhan had rubbed her skin red and raw, but still could not shake the chill of the MacCotters' house. She had locked the door of her little room with its drafty window that overlooked the harbor. Despite her sister-in-law's incessant knocking, Siobhan didn't answer. She tried to lose herself in the rhythm of the squeaking floorboards as she paced. Only when her feet had grown tired did she pour some water into the basin by her bed.

"Show me Bridget," she demanded. The surface of the water rippled, and Bridget's face came into view. She was younger than she had been when they spoke that morning, when she complimented Siobhan's dress. Now a woman in her early thirties, the only wrinkles on Bridget's face were faint laugh lines around her mouth.

Siobhan was sure that Bridget was aging normally in her own time, growing a little older each day. But the mirror carried Bridget back from different parts of her life to this point in Siobhan's. This point was an anchor, a moment of significance, that had affected the fate of Siobhan's line. Siobhan took comfort in this — it was a sign that her marriage to Finn MacCotter would not be for nothing, despite her unsettling visions and his father's frigid, suffocating house.

"Oh! Siobhan! Hi!" Bridget chirped. Her energy never changed — whether she was a girl or a woman or an old lady. She always spoke so fast, Siobhan could hardly understand her. "I'm glad to see you. I've got big news actually, something I think you'd really like to know."

"Go on, my heart," Siobhan said. Even though Bridget appeared older than her now, she was still overwhelmed by a warm rush of affection. There was a maternal fondness for Bridget that Siobhan could not shake, despite the years that separated them.

"I'm pregnant! You're the first person other than my husband to know — weird, right?" Light radiated from Bridget's dewy cheeks. "It's going to be a girl — I just know it."

Siobhan's throat felt tight. Echoing through her head were her own screams of labor that she had scried in the MacCotters' windows.

"Congratulations — that is..." Siobhan murmured. She recalled Gran's story of her birth and her mother's death — the two tangled up together. She clutched the ceramic basin, pressing it into her stomach as a wave of nausea passed over her. As much as Siobhan wanted a daughter, childbirth itself was a nightmare that had haunted her all her life. And to think that Bridget would soon go through it, wherever and whenever she was.

"Are you all right?" Bridget asked. Two deep worry lines creased her forehead.

Siobhan nodded. "My mother..." was all she could manage.

"Shit!" Bridget hissed. "I'm so sorry. Mom told me about your mother. Of course, you're concerned. But I'll be all right, I promise."

Siobhan thought of her conversation with Bridget just this morning. Bridget would live to have crow's feet around her eyes and sleek white hair.

"I know you will, my heart," Siobhan said. Then she swallowed hard, trying to speak through the lump in her throat. "Bridget, do you know if our magic skipped over someone in our line. Did your mom's grandma practice?"

Bridget began to laugh, but caught herself. Siobhan wondered how worry wrote itself on her face — did she have the same deep worry lines as her great-great-granddaughter? "She must have — I've heard stories from my grandma that she was a healer. Why do you ask?"

Siobhan clutched at her stomach. Bridget's words didn't seem to align with her visions at all. "What about when she was young? How did her gift grow?"

Bridget tilted her head. "Siobhan, you already know the answer. Our magic can only grow if we practice it."

The wedding was set for August. Though the date was months away, there was already a flurry of preparation at the Mahoney house. Her sister-in-law and three of Mr. Mahoney's sisters took it upon themselves to tailor Siobhan's mother's wedding dress for the occasion. She could never seem to breathe in her wedding dress, no matter how many times they let it out.

There were arguments over what they should serve at the Mahoney's house following the ceremony, which readings would be best for the mass, whether foxglove or iris would look prettier in a bouquet. Siobhan was seldom asked for her opinion, so she chose not to offer it. Instead, she stood quietly on an overturned soap box, letting herself be pricked with pins, as her mind raced.

The problem had to be Finn. In every vision she'd have of her blonde daughter — Finn's daughter — he stood between them. She had to convince him that their child needed to practice her craft, that this was Siobhan's legacy. She could not let her daughter's magic die.

Whenever one of the aunts held up a mirror for Siobhan to inspect their progress, Siobhan saw the image of her daughter with Finn, with terror in her blue eyes, pulling away from Siobhan.

She breathed deeply until her ribs strained against the seams, and she tugged at the lace against her sweaty neck. The aunts tutted and pinned some more, but Siobhan's dry mouth couldn't form the words to tell them that the problem wasn't the dress — it was her future.

One day, a month into wedding preparations, when the aunts gossiped about a neighbor's daughter leaving for America, Finn MacCotter knocked on the door. The Mahoney women fussed like hens as they barred Finn from entering until Siobhan changed out of her wedding gown.

"Sorry for the trouble," Siobhan said when she finally let him in. She tried to smile at him, but felt more like a wolf bearing its fangs. Each time she saw him, she searched his eyes for the disgust she had seen in her visions. A steady fury, like waves beating against the coast, built up in her for all of the things he had yet to do.

"No trouble. But I have, eh, some news. Well, a request really." Finn removed his cap, wringing it in his hands. "My Da, eh, took a turn. I know there's so much to do, and, eh, I don't want to burden your family. But, do you think we could move up the date?" Finn asked. "To next week?"

Siobhan's stomach clenched so suddenly she thought she'd be sick on Finn's shoes. She'd expected a couple more months to find a way to convince him that she — and their future daughter — needed to be able to practice their craft. But next week? She leaned against the door to steady herself. "I'm not sure. I — "

But then her sister-in-law and the aunts burst from the kitchen where they'd been eavesdropping. "Not a burden at all," her sister-in-law said. "We can manage."

At those words, the mounting fear turned to flame. It started behind Siobhan's navel and spread outward until her fingertips burned. The air around her rippled with heat. She worried that the house would catch fire if she didn't do something. Siobhan cast her gaze toward the harbor.

"Finn, come with me." She grabbed him by the elbow, but Finn yelped in pain and leapt away. His shirt had been scorched.

Siobhan didn't apologize or explain. Instead, she walked out into the bright May morning. His heavy footsteps followed. Only when they were halfway to the harbor, far from her sister-in-law's uncanny hearing, did Siobhan dare to speak.

"Finn, you know what I am, don't you?"

"What do you — " he began.

"Please," she interrupted. "It's a small town. You know the rumors. You know my gran was a wise-woman. You know that I — well — I see things." The fire of her magic grew hotter in the pit of her stomach, as though by speaking it she had fed the flames. She felt her power rippling off her skin. Down the road, the harbor waters grew mirror-still.

Finn tugged at his shirt collar. His neck and cheeks turned splotchy red. "I've heard. But, eh, I'm willing to look past it. We'll have an ordinary life."

"Ordinary?" Siobhan felt the air rush from her lungs.

"Ordinary. We'll run a good house, and raise good children, and no one will say that you're odd."

"What about our daughter? If she sees things too?" Rage and fear were a potent combination for women with her gift. It was like adding whiskey to a flame. Her power flared up, casting a glassy frost across all of the neighbors' windows.

"There's no need to encourage her — abilities. She'll be ordinary, like any other child. What more could she want?" He reached out to hold her hand, but pulled back. "What more could you want?"

"I want her to inherit what is hers." She held Finn's gaze. Long silence hung between them, interrupted only by the sound of groaning ice.

"MacCotter Farm will be her inheritance, if we have no sons." His voice sounded hollow, like the vast rooms of his father's house. "And we are done with this discussion."

He turned away from her, but, just before he did, she saw in his eyes what she had been searching for, for weeks. Disgust. Anger. A shadow of fear.

This was the Finn MacCotter of her visions, the one who shielded her own daughter from her, who banished magic from their home, who cast Siobhan into loneliness. This was not the life she had chosen when she accepted his proposal.

The fire of her magic roared inside her. All of the power that she'd stoked released in a rush. A sudden frost descended on the streets of Schull Harbor, the town encased in a mirrored sheen of ice. And in it, Siobhan finally understood her visions.

On the icy road ahead of her, heading back toward her father's house, she saw the blonde daughter and her fearful eyes. On the road leading down to the harbor, she saw a copper-haired girl, reading in Siobhan's lap.

Siobhan laughed aloud and, with it, icicles crashed to the ground.

How had she forgotten? In her panic at her line dying, she had forgotten the simple truth. The future was not fixed. That blonde-haired daughter she had seen was only one possible child that would come to be — Finn's child. But she remembered the line of copper-haired girls she had first scried in the puddle at the cemetery — those were the daughters of a life and a love yet unknown to her.

✍

Siobhan raced back to her father's house, ignoring the frantic questioning of her aunts and sister-in-law. In her room, she dragged her wardrobe in front of her door, straining and sweating under the effort. She didn't know how long she'd have until her father found out about her fight with Finn. And she needed time to think.

She filled her wash basin, splashing half of the pitcher on the floor with her shaking hands. "What should I do?" she begged of the water.

The water rippled and bubbled, showing her glimpses of every possible future. She could marry Finn MacCotter and have their miserable, magicless daughter. She could stay in Schull Harbor, unmarried, tending the graves of Ma and Gran. She could take the path that traveled past the curve in the coastline that had marked the edge of Siobhan's whole world. Limitless possibilities danced across the water's surface until Siobhan grew dizzy.

She gripped the ceramic basin to steady herself. "Stop," she hissed. The water stilled. She should have known better than to ask the water such an open-ended the question. It could only show her the paths — it could not tell her what to do.

Downstairs, the door slammed. The whole house seemed to rock as her father stormed in.

"Show me Bridget," she demanded. Her voice was tight in her throat. She didn't have much time.

The water rippled, and then Bridget was looking up at her. She was a young woman, nearly Siobhan's age. Her sea blue eyes were watery and red-rimmed, and her coppery hair was disheveled. A few hair pins still clung to her curls. At the edge of the basin, Siobhan glimpsed the neckline of a black dress.

Siobhan's fevered thoughts stilled. Her chest ached as she studied her great-great-granddaughter's quivering chin.

"Oh, my heart, what happened? What's wrong?" Siobhan murmured.

"My grandma — she — " Bridget wiped her eyes. "Could you — could you tell me about yours?" she asked.

But then there was a pounding at the door.

"Siobhan — Siobhan, open this door this instant," her father roared.

"Siobhan, is everything all right?" Bridget asked, drying her eyes.

"Everything is fine, my heart. Don't worry about a thing," Siobhan murmured.

"Finn MacCotter is down at the harbor calling you a — he was calling you a..." Even after all these years, her father still couldn't bring himself to say it.

Siobhan whispered the Old Irish word for 'quiet'. The room stopped rattling, her father stopped thundering. A thick blanket of silence had fallen over everything except Siobhan and her wash basin. Bridget needed her, and Siobhan would let nothing interrupt them.

Siobhan sighed, returning her attention to Bridget. "You wanted to hear about Gran O'Keeffe, yes?"

Bridget nodded, her red-rimmed eyes wide with surprise.

Gran O'Keeffe had been Siobhan's whole heritage — serving as both grandmother and mother. The air around Siobhan crackled with Gran O'Keeffe's memory. Since Gran's death, there was a word Siobhan hadn't spoken. But Bridget deserved to hear it.

"My Gran O'Keeffe was a witch, like us."

Gran O'Keeffe was the one who named Siobhan's ability. Scrying: that was the word for seeing the future in the mirror, in water, in ice. Any witch worth her salt could learn to scry, but only once in several generations was a witch born a natural scryer. Gran O'Keeffe's own mother had been one. It had been enough, to see the look of pride on Gran O'Keeffe's face, rather than ever seeing her own.

In this very house, Siobhan had learned the healing arts at Gran's elbow — borage seed oil for aching bones, honeyed marshmallow root for cough, yarrow tea for fevers. Though the plants would not speak to Siobhan as they had to Gran O'Keeffe, it had been enough to feel the heat of their shared magic ripple through the small kitchen as old and young woman worked side by side.

In this very room, Gran O'Keeffe had brushed and braided Siobhan's copper hair, describing the face that had eluded Siobhan all her life. "You look just like your ma did at this age," Gran O'Keeffe would whisper as she worked her knobby fingers through Siobhan's hair. "Big eyes as blue as the sky."

Schull Harbor was her home, where memories of Gran O'Keeffe were embedded into the grains of the wooden house and the cracks of the cobblestone streets. Schull Harbor was all she had known, and she loved it — despite its smallness that only got smaller — because it was here that she had learned her craft. This town was all she was. Could she really leave it all behind? Leave Ma and Gran O'Keeffe's bones, their memories?

Siobhan watched the lines of grief ease on Bridget's face as she spoke. Siobhan didn't care how many generations stood between her and her daughter's, daughter's, daughter's daughter. Bridget was flesh of her flesh and blood of her blood. She loved her as though she had carried her herself — as Gran O'Keeffe had loved Siobhan.

Gran O'Keeffe would understand.

Siobhan realized then that she did not need the water to tell her what to do. There were hundreds of paths that could lead to copper-haired daughters learning their craft. But she wanted just one path — she wanted the future that led to Bridget.

Her magic smoldered in her stomach. That tugging, fiery sensation behind her navel burned brighter than it had in years. Siobhan had always thought that her power came from this land, from the buried bones of her foremothers. But as she watched her great-great-granddaughter's face — the one she has seen age in the rippling waters of her wash basin — she understood the truth. Their magic was not tied to the land. Their magic was tied to each other.

These abilities were her inheritance and her legacy — hers to remember and hers to leave behind. This young woman who scried the past while Siobhan scried the future was proof of that legacy.

"You come from a long line of extraordinary women." Siobhan's voice crackled with power.

With those words, the wash basin in her hands turned to crystal. The surface of the water stilled into silver glass. The future itself turned solid and clear.

"Bridget," she asked her great-great-granddaughter, "where are you?"

Bridget grinned, because she had known this future all along. "Brooklyn."

"Brooklyn." The word fell from Siobhan's lips like an irreversible spell. It was a place that sounded too big for her wash basin, so Siobhan threw open the window. "Show me," she demanded of the harbor. The blistering heat under her skin seeped out of her, until the air around her hummed. The harbor turned to solid ice — boats were trapped, fisherman's frozen nets were too heavy to pull, children splashing in the shallows skated along a sheen of glass.

Siobhan feared the ice would show her the future of Schull Harbor with wild grass growing over her foremothers' graves. But it didn't. Instead, she witnessed her own line stretch for generations beyond the harbor and across the Atlantic. Tears streamed down Siobhan's cheeks. In those faces, she saw Ma's blue eyes and Gran's knowing smile repeated and changed like an old incantation.

Siobhan tore away from the window to peer back into the crystal basin. Bridget raised her eyebrows, as though to ask Siobhan what she had seen, even though she already knew. How Siobhan loved her, this girl of her line.

"My heart," Siobhan breathed. "I'm on my way."

✍ ✍ ✍

REVISION

Initial feedback

I liked the concept and characters, but felt the story started slowly, and the decisions in it came a little too easily. The end felt a bit flat to me. The rules of the magic could use a little clarification — e.g., why does Bridget show up initially, if the Siobhan is expecting a view of her future with Finn? Who is her child's father?

Author's intent

What do you think the story's about?
What emotions are you trying to evoke?

I think the story is about heritage and legacy; when I was first thinking about this story, I really liked the idea of using scrying as a way to link two distant generations so that Siobhan could see her legacy.

I also think that the story is about choices and the idea of a fluid future — something that I think I can lean into during a rewrite. I want to create a sense of claustrophobia as Siobhan nears the wedding date — she feels trapped by the future and forgets that she has any control over it. I think that will then make her decision to leave for America even more freeing.

Author's note

"The Future in a Wash Basin" was the first piece I had published after a long break from writing short stories — and an even longer break from submitting them. Revising this piece for *Metaphorosis* encouraged me to seriously think of myself as a writer.

To start the rewrite, *Metaphorosis* editor B. Morris Allen asked me what I thought my story was about, and I knew this would be a highly collaborative process. While I had an idea of what was at the heart of the story — heritage, legacy, choice, and fate — I had never needed to articulate those ideas directly. Composing my response to Morris forced me to reduce those big concepts into specifics that I could incorporate into the story. After I better understood the ideas around which I wanted to focus this piece, I could begin addressing structural changes.

The most fruitful part of the revision process was that it allowed me to consider how the use of magic and time affected the shape of the story. As we began the first round of revisions, Morris suggested that I clarify the rules of magic in the story: originally, when Siobhan scries her descendants, Bridget appears immediately, but *why* does Bridget appear if Siobhan is expecting a view of her future with her betrothed? As I considered this, I realized that I had built Siobhan's visions around the idea that the future was fixed and inevitable — Bridget appeared in Siobhan's visions because I knew what decision Siobhan would make at the end of the story. But I didn't want time to work that way. Siobhan says, "The future is not fixed," and this revision process let me restructure the story to reflect that statement.

To allow for a changeable future, I added visions of Siobhan's daughter by her fiancé to juxtapose with visions of Bridget. By laying out two paths for Siobhan, the revised story structure inherently heightened the tension around her decision to stay in Ireland or to emigrate. This restructuring allowed me to better align this story with what I thought it was about: the moment when a decision affects not only one person, but a whole lineage.

Because I tied this story much more closely to Siobhan's decision, I had to cut a concluding section written from Bridget's perspective. I had wanted the readers to see Bridget in her own time and show how her unique ability to scry the past would be used in her day-to-day life. However, it felt like it detracted from the story, especially coming moments after Siobhan's critical choice. I don't regret cutting Bridget's scene, both because it strengthened Siobhan's story and because now Bridget can have her own story.

Ultimately, through the revision process "The Future in a Wash Basin" became more like the piece I had imagined it could be. By articulating what the story was about, I focused my revisions on amplifying those ideas, adding and cutting where necessary. In doing so, I discovered more tenderness between Siobhan and Bridget, which became the beating heart of the story.

Editor's note

I like things to make sense, primarily so that underlying mechanics don't distract from the core narrative of the story. Here, while I liked the concept and characters of the story, I felt that the magic in the piece didn't make sense to me. Instead of empathizing with Siobhan and her choices, I was thinking in part about why Bridget showed up at all (rather than Finn). I also felt that the start and end of the story needed work (one a little slow, the other a little flat), and that some of Siobhan's changes came too easily.

The mechanical issues of the magic were fairly easily cleared up, though as Erin notes, they required some rejiggering of the story on her part. Those changes — in particular the daughter's fear of Siobhan — were things I would not have considered, but that I thought strengthened the story. This is the ideal of revision, from an editor's perspective — to be able to point out an issue and have the author come up with something entirely new that makes the heart of the story even stronger.

Despite my initial concerns about slowness, the start of the story didn't change much. There's an inevitable familiarization process that occurs during editing — I get to know the story better, the author's intent better, the overall arc better. Sometimes, that means I see something in the story that I didn't get initially; sometimes it means that I lose track of my original, first-exposure reaction. There's no way to tell which is happening, and the only thing to do is to try to judge the product as it evolves. In this case, I thought the final version of the start was a good fit to the overall story, despite not being considerably 'faster' than before.

The ending was somewhat more challenging. As Erin notes, the piece originally ended with a scene from Bridget's perspective, which allowed the theme of the family line to come through clearly. However, I find sudden shifts in perspective more often to be awkward, especially toward the end of the story. I felt that the story could lose the final, Bridget-focused scene and still be effective, and I think that approach worked very well.

The Future in a Wash Basin

Co. Cork, 1896

Siobhan O'Keeffe Mahoney had never seen her own reflection. It was not for lack of trying. She would pass the only mirror in the house she shared with her father and brother, then quickly turn around as though she could surprise it into revealing her image. She would stare so long into the gray waters of Schull Harbor on a windless day that, once, one of the rotten neighborhood boys pushed her in. She'd floated, as her kind did. She would press her nose to the long icicles that formed beside their door in January, hoping for the briefest glimpse of the sea blue eyes and coppery hair for which she had received so many compliments. But never once had she seen her own reflection.

Instead, she saw the future.

And from Siobhan's place in the worn armchair by the hearth, the future looked bleak.

Finn MacCotter stood opposite her, wringing his cap in his hands. She had understood all of the words Finn had said individually, but couldn't make sense of them in the order in which he had delivered them.

Siobhan wiped her clammy palms on her skirt. "I'm sorry, Mr. MacCotter. Am I correct that this is a proposal of marriage?"

Finn MacCotter glanced over his shoulder, where Siobhan's father, Cormac Mahoney, stood with his arms crossed.

"I certainly hope you're not sorry to hear it." He let out a wheezy laugh, and his freckled cheeks flushed. "My Da, eh, you know he's not well. He wants to see me, eh, settled. And he and Mr. Mahony being such good friends and all — ."

Siobhan's father cleared his throat. Finn stopped talking.

Siobhan supposed she shouldn't be surprised. She was newly twenty-two and Finn a few years older, but it felt like there were fewer people their age in Schull Harbor by the hour. Finn had been courting Mary Ann Barry last spring, and many expected them to be engaged by St. Paul's Day. But then Mr. Barry packed up his wife and daughters and moved to America. For weeks, Finn sulked up and down Main Street. The news had shaken Siobhan; she couldn't fathom leaving her home behind for a strange world.

Siobhan glanced over Finn's shoulder at the gilded-frame mirror that hung above the hearth. It was the nicest thing in the house — a wedding present from her Ma's gran. Both women were long-gone now.

The clear surface of the mirror rippled as she looked at it. Should she marry Finn MacCotter or refuse? Each time she wavered, a misty image bubbled to the surface. Siobhan saw herself scrubbing cow dung off Finn MacCotter's boots if she accepted or scrubbing her brother's children's dirty nappies if she refused. She would wash butchered blood from the cracks in Finn's leather gloves, or she would wash the blood from her sister-in-law's bedsheets after another birth. She would stare at the ceiling waiting for Finn to finish laboring over her in bed, or she would stare at the ceiling in the attic, displaced from her room, praying her screaming nieces and nephews would fall asleep.

Siobhan gripped the armchair with white knuckles. Her fingernails sank into the worn fabric. Was this it then? Was she trapped by two tiresome fates — the obedient wife or the spinster aunt — without anything to call her own?

But then the image shifted to reveal a copper-haired daughter bouncing on her knee. Siobhan nearly leapt from the armchair, her heart in her throat. If she took this path with Finn, she would have a daughter. Her mother's line would continue.

The vision warped and faded. Siobhan blinked herself back to the present, to this worn armchair. Her father stood directly in front of the mirror. His storm gray eyes stared her down, and one bushy brow raised slowly. Of course, he knew she had been scrying. He looked back and forth between her and Finn MacCotter and nodded twice.

But it wasn't her father's stern look that made her accept. It was the promise of a little girl to whom she would teach her foremothers' arts.

Siobhan managed a smile. "Well, Mr. MacCotter, your proposal is certainly as good as any."

"Lovely! Eh, thank you. I'll, eh, go tell my Da." Finn MacCotter placed the wrung-out cap on his head. As soon as the front door closed, Sean and his wife, Aoife, rushed in from the kitchen.

"Well done, Siobhan! Well done!" Sean smacked her on the shoulder.

"We are so happy for you," Aoife hugged her. Aoife and Sean were married hardly six months, and already Aoife's stomach swelled.

Siobhan looked at her father, but he was studying the mirror closely, as he always did when he caught her scrying, wondering what secrets it revealed to his daughter.

That night, after some revelry with the neighbors, Siobhan put on her wool jacket, took an oil lantern from the hook by the door, and headed out into the dark. The late-March air cooled her flushed cheeks, red with whiskey and the heat of a dozen bodies cramped in their small front room. The oil lantern lit only a small patch of road in front of her. It didn't matter. Her bones knew the way. She trod down Colla Road, away from the yellow, blue, and plum-colored houses of the main street. Between the trees and the shore scrub she could spy the inky water of the harbor and the lone light of a ship.

Soon, she came upon the cemetery. It sat beside the ruins of Saint Mary's Church, a roofless stone structure overgrown with shrubbery and moss. The old gate squeaked as she entered. Two matching headstones on freshly weeded plots sat at the base of the hill, overlooking the harbor. Siobhan settled down in the grass, leaning against the cold stone.

"Ma, Gran, I'm getting married," she whispered.

And somewhere, far away or very near, Bridget O'Keeffe Mahoney and Emer Sullivan O'Keeffe listened. Siobhan felt heat flickering behind her navel — her magic. When she was a girl, she'd felt it strongest in her gran's kitchen, watching the old woman grinding herbs into healing salves. But in the years since Gran's death, it felt the strongest here.

This was the land where her mother and her gran practiced their craft. This was the land where her own daughters would learn their arts. Even though the town seemed to be growing smaller each day, she couldn't bear to leave Schull Harbor and the bones of the women who came before her.

She pressed her fingers to the earth and spoke the Old Irish word for water. It was a tongue lost to nearly all but the wise women, a language she had learned from her gran. The ground yielded to her touch, and soon fresh water bubbled up and pooled at the base of the stones. She would use the water's surface to scry.

She had chosen the path in which she would bear children — even if they were Finn MacCotter's children. Her mother's line would continue. Her daughter would learn magic at her elbow.

Siobhan whispered, "Show me my line."

Then, for the first time in Siobhan's life, she thought she saw her reflection. A sea blue eye stared back at her, too close to the surface of the water. It blinked. Siobhan, startled, tumbled backward into the grass. But she crept forward again, and peered into the pool. The face pulled away from the water's surface, revealing the girl's other eye, a pert freckle-dusted nose, and a crooked smile with new teeth growing in awkwardly.

"Hi!" The girl said. Her face rippled as a gentle breeze skirted across the surface of the water. Her voice was strange, an accent with sharp, narrow sounds that grated Siobhan's ears.

"Hello," Siobhan said cautiously. Often, she could hear the scenes that she scried, but she had never been able to communicate with them. Something about this seemed touched with fae magic.

"Do you see funny things in the mirror too?" the girl asked.

"I do," Siobhan answered.

"Have you ever seen yourself?"

"No."

"Me either." The girl shrugged. "And what did you ask the mirror to see tonight? Oh, I guess you aren't using a mirror, are you? You're all — wavy."

Siobhan laughed, the sound so loud in the silent night that she scared herself. This girl spoke so many words, and so quickly. The flame in Siobhan's stomach grew hotter, white heat rippling through her body. It was a powerful feeling, a prideful and protective affection. She hadn't expected to feel it this suddenly. Perhaps it was because she knelt on her mother and gran's graves — a heritage of blood and bones. This was a girl of her line.

"I asked to see my family," Siobhan said.

The girl grinned, lips parting to reveal her lopsided teeth again. "You're Siobhan, aren't you?" Siobhan must have made a surprised face because the girl laughed. "My mom's told me all about you. I'm Bridget! It's nice to meet you."

Siobhan caught her breath hearing her mother's name spoken in the girl's strange voice.

"Tell me about your mother," Siobhan whispered.

So, she listened to Bridget tell her about her mother, who was attuned to stones and crystals, who used citrine to manifest enough cash to make ends meet, rose quartz to ease her broken heart after Bridget's father left, amethyst under Bridget's pillow to keep bad dreams away.

Hearing these stories reminded Siobhan of the tales she'd heard of her own mother, who could press her hands to a stone and hear its history.

As the moon rose and set, the water slowly dried up. Siobhan finally said goodbye to Bridget — this scried girl with her mother's name — who stared up at her through the water. When Bridget's image was gone, and Siobhan was alone in the cemetery once more, she whispered a prayer of thanks over the graves. Her line would go on. That alone could make a marriage to Finn MacCotter bearable.

The next day, Siobhan and her father donned their Sunday best and walked down the long dirt road toward the MacCotter's Farm. The cows in the pasture lumbered up to them, stretching their heads over the low stone walls as though to inspect Siobhan personally. Milk, cheese, butter, and the highest quality meat came out of MacCotter's Farm. At least a dozen men in town were employed there as farmhands — those who did not go to sea every day, as Siobhan's father did.

The morning was damp and chilly. Siobhan's face was ruddy with cold when they finally reached the MacCotter's stone house. Finn MacCotter answered the door. He was smartly dressed, with his curly blond hair parted and beard newly trimmed.

"Welcome, eh, if you'll follow me this way."

"Is that them?" A voice called from the other room.

"Yes, Da!" Finn shouted back.

Finn led them into the foyer. Siobhan had been inside the MacCotter's house before — they held an annual Christmas party for the whole town — but she hadn't expected it to look so splendid on an ordinary day. The dark wooden banisters gleamed. She followed the stairs with her eyes, generations of blond MacCotter's looking down on her from oil portraits. To their right was a large formal dining room, where the MacCotter's hosted Christmas dinner at a table laden with silver. To their left was a parlor that was twice the size of the Mahoney's front room. There Mr. MacCotter sat in a chair by a roaring fire, wrapped in blankets.

"Cormac, welcome! And Miss Mahoney, come here, come here." Siobhan allowed Mr. MacCotter to kiss her hand.

"Finbarr!" Mr. Mahoney boomed, shaking Mr. MacCotter's liver-spotted hand. "All's well with the farm?"

"Fine, fine," Mr. MacCotter wheezed. "Except I don't know how I'll keep staffing it. America is stealing all my farmhands' sons. It seems a man can't expect his children to stay in one place anymore. We must be the luckiest men in all of Cork."

Though they were the same age, Mr. MacCotter seemed decades older than his friend, stooped and hunched with pain no one could seem to cure. Perhaps Gran O'Keeffe could have cured him, had he fallen ill in her time.

"Now, Miss Mahoney, let me look at you."

Siobhan wore a dress of carnation red, a fawn-colored wool shawl embroidered with rosebuds, and her coppery hair neatly pinned. Of course, there had been no way for her to see how she looked. But, that morning, as she had peered into her wash basin, Bridget's face appeared. Bridget was older than she'd been when they'd spoken in the cemetery — now a woman in her sixties with elegant white hair. Bridget had said that Siobhan looked beautiful. That was better than any reflection.

"Turn please," Mr. MacCotter said. Siobhan gave a girlish twirl and Mr. MacCotter let out a sound of annoyance similar to a cow's loam. "No, girl, slowly please, slowly."

So, Siobhan turned slowly in a full circle, feeling the weight of the men's eyes on her. She tried to make a face to her father, but his arms were crossed, watching Mr. MacCotter closely.

"Very good. Now, if you would please smile," Mr. MacCotter instructed.

Siobhan did her best lady-like smile, demure and closed-lipped. Again, a cow-like sound burst from Mr. MacCotter, sending spittle flying. "No, girl — your teeth. I want to see your teeth."

And then Siobhan realized that she was not a woman, trying to impress her father-in-law, but a cow being inspected at auction. She bared her teeth, curling her lips as far back as she could manage.

"Siobhan!" her father hissed.

But Mr. MacCotter didn't seem to notice the gesture. "She's looks healthy, and any daughter of yours must have a strong constitution. Her hips — wideset — good for child-bearing. We'd hate to see her go the way of her mother."

A flame sparked in the pit of Siobhan's stomach, equal parts magic and rage.

Siobhan tried to keep her voice level. "There was nothing wrong with my mother."

"Siobhan, now is not the time," her father warned, his voice low.

"Of course, my girl, of course. If your kind father had insisted the doctor be present for the whole labor instead of leaving it up to his addled mother-in-law, perhaps she would have made it," Mr. MacCotter said.

Fire spread through Siobhan's core, heat moving up into her chest. Frost began to spread on the windowpane as she balled her fists.

"If my father hadn't called for the doctor at the last minute and let my gran continue her treatment, my mother most certainly would have made it." The frost grew with a low cracking.

Gran O'Keeffe had told her the story. Her father, in his terror, called for the doctor who had thrown Gran O'Keeffe from the room. She had finished brewing ergot tea — a thimbleful of ergot powder brewed in boiling water — that would make her mother's uterine muscles contract and stop the bleeding. The doctor had knocked the teacup from her hand, convinced ergot was poisonous. He packed Bridget O'Keeffe Mahoney full of cotton, which she bled through, and bled through, and bled through, while the tea that could have saved her seeped into the floorboards. Gran O'Keeffe rocked Siobhan, newly born and wailing, outside the door while her daughter died.

"I said not now, Siobhan!" Her father snapped.

The thick ice on the window shone like silver. And in it, Siobhan saw herself in labor, her face red with sweat, screaming in primal pain.

She squeezed her eyes shut, willing the image away.

"There, there, my girl. I did not mean to upset you. Of course, you miss your mother at a time like this," Mr. MacCotter said.

"Of course," Siobhan murmured. The fire inside her had been extinguished, leaving a hollow cold in its wake.

Hours later, Siobhan was still shaking. She had locked the door of her little room with a drafty window that overlooked the harbor. Despite Aoife's incessant knocking, Siobhan didn't answer. She tried to lose herself in the rhythm of the squeaking floorboards as she paced. Only when her feet had grown tired did she pour some water into the basin by her bed.

"Show me Bridget," she demanded. The surface of the water rippled, and Bridget's face came into view. She was younger than she had been when they spoke that morning, and she had complimented Siobhan's dress. Now a woman in her early thirties, the only wrinkles on Bridget's face were faint laugh lines around her mouth. Siobhan was sure that Bridget was aging normally in her own time, growing a little older each day. But the mirror carried Bridget back from different parts of her life to this point in Siobhan's. This point was an anchor, a moment of significance, that had affected the fate of Siobhan's line. Siobhan took comfort in this — it was a sign that her marriage to Finn MacCotter would not be for nothing.

"Oh! Siobhan! Hi!" Bridget chirped. Her energy never changed — whether she was a girl or a woman or an old lady. She always spoke so fast, Siobhan could hardly understand her. "I'm glad to see you. I've got big news actually, something I think you'd really like to know."

"Go on, dear," Siobhan said. Even though Bridget appeared older than her now, she was still overwhelmed by a warm rush of affection. There was a maternal fondness for Bridget that Siobhan could not shake, despite the years that separated them.

"I'm pregnant! You're the first person other than my husband to know — weird, right?" Light radiated from Bridget's dewy cheeks. "It's going to be a girl — I just know it."

Siobhan's throat felt tight. Echoing through her head were her own screams of labor that she had scried in the MacCotter's windows.

"Congratulations — that is — ," Siobhan murmured. She clutched the ceramic basin, pressing it into her stomach as a wave of nausea passed over her.

"Are you all right?" Bridget asked. Two deep worry lines creased her forehead.

Siobhan nodded. "My mother — ," was all she could manage.

"Shit!" Bridget hissed. "I'm so sorry. Mom told me about your mother. Of course, you're concerned. But I'll be all right, I promise."

Siobhan thought of her conversation with Bridget just this morning. Bridget would live to have crow's feet around her eyes and sleek white hair.

"I know you will," Siobhan said. "And I am happy for you, truly. Perhaps your daughter and I will talk like this one day, if she's a seer like us."

Bridget's eyes grew misty. "I would like that very much."

Siobhan smiled, realizing she would like that very much too.

The wedding was set for August. Though the date was months away, there was already a flurry of preparation at the Mahoney house. Aoife and three of Mr. Mahoney's sisters took it upon themselves to tailor Siobhan's mother's wedding dress for the occasion. There were arguments over what they should serve at the Mahoney's house following the ceremony, which readings would be best for the mass, whether foxglove or iris would look prettier in a bouquet.

Siobhan was seldom asked for her opinion, so she chose not to offer it. She stood quietly on an overturned soapbox, wincing at the occasional pinprick. When an aunt held up a mirror for Siobhan to inspect the progress of the gown, Siobhan only saw the image of a copper-haired girl running through a field of tall grass. There was no trace of Finn in the girl's pointed features, only Siobhan's own.

One day, a month into wedding preparations, when the aunts gossiped about a neighbor's daughter leaving for America, Finn MacCotter knocked on the door. The Mahoney women fussed like hens as they barred Finn from entering until Siobhan changed out of her wedding gown.

"Sorry for the trouble," Siobhan said when she finally let him in. She was growing used to his presence — he'd joined them for dinner every Sunday, and he'd twice hosted her family at the farm. But she still felt no emotion when she saw him. He may as well have been some new furniture in the house.

"No trouble. But I have, eh, some news. Well, a request really." Finn removed his cap, wringing it in his hands. "My Da, eh, took a turn. I know there's so much to do, and, eh, I don't want to burden your family. But, do you think we could move up the date?" Finn asked. "To next week?"

Panic tightened in Siobhan's stomach. She'd expected a couple more months to resign herself to him. But to marry Finn MacCotter next week? She leaned against the door to steady herself. "I'm not sure. I — ."

But then Aoife and the aunts burst from the kitchen where they'd been eavesdropping. "Not a burden at all," Aoife said. "We can manage."

At Aoife's words, the mounting fear turned to heat. It started behind Siobhan's navel and spread outward until even her fingertips burned. The air around her rippled with heat. She worried that the house would catch fire if she didn't do something. Siobhan cast her gaze toward the harbor.

"Finn, come with me." She grabbed him by the elbow, but Finn yelped in pain and leapt away. His shirt had been scorched.

Siobhan didn't apologize or explain. Instead, she walked out into the bright May morning. His heavy footsteps followed. Only when they were halfway to the harbor, far from Aoife's uncanny hearing, did Siobhan turn to look at him. There was a trace of fear in his wide blue eyes.

"Finn, you know what I am, don't you?"

"What do you — ," he began.

"Please," she interrupted. "It's a small town. You know the rumors. You know my gran was a wise-woman. You know that I — well — I see things." The fire of her magic grew hotter in the pit of her stomach, as though by speaking it she had fed the flames. She felt her power rippling off her skin. Down the road, the harbor waters grew mirror-still.

Finn tugged at his shirt collar. His neck and cheeks turned splotchy red. "I've heard. But, eh, I'm willing to look past it. We'll have an ordinary life."

"Ordinary?" Siobhan felt the air rush from her lungs.

"Ordinary. We'll run a good house, and raise good children, and no one will say that you're odd."

"What about our daughter? If she sees things too?" Rage and fear were a potent combination for women like Siobhan. It was like adding whiskey to a flame. Her power flared up, casting a glassy frost across all of the neighbors' windows.

"There's no need to encourage her — abilities. She'll be ordinary, like any other child. What more could she want?" He reached out to hold her hand, but pulled back. "What more could you want?"

Siobhan could not put her grief into words, so she said nothing. The fire in her belly died. All of the power that she'd stoked released in a rush. A sudden frost descended on the streets of Schull Harbor, the town encased in a mirrored sheen of ice. That strange May frost would become something of a legend in town in the years to come. But that day, as Siobhan slipped and stumbled home, she saw the vision of that copper-haired, magicless, daughter each time she fell.

That night, as Siobhan searched for the future in her wash basin, Bridget appeared again. She was a young woman, nearly Siobhan's age. Her sea blue eyes were watery and red-rimmed, and her coppery hair was disheveled. A few hair pins still clung to her curls. At the edge of the basin, Siobhan glimpsed the neckline of a black dress.

"My grandma — she — ." Bridget wiped her eyes. "Could you — could you tell me about yours?" she asked.

Siobhan sucked down a sharp breath. Gran O'Keeffe had been Siobhan's whole heritage — serving as both grandmother and mother. The air around Siobhan crackled with Gran O'Keeffe's memory. Since Gran's death, there was a word Siobhan hadn't spoken. But Bridget deserved to hear it.

"My Gran O'Keeffe was a witch, like us."

Gran O'Keeffe was the one who named Siobhan's ability. Scrying: that was the word for seeing the future in the mirror, in water, in ice. Any witch worth her salt could learn to scry, but only once in several generations was a witch born a natural scryer. Gran O'Keeffe's own mother had been one. It had been enough for a while, to see the look of pride on Gran O'Keeffe's face, rather than ever seeing her own.

When Gran O'Keeffe fell ill in Siobhan's thirteenth year, Siobhan cursed her gifts. She had spent her life studying healing at Gran's elbow, but no amount of borage seed oil could relieve Gran's aching bones, no honeyed marshmallow root could ease Gran's cough, no yarrow tea could lower Gran's fever. The plants would not speak to Siobhan as they had to Gran O'Keeffe. Instead, every time Siobhan looked into the basin of cool water beside Gran's bed, she saw a freshly dug grave in the cemetery of St. Mary's ruins.

Siobhan watched the lines of grief ease on Bridget's face as she spoke. Siobhan didn't care how many generations stood between her and her daughter's, daughter's, daughter. Bridget was flesh of her flesh and blood of her blood. She loved her as though she had carried her herself — as Gran O'Keeffe had loved Siobhan.

Siobhan had always thought that her power came from this land, from the buried bones of her foremothers. But now she felt her magic smoldering. That tugging, fiery sensation behind her navel burned brighter than it had in years. Her power did not come from the dirt that held their bones; it came from their memory.

There was another path for her future, Siobhan began to realize, one she hadn't dared consider. A future in which her daughter was not born by Finn MacCotter. A future far from Schull Harbor. A future in which she did not have to be ordinary.

"You come from a long line of extraordinary women." Siobhan's voice crackled with power.

With those words, the wash basin in her hands turned to crystal. The surface of the water stilled into silver glass. The future itself turned solid and clear.

"Bridget," she asked her great-granddaughter, "where are you?"

Bridget grinned, because she had known this future all along. "Brooklyn."

"Brooklyn." The word fell from Siobhan's lips like an irreversible spell. It was a place that sounded too big for her wash basin, so Siobhan threw open the window. "Show me," she demanded of the harbor. The blistering heat under her skin seeped out of her, until the air around her hummed. The harbor turned to solid ice — boats were trapped, fisherman's frozen nets were too heavy to pull, children splashing in the shallows skated along a sheen of glass.

Siobhan feared the ice would show her the future of Schull Harbor with wild grass growing over her foremothers' graves. But it didn't. Instead, she witnessed her own line stretch for generations beyond the harbor and across the Atlantic.

Brooklyn, New York, 1996

Bridget Mahoney Fitzgerald had never seen her own reflection. It was not for lack of trying. She would pass the floor length mirror in her dimly lit apartment, then quickly turn around in a sneak attack. She would stare so long into the gray waters of the Lower Bay that, once, a cop patrolling Brighton Beach accused her of being high on something. When she'd try to swim, she floated, as her kind did. She would press her nose to the frost forming on the windows in November, when the super still hadn't turned up the heat, hoping for the briefest glimpse of the sea blue eyes and coppery hair which she had inherited from her great-grandmother. But never once had she seen her own reflection.

Instead, she saw the past.

And from Bridget's place on the sidewalk in front of the pub, a week after her twenty-sixth birthday, the past was catching up to her.

She stood outside Kitty Kiernan's, a new Irish pub that had opened on Third Avenue. Beyond the open red door, her date sat at the bar with his jittery legs bouncing. She couldn't keep herself from smiling when she saw him. They worked together at the Brooklyn College Library. It had taken him months and several not-so-subtle encouragements between stamping books at the circulation desk, but he finally worked up the courage to ask her out for a drink.

Bridget loved the library because it gave texture to her visions. The past that once only glimmered in the mirror became real beneath the weight of paper and ink. She knew that her great-grandmother Siobhan O'Keeffe Mahoney immigrated in 1896; her colleagues helped her locate Siobhan's name in the ledger of the RMS *Aurania*. Bridget knew that her great-grandmother never married; she held her grandmother's birth certificate where no father's name was listed. She knew that Siobhan and her daughter lived on their talents as witches alone; in the archives, she discovered classified ads in early-aught issues of *The Brooklyn Daily Eagle* which advertised the services of a discrete woman who could help ladies see their futures.

Bridget had found pasts to be as interesting as futures. She opened her compact and whispered her date's name. In the small circular glass, she watched him try on three different shirts, fuss with his hair, and check his breath before he placed his hands on either side of the bathroom mirror. "She is extraordinary," he said.

Bridget smiled. Siobhan had called her that once, "extraordinary," and then her great-grandmother's watery image had turned clear as glass.

Bridget snapped her compact closed and walked towards her future.

✍ ✍ ✍

THE TICK OF THE CLOCK

—

J.C. PILLARD

The Tick of the Clock

The prince followed the sound of ticking. It was not an exact science, and he'd lost his way many times as his ear tricked him with woodpeckers and creaking branches. But he always found his way again, because while the other sounds would die away, the ticking did not.

Tick, tick, tick.

He was more exhausted than he cared to admit, eyes stinging from the effort of keeping them open. His feet dragged, ploughing into the earth as though they meant to sow seeds. His clothes were dirty and sweat-soaked. The long green scarf his mother had made him snagged on every branch, and he had to wrench it loose. He thought, bitterly, that he could simply stop freeing it when it became tangled, but he couldn't bring himself to leave it.

The forest seemed to go on forever, trees growing into obscurity in every direction. The ticking drew him deeper beneath the branches, and before he knew it, the sky itself was blotted out by the tangled canopy.

Tick, tick, tick.

As the days and nights bled together, the prince realized what a foolish thing he'd done, and the dull fury which had driven him began melting to despair, the guilt he'd been keeping at bay creeping in by inches. His fingers tangled in the chain around his neck, the one holding his father's pocket watch against his breast. The voices of the palace advisors echoed in his head.

One foolish act cannot right another. You cannot undo your mother's curse with sheer force of will.

Because that's what this was, wasn't it? His mother's edict, not a law of preservation but a curse. A curse that had trapped the prince — and everyone else in his kingdom — in time for one hundred years.

Tick, tick, tick.

His food had run out two days ago. Or was it two weeks? He wasn't sure. He couldn't remember when he'd last seen a river to fill his canteen. There were many inviting places to lay his head as he trudged on: mossy patches beneath spreading trees that looked like feather beds. But he knew that if he stopped, he would not get up again.

He really did try to keep going. He *had* to keep going. Yet, his feet grew heavier and heavier until he was lifting the entire world with each step.

Step, tick. Step, tick. Step, tick. Fall.

✍

The prince remembered the day his mother had written her edict. It had been a strange day in many ways. Only a week since his father had died, a week of black crepe wrapped over everything, of murmured apologies and condolences, of food gone half cold before he remembered to eat it. A week of his mother staring blankly forward, as though her soul had departed with her husband's.

That morning, when the prince had finally dragged himself out of bed and gone through the motions of preparing for the day, he went down to breakfast only to find his mother was not there. He thought of leaving her alone, wherever she was. God knew all he wanted was to be left in solitude to grieve in peace. But she had been so blank and empty in the past week that worry climbed up his throat and choked him, forcing him out of the dining room to search for her. He found her in what had been his father's study. She was bent over the broad oak desk, a parchment unrolled before her. The only sounds were the scratching of her quill and the ticking of the grandfather clock against the wall.

The prince cleared his throat. "Mother. Have you eaten already?"

She barely glanced at him. "I'll come down in a moment."

"What are you doing?"

She didn't answer. The prince skirted around the desk, studying the parchment beneath her fingers.

Let it here be decreed that whatsoever kills a member of the royal family shall be forever banished from the borders of this kingdom. Any harm that befalls the royal family —

The prince sighed and stepped away, letting his mother continue her writing. His father's death had been sudden — an illness that swept through and took him in less than a week. He mourned his father's gentleness and kindness, but as the days had run on, he'd started to see that he'd lost more than one parent in his father's death. As his mother's grief began to consume her, he wondered if perhaps he'd lost them both.

It won't bring him back. The words were on his tongue, but he bit down, swallowing them, and left her to her writing. At the time, it had seemed like the right thing to do, to leave her alone to carve her grief into paper. But much had happened — or, rather, had not happened — since then, and the prince had come to reflect that perhaps if he'd said something, things would have turned out differently.

Of course, now it was too late to know.

✍

The ticking had stopped. Or, at least, it was much, much softer. That was the first thing the prince noticed upon waking.

He opened his eyes to a pine-wood ceiling whorled with age. He breathed in, evergreens and honey filling his nose. He lay in a feather bed beside an open window that looked out onto a woodland glen. Sunlight glowed through the branches of the trees outside, and he stared at those trees in disbelief. The dense, impossible forest was gone. Had he only dreamed it?

"You're awake."

Starting, the prince turned towards the creaking voice. An old woman sat beside the bed, a stretch of knitting falling on her lap. She did not look up from it as she spoke again, her needles clacking softly.

"I wasn't sure if you were going to live. But you just kept breathing steadily. You've got a strong heart."

"Where am I?" His voice cracked from disuse, and he coughed, sending pain rocketing through his body.

The woman waited for him to finish coughing and settle back against the pillows. "My house," she said, setting her knitting aside. She picked up a worn cup from the side table. "Here. Drink."

Gratefully, the prince took it from her gnarled hand. He nearly groaned as the water hit his tongue, fresh and cool. He'd been thirsty for so long he'd forgotten what water tasted like.

As he looked down at himself, the prince gasped, sloshing water over the white cotton sheets. He wore no shirt. His scarf and pack, too, were gone, as was the watch pendant. His heart began to pound, his hands to shake. No, no, it wasn't possible, it —

"Your things are in there," the old woman said, pointing to a large cedar chest across the room. "I didn't want you getting dirt on my sheets."

The prince sank back into the pillows, relief and confusion and exhaustion all pouring through him. He drew a shaky breath, letting the pine-scented air fill his lungs.

"You'll be weak for some time," the old woman continued, resuming her knitting. "Stay in bed today. Rest. Once you have your strength back, you can tell me where you've come from that would have you collapsing on my doorstep."

The prince did not hear this last part. He'd fallen asleep again, the cup still clutched in his hands.

✍

Later, he was not sure how much time had passed while he slept. The prince slipped in and out of consciousness as easily as day slips into night. The old woman was always there when he woke, often with food and water, sometimes just with her knitting. He grew used to falling asleep to the gentle clack of her needles, the very slight rasp of the yarn being pulled through the stitches.

"I found you unconscious in my garden," the old woman told him upon one of his awakenings. "You were face down in my cabbages."

The prince did not remember a garden. He just recalled the endless forest, the feeling of his feet sliding over the ground.

"Your pardon," he said. "I became lost some time ago, and I thought I was alone in the forest. I — I didn't see your house."

"My house is well hidden, and the forest isn't friendly to outsiders. You should count yourself lucky that you managed to stumble into it. But where were you trying to get to?"

"I'm not sure. I've never been there before." He cleared his throat. "I must be going soon, though." His hand crept up unconsciously to the watch that hung again around his throat. He'd retrieved it from the cedar chest as soon as he'd had the strength to stand.

The old woman made a dismissive noise. "You can barely walk to the door."

It was true. Each time he woke, the prince would stand and walk as far as he could. It was not very far at all for the first few days, and though he chafed at the delay, he couldn't fathom beginning his journey again so soon. Besides, what was a few more days lost? Nothing, not where he came from.

Eventually, the prince was well enough to leave the small bedroom, though not to leave the house. He often sat with the old woman in her parlor. It was a cozy room. She would sit in the rocking chair beside her large hearth, a cloak that reminded the prince of the night sky hanging off the back of her seat. He sat across from her, beneath a cuckoo clock that hung above the crackling fire. He often watched that clock as its pendulum swung with each moment, the bird crying out the hour. He never saw the old woman wind it.

"You're going to wear a hole in my floor if you keep that up," the old woman chided one evening, as the prince's leg bounced impatiently, sending a thumping tempo through the room. He flushed and stilled, chagrined.

"Young people," the old woman grumbled. "You always need to be moving. Take it from me — sometimes it's good to sit still for a spell."

A laugh burst from the prince, and the old woman gave him a chiding look. "My apologies," he said. "It's just...it's an ironic thing to hear. I've been stuck in one place for so long, now that I'm free of it, I can't imagine staying still."

"That would account for you collapsing in my garden," the old woman said. She liked to bring that up at every opportunity, as though driving home a lesson.

The prince leaned back in his chair, staring out towards the growing dusk. "How did you come to live here?"

"Hmmm. It's a long story."

"I'd like to hear it."

She sighed. "Perhaps a small part. I had many homes once. Castles by the sea, townhouses in soaring cities. This was always my favorite retreat. It was forever here, waiting for me. So, when I lost most everything I had, I knew that this house would serve me. Take it from me, prince, you should always have a plan for when everything collapses around you."

"You sound like my mother," the prince said with a half-smile.

"She must be a clever woman."

The prince grimaced, glancing away. "A little too clever, I think. In the end."

"Ah." The old woman reached across the space between them and patted his hand. Her fingers were warm against his skin. "I'm sorry for your loss."

He nodded but said nothing.

✍

A few more weeks saw the prince well enough to begin his journey again. On what was to be his last morning in the cottage, he woke to find a new set of clothes laid out for him. His old clothes had been beyond repair, and he thought with some regret of the long green scarf his mother had made for him. His pack, though, was still in good condition, and he pulled it from the trunk and checked to ensure everything was there. He slid his new clothes on, letting the watch rest against his breastbone. Then he went to the window, peering out over the green forest beyond, trying to fix the image in his mind. Fear and no small amount of guilt pressed on his shoulders, and though he'd gone to fix what his mother had broken, the prince now wished he could live in this moment forever. Eventually, though, his duty could be put off no more. He hefted his bag and went out into the parlor where the old woman sat. He took his usual chair and leaned forward intently.

"I have nothing with which to repay you," the prince began. "I spent my last coin some time ago."

"Hmph," the old woman grunted, her needles moving steadily. The knitting had grown long since the prince's arrival in her house. "Well, perhaps you can repay me another way."

"How?"

"I seldom venture into the outside world," the old woman said. "It has been a long time since I have heard any word of it. Tell me a story from your country, wherever that may be."

The prince glanced at the cuckoo clock above the fire, then back to the old woman's nimble hands as the needles clacked together. He took a deep breath.

"Very well," he said. "I think I have just the one.

"Once upon a time, there was a kingdom with a wise king and a clever queen. The two ruled fairly for many years until, one sad day, the king died of a sudden illness. The citizens of the kingdom mourned for months, none more so than the queen who had loved her husband as a flower loves the sun. But the kingdom had to continue, and so the queen bore the burden alone. Yet, as anyone will tell you, cleverness untempered by wisdom can be a dangerous thing.

"The queen, having felt the pain of her husband's death deeply, decreed that when she died, whatever killed her should be outlawed from the kingdom. Her decree was spread to every corner of the land, and then subsequently forgotten, as she ruled for many years more. When she was old, with decades behind her, the queen went to bed one night and did not wake."

The prince ceased speaking for a moment, his eyes fixed on the pine-board floor. The old woman glanced up from her work, examining him.

"Is that the end?"

He smiled. "Almost. For, you see, the queen's decree was heard, and it was obeyed. That which had killed her was exiled from the kingdom."

"Old age."

"No. Time."

The needles — the ticking — stopped. The old woman peered up at the prince, who studied her with keen eyes.

"Time left the kingdom and has not returned for a hundred years. The people of the realm did not at first realize the price they would pay for their queen's folly. But when it became clear that every day would be the same, they started to understand. Eventually, the queen's son decided he would leave and seek out Time for himself."

The old woman's eyes narrowed. She set her knitting down carefully. "How did you manage to leave without falling to dust?"

The prince who was a king took the watch from around his neck and clicked it open, revealing the broken glass and unmoving hands of the clock. Wordlessly, he gave it to her, and she turned it over in her gnarled hands.

"Clever as your mother," she muttered, handing it back. He returned it to its place around his neck. When he'd woken without it on his person, he'd thought he was only seconds from death. After all, he had lived a single day for nearly one hundred years. But as the days passed in the cottage and he did not crumble, he began to realize whose house he'd stumbled upon.

"Why are you here?" the old woman asked. There was no anger in her tone: just curiosity and perhaps a bit of sadness.

"I am here to plead for my people. My mother made a grave mistake."

"She accomplished her goal. No one else shall die as she did."

"But they linger on when many would rather go," the king returned. "There are those who have been ill for one hundred years. Every breath is agony, but without Time to take them, they cannot die. There are children who long to grow up, lovers who long to have children." The king closed his eyes, seeing once again the pain on his subjects' faces. He blinked them open to meet the old woman's unflinching gaze.

"Without you, we are all trapped. I have come here to ask you to return and help me right my mother's wrong. Please. My people suffer for the decision of someone long dead."

The old woman sat in silence for some time, the only sound the crackle of the flames in the hearth. The king knew to wait, because Time could not be rushed.

At length, she spoke again. "What of you?"

"What of me?"

"Would you dishonor your mother's memory by breaking her final law?"

The king was quiet for a moment. It was a question he had asked himself often over the past hundred years, and never more so than when he left the kingdom to undo her decree. His mother had done what she thought best at the time. But times change.

"I have thought of my mother every day for one hundred years," he said at last. "For the first ten I loved her, for the next ninety I loathed her."

"And now?"

The king heaved a sigh. "Now, I believe I understand her. I think that might be better than either."

The old woman nodded, looking at him sorrowfully. "I would help you, if I could. But there is a price."

"Whatever it is, I'll pay it."

"Listen before you agree, boy," she said harshly. "Within your kingdom are thousands of lives, trapped in time for a hundred years. If I were to return now, everyone would crumble. So much time rushing in so quickly would destroy everything." She paused, studying him. "All that unspent time needs a place to go."

The king sucked in a breath. "Ah."

"Indeed."

The cuckoo clock on the wall began ticking again, and the king let his gaze drift up to it. He had expected a price, of course. He just hadn't realized it would be quite so high. But there was no one else to pay it, and he could not return empty-handed.

He turned back to the old woman, who watched him carefully. "I will pay it. I will take their time."

The old woman's eyes softened. "You would give up all your days for them?"

"It is all I have to give. Besides, I've had time enough to mourn a life unlived."

The old woman nodded once more. With a flourish, she bound off the final stitch of her knitting and pulled it straight. It was a scarf, the king realized, black as night and with cables like constellations running its length. She handed it to him, and he wrapped it around his neck. The wool prickled against his skin.

"I will come with you," she said. "We will right this wrong together."

The prince swallowed and nodded. He stood, hefting his pack, but the old woman's hand wrapping around his wrist stilled him. She watched him with her ancient, ageless eyes, and he saw in them all that had been and all that would be and all that might be, one day, though not for him.

"Remember what I told you, boy: sometimes it's good to sit still for a spell. You needn't be so eager to sell your life. We will go together, but not today." She smiled, releasing him and gesturing to his chair.

"Let us have another day, you and I. We have time enough for that."

≤ ≤ ≤

Initial feedback

I liked the prose and concept. We could do with more context early on, and I'm not sure you benefit from withholding the core conflict for so long. The end feels too easy, without much tension or sacrifice from the boy. I'd have liked to see the underlying relationships (e.g., with the mother) more developed.

Author's intent

What do you think the story's about?
What emotions are you trying to evoke?

My goal in writing the tale was to create something with a bittersweet, fairy tale atmosphere. The thesis of the story is the pain of having to right the wrongs of your parents, and coming to understand why they made the decisions they did, even if they were incorrect in making them. I was partially inspired by the Twilight Zone episode "Nothing in the Dark", which was one of the reasons I concealed the core conflict for so long, but I think there's a way to both engage the core conflict and still have an "aha!" moment around the old woman at the end.

To that end, I want to revise the opening to give more context to the boy's journey, add in a scene after he falls unconscious where he recalls his mother writing the edict in the first place, and add more tension to his thoughts when he awakens in Time's cottage. I'm also considering that he may end up having to pay a steeper price to right his mother's wrong — I haven't fully settled on what yet.

Author's note

The rewrite process with *Metaphorosis* was the first time I'd had rewrites requested. I usually do revisions on my own based on any feedback I might get during the submission process, but being able to work directly with the editor was a new experience.

What struck me most when I first began my rewrite was that Morris had not sent me a marked-up copy of "The Tick of the Clock". Instead, I was given feedback on the story and asked to respond with what I thought the story was about. The initial feedback pointed out a lack of context early on surrounding the boy, his quest, and his relationship with his mother, as well as the easiness of the ending. After percolating on it for a day, I found I agreed with pretty much everything. I tend to write endings that are too nice to my characters, and I realized that I had written the story to be a mystery when it was really a fairy tale. I'm not sure if I would have arrived there on my own if Morris had given me in-text feedback right away.

However, then I had to come up with what my story was 'about'. What a pernicious question! It initially stumped me. As a writer, I tend to get bogged down by details, and I don't necessarily see what larger themes are at play. When I had to sit with the question, though, I realized how much of the story was driven by unintended consequences and the need to right the wrongs of your parents. Once I had that in hand, it helped inform my inclusion of a flashback scene about the prince's mother. It also helped me modify his interactions with Time, though most of those scenes remained fairly intact.

I sent in my second revision after about two weeks of fiddling, and Morris got back to me the next day with revisions (putting to shame what I had thought was a 'quick' turnaround on my part!). The most useful element of the whole process was the structural feedback I received. Little changes — phrasing, etc. — are fine, but it was helpful to have a person who looks at the forest and the trees. The story went through four versions before Morris and I were both happy with it, and the end result is much stronger. While the trajectory of the story didn't change, where it ultimately landed did. Morris's comment about the ending helped fuel a much more satisfying, if much sadder, conclusion to the story, and helped really drive home the thematic elements of the tale.

The only thing, in all of the revisions, that I was sad to lose was the change of 'boy' for 'prince' and 'prince' for 'king'. Boy to prince remains a stronger linguistic leap in my mind, but it's a decision that ultimately made sense for the timeline of the story. The end result, however, remains one of my favorite pieces that I've written to this date.

Editor's note

There was a spread of opinion among my readers about this story, but the joy (and difficulty) of being the editor is that I get to make those decisions, and I thought the story had potential. I liked the prose in particular, and there's no question that I and *Metaphorosis* lean toward strong prose where we can. What I thought was lacking was context — why everything is happening and why. Context is similar to but distinct from worldbuilding. Where worldbuilding tells you how the overall setting works, context tells you something about how and why the characters work the way they do. Sometimes, authors can use worldbuilding to establish context (and vice versa), but they're not the same thing, and lack of context is one of the most frequent issues I see. Often, it can take a few rounds to get the context and balance right, but J.C. resolved the issue fairly quickly.

The rest of the revisions were largely tweaks here and there to the characters and their relationships. Keep in mind that reaching a final version hopefully means that author and editor are both happy, but it doesn't mean agreement on everything. J.C. notes her sorrow at changing 'boy' to 'prince', but — while recognizing her point — I stand by that suggestion; I thought 'boy' too firmly suggested a confusing pre-adult, while in the story, considerable time (even frozen) has gone by. Was that right or wrong? You decide!

The Tick of the Clock

The boy followed the sound of ticking. It was not an exact science, and he'd lost his way many times as his ear tricked him with woodpeckers and creaking branches. But eventually, he always found his way again, following the regular sound, like the steady beating of a heart.

Tick, tick, tick.

His feet dragged, ploughing into the earth as though they meant to sow seeds. His clothes were dirty and sweat-soaked. The long green scarf his mother had made him snagged on every branch, and he had to wrench it free.

The forest seemed to go on forever, trees growing into obscurity in every direction. The ticking seemed to draw him deeper beneath the branches, and before he knew it, the sky itself was blotted out by the tangled canopy.

Tick, tick, tick.

His food had run out two days ago. Or was it two weeks? He was terrible at telling time. He couldn't remember when he'd last seen a river to fill his canteen. There were many inviting places to lay his head as he trudged on: mossy patches beneath spreading trees that looked like feather beds. But he knew that if he stopped, he would not get up again.

Tick, tick, tick.

He really did try to keep going. He *had* to keep going. Yet, his feet grew heavier and heavier until he was lifting the entire world with each step.

Step, tick. Step, tick. Step, tick. Fall.

✍

The ticking had stopped. Or, at least, it was much, much softer. That was the first thing the boy noticed upon waking.

He opened his eyes to a pine-wood ceiling whorled with age. He breathed in, evergreens and honey filling his nose. He lay in a feather bed beside an open window that looked out onto a forest.

Light filtered in through the trees beyond; the sun, which he had not seen in weeks, glowed through their branches.

"You're awake."

He turned his head towards the creaking voice. An old woman sat beside the bed, a stretch of knitting falling from her lap. She did not look up from it as she spoke again, her needles clacking in time with the clock on the far wall.

"I wasn't sure if you were going to. But you just kept breathing so steadily. You've got a strong heart."

"Where am I?"

"My house." The old woman set aside her knitting for just a moment and picked up a worn cup on the side table. "Here. Drink."

Gratefully, the boy took it from her gnarled hand. He nearly groaned as the water hit his tongue, fresh and cool. He'd been thirsty for so long he'd forgotten what water tasted like.

As he looked down at himself, the boy started, sloshing water over the white cotton sheets. He wore no shirt. His scarf and pack, too, were gone. His heart began to pound, his hands to shake.

"Your things are in there," the old woman said, pointing to a large cedar chest across the room. "I didn't want you getting my sheets covered in dirt."

The boy sank back into the pillows, relief and confusion and exhaustion all pouring through him. He drew a shaky breath, letting the pine-scented air fill his lungs.

"You'll be weak for some time," the old woman continued, resuming her knitting. "Stay in bed today. Rest. Once you have your strength back, you can tell me where you've come from that would have you collapsing on my doorstep."

The boy did not hear this last part. He'd fallen asleep again, the cup still clutched in his hands.

✍

Later, he was not sure how much time had passed while he slept. The boy slipped in and out of consciousness as easily as day slips into night. The old woman was always there when he woke, often with food and water, sometimes just with her knitting. He grew used to falling asleep to the gentle clack of her needles, the very slight rasp of the yarn being pulled through the stitches.

"I found you unconscious in my garden," the old woman told him upon one of his awakenings. "You were face down in my cabbages."

The boy did not remember a garden. He just recalled the endless forest, the feeling of his feet sliding over the ground.

"Your pardon," he said. "I think I became lost some time ago but just kept going."

"Where were you trying to get to?"

"I'm not sure. I've never been there before."

"Hmph. Well, that will account for you getting lost from the start."

Eventually, the boy was well enough to get up and move about. He often sat with the old woman in her parlor. It was a cozy room. She would sit in the rocking chair beside her large hearth, a cloak that reminded the boy of the night sky hanging off the back of her seat. He sat across from her, beneath a cuckoo clock that hung above the crackling fire. He often watched that clock as its pendulum swung with each moment, the bird crying out the hour. He never saw the old woman wind it.

At last, he was well enough to begin his journey again. But, being a thoughtful young man, he did not wish to depart without paying his host. On what was to be his last morning in her cottage, the boy woke to find a new set of clothes laid out for him. His old clothes had been beyond repair, and he thought with some regret of the long green scarf his mother had made for him. His pack, though, was still in good condition, and he pulled it from the trunk and checked to ensure everything was there. Then, putting on his new clothes and hefting his bag, the boy went into the parlor where the old woman sat, intent on speaking to her of payment. He sat across from her in the chair he'd begun to think of as his.

"I have nothing with which to repay you," the boy began. "I spent my last coin some time ago."

"Hmph," the old woman grunted, her needles moving steadily. The knitting had grown long since the boy's arrival in her house. "Well, perhaps you can repay me another way."

"How?"

"I seldom venture into the outside world," the old woman said. "It has been a long time since I have heard any word of it. Tell me a story from your country, wherever that may be."

The boy glanced at the cuckoo clock above the fire, then back to the old woman's nimble hands as the needles clacked together.

"Very well," he said. "I think I have just the one.

"Once upon a time, there was a kingdom with a wise king and a clever queen. The two ruled fairly for many years until, one sad day, the king died of a sudden illness. The citizens of the kingdom mourned for many months, none more so than the queen who had loved her husband as a flower loves the sun. But the kingdom had to continue, and so the queen had borne the burden alone. Yet, as anyone will tell you, cleverness untempered by wisdom can be a dangerous thing.

"The queen, having seen the pain that her husband's death brought upon the land, decreed that when she died, whatever killed her should be outlawed from the kingdom. Her decree was spread to every corner of the land, and the subsequently forgotten, as she ruled for many years more. When she was old, with decades behind her, the queen went to bed one night and did not wake."

The boy ceased speaking for a moment, his eyes fixed on the pine board floor. The old woman glanced up from her work, examining him.

"Is that the end?"

He smiled. "Almost. For, you see, the queen's decree was heard, and it was obeyed. That which had killed her was exiled from the kingdom."

"Old age."

"No. Time."

The needles stopped. The old woman peered up at the boy, who studied her with keen eyes.

"Time left the kingdom and has not returned for a hundred years. The people of the realm did not at first realize the price they would pay for their queen's folly. But when it became clear that every day would be the same, they started to understand. Eventually, the queen's son decided he would leave and seek out Time for himself."

The old woman's eyes narrowed. She set her knitting down carefully. "How did you manage to leave without falling to dust?"

The boy who was a prince took a silver chain from his bag. Upon its end dangled a small watch, the glass face of it broken and the hands unmoving in their positions. Wordlessly, he gave it to her, and she turned it over in her gnarled hands.

"Clever as your mother," she muttered, handing it back. He returned it to its place in his bag. When he'd woken without it on his person, he'd thought he was only seconds from death. After all, he had lived a single day for nearly one hundred years. But as the days passed in the cottage and he did not crumble, he began to realize whose house he'd stumbled upon.

"Why are you here?" the old woman asked. There was no anger in her tone: just curiosity and perhaps a bit of sadness.

"I am here to plead for my people. My mother made a grave mistake."

"She accomplished her goal. No one else shall die as she did."

"But they linger on when many would rather go," the prince returned. "There are those who have been ill for one hundred years. Every breath is agony, but without Time to take them, they cannot die. There are children who long to grow up, lovers who long to have children." The prince closed his eyes, seeing once again the pain on his subjects' faces. He blinked them open to meet the old woman's unflinching gaze.

"Without you, we are all trapped. I have come here to ask you to return and help me right my mother's wrong. Please. My people suffer for the decision of someone long dead."

The old woman sat in silence for some time, the only sound the ticking of the cuckoo clock above the hearth. The prince knew to wait, because Time could not be rushed.

At length, she spoke again. "What of you, boy?"

"What of me?"

"Would you dishonor your mother's memory by breaking her final law?"

The prince was quiet for a moment. It was a question he had asked himself often over the past hundred years, and never more so than when he left the kingdom to undo her last decree. His mother had done what she thought best at the time. But times change.

"I have thought of my mother every day for one hundred years," he said at last. "For the first ten I loved her, for the next eighty-nine I loathed her."

"And now?"

The prince heaved a sigh. "Now, I believe I understand her. I think that might be better than either."

The old woman picked up her needles once more. "In that, we are agreed."

With a flourish, the old woman bound off the final stitch of her knitting, pulling the fabric straight. It was a scarf, the prince realized, black as night and with cables like constellations running its length. She handed it to him, and he wrapped it around his neck. The wool prickled against his skin.

The old woman stood, and in the motion she changed. The prince could not say how, for she was still a crone. But she stood tall and straight as an evergreen, and her eyes contained all that had been and all that shall be and all that might be, one day. She raised a withered, ageless hand. For the first time, the prince was afraid. But the woman merely smiled. She donned the black cloak that hung upon her chair, the one that reminded the prince of the night sky, and gestured to the door.

"Lead on."

✍ ✍ ✍

HOPE ON THE VINE

—

R.E. DUKALSKY

Hope on the Vine

It was early August and hope was withering on the vine.

It had withered every year so far for the last eleven, so Nima was disappointed rather than surprised. Disappointed, frustrated, demoralized. She really thought she'd gotten the balance right this time.

She knelt in front of the raised mound of earth that should have been nourishing the hope vine's roots, her dirty boots poking out behind her and the sun glinting gently off her greying curls. By this point in the season, the vine should be about three feet tall, with multiple spurs twining eight to ten feet in every direction. Heavy buds the size of the first knuckle of her thumb should be swelling between pairs of reniform leaves gleaming a lustrous dark jade. She should be out here looking eagerly for the first open blossom, a rich yellow stellate flower the size of her hand, shading to the orange of glowing embers in the center. She hadn't seen one for many years.

Instead, she stared disconsolately at a meager vine supporting a few anemic yellow-green spurs. The remaining leaves, with two notable exceptions, were the same undernourished shade, their ribs showing more starkly every day, while their edges turned brown and flaked away. Only one spur, the one that twisted around the rail of the fence, showed any semblance of health, and Nima was as baffled by its continued vitality as she was by the parent vine suddenly giving up on life. It had seemed to be growing on schedule — perhaps a little undersized but a good color — but instead of progressing to the next stage of growth and putting out buds, it had drooped, retreated, withered. Just like its ten predecessors — those that had even bothered to sprout.

Eleven long years on this struggling piece of earth, trying to tease a hope vine from seed to fruit. So far, this was the closest she had come to success. One fruit was all one could expect from such a young vine, but one was all she needed: proof she could send to her Arbiter that this vine would thrive. Then, at last, she could move on. On to the next impoverished, war-scarred town and the next desiccated, abandoned farm, where the potential for hope or fortitude or patience lay dormant under years of neglect and acres of weeds.

The next, and the next, and the next. One by one until the tired land put the years of war and sorrow behind it for good and all.

But there wouldn't be a next and a next if she couldn't bring this vine back to life. Nima doubted she'd live to see the land restored, but leaving here would be its own reward. She dreaded another roasting summer and dreary winter in the small blue house behind her. Another year of being ignored by her neighbors, loathing them in return, and never forgetting no one wanted her here.

Maybe she hadn't fertilized enough? But no; she'd been side-dressing the vine with the recommended half-cup of the special expensive blend that came from the Wizard's Herbarium, and she marked each application on her calendar so she knew she hadn't missed any. Was the mix itself wrong? They said it was guaranteed, but you never knew what that meant with the wizards you got these days. In her time, guarantees had come with blood, not a letter under shiny gilt seal.

If the mix was good, was water the issue? Possible, but hope vines were notoriously flexible in their water needs. In theory, they could take root and grow anywhere, with minimal tending. That was why they, along with fortitude trees and hedges of patience, were among the first recommended plants for war restoration project sites. Even someone who'd never set finger to a garden should be able to grow one — and once a hope vine established itself, every living thing in the area would flourish as well.

Probably she hadn't figured out the right tending regimen. This was where hope vines could be tricky, according to both her own vague memories and the instructions she received each year with the new seed. Fortitude trees could be watered with either sweat or blood (both of which she had in abundance, particularly in the summer). A hedge of patience would grow well with tears, sighs or, in a pinch, prayers. Hope vines demanded fiddly, intangible things: dreams recounted, promises exchanged, plans laid. But wizards didn't dream, she had no one to make promises to, and under the circumstances plans were not hers to lay. She'd tried making promises to the old farmhouse, to the wasted land around it, to the rickety fence and the empty road, but she wasn't sure they counted. If she were honest, the only promise she meant to keep was the one about leaving.

She'd walk out the gate now and never come back if she hadn't given her word, and not with some fancy seal, but in the old way, with consequences for breaking her oath. She'd promised to stay until she could prove she'd restored local resilience to an acceptable baseline — in plainspeak, until the hope vine was able (or willing?) to reproduce. No one back in the capital knew, or really cared, how long it took or what it asked of the grower. The point was to have wizards scattered across the land, repairing the scars of war where everyone could see them doing it. So here she was until she could cultivate her release.

Nima stroked a finger across one of the limp leaves. "If you stay alive, I leave and you never have to see me again. So save us both some pain and just *grow*," she whispered, putting all the force of her will into it. No effect, of course, except a dull burn up her right arm to complement her aching knees.

"What's wrong with your plant?"

The voice was high-pitched and unfamiliar. Nima looked up to see a girl of about twelve years draped across the fence near the gate ten feet away. Just about where the questing ends of the vine ought to be right now, Nima thought sourly. She'd never seen the girl before, though she had the look of a local: a short, wide body, tawny skin, a blunt nose, and straight, thick black hair cut short above her shoulders. Her eyes were close-set, small, and twinkling with curiosity.

"It isn't growing," Nima said shortly. She was sick to death of these suspicious locals. "Did you need something?"

"I'm Yun," the girl said, completely ignoring the pointed question. "Did you forget to water it?"

"No," Nima replied, trying to rein in her temper. It wouldn't improve her relationship with the locals if she started yelling at children. On the other hand, she didn't care that much about having a relationship with the locals. She turned back to the hope vine, scratching gently in the dirt around the main stalk to see if there was something preying on its roots.

"What about fertilizing? Did you feed it?" Yun asked.

"Yes," Nima said without looking up.

"Did you put it in the right kind of soil?"

"*Yes.*"

"Does it get enough sun?"

Exasperated, Nima gestured at the open sky. Her back twinged, and she looked up with an even more unfriendly expression than she'd intended.

"Hm. Maybe it's getting *too* much sun," Yun mused, unfazed. "Or maybe this isn't a good place for it to grow."

Nima clenched her jaw and bent back down. Maybe the irritating child would get bored and wander away. After a few seconds she heard soft footsteps against the dust and dared to hope. But no luck.

"But I don't know," Yun said, from much nearer, almost right in front of Nima. "It *feels* like it wants to grow here." A brown hand appeared at the corner of Nima's vision, stroking the leaves of the one remaining spur.

Nima looked up sharply. "Don't touch it," she snapped.

Yun whipped her hand away and looked, for the first time, as if she were picking up on Nima's unwelcoming demeanor. "Why not?"

"Because it's *my* vine," Nima replied, hearing how ridiculous she sounded even as the words came out of her mouth. "What I mean is, it's fragile and it isn't polite to touch other people's crops."

This was evidently a new concept to Yun. "I help Aunt Lio with her beans all the time and she says — "

But Nima was done with this conversation she hadn't wanted in the first place. She didn't want what passed for local agricultural expertise, especially from a child, and needed peace and quiet to think about what to try next. "Then I'm sure she would appreciate your help now," she interrupted, then stood up and stalked away, pushing through the stiffness in her knees. "Don't touch my plants," she called over her shoulder without looking back.

✍

Working on a half-baked theory that her bad mood was somehow hampering the vine's growth, Nima stayed away from it for the next few days. She kept a sharp eye on the fence, but the girl had vanished back to whatever ramshackle farmhouse she'd come from. Nima saw her traipsing by once on the road, but the girl showed no inclination to stop or pester the vine.

After a week, Nima woke up having slept well, and decided she'd waited enough time to test her theory. If her mood did somehow affect the vine, she'd given it time to recover and should be able to see the effects. She filled her big watering can, sprinkled in the special water-soluble fertilizer and lugged it out to the fence.

The vine looked exactly the same: anemic stalk and spurs, withered yellow leaves slowly crumbling off their ribs... and one perfectly healthy spur climbing slowly around the fence rail along the road. The good spur had even put out another two leaves while the rest of the plant died.

"What...?" Nima stood there, hands hanging down open at her sides. She had learned to grow things; the profusely healthy vegetable garden behind the house attested to that. She glared at the vine, disregarding the theory she'd been testing. "What do you *want* from me?" There was no reason this should be so hard, no reason this spur should thrive while the parent plant died, no reason the one plant that mattered should wither while the rest of the garden flourished.

A sharp trill pierced her despair. Yun was tromping down the road in heavy boots several sizes too big for her, swinging two empty beaten metal buckets, whistling like the cloudy morning had been made for her alone. There was something odd about the buckets; they were the wrong shape somehow, too rounded on the bottom, with asymmetric sides. Nima squinted at them and realized they were infantry helmets, inexpertly beaten into a slightly more bucket-like shape by a *very* amateur blacksmith.

"Did you figure out how to fix your plant?" Yun asked. She must have taken Nima's attempt to parse the helmets-turned-buckets as an invitation to stop and chat.

"No," Nima said, trying to think of a task that would take her away from the fence but allow her to keep an eye on the girl.

"It looks better, though," Yun said, waving one of the buckets at the flourishing spur. At least she wasn't trying to touch it. She wrinkled her nose. "That part, at least."

Nima picked up her watering can and began dribbling the water gently around the roots of the vine. Yun didn't take the hint. She tromped a few steps closer, set the buckets down with a dusty *thump*, and squatted on her haunches in front of the vine. "I think it's happier on this side of the fence."

"Plants don't feel happy or sad," Nima said repressively. She saw Yun shrug out of the corner of her eye.

"Aunt Lio says they do." Aunt Lio was evidently the arbiter of reality. She leaned closer. "What kind of plant is this anyway?"

"A hope vine," Nima said shortly, then surprised herself by continuing, "at least, it's supposed to be."

"I never saw one of those before," Yun said, scrunching up her nose and peering at the plant with renewed interest.

"They aren't very common after the war," Nima found herself explaining.

"Ah," Yun said sagely, although she wasn't old enough to remember even the final years of the war and couldn't possibly understand what lay behind the disappearance of the country's native resilient vegetation. "What's it for?"

For giving you and all your ungrateful kin a future worth growing into, Nima thought but did not say. The last thing she wanted was this girl's irate aunt descending to put the wizard in her place. "If it grows," she said, biting off each word, "it will reinforce the local ecosystem — that means the soil, the water, other plants, the animals that eat those plants, and people who rely on the plants and animals," she added, confident that the local school, if one even existed, did not cover the ecology of resilience.

"We have been having some problems," Yun agreed thoughtfully, just as if she were a grizzled veteran farmer. She leaned even closer to the vine, body rolling at such an angle that Nima feared she would pitch face first into the plant — and the railing.

"Be careful," she said, more harshly than she had intended.

Yun straightened up, but didn't look abashed. "I think maybe this part of the plant isn't bothered by something that's messing with the rest of it," she said. "Or maybe it just likes that I talk to it."

Yun's comment niggled at the back of Nima's brain. Maybe there *was* something affecting the roots or the leaves on the parent vine that hadn't spread to the healthy spur yet — or maybe the spur had some kind of natural resistance…

"I have to go restake the beans," Yun was saying in the background, but Nima was no longer paying attention. She didn't even notice the girl stretching out a stealthy hand to give the new leaves a friendly tap. "I'll be back tomorrow."

✍

Yun kept turning up after that. Sometimes for an hour, sometimes for ten minutes, sometimes carrying her ridiculous repurposed buckets, sometimes hauling a feed sack on a little wagon, frequently with her arms full of hollow reeds as wide as her wrist and as tall as she was. She never seemed to be in a hurry or fear that whoever sent her on these tasks would be impatient at her dawdling. Aunt Lio either ran a slipshod operation or didn't particularly care what this niece was up to. Yun never mentioned her parents, so maybe she was a war orphan dumped on her only known relative. Maybe Lio had so much help on her farm that one lolly-gagging child made no difference. Or maybe they were just relieved to get a break from her questions.

"Do they have hope vines where you come from?" she asked one time.

"No," Nima said.

"Then how do you know how to grow one?"

I don't, Nima thought. "Resilient plants need the same things as any other plants — "

"Where *do* you come from anyway?" Yun interrupted.

"Not here," Nima said, picking up her rake and walking away.

✍

"I know this isn't your farm," Yun said another time.

Nima was pruning back the dead leaves on the spurs closest to the healthy one, in case the problem was some kind of spore or mildew. Her shears jumped and nearly clipped a healthy leaf. "What is that supposed to mean?" she demanded.

"Everyone knows you aren't from here, even though you've lived here forever," Yun said with a limber shrug. "When are the people who belong to this farm coming back?"

"They aren't," Nima snapped.

"Maybe this would grow better if they did," Yun said, bumping the vine with grimy knuckles.

"Don't touch," Nima said, but she'd long since given up on the idea that Yun would listen.

"Don't worry, *I'm* not going away," Yun said, more to the vine than to Nima. "Hey look, there's a new grabby bit here!"

✍

"How does a hope vine help the... ecosystem?" Yun asked after she'd been coming by regularly for almost a month.

"Different ways," Nima said distractedly, her words punctuated by the *thonk-crunch* of her trowel. She was digging some small trenches to drain excess water away from the hope vine's mound just in case the roots were becoming waterlogged. "Other things ... grow better ... near a hope vine. Fewer diseases ... more abundant production. Roots ... stop erosion and make dead soil fertile again. You can live ... off a single fruit ... for a long time. Healing tea or tincture from the leaves. And just being around the flowers..." she sat back on her heels and wiped her forehead, "I really can't explain what that feels like, you have to experience it for yourself."

"We could really use one of those," Yun said. "Aunt Lio says the beans need a miracle."

"Hope vines aren't miracles, they're applied magic," Nima said sternly. "And you shouldn't expect either to do your work for you."

"I am doing the work," Yun said, but without heat. "But there's a bug that came and it eats the buds before they can bloom." She reached a finger out toward the vine, then pulled it back again.

✍

"What's it like?" Yun asked on one unreasonably hot day.

"What's what like?" Nima replied, only half listening as she teased a tendril gently through a gap in the climbing frame.

"Being a bad wizard."

Nima froze with the tendril balanced on one finger. "What do you mean by that?" she asked carefully. Sweat trickled between her shoulder blades.

"Everyone knows," Yun said without noticeable concern. "You're a bad wizard who made all the bad stuff happen in the war."

Nima snatched her hand away from the vine so she wouldn't transmit her feelings through the tender shoots. "That's a gross exaggeration."

"Also, I saw your thing," Yun pointed at Nima's right arm, where the geas runes constraining Nima's magic and her free movement crawled with slow abandon. She'd probably spotted it the first time they met, but Nima found herself tugging her sleeve down anyway, angry at her own shame. She hated any reminder that she was permanently separated from her magic, even though she'd accepted the geas binding to avoid lifetime imprisonment.

"Aunt Lio says getting a nice farm to run isn't a real punishment," Yun persisted. She reached out and casually flicked the vine. Nima winced, but the vine held firm. In fact, it flexed a tendril toward the sun.

Nima picked up her trowel, hefted it, set it down. She didn't like the idea of Yun and her aunt discussing her sentence as if were just moderately interesting village gossip. "Your Aunt Lio doesn't know everything. It's not a punishment. It's a collective obligation."

"Hah!" Nima wasn't sure whether Yun's hard, fierce laugh was meant to dismiss the possibility that Aunt Lio could be wrong or the official line that felt flat even to the wizard herself. "Then why do you have that?" Yun jabbed a finger at the geas runes.

"Yes, fine, technically it's a punishment," Nima said sharply, "but I *cooperated*. I *agreed* to community service. I could have just done my time, but I entered the program voluntarily to try to make amends for what happened. Nobody forced me to wear this." She shook her right arm at the girl. "Nobody forced me to be here."

"Then why don't you leave?" Yun asked in genuine curiosity.

In all the years she'd endured in this place, no one had ever asked Nima what she thought about her situation. It was humiliating to be grateful for a child's fickle attention, but her life was nothing but humiliations now.

"Because what the wizards did was wrong," Nima said, striving for patience. Not native to this farm and not native to her either. "We had the right — we had good intentions. But we did things that had consequences far beyond what we intended, beyond what we could have imagined when we started."

"What were you trying to do?" Yun asked. "Aunt Lio says all you wizards just wanted to keep your power and when the war happened you decided to burn the country down instead of sharing even one good thing with regular people."

There had been a time where Nima would have drowned in their own sweat anyone who dared speak so harshly, so honestly. "How fortunate that a bean farmer knows the absolute truth!" she snapped, then reined herself in. "Look, the war was complicated and you're too young to understand most of what happened."

Yun crossed her arms, stubborn. "Aunt Lio says the wizards hoarded all the best food and medicine and magic in their towers," she persisted. "She says the headwomen of all the villages went to the towers and asked for the wizards to share, but the wizards said they had nothing valuable to trade. So the villages stopped sending tithes to the towers and then the wizards came out of their towers and ruined everything. And Tonji says the wizards never loved anything but themselves and that's why they could do what they did to the land and the rivers and everything."

Nima had no idea who Tonji was and she didn't like their assessment of the war. "That's not an accurate picture," she said stiffly, although it was, if boiled down to its essence and told through the eyes of the victors. "There was... more to it." In the back of her mind she heard, was always hearing, the soul-shattering crack of her tower's foundations.

"Like what?" Yun asked pugnaciously.

Nima thought of her tower, its dimensions aligned precisely with the planes and angles of her interior self. Like a phantom limb, she could feel vast power seeping from the land into her tower's stones, and from its stones into her. Power that extended the reach of her hand as far as thought could take it, that honed her vision, peering keen-edged with magic into any secret she desired. When her tower stood, she was the secret composer of the song beneath everything... and then they had pulled her tower down and she was nothing. Keeper of a withered garden in a mutilated land. Bitterness welled up in her.

"I couldn't possibly explain it to you in a way you could comprehend," she said, aiming for austere, but coming no higher than cruel.

Yun gave her a very straight look then shrugged deliberately. "Well, it's not like you know the first thing about growing beans," she replied.

It toppled Nima like she was a tower herself. Yun hadn't spoken in pettiness, but rather with the world-weary familiarity of someone who often had to defend her own worth. Maybe she'd heard her aunt use the line and seen the seed of truth it held. Yun didn't know what it was like to wield power that could make and unmake the world. Nima didn't know how to grow beans. Once, the difference between them would have been too vast to comprehend. Now, it meant that between the two of them, Nima was merely the less capable subsistence farmer.

Nima was used to wrapping prickly defensiveness around herself like armor, but she suddenly couldn't reach it. They just sat there looking at each other, black eyes to brown. "I never had any reason to grow beans before," Nima said, conceding.

The silence stretched for several more minutes while Nima pretended to rearrange the dirt at the base of the vine's main stalk. "Wizards cared for the land a long time," she continued at last. "People couldn't see what we did. For generations we kept the soil fertile, managed the weather, sustained the forests...we didn't intend to destroy so much, not when the rebellion started and not after. We were just desperate to make the war stop."

Yun tilted her head skeptically. "If you wanted the war to stop, you could have just given the headwomen what they asked for. You didn't have to do all that bad stuff," she said.

Nima had used a lot of noble sentences and fine words to get her through the dark nights of doubt, but none of them volunteered to stand up against that unflinching logic. "You're right," she said, after a long minute. "But we did do it. I. I did it. All I can do now is try to repair what I can."

Yun glanced away as if the subject had never really been that interesting in the first place. "So why is this vine so important?"

Nima scrubbed her hands over her face. "This land, one of the things it has — had — " she paused. Started again. "A long time ago, wizards found a way to cultivate resilience. *Yes, wizards,*" she snarled at the skeptical look on Yun's face. "They taught seeds to grow hope, patience, and fortitude. They infused rivers with trust and stocked lakes with solidarity. They showed the land how to produce the things that would sustain it, no matter what came." She pressed her lips together and bit down hard on the sour feeling twisting her belly. "But the hope vines and trees of fortitude and all the rest of it didn't survive the war."

"Because of you," Yun interrupted. "You wizards, I mean. Right?"

"It wasn't just — " But it was. They had stretched out their hands and stripped the land of everything their forebears had grafted into it. She was out here trying to make amends for her role in that enormous crime, so what was the point of spinning a sweeter-sounding version of the truth to this child who wasn't buying it anyway? "Yes. Wizards weren't responsible for all the bad things that happened in the war, but they — we — did destroy the resiliency ecosystem. We did that."

"Why?" Yun asked.

A simple, deadly question. Nima had answers she'd given herself, answers she'd given her colleagues who doubted their course of action, answers she'd given the court that sentenced her.

Only we have the knowledge and experience to guide this country to its better future. Our better future requires peace and peace requires order, and order can only come when the villages bow to our authority.

These rebel armies are destroying the land — perhaps if they see harsh consequences they will surrender before we have to kill them all.

Some of the Wizard's Consortium chose to cross that final line and the rest of us let ourselves get pulled across.

So many answers. But none of them sufficient, in the end, to justify stripping the land of everything that held it together and helped it thrive. Not when you boiled it down to a young girl and an old wizard crouched on opposite sides of a fence in a dusty nowhere trying to understand why nothing good could grow.

"Because we forgot that wizards first built towers to serve and protect the land," she said at last. She suddenly became aware of how stiff and heavy her legs had become. "We thought of the land as something under our rule, not under our care. So when the rebels — when the war came, it was easy to use the land as a weapon."

Nima remembered standing atop her tower filled with grim righteousness as she stretched out her hands and drained the Ko River into the bedrock. She remembered the sense of urgency that filled her heart when she walked in the fortitude groves, blighting the ancient trees to strip the rebels of their will to fight. She remembered having those feelings, but she couldn't reproduce them. Now, all she could feel was shame and despair at the enormity of what they had done. How could she ever have thought that growing one stupid hope vine would mean anything in the face of their atrocities? Even if she lived to be the oldest wizard in history and grew a new vine or tree every year, it would be a pitiful drop in the desert their crimes had created.

"And now wizards must undo what wizards did," Yun chanted the first line of the decree that doomed all surviving wizards to a lifetime of penal restitution — out here in the backlands, it was probably the only part of the decree she'd ever heard. She bopped one of the withered leaves unceremoniously. "You're not very good at it, huh?"

Nima lurched forward to cup the leaf, jerked herself back, then stared at it as it seemed to stretch out luxuriously. Was a deeper green flushing outward from the central rib, or were her eyes lying to her? "This work is much harder than I expected," she admitted.

Yun nodded sagely. "I bet it's hard to make this place hopeful when you aren't." Then her head shot up as if hearing a voice calling her. "Whoops, gotta go," she said. She hopped to her feet, scooped up her buckets, and took off at a steady trot down the road.

Nima watched her go, rolling her last words around and around. *It's hard to make this place hopeful when you aren't.* That could be the problem. Perhaps the hope vine couldn't grow if its tender had no hope of her own to share.

But then — Nima leaned over the leaf Yun had bopped, without touching it herself. It was noticeably greener and drooped less. And then — she peered down where Yun had been flicking her careless fingers, and there was one, no two! new tendrils peeking out. Nima thought about all the times she'd scolded Yun for touching the vine. Was it a coincidence that the healthy spur was the one closest to the road, the easiest one for Yun to reach? Was the vine nourishing itself off her innate hope for the future, a future Yun expected to be part of in exactly the way Nima didn't?

Nima brooded on it all night.

✍

Yun came back the next day, and the next, chattering about the problem with Aunt Lio's bean crop. Nima made noncommittal noises or gave answers she forgot even as they came out of her mouth. The beans weren't her problem. She was watching Yun and the vine, trying to learn the secret of how she made it grow.

The girl didn't appear to be doing anything special. She didn't even seem to be paying attention to the vine most of the time, although she always crouched by it when she stopped, even though it meant she had to perch in the ditch on the side of the road. She would bump or stroke or tap the leaves or tendrils to emphasize a point or sometimes as if it were agreeing with her, but she might have done the same thing with her buckets or the wagon. She certainly didn't treat the vine with the care or deference that Nima herself did. Nima couldn't see any one thing that set Yun's interactions with the hope vine above her own — except, of course, that the vine grew where Yun touched it and withered everywhere she did not.

And 'grow' was a bit of an understatement. On Nima's side of the fence, the other spurs had desiccated into dry, spindly stalks, their leaves long since crumbled into the dirt. On Yun's side, seven feet of rich jade green sprouted leaves the size of Nima's palm, twisted tendrils around every surface of the climbing frame and the fence rails, and were sending out new spurs in two places. There was even one tiny green nub that, given time, would become a bud.

Nima never, ever touched the healthy spur. She even stood on the dead side of the plant to water and dress it, hoping not to poison it with indirect contact. She didn't encourage Yun to touch it either, superstitiously worried that the vine would pick up on her desperation and stop responding to Yun's presence. She just held herself in nervous stasis, waiting for the bloom.

✍

Maybe it was the empty rattling of the sledge that drew Nima's attention, or maybe it was how Yun's feet dragged in the dusty road as she approached. Whatever it was, Nima looked up one day to see a new expression on Yun's face: despair.

The girl squatted in her usual place on the other side of the fence, her hands flopped over her knees and her black hair sticking to her sweaty temples. She didn't touch the vine.

"What's wrong with you?" Nima said, more harshly than she'd intended. But then, she'd never been a gentle person.

"The bean crop failed," Yun said, looking burdened in a way Nima had never seen her. "Aunt Lio says there's no way to save it now, even though we built reed irrigation all the way from the river and I pick off all the bugs I can find."

"I guess you'll have to eat something other than beans this winter," Nima said, trying to remember if beans had some sort of local cultural significance. "Variety is good for you."

Yun looked at her like Nima had just suggested they try to eat the sun. "We don't eat beans, we sell them," she said. Then, in a cadence that sounded like something she'd heard from someone else many times, "No beans, no money. No money, no winter stores, no shoes, no seeds for spring."

"Oh," Nima said. Of course Yun's entire livelihood hung on those stupid beans. "That's...bad."

Yun sighed heavily and gave the swollen bud close to her face the gentlest of caresses. Nima sucked in her breath, but Yun didn't notice and the vine didn't show any immediate negative effects. "Do you know any way to fix the beans?" she asked suddenly, looking a little nervous for the first time Nima could remember. "I mean...I know you said we shouldn't expect magic to fix our problems, but you also said wizards used to take care of the land..."

"Not with this," Nima said, jerking her right arm in a sharp motion so the geas runes caught the light.

"Oh, right," Yun said, subsiding back despondently. She sighed again. "We sure could use one of these hope vines right now." Nima suddenly recognized the line as something she'd heard Yun saying a lot lately.

That night, Nima found herself thinking of Yun's beans instead of the hope vine. There wasn't any reason to be thinking about either one — all she could do for the vine was what she'd done, and Yun was someone else's problem — but she kept coming back to it like a piece of food stuck between her molars. It wasn't just the girl's despair; Nima hadn't spent a century as a powerful wizard with a tower of her own because she was susceptible to sad peasant children. But what if the bean crop's failure forced Yun and her family to leave the farm? What if they starved? What would happen to the hope vine if Yun suddenly stopped coming by, telling her cheerful stories and helping pass the long weary days with impertinent questions?

And more than that — Yun's intervention, however unintentional, had resuscitated Nima's own hope of escaping this pastoral prison. Which, in a way, put her in Yun's debt.

And that was the nub of the problem, Nima realized as she dried her dinner dishes. She felt indebted to Yun, who had helped her while enduring Nima's constant unwelcoming attitude. And there was a way to repay her. But it would cost Nima the one thing she valued: the opportunity to leave.

On the other hand, if she didn't pay this debt, Nima would be proving Aunt Lio and Tonji right: that wizards would rather let the land and everyone who depended on it suffer than share even one good thing. And even more than she hated being in debt, more than she hated being here, Nima found she hated the idea that Lio and her ilk could be right about her after all. If they were, then Yun would keep believing they were right about the war, would keep thinking wizards were bad people who embraced destruction to feed their own selfishness.

"Damn and damn!" she swore, looking down to discover she'd worried her washing cloth into threads.

She couldn't repair the land. She couldn't undo the systemic destruction they'd wrought, not even in a wizard's lifetime.

She could save one bean farm. She could persuade one girl — maybe one family — that wizards could help as well as harm. Not just for show, or to win release, but because she wanted Yun to welcome a future with wizards in it as enthusiastically as she welcomed everything else. It would cost at least a year of her life; there was no guarantee that this hope vine would fruit two years in a row. But after eleven years of loneliness and failure, was one more really such a sacrifice?

"Yes it *is*," Nima snarled to the empty room, to herself. "But wizards must undo what wizards did." Then she picked up her lamp and stomped out of the house.

Hope vines thrived on promises, after all.

✍

Nima waited with characteristic impatience for Yun to arrive the next morning, but the girl didn't appear until mid-afternoon, trudging along in her too-big boots and carrying her mangled helmet buckets. She flashed Nima a wan smile as she crouched down by the vine, petting it as if seeking comfort from the silky leaves.

"How are the beans?" Nima asked awkwardly after a minute. She hadn't thought about this part, not once she'd made her decision. And, she realized, she'd never started one of their conversations before today. It was always Yun, interrupting her work with a question or observation.

"Still bad," Yun said. "Aunt Lio says we'll be lucky to get a quarter of the crop."

"Well, look," Nima said, her eyes fixed on the hope vine while her hands fiddled anxiously in the dirt. "This thing is about to flower. If it fruits, I could — you could have it. You could plant it near your beans. I'm sure it would grow for you."

Yun looked up, her eyes shining in a way Nima had never seen. It was like all the dust had washed right out of her world. "You mean it? We could have a hope vine of our own?"

"It won't make your bean plants come back," Nima warned. "Probably."

"But it means they'll grow good next year!" Yun said with an enormous grin. "That's right, isn't it? Everything grows better where a hope vine grows?"

"That's the theory," Nima agreed. She felt surprisingly guilty giving the girl hope when she wasn't sure the vine was capable of producing a fruit this late in the season. But then, hope was all she had to offer, from beginning to end.

"But... wait." Yun crinkled up her face around her nose. "Don't you have to send that fruit to your Arbiter? So they send you on to your next place?"

"There will be another fruit, in another year," Nima said with forced calm, giving the vine an affectionate little stroke with the back of her hand. And to her utter astonishment, a tiny bright green tendril unfurled from beneath her knuckles.

✑

The vine bloomed four days later, opening like a star and drawing the eye from anywhere in the garden. Nima found herself staring at it for uncounted time, just tracing its silky depths with her eyes. She could see, if she looked closely in the way wizards were trained to do, runes tracing and retracing themselves deep within the flower's genetic structure. But mostly she just stood beside the vine, falling into its radiance.

Two days after the bloom, Nima came out early to gaze at the flower. It was a habit she'd fallen into immediately, getting in close to the luminous petals, tracing the dew that beaded gently on their surface, filling her lungs with the flower's scent before facing the tasks of the day. It made the whole day seem more bearable; no, it made tomorrow seem so promising it was worth today's labor.

At the cottage door she gasped in horror; even from that distance she could see the blossom was withered, almost completely gone after only two days. What would she tell Yun? How had she killed the flower so quickly even when everything seemed to be going well?

But when she drew close, crouching down and parting the leaves with trembling hands, she saw the flower had died a purely natural death. Hope blossomed fleetingly, it seemed, or perhaps her decision had hurried it along. There, glowing greeny-golden as a brand-new promise, a small orb poked up from the heart of the crumpled petals.

The vine's first fruit.

✑ ✑ ✑

Initial feedback

I liked the prose and concept. We could do with more initial context (what is a hope vine? why is she surprised after 11 years of trying? how many towns can she hope to cover?) and foundation for later revelations. Her turnaround re Yun is a bit rapid. I found the end on the thin side, and would have liked to see it developed more. She's visiting the vine every day to water it, so the 'reveal' of how it's doing is awkward. Why is there only one fruit?

Author's intent

What do you think the story's about?
What emotions are you trying to evoke?

To give you a sense of what I think the story is about: in my (other) professional life, I advise groups in conflict-affected countries on negotiating and implementing political transitions. Because of that work, I spend a lot of time thinking about transitional justice and how to recover from conflict. One of the most difficult elements to rebuild after conflict are the characteristics that help societies hold together — these intangibles are often vaguely categorized as "resiliency" in the post-conflict field. This story is an attempt to envision what transitional justice might look like in a world with magic, where resiliency factors are tangible things. More specifically, I'm trying to explore two themes: (1) how perpetrators can be part of a restorative process (but only if they acknowledge their own culpability); and (2) the challenge of being able to repair only a small fraction of the harm you caused. Hopefully that gives you a sense of what I'm trying to do with this piece, but please let me know if you have any further questions.

Author's note

I always look forward to being edited because it means I get a completely fresh set of eyes on characters and settings that I have inhabited for so long that I can't see them clearly anymore. "Hope on the Vine" is a perfect example of why an editor's eye is so necessary.

When Morris, *Metaphorosis'* editor, initially asked me to revise and resubmit this story, he asked for a brief paragraph explaining what I though the story was about. That was crucial to the editing process, because it meant that he and I approached future edits with same goal in mind. He knew what I was trying to do with "Hope on the Vine" and he was able to identify places where the narrative wasn't supporting the central theme of the story. After two months of drafting and four or five rounds of solo editing, I was too close to the story and the characters to recognize where the words on paper weren't as developed as the images in my head.

I wrote "Hope on the Vine" to explore transitional justice in a fantasy setting. Transitional justice is a collective term referring to efforts to document, memorialize, and hold people accountable for crimes committed during conflict or political upheaval. It's a long, slow, difficult process, partly because the crimes are often so huge or so widespread that punishing single perpetrators can never restore what was lost. Knowing this, how do victims and perpetrators convince themselves to strive for justice anyway?

My war criminal wizard Nima has 'voluntarily' agreed to a lifetime of community service rebuilding the environment she and other wizards magically stripped of its resiliency. She isn't in prison, but she's been cut off from her magic and she's gone from being a powerful ruler to a manual laborer in a rural hinterland. In my original draft, I intended to show her journey — first to understand that her actions were crimes, and second that she had a duty to repair them beyond simply fulfilling the sentence imposed on her.

The editing process helped me see that I was only telling half her journey. Yes, Nima needed to recognize her guilt and the need for restitution. But that's not justice, that's just accepting punishment. Achieving justice meant she also needed to confront the fact that she could never fully repair the harm she had done and yet choose to try to do what she could where she could. And finally, she had to see herself as part of the world she was repairing, not an outcast from it.

In the original draft, Nima doesn't understand why she offers to help Yun's family by giving them the fruit from the hope vine. I'd tried to give her a moment of revelation and change, but neither she nor the reader were ready for it. Morris asked questions about Nima's motivations in this and other scenes that helped me see why her decision felt shallow rather than transformative. In the final draft, she wrestles with the decision; she understands the stakes; she knows that helping will cost her, with no guarantee that it will help Yun. Editing transformed this hinge point from an unexamined impulse that might change Nima after the story was over to a considered decision that could only happen because the events of the story were already changing her.

Editor's note

While a little knowledge is a dangerous thing, every now and then a story comes in that connects to what I actually do for a living. I can't say that it was essential to the process here, but at the least, when R.E. mentioned 'restorative justice, we had a common vocabulary to work with. Here, I thought the restorative justice element was fairly clear from the start, but the idea that only partial restitution may be possible was a bit muddled by Nima's personal arc. I felt that fixing one would help fix the other, and R.E. resolved them quite early on.

There was relatively little other substantive work to do — the structure and balance of the piece largely worked well from the start. However, I had concerns about some of the mechanisms of the hope vine and Nima's powers that took a few exchanges to work out. Some of those touched lightly on the backstory — who had sent Nima out, and how — but largely it was details about the number of hope fruit, what effect they had, and how Nima interacted with it in daily watering.

Plus, we argued for a while about the difference between a sledge and a cart. Sometimes it's all about the details. :-)

Hope on the Vine

It was early August and hope was withering on the vine.

It had withered every year so far for the last eleven, so Nima wasn't surprised, only disappointed. She really thought she'd gotten the balance right this time.

She knelt in front of the raised mound of earth that should have been a strong, nourishing foundation for the hope vine's roots, her dirty boots poking out behind her and the sun glinting gently off her greying curls. The vine should be about three feet tall and eight feet wide by this point in the season. Heavy buds the size of the first knuckle of her thumb should be swelling between pairs of reniform leaves gleaming a lustrous dark jade. She should be out here looking for the first open blossom, a rich yellow stellate flower the size of her hand shading to the orange of glowing embers in the center.

Instead, she was kneeling in front of a meager three-foot by four-foot vine with anemic yellow-green spurs. The remaining leaves, with two notable exceptions, were the same undernourished shade, their ribs showing through more starkly with every passing day while their edges turned brown and flaked away. Only one spur, the one that twisted around the rail of the fence, showed any semblance of health, and Nima was as baffled by its continued vitality as she was by the parent vine suddenly giving up on life.

Eleven long years on this struggling piece of earth, trying to tease a hope vine from seed to fruit. If she could figure out the right combination and get this vine to thrive, she could move on. On to the next tired, war-scarred town and the next desiccated, abandoned farm, where the potential for hope or fortitude or patience lay dormant under years of neglect and acres of weeds.

The next, and the next, and the next. One by one until the tired land put the years of war and sorrow behind it for good and all.

But there wouldn't be a next and a next if she couldn't bring this vine back to life. She'd have to spend another roasting summer and dreary winter in the small blue house behind her. Her neighbors would ignore her, she'd quietly loathe them, and she'd never forget she wasn't wanted here.

Maybe she hadn't fertilized enough? But no; she'd been side-dressing the vine with the recommended half-cup of the special expensive blend that came from the Wizard's Herbarium, and she marked each application on her calendar so she knew she hadn't missed any. Was the mix itself wrong? They said it was guaranteed, but you never knew what that meant with the wizards you got these days. In her time, guarantees had come with blood, not a letter under shiny gilt seal.

If the mix was good, was water the issue? Possible, but hope vines were notoriously flexible in their water needs. In theory, they could take root and grow anywhere, with minimal tending. That's why they were among the first recommended plants for war restoration projects.

Probably she hadn't figured out the right daily tending regimen. This was where hope vines could be tricky. The fortitude tree could be watered with either sweat or blood (both of which she had in abundance, particularly in the summer). A hedge of patience would grow well with tears, sighs or, in a pinch, prayers. But hope vines demanded fiddly, intangible things: dreams recounted, promises exchanged, plans laid. But wizards didn't dream, she had no one to make promises to, and under the circumstances plans were not hers to lay. She'd tried making promises to the old farmhouse, to the wasted land around it, to the rickety fence and the empty road – but they had clearly been insufficient.

Nima stroked a finger across one of the limp leaves. "Grow," she whispered, putting all the force of her will into it. No effect, of course.

"What's wrong with your plant?"

The voice was high-pitched and unfamiliar. Nima looked up to see a girl of about twelve years draped across the fence near the gate, about ten feet away from her. Just about where the questing ends of the vine ought to be right now, she thought sourly. She'd never seen the girl before, though she had the look of a local: a short, wide body, tawny skin, a blunt nose, and straight, thick black hair cut short above her shoulders. Her eyes were close-set, small, and twinkling with curiosity.

"It isn't growing," Nima said shortly. She was sick to death of these suspicious locals. "Did you need something?"

"I'm Yun," the girl said, completely ignoring the pointed question. "Did you forget to water it?"

"No," Nima replied, trying to rein in her temper. It wouldn't improve her relationship with the locals if she started yelling at children. On the other hand, she didn't care that much about having a relationship with the locals. She turned back to the hope vine, scratching gently in the dirt around the main stalk to see if there was something preying on its roots.

"What about fertilizing? Did you feed it?" Yun asked.

"Yes," Nima said without looking up.

"Did you put it in the right kind of soil?"

"*Yes.*"

"Does it get enough sun?"

Exasperated, Nima thrust a hand out toward the unimpeded sky. Her back twinged, and she looked up with an unfriendly expression on her unschooled face.

"Hm. Maybe it's getting *too* much sun," Yun mused, unfazed. "Or maybe this isn't a good place for it to grow."

Nima clenched her jaw and bent back down. Maybe the irritating child would get bored and wander away. After a few seconds she heard soft footsteps against the dust and dared to hope. But no luck.

"But I don't know," Yun said, from much nearer, almost right in front of Nima. "It *feels* like it wants to grow here." A brown hand appeared at the corner of Nima's vision, stroking the leaves of the one remaining spur.

Nima looked up sharply. "Don't touch it," she snapped.

Yun whipped her hand away and looked, for the first time, as if she was picking up on Nima's unwelcoming demeanor. "Why not?"

"Because it's *my* vine," Nima replied, hearing how ridiculous she sounded even as the words came out of her mouth. "What I mean is, it's fragile and it isn't polite to touch other people's crops."

This was evidently a new concept to Yun. "But I help my Aunt Lio with her beans all the time and she says-"

But Nima was done with this conversation she hadn't wanted in the first place. She didn't want what passed for local agricultural expertise, didn't particularly like children, and needed peace and quiet to think about what to try next. "Then I'm sure your aunt would appreciate your help now," she interrupted, then stood up and stalked away, trying to ignore the ache in her knees. "Don't touch my plants," she called over her shoulder without looking back.

✍

Working on a half-baked theory that her bad mood was somehow hampering the vine's growth, Nima stayed away from it for the next few days except for watering. She kept a sharp eye on the fence, but the girl had vanished back to whatever ramshackle farmhouse she'd come from. She saw her traipsing by once on the road, but she showed no inclination to stop or pester the vine.

After a week, Nima woke up having slept well and decided she'd waited enough time to test her theory. If her mood did somehow affect the vine, she'd given it enough time to recover and should be able to see the effects. She filled her big watering can, sprinkled in the special water-soluble fertilizer and lugged it out to the fence.

The vine looked exactly the same: anemic stalk and spurs, withered yellow leaves slowly crumbling off their ribs...and one perfectly healthy spur climbing slowly around the fence rail along the road. The good spur had even put out another two leaves while the rest of the plant died.

"What...?" Nima stood there, hands hanging down open at her sides. She could grow things; the profusely healthy vegetable garden behind the house attested to that. There was no reason this should be so hard, no reason this spur should thrive while the parent plant died, no reason the one plant that mattered should wither while the rest of the garden flourished.

Whistling pierced her despair. Yun was tromping down the road in heavy boots several sizes too big for her, swinging two empty beaten metal buckets, whistling like the cloudy morning had been made for her alone. There was something odd about the buckets; they were the wrong shape somehow, too rounded on the bottom with asymmetric sides. Nima squinted at them and realized they were infantry helmets, inexpertly beaten into a slightly more bucket-like shape by a *very* amateur blacksmith.

"Did you figure out how to fix your plant?" Yun asked. She must have taken Nima's attempt to parse the helmets-turned-buckets as an invitation to stop and chat.

"No," Nima said, trying to think of a task that would take her away from the fence but allow her to keep an eye on the girl.

"It looks better, though," Yun said, waving one of the buckets at the flourishing spur. At least she wasn't trying to touch it. She wrinkled her nose. "That part at least."

Nima picked up her watering can and began dribbling the water gently around the roots of the vine. Yun didn't take the hint. She tromped a few steps closer, set the buckets down with a dusty *thump*, and squatted on her haunches in front of the vine. "I think it's happier on this side of the fence."

"Plants don't feel happy or sad," Nima said repressively. She saw Yun shrug out of the corner of her eye.

"My Aunt Lio says they do." Aunt Lio was evidently the arbitrator of reality. She leaned closer. "What kind of plant is this anyway?"

"A hope vine," Nima said shortly, then surprised herself by continuing, "at least, it's supposed to be."

"I never saw one of those before," Yun said, scrunching up her nose and peering at the plant with renewed interest.

"They aren't very common after the war," Nima found herself explaining.

"Ah," Yun said sagely, although she wasn't even old enough to remember the final years of the war and couldn't possibly understand what lay behind the disappearance of the country's native resilient vegetation. She leaned even closer to the vine, body rolling at such an angle that Nima feared she would pitch face first into the plant – and the railing.

"Be careful," she said, more harshly than she had intended.

Yun straightened up but didn't look abashed. "I think maybe this part of the plant isn't bothered by something that's messing with the rest of it," she said. "Or maybe it just likes that I talk to it."

Yun's comment niggled at the back of Nima's brain. Maybe there *was* something affecting the roots or the leaves on the parent vine that hadn't spread to the healthy spur yet – or maybe the spur had some kind of natural resistance...

"I have to go," Yun was saying in the background, but Nima was no longer paying attention. She didn't even notice the girl stretching out a stealthy hand to give the new leaves a friendly tap. "I'll be back tomorrow."

✍

Yun kept turning up after that. Sometimes for an hour, sometimes for ten minutes, sometimes carrying her ridiculous repurposed buckets, sometimes hauling a feed sack on a little rolling sledge, once with her arms full of hollow reeds as wide as her wrist and as tall as she was. She never seemed to be in a hurry or fear that whoever sent her on these tasks would be impatient at her dawdling. Aunt Lio either ran a slipshod operation or didn't particularly care what this niece was up to. Yun never mentioned her parents, so maybe she was a war orphan dumped on her only known relative. Maybe Lio had so much help on her farm, wherever it was, that one lolly-gagging child made no difference. Or maybe they were just relieved to get a break from her questions.

"Do they have hope vines where you come from?" she asked one time.

"No," Nima said.

"Where do you come from?" Yun asked.

"Not here," Nima said, picking up her rake and walking away.

✑

"I know this isn't your farm," Yun said another time.

Nima was pruning back the leaf husks on the spurs closest to the healthy one, in case the problem was some kind of spore or mildew. Her shears jumped and nearly clipped a healthy leaf. "What is that supposed to mean?" she demanded.

"Everyone knows you aren't from here even though you've lived here forever," Yun said with a limber shrug. "When are the people who belong to this farm coming back?"

"They aren't," Nima snapped.

"Maybe this would grow better if they did," Yun said, bumping the vine with grimy knuckles.

"Don't touch," Nima said, but she'd long since given up on the idea that Yun would listen.

"Don't worry, I'm not going away," Yun said, more to the vine than to Nima. "Hey look, there's a new grabby bit here!"

✑

"What's it like?" Yun asked on one unreasonably hot day.

"What's what like?" Nima replied, only half listening as she teased a tendril gently through a gap in the climbing frame.

"Being a bad wizard," Yun said, as if that should have been obvious.

Nima froze with the tendril balanced on one finger. "What do you mean by that?" she asked carefully.

"Everyone knows," Yun said without noticeable concern. "You're a bad wizard who made all the bad stuff happen in the war."

Nima snatched her hand away from the vine so she wouldn't transmit her feelings through the tender shoots. "That's a gross exaggeration. I'd never been here before – before I was assigned this farm."

"Also, I saw your thing," Yun pointed at Nima's right arm, where the geas runes constraining Nima's magic and her free movement crawled with slow abandon. She'd probably spotted it the first time they met, but Nima found herself tugging her sleeve down anyway, angry at her own shame.

"But you were responsible for bad stuff somewhere," Yun persisted. "Aunt Lio says getting a nice farm to run isn't a real punishment." She reached out and casually flicked the vine. Nima winced but the vine held firm. In fact, it flexed a tendril toward the sun.

Nima picked up her trowel, hefted it, set it down. "Your Aunt Lio doesn't know everything. It's not a punishment. It's a collective obligation."

"Hah!" Nima wasn't sure whether Yun's hard, fierce laugh was meant to dismiss the possibility that Aunt Lio could be wrong or the official line that felt flat even to her. "Then why do you have that?" She jabbed a half-closed fist at the geas runes.

"Yes, fine, technically it's a punishment," Nima said sharply, "but I *cooperated*. I *agreed* to be tried. I could have just done my time, but I entered the program voluntarily to try to make amends for what happened during the war. Nobody forced me to wear this." She shook her right arm at the girl. "Nobody forced me to be here."

"Then why don't you leave?" Yun asked in genuine curiosity.

In all the years she'd endured in this place, no one had ever asked Nima what she thought about her situation. It was humiliating to be grateful for a child's fickle attention, but her life was nothing but humiliations now.

"Because what the wizards did was wrong," Nina said, striving for patience. Not native to this farm and not native to her either. "We had the right- we had good intentions. We thought we were preserving order in the world. But we did things that had consequences far beyond what we intended, beyond what we could have imagined when we started."

"What were you trying to do?" Yun asked. "Aunt Lio says all you wizards just wanted to keep all their power and when the war happened you decided to burn the country down instead of sharing even one good thing with regular people."

There had been a time where Nima would have drowned in their own sweat anyone who dared speak so harshly, so honestly. "How fortunate a bean farmer knows the absolute truth!" she snapped, then reined herself in. "Look, the war was complicated and you're too young to understand most of what happened."

Yun was undeterred. "Aunt Lio says the wizards hoarded all the best food and medicine and magic in their towers," she persisted. "She says the headwomen of all the villages went to the towers and asked for the wizards to share, but the wizards said they had nothing valuable to trade. So the villages stopped sending tithes to the towers and then the wizards came out of their towers and ruined everything. And Tonji says the wizards never loved anything but themselves and that's why they could do what they did to the land and the rivers and everything."

Nima had no idea who Tonji was and she didn't like his assessment of the war. "That's not an accurate picture," she said stiffly, although it was, if boiled down to its essence and told through the eyes of the victors. "There was...more to it." In the back of her mind she heard, was always hearing, the soul-shattering crack of her tower's foundations.

"Like what?" Yun asked pugnaciously.

Nima thought of her tower, its dimensions aligned precisely with the planes and angles of her interior self. She recalled vast power seeping from the land into her tower's stones, and from its stones into her. Power that extended the reach of her hand as far as thought could take it, that honed her vision, peering keen-edged with magic into any secret she desired. When her tower stood, she was the secret composer of the song beneath everything...and then they pulled her tower down and she was nothing. Keeper of a withered garden in a mutilated land. Bitterness welled up in her.

"I couldn't possibly explain it to you in a way you could comprehend," she said, aiming for austere but coming no higher than cruel.

Yun gave her a very straight look then shrugged deliberately. "Well, it's not like you know the first thing about growing beans," she replied.

It toppled Nima like she was a tower herself. Yun hadn't spoken in pettiness, but rather with the world weary familiarity of someone who often had to defend her own worth. Maybe it was a line she'd heard her aunt use. It didn't matter; she'd seen the seed of truth it held. Yun didn't know what it was like to wield power that could make and unmake the world. Nima didn't know how to grow beans. Once, the difference between them would have been too vast to comprehend. Now, it meant that between the two of them, Nima was merely the less capable subsistence farmer.

Nima was used to wrapping prickly defensiveness around herself like armor, but she suddenly couldn't reach it. They just sat there looking at each other, black eyes to brown. "I never had any reason to grow beans before," Nima said, conceding.

The silence stretched for several more minutes while Nima pretended to rearrange the dirt at the base of the vine's main stalk. "We cared for the land a long time," she continued at last. "People couldn't see what we did. We worked to keep the soil fertile, to manage the weather, to sustain the forests... We weren't trying to destroy the land. We were just desperate to make the war stop."

Yun crossed her arms over her chest. "Seems to me like if you didn't want all that bad stuff to happen, the best thing would have been for you not to do it," she said.

Nima had used a lot of noble sentences and fine words to get her through the dark nights of doubt, but none of them volunteered to stand up against that unflinching logic. "You're right," she said, after a long minute. "But we did do it. I. I did it. So all I can do now is try to repair what I can."

Yun glanced away as if the subject had never really been that interesting in the first place. "So why is this vine so important?"

Nima scrubbed her hands over her face. "This land, one of the things it has – had-" she paused. Started again. "A long time ago, wizards found a way to cultivate resilience. *Yes, wizards*," she snarled at the skeptical look on Yun's face. "They taught seeds to grow hope, patience, and fortitude. They infused rivers with openness and stocked lakes with solidarity. They showed the land how to produce the things that would sustain it, no matter what came." She pressed her lips together and bit down hard on the sour feeling twisting her belly. "But the hope vines and trees of fortitude and all the rest of it didn't survive the war."

"Because of you," Yun interrupted. "You wizards, I mean. Right?"

"It wasn't just-" But it was. They had stretched out their hands and stripped the land of everything their forebears had grafted into it. She was out here trying to make amends for her role in that enormous crime, so what was the point of spinning a sweeter-sounding version of the truth to this child who wasn't buying it anyway? "Yes. Wizards weren't responsible for all the bad things that happened in the war, but they – we- did destroy the resiliency ecosystem. We did that."

"Why?" Yun asked.

A simple, deadly question. Nima had answers she'd given herself, answers she'd given her colleagues who doubted their course of action, answers she'd given the court that sentenced her.

Only we have the knowledge and experience to guide this country to its better future. Our better future requires peace and peace requires order and order can only come when the villages bow to our authority.

These rebel armies are destroying the land – perhaps if they see harsh consequences they will surrender before we have to kill them all.

Some of the Wizard's Consortium chose to cross that final line and the rest of us let ourselves get pulled across.

So many answers. But none of them sufficient, in the end, to justify stripping the land of everything that held it together and helped it thrive. Not when you boiled it down to a young girl and an old wizard crouched on opposite sides of a fence in a dusty nowhere trying to understand why nothing good could grow.

"Because we forgot that wizards first built towers to serve and protect the land," she said at last. She suddenly became aware of how stiff and heavy her legs had become. "We thought of the land as something under our rule, not under our care. So when the rebels – when the war came, it was easy for us to start thinking of the land as a weapon."

Nima remembered standing atop her tower filled with grim righteousness as she stretched out her hands and drained the Ko River into the bedrock. She remembered the sense of urgency that filled her heart when she walked in the fortitude groves, blighting the ancient trees to strip the rebels of their will to fight. She remembered having those feelings, but she couldn't reproduce them. Now, all she could feel was shame and despair at the enormity of what they had done. How could she ever have thought that growing one stupid hope vine would mean anything in the face of their atrocities? Even if she lived to be the oldest wizard in history and grew a new vine or tree every year, it would be a pitiful drop in the desert their crimes had created.

"And now wizards must undo what wizards did," Yun chanted the first line of the decree that doomed all surviving wizards to a lifetime of penal restitution – out here in the backlands, it was probably the only part of the decree she'd ever heard. She bopped one of the withered leaves unceremoniously. "You're not very good at it, huh?"

Nima lurched forward to cup the leaf, jerked herself back, then stared at it as it seemed to stretch out luxuriously. Was a deeper green flushing outward from the central rib, or were her eyes lying to her? "No," she admitted. "I'm not. All I have to do is grow one fruit to send to the parole board so I can move on. But this work is much harder than I expected."

Yun nodded sagely. "I bet it's hard to make this place hopeful when you aren't," she said. Then her head shot up as if hearing a voice calling her. "Whoops, gotta go," she said. She hopped to her feet, scooped up her buckets, and took off at a steady trot down the road.

Nima watched her go, rolling her last words around and around. *It's hard to make this place hopeful when you aren't.* Could that be the problem? The hope vine couldn't grow if its tender had no hope of her own to share?

But then – Nima held her hand out to the leaf Yun had bopped, without touching it herself. It was noticeably greener, and drooped less. And then – she peered down where Yun had been flicking her careless fingers, and there was one, no two! new tendrils peeking out. Wherever the child had touched the plant it was thriving. Nima thought about all the times she'd seen Yun touching the vine (and scolded her for it). Was a coincidence that the one healthy spur was the one closest to the road, the easiest one for Yun to reach? Was the vine nourishing itself off of her innate hope for the future, a future Yun expected to have a place in in exactly the way Nima didn't?

Nima brooded on it all night.

✍

Yun came back the next day, and the next, chattering about some issue with Aunt Lio's bean crop. Nima made noncommittal noises or gave answers she forgot even as they came out of her mouth. She was watching what happened to the vine where Yun touched it, trying to learn the secret of how she made it grow.

The girl didn't appear to be doing anything special. She didn't even seem to be paying attention to the vine most of the time, although she always crouched by it when she stopped, even though it meant she had to perch in the ditch on the side of the road. She would bump or stroke or tap the leaves or tendrils to emphasize a point or sometimes as if it were agreeing with her, but she might have done the same thing with her buckets or the rolling sledge. She certainly didn't treat the vine with the care or deference that Nima herself did. Nima couldn't see any one thing that set Yun's interactions with the hope vine above her own – except, of course, that the vine grew where Yun touched it and withered everywhere she did not.

And "grow" was a bit of an understatement. On Nima's side of the fence the other spurs had desiccated into spindly dry stalks, their leaves long since crumbled into the dirt. On Yun's side, seven feet of rich jade green sprouted leaves the size of Nima's palm, twisted tendrils around every surface of the climbing frame and the fence rails, and were sending out new spurs in two places. There were even four tiny green nubs that, given time, would become buds.

Nima never, ever touched the healthy spur. She even stood on the dead side of the plant to water and dress it, hoping not to poison it with indirect contact. She didn't encourage Yun to touch it either, superstitiously worried that the vine would pick up on her desperation and stop responding to Yun's presence. She just held herself in nervous stasis, waiting for the bloom.

✍

"What does a hope vine actually do?" Yun asked.

"It's hard to explain," Nima said distractedly. "They have many effects, but not always all of them at the same time. Other things grow better when a hope vine grows somewhere nearby. The roots prevent erosion and return nutrients to dead soil. The fruits can feed people much longer than their size would suggest. And just being around the flowers – I really can't explain what that feels like, you'll just have to experience it for yourself."

"We could really use one of those," Yun said. But Nima was measuring the length of an unfurled bud and didn't ask a follow-up question.

✍

Maybe it was the empty rattling of the sledge that finally forced Nima to admit that something was wrong. Or maybe it was that Yun's feet dragged in the dusty road as she approached. Whatever it was, Nima looked up one day to see a new expression on Yun's face: despair.

The girl squatted in her usual place on the other side of the fence, her hands flopped over her knees and her black hair sticking to her sweaty temples. She didn't touch the vine.

"What's wrong with you?" Nima said, more harshly than she'd intended. But then, she'd never been a gentle person.

"The bean crop is failing," Yun said, looking burdened in a way Nima had never seen her. "Aunt Lio says there's no way to save it now, even though we built reed irrigation all the way from the river and I pick off all the bugs I can find."

"The bean crop?"

"I told you," Yun said, but without heat. "There's a bug that came and it eats all the buds before they can bloom." She reached a sad little finger out toward one of the swelling buds of the hope vine, then pulled it back again.

"I guess you'll have to eat something other than beans this winter," Nima said, trying to remember if beans had some sort of local cultural significance. "Variety is good for you."

Yun looked at her like Nima had just suggested they try to eat the sun. "We don't eat beans, we sell them," she said. Then, in a cadence that sounded like something she'd heard from someone else many times, "no beans, no money. No money, no winter stores, no shoes, no seeds for spring."

"Oh," Nima said. Of course Yun's entire livelihood hung on some stupid beans. What if they had to leave the farm? What if they starved? What would happen to the hope vine if Yun suddenly stopped coming by, telling her cheerful stories and helping pass the long weary days with impertinent questions? "That's...bad."

"Yes." Yun sighed heavily and gave the swollen bud close to her face the gentlest of taps. Nima sucked in her breath, but Yun didn't notice and the vine didn't show any immediate negative effects. "We sure could use one of these hope vines right now," she repeated. Nima suddenly recognized the line as something she'd heard Yun saying a lot lately.

She was never entirely sure why she did what she did next. Some of it was self-interest, but her memory of the day was tinged with several shades of guilt as well – guilt for disregarding the problem growing in front of her eyes, guilt for her abrasive attitude toward Aunt Lio, guilt for her failure year after year to restore the land in this area. And perhaps there was the smallest hope that just one thing could be made to grow in these forsaken backlands.

"Look, this is about to flower. If it fruits afterward I'll give you the very first one," Nima said, completely surprising herself. "Then you can take it home to your Aunt Lio and plant it. I'm sure it will grow for you. And...I could teach you what I've learned about it."

Yun looked up, her eyes shining in a way Nima had never seen. It was like all the dust had washed right out of the world. "You mean it? We could have a hope vine of our own?"

"It won't make your bean plants come back," Nima warned. "Probably."

"But it means they'll grow good next year!" Yun said with an enormous grin. "That's right, isn't it? Everything grows better where a hope vine grows?"

"That's the theory," Nima agreed. She felt guilty giving the girl hope when she wasn't sure the vine was capable of producing a fruit this late in the season, no matter how nicely it was filling out. But then, hope was all she had to offer, from beginning to end.

"But...wait." Yun crinkled up her face around her nose. "Don't you have to send the fruit to the parole board? So they send you on to your next place?"

"There will be another fruit, in another year," Nima heard herself say, giving the vine an affectionate little stroke with the back of her hand. And to her utter astonishment, a tiny bright green tendril unfurled from beneath her knuckles.

✍

The vine bloomed four days later, opening like a star and drawing the eye from anywhere in the garden. Nima found herself staring at it for uncounted time, just tracing its silky depths with her eyes. She could see, if she looked closely in the way wizards were trained to do, runes tracing and retracing themselves deep within the flower's genetic structure. But mostly she just wanted to stand beside the vine, falling into its radiance.

Two days after the bloom, Nima came out early to gaze at the flower. It was a habit she'd fallen into immediately, getting in close to the luminous petals, tracing the dew that beaded gently on their surface, filling her lungs with the flower's scent before facing the tasks of the day. But she hadn't taken more than a half-dozen steps from the cottage door before she gasped in horror; even from that distance she could see the blossom was withered, almost completely gone after only two days. What would she tell Yun? How had she killed the flower so quickly even when everything seemed to be going well? Or worse, had it been stolen?

But when she drew close, crouching down and parting the leaves with trembling hands, she saw the flower had died a purely natural death. Hope blossomed fleetingly, it seemed. But there, glowing greeny-golden as a brand-new promise, a small orb poked up from the heart of the crumpled petals.

The vine's first fruit.

✍ ✍ ✍

THE WIFE OF FABIAN VITALIK

—

MARIAH MONTOYA

The Wife of Fabian Vitalik

The day that Fabian Vitalik's wife left, rain masked the roar of the sea just beyond their rock garden. Fabian ended fishing early because of the storm, and came home to find his wife dozing on the sofa by the window, unfazed by the sharp *pat pat pat* of rain fingers on glass.

He found her enthralling when she was still and senseless like this, so he sat down and watched her breathe, the pearl necklace that rested on her chest rising and falling like waves. Their handmade string of seashells hanging from the ceiling tinkled above her head.

"I love you," Fabian whispered to her sleeping figure, rubbing fish grease on his pants. He thought his wife was most beautiful when she was human.

Of course, she was famous for her shape-shifting. When he'd first seen her high up on the stage, twirling and morphing into other things, the audience had gone wild for the black sleekness of her cat's fur, the shine of her teapot porcelain surface, the perfume that wafted from her petals when she mutated into a lilac bush. Oh yes, he remembered the hoots and howls of men when she danced her way across the stage as only a dress, the movement of shimmering fabric emphasizing the curves of the woman that would be underneath.

He had stared up at her in that crowd, marking the flashes of skin when she would have to, for a moment, be herself again before transforming into something she was not.

Now her overalls were fraying, her hair graying at the roots, the creases of fake smiles ebbing over her face. But so beautiful. Perhaps that was why she had married him, a simple fisherman living in Camber who'd tracked her down when the rain started pouring and the audience dispersed with newspapers over their heads. Nobody had glanced her way after she converted back into a woman, rain-soaked and delicate and normal. Nobody but him. And thirty years later, Fabian could not stop staring.

It was only when the rain stopped that she tensed and shifted her body on the sofa, as if the lack of pattering on the window was an alarm. The seashells clinked to a still. Her eyelids fluttered open.

"How did you sleep, love?" Fabian asked from his armchair, drinking in her presence.

She blinked at him, flexed her fingers as if amazed that she had fingers at all. Far off, they could finally hear the ocean again, roaring and crashing onto the beach. She looked back up at him. "What have you been doing this whole time?"

"Reading," Fabian said, although his book lay unopened on the other end of the coffee table.

"How'd fishing go? I assume the rain ruined things."

"Caught some, but not much. Had to come back early."

"Hmm." His wife glanced out the windowpane, where the rainstorm had leaked into a gray drizzle. The stones in their garden glistened with the residue of the storm. "You know," she said, "I have always wanted to shift into wind. Or fire. An element of some sort, but I don't know how. Which muscle do I reach for? Which thought do I think? Which color do I let fill me up?"

Fabian did not answer, only stared at the curve of her mouth, thinking about love and fishing and the sea. How many times had he woken from a night of lovemaking to find something else on his wife's pillow — a dusty book, a glass doll, a starfish? When she was transforming, she was so much like the sea, wild and unpredictable. But when she was human, she moved like a butterfly, gently, gracefully...

" — simply rise and plummet where I please."

Fabian nodded, not knowing what she had just said. He remembered his wife giving birth to their three children, who were all grown and traveling now — Josiah had come out covered in fur, his shape-shifting abilities stuck between some kind of animal and the baby he was. The doctors had panicked until the little guy had given a sharp, sputtering cry and shifted back into baby skin.

None of their other children could shape-shift, and Josiah never did again. The curse, the blessing, of having an ordinary father.

" — hear me, Fabian? Does it not faze you, what I just said?"

"What?" Fabian jolted out of his visions, refocusing on the woman before him.

"I don't want to stay here anymore. With you, with this dratted, God-forsaken house." His wife stared at him with the haltingness of a sand crab caught by a seagull eye. "I want to simply rise and plummet where I please. You, Fabian, do not appreciate my needs to escape confinement, and — "

The crash of the ocean. Fabian's ears roared with the sound. He did not know whether his wife meant confinement in his house, or in her body, or both. She was touching the pearls on her neck, the pearls he had plucked from shored oysters himself.

" — and my love has crumpled inside me, Fabian. I feel like a rock when I am with you. You never admire me when I'm a cricket singing you songs at night, or when I'm a vase of flowers in our kitchen, or when I'm a wardrobe holding our clothes." Angry blotches were rising on her cheekbones now. "I feel like a rock," she said again. "I have since I met you. I want to feel like — I don't know, *something* lighter, something more free and beautiful and untamed than I am now."

Fabian stared at her. He wanted to say he didn't *need* a cricket to sing him songs, her human heartbeat was enough at night. He didn't *want* a vase of flowers to make their kitchen pretty, his wife cooking was enough. He didn't need another wardrobe to hold his clothes. He wanted to hold *her*. That was all he'd ever wanted. Why couldn't she appreciate it, the boundless depth of his love?

But the words curled inside him, drowned by hers. *I want to feel like — something lighter, something more free and beautiful and untamed than I am now.* Flashes of soft butterfly wings fluttered behind his eyelids.

"Do you understand, Fabian?"

He blinked. Those seashells above her head turned on their strings, but did not touch each other, and so were silent. "I understand," he said. "I want you to feel like a b- to feel beautiful too, darling."

She did not reply, only rose from her seat and wafted toward the kitchen, wispy like wind. He could hear her clanging in their cupboards and fridge, bringing out wrapped tuna and a knife. He could hear the metal of the knife slicing through scales and skin, the smell of innards floating into the living room. Fabian only stared down at his fishing calluses.

I feel like a rock. Did she really think all his fishing and hard work and love only amounted to rocks? Was she really so cold to his efforts?

Long after the knives quit chopping, he heard the sudden disappearance of his wife and the padded prowling of some creature that took her place. But for all his curiosity, he did not look back to see what his wife, in her disguised grief, had transformed into this time. He only knew that no butterfly was about to flutter over to him and rest gently, silently on his shoulder.

Fabian lugged his empty fishing bag through Camber, past the barber shop and post office and butcher's, all vacant in the grayish night. His footsteps splashed in cobblestone mud. He didn't know why he was making his usual daytime trek through town in the dead of night, especially when he'd spent the last few weeks simply staring at the sea, not brave enough to face fishing with his wife disappeared. But he'd heard the fishermen talk of her performing again and wanted to know, wanted to *see* her one more time....

Up ahead, lights and shouts from Patty's Tavern grew with every step. Music, clapping, hollering, a man stumbling onto cobble with his boots on his hands. Fabian slunk to the open front door and peered inside, where an audience was roaring and hooting, circled around a spectacle in the center of the bar.

She danced and twirled and morphed. She was a spinning wheel, polished, rotating, churning out strands that a few men reached forward to touch... Fabian felt a sharp prick of jealousy... and then the thread was gone. The men staggered forward, fell on their knees to the roar of audience laughter, and there was a split moment when Fabian saw his wife again, her glowing face and upturned smile and brief mien of concentration, the pearl necklace he'd made for her still dangling around her neck.

Then she was a violin playing itself, a bluebird that screeched and spiraled into a waterfall of buttons, which exploded and clattered to the rotted floorboards. A single button rolled to the doorway. Fabian bent to pick it up, but just as he touched the button's smooth, rounded edge, it disappeared between his fingers, and in the center of the bar there was suddenly a fishing boat, rocking as if on a boiling sea.

She knew he was there. Knew his touch.

The empty fishing sack slipped through Fabian's fingers. He left it there, left it at the open doorway where his wife was performing, and staggered around like a drunk, away from the tavern, back toward his home. The world spun around him. Shapes bloomed in the darkness — buttons, birds, spinning wheels, flowers, teapots. Even the eyes of some nighttime cat seemed to glow green in the darkness between two run-down houses. Fabian yelled at them. The eyes blinked and vanished, but other shapes continued to blossom in the darkness, haunting Fabian until he made it to his doorway. He reeled inside and ran to his bed, where, for a moment, he thought he saw his wife's sleeping figure breathing on the bedsheets.

But no, she was long gone, entertaining other men, transmuting into other things.

Fabian stumbled to their closet and rummaged through shoes, coats, dresses, anything that his wife might like to turn into, anything that he could pretend was her until morning. He knew she would never morph into anything simple; his fingers clasped something cold, and he pulled out an old candlestick she had used to hold candles during winter storms. With its twisted, ornate silver twining around the hilt, the candlestick was intricate enough that it would do. Fabian brought it to his bedside and gently placed it on his wife's pillow.

Then he crawled into bed. The coldness pressed in all around him, but he looked at the candlestick where his wife should be, and its shape comforted him.

"Goodnight, my love," he said to the candlestick. It did not reply, but he placed his fingers on its silver and soon found himself sinking into dreams, dreams where his wife was not betraying him in the tavern; instead, she drifted back home to lie by his side once more.

✍

He awoke to her meow.

He mumbled, reached out across his pillow, found the cold hilt of the candlestick. Something wet touched his hand. He opened his eyes to see a cat staring at him on its haunches — his wife, *his wife was finally back*. Fabian's chest leapt with a burst of adrenaline. He wiped his eyes and sat up to look at the cat better.

But his wife was always a sleek, black cat when she morphed, not this dirty tabby nudging his hand, its ears crooked and nose scarred.

"What...?" Fabian asked. The cat jumped off his bed, knocking the candlestick to the floor.

Perhaps she had aged so much that her cat form had aged too. Fabian tried to think back to the last time his wife had become a cat and couldn't recall. Suddenly he wished very much that he had turned around to see what she had become in the kitchen the day she'd left.

The cat yowled, racing into the living room and out his front door, which Fabian must have left wide open last night. He staggered after it, every step making his stomach plummet as he realized that the cat was not his wife, and the candlestick was not his wife, and all the chairs and windows and outside trees were not his wife. When he saw the tabby waiting for him in his rock garden, he could have kicked it away.

But then he noticed what was resting at the tabby's feet in the rocks, like a mouse that the cat had dragged to his doorstep as a prize: his wife's pearl necklace.

"What did you do to her?" Fabian said slowly, bending to pick up the necklace. The cat meowed again. Fury tumbled inside him. "*Where is she?*" he said. "*Where the hell is my wife?*"

The cat turned and streaked down his yard toward Camber.

Fabian ran after it, past all his neighbors' houses and onto the main street of the town, through the daytime vendors who shoved flower seeds and shish kebabs and painted seashells in his face.

The cat weaved through the crowd, past the dry and emptied Patty's Tavern, shooting down a shabbier, muddier avenue, where hedges lined the yards of run-down hovels. Fabian followed it to the furthest hut, where the cat slipped inside the open doorway and meowed a greeting to whoever was stirring inside.

"Fabian Vitalik?" somebody called.

"Who...?"

A man from beyond the open doorway shifted, then emerged onto his front steps with a wan smile. Fabian recognized, with a jolt, the town herbalist, whom he'd only ever met once at a neighborhood funeral.

"Come in, Fabian Vitalik," the herbalist said with a beckoning hand. "Your wife — she is here."

Fabian did not hesitate as he ran into the depths of the house after the man. Soil caked the floor, moss was growing on the molding, and sunlight surged through a vast open window toward the back of the house. Sitting on an earthy rug below this window, surrounded by an array of plants in clay pots, was his wife. She was human.

She was also swaying, as if to music that Fabian couldn't hear.

"Darling," Fabian said, but the herbalist put a hand on his shoulder. The cat was twisting itself around his wife's rocking body, meowing.

"We found her in an alleyway last night, Fabian Vitalik, soaking wet and unable to speak. My little helper here — " He nodded at the cat. " — is adept at sniffing out illnesses, and brought me to her. I believe she has suffered some kind of stroke from excessive shifting."

Fabian clutched the pearl necklace tighter. The herbalist moved toward a rounded table, where he swept a hand across bowls of powder and jars of dark green liquid. "I have given her turmeric stewed at midnight, but she still won't speak. Ashwaganda ground in halibut. Thyme and flax seeds. Her condition has not changed. She has the mind of a three-year-old, and I fear — "

" — Darling," Fabian said again, crouching low, not wishing to hear the rest of the herbalist's prediction. His wife looked up at him. Docile eyes. A sweet expression that softened her wrinkles. She would not stop swaying.

"She needs someone to take care of her, Fabian Vitalik. I fear she will not get better." The herbalist crouched beside him and peered into her face. "She certainly cannot shift anymore, and if she attempted to it would be catastrophic. She needs fed, bathed, dressed, put to bed — "

"She's not my wife anymore," Fabian said for the first time. "She left me. Somebody else has to take care of her." He felt the coldness rush up his spine at these words, desire and anger clashing like crests against a boat. His wife smiled sweetly at him, and he felt bile in his throat. If he had just stayed at Patty's Tavern last night and stopped her from continuing to perform... of course she would have hated him for it, but she *already* hated him.

The herbalist was watching him steadily. His wife swayed like waves.

"There is no one else to take care of her, Fabian. No one else that cares for her when she is stuck in this form."

"She left me," Fabian said again, the pearl necklace in his hand slipping in sweat. He did not want this to be so valid an excuse that she couldn't stay with him, but he wanted an apology, a sad sheen of understanding in her eyes, some subtle sign that she was sorry, and that even if she had not gotten sick, she would be returning to him.

But vacancy stayed spewed across her face.

"She is the mother of your children," the herbalist said gently.

And at this, Fabian felt himself break down. Of course. Of course he would take her in. He would slave over her until she got better, because she *had* to get better. And then he would let her go, for surely, even if she couldn't shift, she would want to leave him again when she healed.

"Fabian," the herbalist said, as if in reply to his thoughts. The tabby meowed. "She *mustn't* try to shift. I doubt she would be able to, but if she *did* manage it... she would be stuck. Stuck in another form forever."

"There'd be no way of bringing her back?" Fabian asked, finally standing up. He tried to imagine his wife stuck in her cat form, or worse — some kind of inanimate object. A decoration, or a candlestick.

The herbalist bowed his head. "If she shifted, there would be no way of bringing her back, no."

A cloud must have passed over the sun, because in that moment, the room was cloaked in eerie, greenish shadows. Fabian bent, strung the pearl necklace around his wife's neck once more, and heaved her into his arms. She allowed this as if she were little more than a rag doll. Fabian started toward the door, then hesitated.

"Isn't there anything that can be *done*? She — she hates her human body." His wife seemed to feel the tremor that ran through him, because although she did not stop smiling, a flicker of unease ran across that strangely vacant face.

"As far as concoctions go, none that I know of. Just love her, Fabian Vitalik."

Fabian nodded, turned away from the herbalist and the cat, and stepped back into broad daylight. His wife's dead weight threatened to bring him to his knees, but he did not stop carrying her, not when he made it to Camber's main street again, not when pedestrians stopped their market trading to stare. He hauled his wife all the way to their house at the shore, sweat beading on his forehead. When he finally made it through their rock garden and set her down underneath their string of seashells, she began swaying again.

His wife was back.

Yet Fabian wanted her to be capable of talking. Of shifting. Of leaving him again. Because only if she was capable of leaving would her staying mean she loved him back.

✍

Shouts, music, and the clanking of glasses washed over him in a buzzing void, but Fabian, sitting at the bar in Patty's Tavern, concentrated on one sound. A pepper-haired man was giggling as he and some comrades danced around an empty plastic pail by the smoke pit, chanting, "Shape-shifter, shape-shifter, alter faster! Quicker! Swifter!" They hooted, hollered, whistled like they had that first night Fabian had peeked into the bar, and eventually a guitarist began strumming his instrument in tune to the mantra. Soon, so many men turned on their stools that half the bar was singing to the plastic pail, slopping beer down their shirts, believing the pail to be Fabian's wife.

"You know what I think?"

A woman slid onto the stool next to him. Tall, long legs. Her jacket swelled where it buttoned up over her breasts, and oh, she smelled good, like lilacs and shellfish and wine. His wife used to smell like that, whenever Fabian would come home exhausted and lay his head down on her lap and listen to her hum songs.

"Well, if you're not going to answer," the woman said, fingering her shot glass, and now, at last, Fabian was zeroed in on something other than those wretched men fawning over a plastic pail. "The name's Zoey. And that bucket was being used to catch a leak in the roof long before those assholes came in. If you ask me, the shape-shifter's anywhere but here. After that one fiasco last month? I'd say she's out of the continent."

Fabian grunted, took a swill out of his mug as he pictured the shape-shifter lying on his bed half a mile away, taking her daytime nap, very much in the continent. A word surfaced to his brain.

"Fiasco?" he repeated.

"Yeah, I was there." The woman brought her glass to her lips and drained it in one gulp. She wiped her lips. "The girl — well, she's more an old lady now — she was performing, you know? And she was turning into all kinds of things, vines and animals and all that drat. She said to get ready for her grand finale, that she was going to turn into wind — and then she just... exploded. Into all these butterflies"

"Exploded into butterflies," Fabian said. In his mind, he heard, *I want to feel like a butterfly again,* although he wasn't sure if his wife had actually said it or if he had simply fabricated those words in his mind.

"Yes, and the butterflies began twirling like a tornado. Almost wind, but not quite. Only, the tornado was screaming. God, it hurt my ears. Then the whole thing just disappear — hey! Where are you going?"

Fabian had fished into his pocket, smacked some coins on the counter, and started toward the door, leaving the woman and her long legs behind. Once out on the street, he targeted the peddler's cart that sold flower seeds, and asked the vendor which flowers attracted butterflies.

For the past few weeks, he had been trying to get his wife to talk. Shifting would be, as the herbalist put it, catastrophic, but *talking?* Fabian had thought she'd find her voice again if he read to her, but maybe she needed a reminder of what was beautiful before she found herself again. Maybe she needed butterflies in their garden instead of rocks.

Once the vendor had sold him a packet of daylily seeds, Fabian hurried to the house, where his wife would be waking up from her nap. He left the seeds on the kitchen table and rushed into the bedroom, where his wife was sitting up in bed, swaying, smiling pleasantly.

"Hello, beautiful," Fabian said, opening the window blinds to let sunlight through. "Are you hungry? I've finally gone fishing again, and I found some mussels with nice, hearty meat in them. You love mussels, remember? And I have a surprise for you, too. It might take a while — they need to grow first, but you're going to love it."

His wife just smiled.

Fabian began his usual routine of setting his wife near the sofa where he slept at night, cooking, cleaning, talking to her as if he expected a reply. Occasionally, when he had the spare money, he would buy some paper and finger paints and place them on the floor in front of her. These were the only times she would finally quit swaying, dip her fingers into the paints, and create.

The pictures were crude, to say the least, as if a toddler had painted them. But Fabian had still been able to decipher wind, fire, earth. Today, as he popped open the mussels and set them over a small kitchen fire to sizzle, she was drawing a distorted ocean. Sun glaring down on miniature whitecaps, seashells as big as ships, curling, spiraling waves.

It happened after feeding her supper and taking the trash out. Fabian came back inside to find his wife's pictures abandoned on the floor. For one jolting moment, he thought she was gone.

Then he saw her swaying in the kitchen. She was sitting neatly in their tarnished tin tub that he bathed her in at nights. Her clothes were in a pile on the floor, so that only her pearl necklace gleamed on her bare chest.

"It's not bath time yet, darling," Fabian said, shaken. He started forward to pick up her clothes and dress her when a change flashed over her face. A frown. Then that soft, sweet smile again. But for a brief moment, he had seen the crunch of her eyebrows, that concentration she wore when she was trying to shift.

"How about we just have bath time now, then?" Fabian said slowly. But even as he walked toward the faucet, he saw that flash of concentration again, heard the small whimper escape her mouth. They stared at each other. His wife's smile was still etched on her face, but the corners of her mouth were quivering. And suddenly, Fabian knew that he needed to plant those seeds *now*.

"I'll be right back," he whispered, backing away. "*Right* back. Please don't go anywhere."

He grabbed the packet of seeds from the table and in a flash, leaving his wife in the tub, was on his knees in the rock garden. The sky overhead was churning and the sea's high tide was a sharp crash in his ears, but Fabian dug rock after rock out of the dirt and threw them to the side. He felt the sharp plop of water on the back of his neck, but he welcomed the rain that splashed onto the soil beneath his fingers.

"Butterflies," he murmured, ripping open the packet and pouring beetle-black seeds onto his palm. He dug into the dirt, feeling the prickle of time pepper his head, as if he could only save his wife by planting fast enough. He dropped the seeds into those little cavities in the earth, covered them back up, and stood, panting.

His front door was still ajar.

Fabian crept back into the doorway and peered inside, where the shadowed sky cloaked their living room and kitchen in dim shades. His wife's picture was flapping in a sudden wind that swooped past Fabian, into the house. Her clothes still lay discarded on the floor.

But the tarnished tub was empty.

"Hello? Where — where are you, darling?" Fabian called. The paper flapped, moving across the floor. The sea still sounded in his ears, but otherwise there was no sound.

Fabian moved further inside and called his wife's name. He went into the bedroom, but she was not there either. And now his heart was crashing in his chest, and he began racing to every corner of the house, calling for her, trying to find her again, and the sound of the sea was slapping against the shore, slapping against tin...

Against tin?

Fabian halted. He turned, looked at the tub still sitting in the kitchen. The slapping sound was coming from the tub's direction, so Fabian took a step toward it, then another. When he was finally hovering over it, he looked down and saw that the tub was not, as he had thought, empty.

Water was sloshing inside, sloshing as if desperate to free itself. His wife's pearl necklace bobbed on the uneasy surface, tossed back and forth by miniature waves.

Fabian fell with a thud to his knees. He clutched the edge of the tub and moaned into it. The water shuddered, rippled, whirled like the sky and sea outside.

If she shifted, there would be no way of bringing her back, the herbalist had said. When Fabian had thought of all the things she might turn into, he had pictured animals, objects... things he could continue to protect and serve if need be. He had never imagined *water*, wild and ancient, something he could not contain even if he wanted to.

But deep within himself, he had known she would never be satisfied in her human form. Not when the whole world waited for her.

Love her, the herbalist had said.

So Fabian grabbed hold of the edge of the tub, dragging it across his living room and over the threshold of his front door. The cleared circle of soil in their garden was soaking up the rain, but his wife would never see it. Never see it, unless —

The tub flinched forward in his hands, her water centimeters from slopping over the edge and splashing onto the soil.

He could water the flowers with her, and when the first buds poked through the earth, when the first petals uncurled themselves, stretching toward the sun, they would *be* her. The butterflies that came to rest gently, silently among the flowers would be her, too, and when he drank coffee on his morning porch he might feel their weightless presence rest upon his shoulder, as if his wife was touching a delicate hand on him once more...

Love her, the herbalist had said.

He just wanted to *be* with her, but she wanted to be a butterfly, or something like a butterfly, free, beautiful, untamed, always stationed in his garden, always with him...

The realization bubbled up inside Fabian just as he was tipping the tub to pour it over his seeds. She did not want to be a butterfly captive in a garden. She never had. She had morphed into an element for a reason.

Love her, love her, love her.

Fabian looked down into the contents of the tub, saw her water drinking up the rain. He had always loved her how he wanted to love her, not how she wished to be loved.

With a sudden surge of will, he put both hands on either side of the tub and lifted the whole thing. It was heavier than his wife's human weight, but he blundered toward the roiling shore, the tub pressed up against his chest, the sound of her waves mingling with the sea's. Pebbles turned to sand. Water lapped up to his boots. Sea foam sprayed his cheeks like tears.

Fabian collapsed. The tub overturned on its side, and he watched as the water within gushed out, joining with the sea he loved. The pearl necklace caught on the tub's handle, and for a moment, Fabian had an urge to snatch it, to keep that last remnant of his wife.

But he found his fingers untangling it, feeding it to the sea. The waves dragged it underwater and out of sight, and then she was truly gone, freed as she had always desired. He exhaled, touched his lips to the surface of the water to give her a last kiss.

Then he retreated, leaving the tub lying by the shoreline, using the last of his strength to get to his feet and limp back to the house alone. Once inside, he eased the door shut and looked past the string of seashells out the window. In that garden, flowers would still grow. Butterflies would come to rest among them, although they would only be fluttering reminders of what he had wanted his wife to be.

But past the garden, Fabian would always be able to see his wife in her true form: a dazzling ocean, swaying, untamed, free — constantly ebbing to kiss the shoreline where he'd stand.

🐚🐚🐚

Initial feedback

I liked the concept and the characters. The start is nice, but felt muted, and some of the prose was a bit clumsy. The characters' emotions felt uneven, and they/the prose were occasionally overwrought.

Fabian's desires seemed inconsistent; he wanted her to stop shifting. I expected him to pour her onto the seeds. The butterflies felt like an unfair red herring.

Author's intent

What do you think the story's about?
What emotions are you trying to evoke?

The purpose of the story is to explore a deeper facet of love from one human being to another, focusing on Fabian's love for his wife. In the beginning, he believes that love means to love another person for who they 'truly' are, their bare essence, the form they take when they are not morphing.

But Fabian's wife's whole soul was in love with morphing, so her 'true' self, actually, was not the form she took when she was human, but rather the act of exploring different forms and being free. No matter how much she hurts him or how wrong she is in most of her actions, Fabian realizes in the end that to truly love his wife, to 'give up his life for her', he should let her go and let her be what she chooses rather than drown himself to be with her, physically or metaphorically. In the end, limping back to his house was a bigger, more loving sacrifice for Fabian than drowning himself would ever be.

That being said, the reason he didn't water the seeds with her is because he understood that she would never want to be contained within a garden. In the beginning, his wife said she wanted to be/feel like two different things — a butterfly, and an element. This is faulty on my part because I didn't connect the two to show the reader what she really wanted — to be beautiful, wild, and free. I could fix this by changing the wording in the beginning to demonstrate that it is less about the butterflies and more about his wife being free. I could also change the ending's final decision by having Fabian contemplate watering the seeds rather than contemplating drowning himself. He could imagine a future in which his wife would *be* the garden and the butterflies that came to rest on his shoulder would be part of his wife, too, and he might finally have peace. But in the end, he'd realize that to love his wife fully is to understand what parts of her she *wants* him to love. And he would realize that to free her, he needs to give her to the sea instead of containing her in a garden.

Author's note

Metaphorosis was one of the first magazines I sent "The Wife of Fabian Vitalik" to. I always submitted my stories to awesome publishers I didn't think I had a chance with, just to get that 'what if they *do* accept me?' scenario out of the way. In this case, the 'what if' became a sort-of-almost reality when B. Morris Allen responded saying he would consider a rewrite.

My initial thought when reading his request was "Wow, nobody's ever paid this much attention to the content of my writing before" — even the magazines that had published my previous stories had done little more than a line edit here or there. My next thought was "Shit", because I'd never been asked to revise to such depth and I wasn't sure I could do it.

Turns out, I could, but it was easier to find a direction using Morris's specific question as a guide: What is the story about, or what emotion are you trying to evoke? Of course, *I* knew what "The Wife of Fabian Vitalik" was about, but it helped to write down these thoughts and turn my intentions into something more concrete. I realized I had been assuming my audience would inherently grasp these shapeless intentions even in the midst of inconsistent distractions and misleading symbols.

That being said, my main intention for this story was to demonstrate how you should love someone how *they* want to be loved. Yet for some reason, in the original version, the shape-shifter cheated on Fabian with a man who could speak two hundred languages. Why did I do that? What was I thinking? The cheating meant nothing, had no use besides providing a shallow catalyst for the couple's split. The 'two hundred languages' meant nothing, either. I wanted my audience to understand that Fabian had been loving his wife in the wrong way, but by adding the infidelity, I only 'muddied the waters', as Morris rightly told me. Thankfully, in the final version, there is no man who can speak two hundred languages, only a fisherman obsessed with loving his wife's true form without fully understanding what that true form is.

The other major change between my first and final draft comes at the end. In the original submission, Fabian pours his wife as water into the ocean, then decides to go back to his house instead of...drowning? Really, Mariah? Way to be dramatic and insensitive for no reason whatsoever. Drowning wasn't symbolic in this particular story. Fabian's decision to live only distracts the reader from the lessons he learns about love. In the final version, his ultimate choice is whether to pour his wife's water into their garden or into the sea. I'm happy to say he ends up pouring her into the sea, finally coming to terms with the form his wife wanted for herself rather than trying to contain her in a garden of butterflies. This choice aligns so much better with the intention of the story, and I have Morris's critiques to thank for that.

Overall, the revision process with *Metaphorosis* was uncomfortable. It's scary to change your story — not just your words, but the bones beneath your words, as well. I used to think I'd never let an editor change the heart of my work, but this experience taught me that sometimes, an editor is only helping you *find* the heart. And no matter how uncomfortable that may be, it's worth it if you want to deliver your story in its truest form.

Editor's note

There's a distinction between how you feel about a story in the moment, and how it stays with you, how you remember it in the long term. I remember "The Wife of Fabian Vitalik" as a deft, poignant story (which it is), and Mariah as a smooth prose stylist (which later experience has borne out). Yet my notes from the time are more critical. I felt the prose needed work in places, that Fabian's desires were inconsistent, that the butterflies were a red herring.

It's hard to say now, of course, which version I remember, but I think the story didn't change dramatically between versions — it smoothed and connected things that were already there. Interestingly, butterflies and Fabian's desires were the points that took the longest to work out — the former a nice, metaphorical image, the latter central to the flow of the story, but both working toward the same end — demonstrating the force and nature of Fabian's wife's will.

For me, Fabian's desires and actions didn't come out clearly in the original — what it was he wanted, and why it drove him to the actions it did. For example, in the original, I felt his strongest desire was for her to stop shape-shifting, and I didn't see a strong enough foundation for his decision to pour her into the sea; I expected him to pour her into the garden instead. The final version brought out much more clearly that his deep love for her led him to recognize her desires, and choose them over his own.

The butterflies were an interesting study. I originally suggested to Mariah that they were more distraction than contribution, and that they be removed entirely, or their role diminished. Mariah, on the other hand, saw them as a key metaphor, and, happily, stuck to her guns. In the final version, I think they work very nicely, and provide an apposite image through which to examine Fabian's dilemma. Conveniently, they also illustrate a key lesson about revision: the editor is not always right. It's important for writers to know when to accept guidance and when to stick to their original vision. In this case, Mariah made her case, made changes responsive to the concerns I raised, and kept a key image that I would have removed. She was right (editors have their own lessons in humility, and plenty of opportunities to learn them).

The Wife of Fabian Vitalik

The day that Fabian Vitalik's wife left, rain masked the roar of the sea just beyond their rock garden. Fabian ended fishing early because of the storm, and came home to find his wife dozing on the sofa by the window, unfazed by the sharp *pat pat pat* of rain fingers on glass.

He found her enthralling when she was still and senseless like this, so he sat down and watched her breathe, the pearl necklace that rested on her chest rising and falling like waves. Their handmade string of seashells hanging from the ceiling tinkled above her head.

"I love you," Fabian whispered to her sleeping figure, rubbing fish grease on his pants. He thought his wife was most beautiful when she was human.

Of course, she was famous for her shape-shifting. When he'd first seen her high up on that stage, twirling and morphing into other things, the audience had gone wild for the black sleekness of her cat's fur, the shine of her teapot porcelain surface, the perfume that wafted from her petals when she mutated into a lilac bush. Oh yes, he remembered the hoots and howls of men when she danced her way across the stage as only a dress, the movement of shimmering fabric emphasizing the curves of the woman that would be underneath.

He had stared up at her in that crowd, marking the flashes of skin when she would have to, for a moment, be herself again before transforming into something she was not.

Now her overalls were fraying, her hair graying at the roots, the creases of fake smiles ebbing over her face. But so beautiful. Perhaps that was why she had married him, a simple fisherman living in Camber who'd tracked her down when the rain started pouring and the audience dispersed with newspapers over their heads. Nobody had glanced her way after she converted back into a woman, rain-soaked and normal. Nobody but him. And thirty years later, Fabian could not stop staring.

It was only when the rain stopped that she tensed and shifted her body on the sofa, as if the lack of pattering on the window was an alarm. The seashells clinked to a still. Her eyelids fluttered open.

"How did you sleep, love?" Fabian asked from his armchair, drinking in her presence.

She blinked at him, flexed her fingers as if amazed that she had fingers at all. Far off, they could finally hear the ocean again, roaring and crashing onto the beach. She looked back up at him. "What have you been doing this whole time?"

"Reading," Fabian said, although his book was unopened on the other end of the coffee table.

"How'd fishing go? I assume the rain ruined things."

"Caught some tuna, but not much. Had to come back early."

"Hmm." His wife glanced out the windowpane, where the rainstorm had leaked into a gray drizzle. The rocks in their garden glistened with the residue of the storm. "You know," she said, "I have always wanted to shift into wind. Or fire. An element of some sort, but I don't know how. Which muscle do I reach for? Which thought do I think? Which color do I let fill me up?"

Fabian did not answer, only stared at the curve of her mouth, thinking about love and fishing and the sea. How many times had he woken from a night of lovemaking to find something else on his wife's pillow — a dusty book, a glass doll, a starfish? His wife was so much like the ocean, wild, changing, unpredictable. Lovely. He wished he could meld her and the sea into one so that he could sink into both and drown in his love.

" — with the man who can speak two hundred languages."

Fabian nodded, not knowing what she had just said. He remembered his wife giving birth to their three children, who were all grown and traveling now — Josiah had come out covered in fur, his shape-shifting abilities stuck between some kind of animal and the baby he was. The doctors had panicked until the little guy gave a sharp, sputtering cry and shifted back into baby skin.

None of their other children could shape-shift, and Josiah never did again. The curse, the blessing, of having an ordinary father.

" — hear me, Fabian? Does it not phase you, what I just said?"

"What?" Fabian jolted out of his visions, refocusing on the woman before him.

"I slept with the man who can speak two hundred languages." His wife stared at him steadily. "I figured it was time. You, Fabian, cannot shape-shift or fly or go invisible or do anything besides be yourself. I want someone more interesting. I have for years."

The crash of the ocean. Fabian's ears roared with the sound.

His wife touched the pearls on her neck, the pearls he had picked from shored clams himself.

"My love has faltered and crumpled inside me, Fabian. I feel like a rock when I am with you. You never admire me when I'm a cricket singing you songs at night, or when I'm a vase of flowers in our kitchen, or when I'm a wardrobe holding our clothes." Angry blotches were rising on her cheekbones now. "You — I feel like a rock," she said again. "I have since I met you. I want to feel like a butterfly again."

Fabian stared at her. He wanted to say he didn't need a cricket to sing him songs, her human heartbeat was enough at night. He didn't *need* a vase of flowers to make their kitchen pretty, his wife cooking was enough. He didn't need another wardrobe to hold his clothes. He wanted to hold her. That was all he'd ever wanted.

But the words curled inside him, drowned by hers. *I want to feel like a butterfly again. I want to feel like a butterfly.*

"Do you understand, Fabian?"

He blinked. Those seashells above her head turned on their strings, but did not touch each other, and so were silent. "I understand," he said. And then — "I want you to be — to feel like a butterfly too, darling."

She did not reply, only rose from her seat and wafted toward the kitchen, wispy like wind. He could hear her clanging in their cupboards and fridge, bringing out the wrapped tuna and a knife. He could hear the metal of the knife slicing through scales and skin, the smell of innards floating into the living room. Fabian only stared down at his fishing callouses.

A butterfly. *A butterfly.*

Long after the knives quit chopping, he heard the sudden disappearance of his wife and the padded prowling of some creature that took her place. But for all his curiosity, he did not look back to see what his wife, in her disguised grief, had transformed into this time. He only knew that no butterfly was about to flutter over to him and rest gently, silently on his shoulder.

✍

Fabian lugged his empty fishing bag through Camber, past the barber shop and post office and butcher's, all vacant in the grayish night. His footsteps splashed in cobblestone mud. He didn't know why he was making his usual daytime trek through town in the dead of night, especially when he'd spent the last few weeks simply staring at the sea, not brave enough to face fishing with his wife gone. But he'd heard the fishermen talk of her performing again and wanted to know, wanted to *see* her one more time...

Up ahead, lights and shouts from Patty's Tavern grew with every step. Music, clapping, hollering, a man stumbling out with his boots on his hands. Fabian slunk to the open front door and peered inside, where an audience was roaring and hooting, circled around a spectacle in the center of the bar.

She danced and twirled and morphed. She was a spinning reel, polished, rotating, churning out fabric that a few men reached forward to touch... and then the fabric was gone. The men staggered forward, fell on their knees to the roar of audience laughter, and there was a split moment when Fabian saw his wife again, her glowing face and upturned smile and brief mien of concentration, the pearl necklace he'd made for her still dangling around her neck.

Then she was a violin playing itself, a bluebird that screeched and spiraled into a waterfall of buttons, which exploded and clattered to the rotted floorboards. A single button rolled to the doorway. Fabian bent to pick it up, but just as he touched the button's smooth, rounded edge, it disappeared between his fingers, and in the center of the bar there was suddenly a fishing boat, rocking as if on a boiling sea.

She knew he was there. Knew his touch.

The empty fishing sack slipped through Fabian's fingers. He left it there, left it at the open doorway where his wife was performing, and staggered around like a drunk, away from the tavern, back toward his home. The world spun around him. Shapes bloomed in the darkness — buttons, birds, spinning wheels, flowers, teapots. Even the eyes of some nighttime cat seemed to glow green in the darkness between two run-down houses. Fabian yelled at them. The eyes blinked and vanished, but other shapes continued to blossom in the darkness, haunting Fabian until he made it to his doorway. He reeled inside and ran to his bed, where, for a moment, he thought he saw his wife's sleeping figure breathing on the bedsheets.

But no, she was long gone, entertaining other men, transmuting into other things.

Fabian stumbled to their closet and rummaged through shoes, coats, dresses, anything that his wife might like to turn into, anything that he could pretend was her until morning. His fingers clasped around something cold; he pulled out an old candle she used to light during winter storms. Of course, his wife would rather become a flame than the candle itself, but with its twisted, ornate silver twining around the wax, the candle was intricate enough that it would do. Fabian brought it to his bedside and gently placed it on his wife's pillow.

Then he crawled into bed. The coldness pressed in all around him, but he looked at the candle where his wife should be, and its shape comforted him.

"Goodnight, my love," he said to the candle. The candle did not reply, but he placed his fingers on its silver and soon found himself drifting into dreams, dreams where his wife was still lying by his side.

✍

He awoke to her meow.

He mumbled, reached out across his pillow, found the cold hilt of the candle. Something wet touched his hand. He opened his eyes to see a cat staring at him on its haunches — his wife, *his wife was finally back.* Fabian's chest leapt with a burst of adrenaline. He wiped his eyes and sat up to look at the cat better.

But his wife was always a sleek, black cat when she morphed, not this dirty tabby nudging his hand, its ears crooked and nose scarred.

"What...?" Fabian asked. The cat jumped off his bed, knocking the candle to the floor.

Perhaps she had aged so much that her cat form had aged too. Fabian tried to think back to the last time his wife had become a cat and couldn't recall. Suddenly he wished very much that he had turned around to see what she had become in the kitchen the day she'd left.

The cat yowled, racing into the living room and out his front door, which Fabian must have left wide open last night. He staggered after it, every step making his stomach plummet as he realized that the cat was not his wife, and the candle was not his wife, and all the chairs and windows and outside trees were not his wife. When he saw the tabby waiting for him in his rock garden, he could have kicked it away.

But then he noticed what was resting at the tabby's feet in the rocks, like a mouse that the cat had dragged to his doorstep as a prize: his wife's pearl necklace.

"What did you do to her?" Fabian said slowly, bending to pick up the necklace. The cat meowed again. Fury tumbled inside him. *"Where is she?"* he said. *"Where the hell is my wife?"*

The cat turned and streaked down his yard toward Camber.

Fabian ran after it, past all his neighbors' houses and onto the main street of the town, through the daytime vendors who shoved flower seeds and shish kebabs and painted seashells in his face.

The cat weaved through the crowd, past the dry and emptied Patty's Tavern, where just outside, a tall, lean man with an upturned hat at his feet called out, "I am the polyglot! I can speak two hundred languages! You name it and I'll say it. I can speak Yupik, Pawnee, Xhosa, Archi — "

Perhaps the audience would have heard a fifth language that the polyglot spoke, but Fabian stopped chasing the cat long enough to whip toward the man and punch him in the jaw with the fist clenching the pearls. Then he continued his pursuit, tuning out the gasps from the street crowd or the sharp scream from the polyglot's smartass linguistic mouth.

The cat had shot down a shabbier, muddier avenue, where hedges lined the yards of run-down hovels. Fabian followed it to the furthest hut, where the cat slipped inside the open doorway and meowed a greeting to whoever was stirring inside.

"Fabian Vitalik?" somebody called.

"Who...?"

A man from beyond the open doorway shifted in shadows, then emerged onto his front steps with a wan smile. Fabian recognized, with a jolt, the town herbalist, whom he'd only ever met once at a neighborhood funeral.

"Come in, Fabian Vitalik," the herbalist said with a beckoning hand. "Your wife — she is here."

Fabian did not hesitate as he ran into the depths of the house after the man. There were no windows, so the only light came from the simmering ashes of a stone fireplace. And sitting on a rug in front of it, surrounded by an array of clay pots and pans, was his wife. She was human.

She was also swaying, as if to music that Fabian couldn't hear.

"Darling," Fabian said, but the herbalist put a hand on his shoulder. The cat was twisting itself around his wife's rocking body, meowing.

"We found her in an alleyway last night, Fabian Vitalik, soaking wet and unable to speak. My little helper here — " He nodded at the cat. " — is adept at sniffing out illnesses, and brought me to her. I believe she has suffered some kind of stroke from excessive shifting."

Fabian clutched the pearl necklace tighter. The herbalist moved toward a rounded table, where he swept a hand across bowls of powder and jars of bubbling liquid. "I have given her turmeric stewed at midnight, but she still won't speak. Ashwaganda ground in halibut. Thyme and flax seeds. Her condition has not changed. She has the mind of a three-year-old, and I fear — "

" — Darling," Fabian said again, crouching low, not wishing to hear the rest of the herbalist's prediction. His wife looked up at him. Docile eyes. A sweet expression that softened her wrinkles. She would not stop swaying.

"She needs someone to take care of her, Fabian Vitalik. I fear she will not get better." The herbalist crouched beside him and peered into her face. "She certainly cannot shift anymore, and if she attempted to it would be catastrophic. She needs fed, bathed, dressed, put to bed — "

"She's not my wife anymore," Fabian said for the first time. "She left me. Somebody else has to take care of her." He felt the coldness rush up his spine at these words. All his wife would do is smile sweetly at him, and he felt bile in his throat. If he had just stayed at Patty's Tavern last night and stopped her from continuing to perform... of course she would have hated him for it, but she *already* hated him.

The herbalist was watching him steadily. His wife swayed like waves.

"There is no one else to take care of her, Fabian. No one else that cares for her when she is stuck in this form."

"She left me," Fabian said again, the pearl necklace in his hand slipping in sweat.

"She is the mother of your children."

And at this, Fabian felt himself break down. Of course. Of course he would take her in. He would slave over her until she got better, because she *had* to get better. And then he would let her go again, for surely, even if she couldn't shift, she would still want to leave him.

"Fabian," the herbalist said, as if in reply to his thoughts. The tabby meowed. "She *mustn't* try to shift. I doubt she would be able to, but if she *did* manage it... she would be stuck. Stuck in another form forever."

"There'd be no way of bringing her back?" Fabian asked, finally standing up. He tried to imagine his wife stuck in her cat form, or worse — some kind of inanimate object. A decoration, or a candle.

The herbalist bowed his head. "If she shifted, there would be no way of bringing her back, no."

The dying embers were flickering into an eerie, yellowish dark. Fabian bent, strung the pearl necklace around his wife's neck once more, and heaved her into his arms. She allowed this as if she were little more than a rag doll. Fabian started toward the door, then hesitated.

"Isn't there anything that can be *done*? She — she hates her human body." His wife seemed to feel the tremor that ran through him, because although she did not stop smiling, a flicker of unease ran across that strangely vacant face.

"As far as concoctions go, none that I know of. Just love her, Fabian Vitalik."

Fabian nodded, turned away from the herbalist and the cat, and stepped back into broad daylight. His wife's dead weight threatened to bring him to his knees, but he did not stop carrying her, not when he made it to Camber's main street again, not when pedestrians stopped their market trading to stare. He hauled his wife all the way to their house at the shore, sweat beading on his forehead. When he finally made it through their rock garden and set her down underneath their string of seashells, she began swaying again.

His wife was back.

Yet all Fabian wanted was for her to be capable of talking. Of shifting. Of leaving him again.

✍

Shouts, music, and the clanking of glasses washed over him in a buzzing void, but Fabian, sitting at the bar in Patty's Tavern, concentrated on one sound. A pepper-haired man was giggling as he and some comrades danced around an empty cardboard box by the smoke pit, chanting, "Shape-shifter, shape-shifter, alter faster! Quicker! Swifter!" They hooted, hollered, whistled like they had that first night Fabian had peeked into the bar, and eventually a guitarist traipsed nearby to string out the mantra. Soon, so many men turned on their stools that half the bar was singing to the cardboard box, slopping beer down their shirts, believing the box to be Fabian's wife.

"You know what I think?"

A woman slid onto the stool next to him. Tall, long legs. Her jackets swelled where it zipped up over her breasts, and oh, she smelled good, like lilacs and shellfish and wine. His wife used to smell like that, whenever Fabian would come home exhausted and lay his head down on his wife's lap and listen to her hum songs.

"Well, if you're not going to answer," the woman said, fingering her shot glass, and now, at last, Fabian was zeroed in on something other than those wretched men fawning over a cardboard box. "The name's Zoey. And that box was being used to catch a leak in the roof long before those assholes came in. If you ask me, the shape-shifter's anywhere but here. After that one fiasco last month? I'd say she's out of the continent."

Fabian grunted, took a swill out of his mug as he pictured the shape-shifter lying on his bed half a mile away, taking her daytime nap, very much in the continent. A word surfaced to his brain.

"Fiasco?" he repeated.

"Yeah, I was there." The woman brought her glass to her lips and drained it in one gulp. She wiped her lips. "The girl — well, she's more an old lady now — she was performing, you know? And she was turning into all kinds of things, vines and animals and all that drat. She said to get ready for her grand finale, that she was going to turn into wind — and then she just... exploded. Into all these butterflies"

"Exploded into butterflies," Fabian said. In his mind, he heard, *I want to feel like a butterfly again.*

"Yes, and the butterflies began twirling like a tornado. Almost wind, but not quite. Only, the tornado was screaming. God, it hurt my ears. Then the whole thing just disappear — hey! Where are you going?"

Fabian had fished into his pocket, smacked some coins on the counter, and started toward the door, leaving the woman and her long legs behind. Once out on the street, he targeted the peddler's cart that sold flower seeds, and asked the vendor which flowers attracted butterflies.

For the past few weeks, he had been trying to get his wife to talk. Shifting would be, as the herbalist put it, catastrophic, but *talking*? Fabian had thought she'd find her voice again if he read to her, but maybe she needed a reminder of what she loved, what she thought was beautiful, before she found herself again. Maybe she needed butterflies in their garden instead of rocks.

Once the vendor had sold him a packet of daylily seeds, Fabian hurried to the house, where his wife would be waking up from her nap. He left the seeds on the kitchen table and rushed into the bedroom, where his wife was sitting up in bed, swaying, smiling pleasantly.

"Hello, beautiful," Fabian said, opening the window blinds to let sunlight through. "Are you hungry? I've finally gone fishing again, and I found some mussels with nice, hearty meat in them. You love mussels, remember? And I have a surprise for you, too. It might take a while — they need to grow first, but you're going to love it."

His wife just smiled.

Fabian began his usual routine of setting his wife near the sofa where he slept at night, cooking, cleaning, talking to her as if he expected a reply. Occasionally, when he had the spare money, he would buy some paper and finger paints and place them on the floor in front of her. These were the only times she would finally quit swaying, dip her fingers into the paints, and create.

The pictures were crude, to say the least, as if a toddler had painted them. But Fabian could still decipher the wind, the fire. Today, as he popped open the mussels and set them over a small kitchen fire to sizzle, she was drawing earth. Flowers and butterflies and the sun.

It happened after feeding her supper and taking the trash out. Fabian came back inside to find his wife's pictures abandoned on the floor. For one jolting moment, he thought she was gone.

Then he saw her swaying in the kitchen. She was sitting neatly in their tarnished silver tub that he bathed her in at nights. Her clothes were in a pile on the floor, so that only her pearl necklace gleamed on her bare chest.

"It's not bath time yet, darling," Fabian said, shaken. He started forward to pick up her clothes and dress her when a change flashed over her face. A frown. Then that soft, sweet smile again. But for a brief moment, he had seen the crunch of her eyebrows, that concentration she wore when she was trying to shift.

"How about we just have bath time now, then?" Fabian said slowly. But even as he walked toward the faucet, he saw that flash of concentration again, heard the small whimper escape her mouth. They stared at each other. His wife's smile was still etched on her face, but the corners of her mouth were quivering. And suddenly, Fabian knew that he needed to plant those seeds *now*.

"I'll be right back," he whispered, backing away. "*Right* back. Please don't go anywhere."

He grabbed the packet of seeds from the table and in a flash, leaving his wife in the tub, was on his knees in the rock garden. The sky overhead was churning and the sea's high tide was a sharp crash in his ears, but Fabian dug rock after rock out of the dirt and threw them to the side. He felt the sharp plop of water on the back of his neck, but he welcomed the rain that splashed onto the soil beneath his fingers.

"Butterflies," he murmured, ripping open the packet and pouring beetle-black seeds onto his palm. He dug into the dirt, feeling the prickle of time pepper his head, as if he could only save his wife by planting fast enough. He dropped the seeds into those little cavities in the earth, covered them back up, and stood, panting.

His front door was still ajar.

Fabian crept back into the doorway and peered inside, where the shadowed sky cloaked their living room and kitchen in dim shades. His wife's picture was flapping in a sudden wind that swooped past Fabian, into the house. Her clothes still lay discarded on the floor.

But the tarnished tub was empty.

"Hello? Where — where are you, darling?" Fabian called. The paper flapped, moving across the floor. The sea still sounded in his ears, but otherwise there was no sound.

Fabian moved further inside and called his wife's name. He went into the bedroom, but she was not there either. And now his heart was crashing in his chest, and he began racing to every corner of the house, calling for her, trying to find her again, and the sound of the sea was slapping against the shore, slapping against tin...

Against tin?

Fabian halted. He turned, looked at the tub still sitting in the kitchen. The slapping sound was coming from the tub's direction, so Fabian took a step toward it, then another. When he was finally hovering over it, he looked down and saw that the tub was not, as he had thought, empty.

Water was sloshing inside, sloshing as if desperate to free itself. His wife's pearl necklace bobbed on the uneasy surface, tossed back and forth by miniature waves.

Fabian fell with a thud to his knees. He clutched the edge of the tub and moaned into it. The water shuddered, rippled, whirled like the sky and sea outside.

If she shifted, there would be no way of bringing her back, the herbalist had said. When Fabian had thought of all the things she might turn into, he had pictured animals, objects... things he could continue to protect and serve if need be. He had never imagined *water*, wild and ancient, something he could not contain even if he wanted to.

But deep within himself, he had known she would never be satisfied in her human form. Not when the whole world waited for her.

Love her, the herbalist had said.

So Fabian did.

He began his trek toward the sea, standing up and grabbing hold of the edge of the tub, dragging it across his living room and over the threshold of his front door. The cleared circle of soil in their garden was soaking up the rain, but his wife would never see it.

Fabian looked down into the contents of the tub, saw her water drinking up the rain too. With a sudden surge of will, he put both hands on either side of the tub and lifted the whole thing. It was heavier than his wife's human weight, but he shoved the thought aside and blundered toward the roiling shore, the tub pressed up against his chest, the sound of her waves mingling with the sea's. Pebbles turned to sand. Water lapped up to his boots. Sea foam sprayed his cheeks like tears.

Fabian collapsed. He collapsed, and the tub overturned on its side, and Fabian watched as the water within gushed out, joining with the sea he loved. The pearl necklace caught on the tub's handle, and for a moment, Fabian had an urge to snatch it, to keep that last remnant of his wife.

But he found his fingers untangling it, feeding it to the sea. The waves dragged it underwater and out of sight, and then she was truly gone, freed as she had always desired.

Fabian stared, soaked, at the rolling vastness before him. During a storm like this, he always ended fishing early. The waves could kill a man, drag him under and drown him in its crushing immensity. The thought had always alarmed Fabian before, but now...

Beautiful, he thought.

Fabian could stand if he wanted to. He could take a step forward so that his feet were underwater. Then another step, and another. The waves would lick his knees, drench his pants. He could move further into it, letting the tide smash against his torso, his chest. The current beneath the surface would be so strong that Fabian would lose his footing, and then the sea, his wife, would fill his lungs and suck him under.

Perhaps they could fall in love again if he joined her. *She* might fall in love with *him* again.

Fabian trembled, trying to stand.

Love her, the herbalist had said.

Love her, love her, love her. He loved her. He would give his life for her.

So as he exhaled, Fabian touched his lips against the surface of the water, giving his wife one last kiss.

Then he retreated, leaving the tub lying by the shoreline, using the last of his strength to get to his feet and limp back to the house. Once inside, he eased the door shut and looked past the string of seashells out the window. In that garden, flowers would grow. Butterflies would come to rest gently, silently among the rocks.

And past the butterflies, he'd always be able to see his wife from here: swaying, untamed, free — constantly ebbing to kiss the shoreline where he'd stand.

✍ ✍ ✍

THE LONELY KING

—

GUNNAR DE WINTER

The Lonely King

Once, he'd had loyal subjects.

Now he only had bricks and sand.

Immortality was not a blessing.

He had dragged his throne to the highest tower of town. It had been an arduous task, but he'd had – quite literally – all the time in the world.

The top of the tower had long since crumbled, exposing king and throne alike to the elements. Mocking desert winds threw hails of sand at the king's weathered face. He clutched a parchment in his lap, a letter from a love long lost, but that too became taunting sand. The king squinted but stubbornly refused to yield to the desert.

Everything blurred to yellow. Fierce, burning yellow. Even the decrepit town buildings had taken on the color of the desert that surrounded them.

Then, a change.

This is it, thought the king. *Madness has finally found me.*

His kingdom, after all, was devoid of humanity. He was all that was left.

And yet, the flicker on the horizon persisted. Multiplied.

The king blinked rapidly, thinking grains of sand stuck to the surface of his eyes.

But the distant dots continued to come closer. They could have been animals, hunting for rare prey. No, the specks were too... intent, too strongly aimed at him.

He maintained his composure even though his heart almost leapt out of his chest. The dots were human – unmistakable now. A few dozen. Even beasts of burden trundled alongside. Druks, judging by the typical swaying gait of the massive brawny hexapods.

Their goal was clear now. They were headed straight for him.

Alone no longer.

Let my reign find breath again.

The king's joints creaked into activity after eons of statuesque silence. He descended two steps at a time. How his mother would have chided him. Such expression of haste was not royal. There was no such thing as imperial impatience, she always said.

But there was no one to witness the childish giddiness of an ancient monarch. Not yet, anyway.

One half of the town's large wooden gate was rusted shut, a giant rooted in the dry earth. The other half barely held on, another giant, one that hovered over an abyss with only a fraying rope to clutch at.

The king stood waiting in the triangular opening that remained. His heavy coat had left a wide trail through the sand that covered every bare surface in the town.

"Welcome," he bellowed when he thought his new subjects were within earshot.

They stopped and looked at each other. Surprised. Uncomfortable. As if they weren't expecting the king to welcome them.

Nonsense, the king thought. *A good ruler acknowledges his subjects. If they do not know this, they were right to flee their faltering sovereign.*

Following a huddle amongst the travelers, the caravan set in motion again.

Then king felt a broad grin appear within the crags of his weathered face.

The leader of the caravan was a tall man – certainly for a mortal. A full head shorter than the king, he came to a halt a few paces away. His eyes couldn't meet those of his new monarch. He rubbed the back of his head, messing up his thick brown locks.

"Uhm... we didn't expect to..."

The king swung his arm. "Leave it be, good man. Say no more. You are all welcome here." He looked down on his new loyal follower and put a hand on the man's shoulder. Muscles tensed under the king's touch. *Nervous, no doubt.*

"Together, we shall rebuild this kingdom."

✍

That night, the thrill of once again ruling more than an empire of solitude spurred the king's rusted memory. He remembered...

The king remembered a time when the desert was dappled with small king- and queendoms, when immortal houses of rulers formed a robust tree of genealogical ties. Each adult immortal had its town of subjects, but kings and queens frequently visited each other. Squabbles were few and the lives of kings and subjects alike were – generally – good. The desert and its creatures were always a looming threat, but the kingdoms were oases of civilization. The king relished the memory. It had been a time of happiness, even of love. Once, he had had a queen.

Then, one day, those lights of culture faded one by one, in the blink of an immortal's eye. Kings and queens increasingly yielded to the desert, leaving their subordinates helpless. Kingdoms crumbled, eagerly swallowed by the encroaching sea of sand. The rulers that remained turned in on themselves, protecting their own above all else. So too did the king. Contact dwindled. Isolation flourished.

There were no more visits.

✍

A true king intervenes as little as possible.

He let them settle in at their own pace, let them find their own place. After all, except for his tower, all buildings were available for use and occupation.

The morning came with new sounds. The grating creaks of rusted hinges, the crunch of sand under boots. The wail of a child.

And was that...? Yes, the smell of freshly baked bread. The king's withered salivary glands refilled, rejoiced. Though monarchs didn't require sustenance, they appreciated complex flavors.

Patience.

For the first weeks, the king simply watched them from his tower. They seemed like ants scurrying under his gaze. When you were outside time, time became malleable. The king's excitement, though, was immortal. Atemporal.

His new flock had established itself and had begun rebuilding the town. Hinges stopped creaking, sand was swept out of buildings and compacted into avenues. A productive lot.

They would need guidance. And he would be their guide. As he was meant to be.

He walked down the stairs for the second time since the new arrivals had entered his realm. Slowly now, regal.

Sand no longer screeched beneath his sandals as he strode across the cleaned streets, a sound he was glad to miss. There was another sound, though, that died as he emerged from his tower. A sound he did miss.

The sound of laughter, of conversation, of life.

The people were still apprehensive.

But I have given them time. Oh, how their previous monarch must have been monstrous. My task is larger than I thought. I shall not waver.

He smiled, ancient creases in his face performing movements they were still unused to.

"Good day!" His voice rang across town. The people cowered.

Enthusiasm can be frightening for those that are not enthused, he reminded himself. *Slowly. Even the timeless can go too fast.*

He took a deep breath. The air was cleaner, full of aromatics. The taste, the smell of everyday activity, of habitation, soothed him.

"I am pleased," he said – softer now. "You have made tremendous progress. This place," he swept a long, emaciated arm, "has not looked this good, this vibrant since... a very long time." *Ward off the sadness, it is not their burden.*

The caravan's leader – unofficial mayor now – frowned with worry as his kinsmen slowly retreated, eyes averted from the king in their midst.

Poor things. How they must have suffered.

"Tell me, good man," the king spoke softly, containing the royal strength in his voice, "what is your name?"

The man swallowed and sighed. "I am Bramm."

"Bramm." The king stepped closer but halted as soon as he saw the muscles in Bramm's arms tense like cables being pulled too hard. "I am no fool. Tell me what worries you."

Bramm's cheeks clenched so hard the king feared his teeth might shatter.

"Fear not, you are safe here. Speak freely."

Another sigh. "We... Our town was ruined by our monarch. He was... not right. So, we fled, looking for a place to be free."

"A wise choice."

"A place without king or queen."

The thought struck the king like a punch to the gut. He stepped back unwillingly. *Heresy!* Rage bubbled. *No. Control. Restraint. Do not lash out. Their trauma is not their own creation.*

"I see." The king closed his eyes and took another deep breath. *Life, joy, the air is full of it. Do not squander it.* "I can assure you that your tribulations are over. Not only will you be safe here, together we will make this place a thriving community where all can flourish."

Why do they not cheer, why do they not revel in their newfound peace?

Bramm mumbled something, the meaning lost in the song of wind and sand.

"What was that, my friend?"

"But we would not be free."

"I... You are mistaken, Bramm. But I understand. You need time to heal from oppression. I can give you time." The king turned a deaf ear to Bramm's mumbling and blind eyes to the man's shaking head. The immortal headed back to his tower. *Free? How can they be free without ruler, without rules?*

✍

The royal mind was in turmoil. Heaving emotions threw up another memory from eons past.

The king recalled one of his mentors, a king among kings, an immortal ruler that had been around when consciousness congealed out of the mists of the universe. As was custom, visiting monarchs often spent time with those in training.

Those with the most thriving, resilient kingdoms preached patience as the main virtue of a good ruler. The king-to-be spent many nights ruminating on his mentors' teachings about the idiosyncratic minds of the ephemerals, the differences that separated rulers from their subjects, and how a true king embraced this gap for the betterment of all.

✍

Days passed in a fever dream as the king's thoughts went back and forth in an endless pursuit of each other. A pursuit without victor. There was conflict inside the king. What he wanted was right there, yet out of reach. *If you can't rule their hearts, your kingdom is empty.*

From his tower, the king saw Bramm hug his wife and ruffle his son's hair. They were laughing, looking longingly at each other. Complete.

There was love, family among his subjects.

Perhaps a queen could remedy the loneliness. Bah, banish the thought. There was only one queen for me, and she is no more.

Now, his subjects were his children, his recalcitrant lovers, his purpose.

Still...

His subconscious violently pulled him out of his reverie.

Something was amiss.

There.

On the horizon something moved. Aggressively, with predatory purpose. Only one thing could move like that. Sandpards, with six strong legs and a muscular body to support a large triangular head that was more jaw than brain.

The king sprang from his chair, ready to warn his people.

Wait. Not yet. Within the blink of an eye, he stopped moving and turned still as a sculpture. *This will teach them they need me. When they see the value of my presence, they will have no other option but to come to me for protection.*

Sandpards always moved in sixes. They were fast. Very fast.

The king chewed his bottom lip. *Come on, misguided mortals, you must see now that you need me.*

Shouts washed towards him like salve being applied to a fresh wound. His elation grew with the panic below.

Any second now, they will run up the stairs, to me.

But no, they ran outwards, towards the feeble cracked ramparts they had not yet completely fixed.

Fools.

A sandpard could scale those easily. A king knew these things. After all, kings and beasts were made from the same sand.

His flock was in danger.

The king roared and jumped from his tower. He called on the power of the sand to guide his descent. Every grain in the town sang to him, danced for him. A small tornado cushioned his feet and lessened the impact on his joints as he landed. He shot forward.

Slow. Too slow. Rest rusts.

Backed by a wave of sand, he reached the edge of town, where two sandpards had already leapt across the barricades. He struck one beast with his scepter. The other one bit his free arm, nearly swallowing half of it. The king looked at the creature and growled.

"I am the sand, I am the desert." The king's arm turned to sand. The sandpard wheezed until its triple double-lobed lungs were saturated. The beast suffocated and collapsed.

The king fell to his knees, unaware of the shocked silence around him. Then came the scream.

The sandpard matriarch had found a victim. The king surged to his feet and pulled his newly forming arm out of the sand. His new limb was still coalescing when he saw Bramm lunge at the sandpard. The man's son lay limp beneath the beast's hungry jaws.

Brave but foolish.

The king knocked Bramm aside as the sandpard leapt. Beast and king locked in a lethal embrace, a deathly dance within a whirlwind. The inertia of eternity became the flash of violence. Sand settled. Royalty and savagery stared at each other, panting.

The sandpard mewled. Its smooth skin granulated, cracked. Beast became sand. It crumbled and collapsed.

Sandpards weren't clever, except when it came to hunting. The three remaining sandpards, about to finish the circling movement that would bring them to the other side of town, lost heart. With the matriarch out of the picture, they howled and ran off.

The king straightened and rubbed the sand from his sweaty face.

Now they will understand they need me.

"You demon!" Bramm came towards him, his eyes boring into the king's face for the first time. Anger and grief reddened his face and streaked his cheeks with tears. "We do not want you here. We never wanted you here. My son..." Bramm's voice cracked. "You couldn't even save my son," he continued softly, sinking to his knees. "You can't protect us. You... you are nothing. Go. Just go."

The king's chest heaved. *But I waited for your love, your respect. You want protection without rule? You want the protection of a king without accepting his rule?*

The eternal being bellowed. "You ungrateful bastards! Without me, you would have all perished." The town trembled as the sand shifted. "There can be no kingdom without king. We monarchs are life, we are guardians. Without us the desert would swallow you all." The wind wailed along with him.

The fear in the people's eyes stabbed the king's old heart. Anger and wind subsided in tandem.

As befit a king, he strategically redeployed to his sanctuary.

✍

Suppressed anger and a wounded heart birthed another memory from the sands of time.

The king remembered a queen. A queen many ages his senior, but as striking as any immortal could aspire to be. A well of knowledge that only few possessed. As young king and new ruler of his own small kingdom, he often went to visit her. In his dreams, he already saw their children building a new network of prosperous kingdoms.

The king remembered the first night they had lain together. After the throes of passion had ebbed away, the queen whispered stories to him about the birth of the immortals, myths of how the earth itself – the one true parent of the immortals – had begotten them to keep the desert from spreading over the entirety of the world. The desert, so the queen told her devoted listener, was a cancer, always looking to spread and consume. The immortals were scattered across it to stunt its growth, to provide a counterweight and establish balance. The king and his kin accepted this duty and made it their purpose.

✍

They would not dare!

Bramm's rage had lit a fire in the townspeople. They knew they couldn't best a monarch. But they also knew that without kingdom, kings perished. A monarch would never – could never – leave his town except for a visit to another monarch. His people, though, could travel as they pleased.

Will they really choose the cancerous desert over me? Am I so terrible? Do they truly prefer the uncertainty and struggles of being free from rule over the peace and order provided by a king? Bah, good riddance, I shall withstand the desert without them.

The people packed quickly, and the caravan seemed to tremble with the anticipation of movement, like an animal yearning to run. Wooden carts were stuffed and decked with tarps. Druks were corralled out of their enclosure and guided into broad tailored yokes. Before the night fell and the chill of darkness could grab hold, the caravan set in motion.

A few people looked back. But not Bramm.

He must be a good leader, to achieve consensus like this, in the face of danger and uncertainty.

Everyone was willing to follow Bramm wherever he might lead them.

Surely, they will not venture into the desert night, the time of djinns and ghouls?

The wind began to pick up, tugging at the caravan. The king heard the story in the sound, the soliloquy of solitude. A layer of liquid formed on his eyes, not due to the pricking sand this time, but due to the sadness of impending loss.

They would. They actually would. Perhaps the time of monarchs truly is over. Perhaps there are new kings and queens, walking among the people.

Maybe this is my legacy. Maybe they are my legacy.

The king cried unabashedly.

This should not have taken a child's life. I feel the weight of the young one's death.

When the last cart rolled across the town's boundary, a tremor made people's heads turn.

The king's tower shook. From the seams between the stones, small puffs of sand emerged and coalesced into a dense curtain that obscured the tower from sight. A deep rumble.

When the sand dissipated, the tower had gone.

✍

In withdrawal and solitude, another memory reformed.

Then king remembered one of his mentors' final visits and lessons, the last argument before the desert had swallowed the king's only remaining ancient mentor.

Many immortals had already vanished by then, including the king's family and the queen he had loved. Apprehension gripped the king, prompting him to transform his kingdom into a stronghold, impenetrable and towering in seclusion.

His mentor tried to convince him to reconsider. The old one told the king of how, even though they were immortal, they were not meant to be eternal. The greatest ruler, his mentor said, eventually obviates the necessity of his or her own being. Their subjects were the true inheritors of the earth and the salve that could tame the desert. The king had scoffed and scorned his ancient relative.

Their parting had not been not amicable and turned out to be final.

✍

So they have some sense after all.

When the tower had vanished, and the king along with it, the people had returned. Suspicious at first, searching through all the houses and buildings.

They had forgotten that monarchs were creatures of the sand, denizens of the desert. If the king could not watch them from above, he would do so from below.

From his subterranean enclave, the king heard their footsteps, felt them live their lives. Grains of sand were the spies that kept him apprised of all that occurred in his kingdom.

He would build and protect his kingdom. He always would. But carefully now, unnoticed.

The king coerced layers of sand in intricate patterns to shepherd dew into underground canals. Soon, his people would discover a hidden source of irrigation, an oasis seemingly sprung from nothing. When sandpard vibrations woke him from his slumber, he would lay quicksand traps.

My people will thrive. I will protect them.

They will not know. They will not supplicate. So be it. It will suffice for me.

A terrible ruler has iron hands, a good ruler velvet ones. A great ruler needs none.

✍ ✍ ✍

Initial feedback

I very much liked the concept. The tone was a bit dry, and I'd have liked to know more about the king and his background. It could be a little about what he is, but my main concern is *who* he is — what he feels, wants, what happened to him, etc. His eventual decision to stay in the background could use more foundation.

Author's intent

What do you think the story's about?
What emotions are you trying to evoke?

As for the themes I hoped to explore with this story: for me it's about a fundamental tension between the immortal ruler and his mortal subjects. Something I also wanted to stress is that things are often more complex than the hero vs. villain dynamic that drives a lot of stories. Basically, it's about a ruler who has never known anything else and who genuinely wants to be a beneficent leader but who comes up against a desire for freedom among those he wants to rule that fundamentally renders his overt presence useless, and possibly damaging.

Author's note

It's a truism that no story is ever perfect. It's also a truism that a good editor can make your story better, no matter how much you've gone through, polished, and rewritten it.

In the case of "The Lonely King", I wanted to explore the fundamental tension between the (immortal) ruler and his (mortal) subjects. I also hoped to stress that things are often more complex than the hero vs. villain dynamic that drives a lot of stories. The story's king is a benevolent ruler, but no amount of intended benevolence can fully quash the desire for freedom in those that are ruled. This is the conflict that drives the story.

The external conflict was clear in the story's first version, but the — arguably more important — inner conflict of the king wasn't. The world and characters of my stories are always quite vivid in my mind. Bringing that to the page, however, can be challenging because of this. I can feel the desert sand dance across my face and I experience the emotions of the lonely king as they stretch across ages. Since all this is so obvious to me, my first story versions tend to be relatively sparse, as if scratching the surface of something deeper but not quite getting there.

So, the main editorial suggestion was to give the king more proverbial flesh on his sand-scoured bones. We settled on the tried-and-true method of flashbacks to do so. The story lost a few vague allusions and a royal family member, but it got a fuller king in return. We went back and forth a few times to settle on the right balance between detail about the royals and the mystery about them. I like to think we landed on a good spot.

For me, the editorial process is not so much about coming up with new things, but about dragging out what's already rumbling around in my head. A great editor can do so by asking the right questions. That was certainly the case here. With pointed editorial questions about the king and his kin, I managed to whet the blunted edge of the story into a sharper narrative. That is the great challenge for every fiction writer, painting the world you envision and the emotions of the characters that inhabit it using nothing but words. A great editor helps you select the right set of brushes.

When you read the final version of "The Lonely King", I hope you feel the desert wind on your skin and the king's inner turmoil in your mind.

Editor's note

Most of my concerns about "The Lonely King" were about mechanics — the lifecycle of the rulers, the failure of the towns, etc. These were things that distracted me from the primary story. And I thought that the story would benefit from learning more about the king's character and history — what drives him. Those things took a few exchanges to get to a point where it all made good sense and flowed smoothly. Beyond that, it was largely a question of clarifying and polishing. That doesn't necessarily mean quick, however. We went through several exchanges tweaking this and that to get the story to its final state.

As Gunnar notes, it's possible to go through endless iterations with any story. I find that there are three kinds of ending to the editorial process. First, there's a clear problem that's clearly fixed, then a little polishing and you're done. Second, one or both sides simply wears out, and when the story is acceptable to both, you stop. Third, you start looking at smaller and smaller tweaks to a story that's definitely good enough, but not yet perfect. That's the hardest kind to stop, because it will never be perfect, but the changes are small enough that there's no dramatic demarcation to go by. I think that, in this case, the story kept getting better with each iteration, but that we could have stopped one or two versions earlier. I'm glad we kept going as far as we did, but I'll admit that the later gains were minor.

The Lonely King

Once, he'd had loyal subjects.

Now he only had bricks and sand.

Immortality was not a blessing.

He had dragged his throne to the highest tower of town. It had been an arduous task, but he'd had – quite literally – all the time in the world.

The top of the tower had long since crumbled, exposing king and throne alike to the elements. Mocking desert winds threw hails of sand at the king's weathered face. He clutched the parchment in his lap, but that too became taunting sand.

Everything blurred to yellow. Fierce, burning yellow. Even the decrepit town buildings had taken on the color of the desert that surrounded them on all sides.

Then, a change.

This is it, thought the king. *Madness has finally found me.*

His kingdom, after all, was devoid of humanity. He was all that was left.

And yet, the flicker on the horizon persisted. Multiplied.

The king blinked rapidly, thinking grains of sand stuck to the wet surface of his eyes.

But the distant dots continued to come closer. They could have been animals, hunting for rare prey. No, the specks were too... intent, too strongly aimed at him.

He maintained his composure even though his heart almost leapt out of his chest. The dots were human – unmistakable now. A few dozen. Even beasts of burden trundled alongside. Druks, judging by the typical swaying gait of the massive brawny hexapods.

Their goal was clear now. They were headed straight for him.

Alone no longer.

Let my reign find breath again.

The king's joints creaked into activity after eons of statuesque silence. He descended two steps at a time. How his mother would have chided him. Such expression of haste was not royal. There was no such thing as imperial impatience, she always said.

But there was no one to witness the childish giddiness of the ancient monarch. Not yet, anyway.

One half of the large wooden gate was rusted shut, a giant rooted in the dry earth. The other half barely held on, another giant, one that hovered over an abyss with only a fraying rope to clutch at.

The king stood waiting in the triangular opening which was all that remained of the once large gate. His heavy coat had left a wide trail through the sand that occupied every bare surface in the town.

"Welcome," he bellowed when he thought his new subjects were within earshot.

They stopped and looked at each other. Surprised. Uncomfortable. As if they weren't expecting the king to welcome them.

Nonsense, the king thought. *A good ruler acknowledges his subordinates. If they do not know this, they did well to flee their undoubtedly oppressive sovereign.*

The caravan set in motion again.

A broad grin appeared within the crags of the king's weathered visage.

The leader of the caravan was a tall man – certainly for a mortal. He came to a halt in front of the king. His eyes couldn't meet his new monarch. He rubbed the back his head, messing up his thick brown locks.

"Uhm... we didn't expect to..."

The king swung his arm. "Leave it be, good man. Say no more. You are all welcome here." He looked down on his new loyal follower and put a hand on the man's shoulder. Muscles tensed under the king's touch. *Nervous, no doubt.*

"Together, we shall rebuild this kingdom."

✍

A true king intervenes as little as possible.

He let them settle in at their own pace, let them find their own place. After all, except for his tower, all buildings were available for use and occupation.

The morning came with new sounds. The grating creaks of rusted hinges, the crunch of sand under boots. The wail of a child.

And was that... Yes, the smell of freshly baked bread. The king's withered salivary glands refilled, rejoiced.

Patience.

For the first weeks, the king simply watched them from his tower. They seemed like ants scurrying under his gaze. When you are outside time, time becomes malleable. Excitement, though, is immortal. Atemporal.

His new flock had established itself and had begun rebuilding the town. Hinges stopped creaking, sand was swept out of buildings and compacted into avenues. A productive lot.

They would need guidance. And he would be their guide. As he was meant to be.

He walked down the stairs for the second time since the new arrivals had entered his realm. Slowly now, regal.

Sand no longer screeched beneath his sandals as he strode across the cleaned streets. A sound he was glad to miss. There was another sound, though, that died as he emerged from his tower. A sound he did miss.

The sound of laughter, of conversation, of life.

The people were still apprehensive.

But I have given them time. Oh, how their previous monarch must have been monstrous. My task is larger then I thought. I shall not waver.

He smiled, ancient creases in his face performing movements they were still unused to.

"Good day," he exclaimed forcefully – seeing the sudden cowering, perhaps too forcefully.

Enthusiasm can be frightening for those that are not enthused, he reminded himself. *Slowly.* Even the timeless can go too fast.

He took a deep breath. The air was cleaner, full of aromatics. The taste, the smell of everyday activity, of habitation, soothed him.

"I am pleased," he said – softer now. "You have made tremendous progress. This place," he swept a long, emaciated arm, "has not looked this good, this vibrant since... a very long time." *Ward off the sadness, it is not their burden.*

The caravan's leader – unofficial major now – frowned with worry as his kinsmen slowly retreated, eyes averted from the king in their midst.

Poor things. How they must have suffered.

"Tell me, good man," the king spoke softly, containing the royal strength in his voice, "what is your name?"

The man swallowed and sighed. "I am Bramm."

"Bramm." The king stepped closer but halted as soon as he saw the muscles in Bramm's arms tense like cables being pulled too hard. "I am no fool. Tell me what worries you."

Bramm's cheeks clenched so hard the king feared his teeth might shatter.

"Fear not, you are safe here. Speak freely."

Another sigh. "We... Our town was ruined by our monarch. He was... not right. So, we fled, looking for a place to be free."

"A wise choice."

"A place without king or queen."

The thought struck the king like a punch to the gut. He stepped back unwillingly. *Heresy!* Rage bubbled. *No. Control. Restraint. Do not lash out. Their trauma is not their own creation.*

"I see." The king closed his eyes and took another deep breath. *Life, joy, the air is full of it. Do not squander it.* "I can assure you that your tribulations are over. Not only will you be safe here, together we will make this place a thriving community where all can flourish."

Why do they not cheer, why do they not revel in their newfound peace?

Bramm mumbled something, the meaning lost in the song of wind and sand.

"What was that, my friend?"

"But we would not be free."

The king's mouth moved, but the words failed to come out. He stumbled back to his tower. *Free? How can they be free without ruler, without rules?*

✍

Days passed in a fever dream. There was conflict inside the king. What he wanted was right there, yet out of reach. *If you can't rule their hearts, your kingdom is empty.*

From his pedestal, the king saw Bramm hug his wife and ruffle his son's hair. They were laughing, looking longingly at each other. Complete.

There was love, family among his subjects.

Perhaps a queen could remedy the loneliness. Bah, banish the thought. Kings and queens are not meant to be together. We are infertile anyway. No lineage. Besides, rulers could not be distracted.

Their subjects were their children, their lovers, their purpose. Still...

His subconscious violently pulled him out of his reverie.

Something was amiss.

There.

On the horizon something moved. Aggressively, with predatory purpose. Only one thing could move like that.

Sandpards, with six strong legs and a muscular body to support a large triangular head that was more jaw than brain.

The king sprung from his chair, ready to warn his people.

Wait. Not yet. Within the blink of an eye, he had stopped moving and turned still as a sculpture. *This will teach them they need me. When they see, they will have no other option but to come to me for protection.*

Sandpards always moved in sixes. They were fast. Very fast.

The king chewed his bottom lip. *Come on, you must see now.*

Shouts washed towards him like salve being applied to a fresh wound. His elation grew with the panic below.

Any second now, they will run up the stairs, to me.

But no, they ran outwards, towards the feeble cracked ramparts they had not yet completely fixed.

Fools.

A sandpard could scale that easily. A king knows these things. After all, kings and beasts are made from the same sand.

His flock was in danger.

The king roared and jumped from his tower. He called on the power of the sand to guide his descent. Every grain in the town sang to him, danced for him. A small tornado cushioned his feet and lessened the impact on his joints as he landed. He shot forward.

Slow. Too slow. Rest rusts.

Backed by a wave of sand, he reached the edge of town, where two sandpards had already leapt across the barricades. He struck one beast with his scepter. The other one bit his free arm, nearly swallowing half of it. The king looked at the creature and growled.

"I am the sand, I am the desert." The king's arm turned to sand. The sandpard wheezed until its triple double-lobed lungs were saturated. The beast suffocated and collapsed.

The king fell to his knees, unaware of the shocked silence around him. Then came the scream.

The sandpard matriarch had found a victim. The king surged to his feet and pulled his newly formed arm out of the sand. His new limb was still coalescing when he saw Bramm lunge at the sandpard. The man's son lay limp beneath the beast's hungry jaws.

Brave but foolish.

The king knocked Bramm aside as the sandpard leapt. Beast and king were locked in a lethal embrace, a deathly dance within a whirlwind. The inertia of eternity became the flash of violence. Sand settled. Royalty and savagery stared at each other panting.

The sandpard mewled. Its smooth skin granulated, cracked. Beast became sand. It crumbled and collapsed.

With the matriarch out of the picture, the three remaining sandpards, that were about to finish the circling movement that bright them to the other side of town – sandpards weren't too clever, except when it came to hunting – howled and ran off.

The king straightened and rubbed the sand from his sweaty face.

Now they will understand they need me.

"You demon!" Bramm came towards him, eyes boring into the king's face for the first time. Anger and grief reddened his face and streaked his cheeks with tears. "We do not want you here. We never wanted you here. My son..." Bramm's voice cracked. "You couldn't even save my son," he continued softly, sinking to his knees. "You can't protect us. You... you are nothing. Go. Just go."

The king's chest heaved. *But I waited for your love, your respect. You want protection without king? You want me to give everything without getting anything?*

The eternal being bellowed. "You ungrateful bastards! Without me, you would have all perished." The town trembled as the sand shifted. "There can be no kingdom without king. We monarchs are life, we are guardians. Without us the desert would swallow you all." The wind wailed along with him.

The fear in the people's eyes stabbed the king's old heart. Anger and wind subsided in tandem.

As befit a king, he strategically redeployed to his sanctuary.

✍

They would not dare!

Bramm's rage had lit a fire in the townspeople. They knew they couldn't best a monarch. But they also knew a monarch would never – could never – leave his town. His people, though, could.

Will they really choose the desert over me? Am I so terrible? Do they truly prefer the uncertainty and struggles of being free from rule over the peace and order provided by a king? Bah, good riddance.

The people packed quickly, and the caravan seemed to tremble with the anticipation to move, like an animal yearning to run. Wooden carts were stuffed and decked with tarps. Druks were corralled out of their enclosure and guided into broad tailored yokes. Before the night fell and the chill of darkness could grab hold, the caravan set in motion.

A few people looked back. But not Bramm.

He must be a good leader, to achieve consensus like this, in the face of danger and uncertainty.

Everyone was willing to follow Bramm wherever he might lead them.

Surely, they will not venture into the desert night, the time of Djinns and Ghouls?

The wind began to pick up, tugging at the caravan. The king heard the story in the sound, the soliloquy of solitude. A layer of liquid formed on his eyes, not due to the pricking sand this time, but due to the sadness of impending loss.

They would. They actually would. Perhaps the time of monarchs truly is over. Perhaps there are new kings and queens, walking among the people, being one of them.

Maybe this is my legacy. Maybe they *are my legacy.*

The king cried unabashedly.

This should not have taken a child's life.

When the last cart rolled across the town's boundary, a tremor made people's heads turn.

The king's tower shook. From the seams between the stones, small puffs of sand emerged and coalesced into a dense curtain that obscured the tower from sight. A deep rumble.

When the sand dissipated, the tower had gone.

*

So they have some sense after all.

When the tower had vanished, and the king along with it, the people had returned. Suspicious at first, searching through all the houses and buildings.

They had forgotten that monarchs were creatures of the sand, denizens of the desert. If the king could not watch them from above, he would do so from below.

From his subterranean enclave, the king heard their footsteps, felt them live their lives. Grains of sand were the spies that kept him apprised of all that occurred in his kingdom.

He would build and protect his kingdom. He always would. But carefully now, unnoticeable.

The king coerced layers of sand in intricate patterns to shepherd dew into underground canals. Soon, his people would discover a hidden source of irrigation, an oasis seemingly sprung from nothing. When sandpard vibrations would wake him from his slumber, he would lay quicksand traps.

My people will thrive. I will protect them.

They will not know. They will not supplicate. So be it. It will suffice for me.

A terrible ruler has iron hands, a good ruler velvet ones, a great ruler needs none.

✍ ✍ ✍

GRAVEYARD

—

ARLEN FELDMAN

Graveyard

The crew had already started calling it the *graveyard*.

If it was a graveyard, it would be hard to choose a bleaker site for it, on a planet pretty much made up of bleak sites. I walked as close as I dared to the edge of the cliff, and looked down over a thousand meters of sharp gray crags spreading out all around under a dark, thunderous sky. I felt the wind tugging at me, and hastily stepped back.

Merrick was watching over the technicians — as though they needed or wanted his help. To be fair, he did know a lot about the scanning equipment.

Not that I wanted to be fair.

I tugged at my breathing mask, trying to make it more comfortable, and turned to examine the site. Thirty-seven upright stones, spread over a clearing about forty meters wide. The shortest stone was 22 centimeters and the tallest was 196 centimeters — almost two meters. From three sides, they just looked like rocks.

It was because of the fourth sides that we were here. They had been carved flat, and a pattern had been deeply etched into each. The designs were different from stone to stone, but they all followed a similar design — a spiral of shapes spreading out from a central point. The shapes were small circles and rounded rectangles of different lengths. It sort-of reminded me of Morse code, except that there were at least eight different lengths. Unless, of course, the "dashes" all meant the same thing, and the carver wasn't particularly careful about length.

"Jenna?"

I jumped, then turned around. Sean, the other member of the research team, was standing less than sixty centimeters behind me. Hard to hear with the wind and the masks and the warm-weather gear.

Sean held up his hands. "Sorry. Didn't mean to startle you."

"No worries." I grinned at him, putting my hand to my chest. "Whatever doesn't make your heart explode makes you stronger. What's up?"

"We're about ready."

I nodded and followed him over to the "command post", which was really just a stack of plastic crates with some ruggedized computers sitting on top. Sean typed something on a keyboard and I felt the thrum as power ran to the imaging lasers mounted on collapsible pylons positioned all around the site.

For a while, we watched the progress display on the screen, then I turned and walked back towards the stones. Not much point looking at a picture when the real thing was right there.

"You know," said Merrick, who had followed me, and was now standing right next to me. "If it is a graveyard, then the inscriptions would make a certain amount of sense."

I took a half step away from him. "How so?"

"Well, the little one there might be *To Aunt Maggie*, while that one," he pointed to the largest stone with two separate swirls of symbols," might be the Grayon-Alpha-3 equivalent of the Lord's Prayer or *Do Not Go Gentle*."

I laughed, though in truth the idea had already occurred to me. "You know what the Professor would say, don't you?"

"Don't get ahead of the facts," we intoned in unison, and laughed.

Professor Kineson should have been here. He was Earth's foremost xeno-anthropologist, but he was now too old for major journeys. Instead he'd sent his grad students — me and Merrick — arguably Earth's only *other* xeno-anthropologists. To date, it wasn't a very popular or useful field, although Grayon-Alpha-3 might change that.

Life was pretty common on the worlds that had been explored — plants and insectoids being the most common, but larger forms as well. Grayon-Alpha-3 was no different, covered in small ugly plants and a number of beetle-like insectoids that were currently being intensely studied by the biology team.

On two previously explored worlds, we'd found indications of intelligence — remnants of crude settlements — but no actual settlers. Professor Kineson had been the main researcher for both of those.

But writing — that was a first. If the designs on these stones turned out to be a form of language, that would be a game changer. And it had to be writing. How could it be anything else?

"It could be art," said Merrick, as though reading my mind — a very annoying habit of his. "Like Celtic knotwork."

I shrugged. Even artwork would be exciting, but in my gut, I knew that it was writing — an attempt to communicate. Not that I would ever admit to anything so unscientific as a gut feeling.

The hum of the scanners shut down at the same time as a lull in the wind, and for a few seconds it was eerily quiet. That might have been the moment when the reality of what we were doing set in. We were standing on an alien world in the presence of unquestionable evidence of intelligence. Even knowing nothing about who or what they were, when and how they lived, I felt an almost physical connection to the creators of these stones.

I looked up to see Merrick staring at me.

"What?" I asked.

"Nothing. You just had a look."

He reached out an arm towards my shoulder, but I took another half-step away.

Sean came up to us, his hand brushing against his breathing mask, as though he wanted to scratch his chin. It was hard to get used to Sean having a visible face. On the trip here, he'd had a huge, ragged, Santa-Claus beard, but he'd had to shave it off so that the breathing mask would fit. Although he was in his forties, he now looked like a teenager. I'd studiously avoided saying anything, although the rest of the crew had teased him mercilessly about it.

"Scan's done," he said. "We only have about another hour of daylight. We should probably get back to the lander."

I nodded, but didn't move. I was looking at the smallest stone — the one that Merrick had called *Aunt Maggie*. I'd spent a lot of time in old graveyards, and the smallest, saddest stones were always for babies and children. In my head, I mentally shortened the label to just *Maggie*.

I turned, grabbed my kit, and followed the others back to the lander.

✍

The next day was all about scanning underground. If these were gravestones, then there should be something underneath them. The Ground Penetrating Radar setup was finicky, and we were all sweating profusely by the time we had it working, despite the cold.

Nothing. There was nothing beneath any of the stones.

"It doesn't mean they're not grave markers," I said, although without much conviction. "They could be cenotaphs — memorials without the bodies."

No one argued, but I doubted that anyone was convinced.

"There is one weird thing," said Sean.

Merrick and I both turned to face him.

"The stones look rough-carved, but they each extend at least twenty centimeters below the surface, and the fit is precise. I mean, *really* precise — within five microns." He pointed at the display. "I could *probably* do it with a laser and a bunch of time, but it's hard to see how you could do it with primitive tools. Also, there would be tool marks, and there aren't any."

Merrick shook his head. "If they were an advanced culture with lasers, then there would be some other evidence on the planet. Roads, buildings, something. The satellites have found squat."

"That depends on how old they are," said Sean, scratching ineffectually at his breathing mask.

"Maybe they lived underground," I suggested. "That would explain the lack of anything on the surface."

Merrick shook his head. "*Don't get ahead of the facts,*" he said. "The satellites would have found some evidence of any sort of sophisticated underground settlement. We found the spot where the stones for the monuments came from, which is less than half a kilometer from here, but that's literally the only non-natural variance on the planet — other than this place."

I sighed. Without any other sites, we didn't have a lot to go on. We'd hoped to find something buried beneath the stones that we could use to figure out a date. Then, suddenly, I had an idea.

"You know, there might be a way of figuring out a date — from the stones themselves."

"The stones are granite," said Merrick, sounding exasperated. "They are the same age as the surrounding rocks. You can't get an age off of them separate from that."

"Thanks for the Geology 101 lecture." I didn't bother trying to keep the sarcasm from my voice. I turned to Sean. "Weathering patterns. The stones further away from the cliff are weathered less than those nearer to it. We know how granite breaks down, what chemicals are present in the atmosphere, weather patterns — at least for the few years that the satellites have been in place. We should be able to at least get a rough estimate from that."

"Clever," said Merrick, suddenly interested.

Sean stroked at his chin. "Rough is the word."

"The faces and the designs haven't really worn down," said Merrick.

"No," said Sean, thinking, "but the edges have. We'll have to analyze some other rocks as well for control, pull atmospheric data from the satellites, but...it could work." He looked up. "Yeah — at least within a few hundred years." He grinned at me. "Nice!"

It was four days later, early in the morning, when Sean knocked on the door of my cabin.

"Yeah?" I answered blearily.

He handed me a piece of paper. "Between 700 and 1200 years."

For several seconds I had no idea what he was saying, and then suddenly neurons started firing in my brain. "You did it? You did it!" I gave him a hug, and he turned bright red. I noticed that he'd started growing a beard again, but that it was carefully trimmed to the shape of a breathing mask.

"This is awesome," I told him. "It's the first concrete thing we really know about the site. The post-project report was looking awfully bare."

Sean suddenly looked nervous. "So, you won't be reporting anything until the end of the trip?"

"Of course not. That would be...why?"

"Well, it's just that..."

But I didn't need to hear it. I already knew.

"Merrick? You told Merrick first?"

"I didn't...he was in the lab when the computer spat out the results. I couldn't — "

But I was already halfway down the passage.

My thoughts were on events from a year ago. Me, curled up on the sofa next to Merrick while he read my research notes on the ancient settlement found on Gliese 837c, telling me how great my work was. Late nights, lying next to one-another, endlessly discussing *my* ideas...

I practically slammed into him coming the other way down the passage.

He oofed, then backed away. "Oops, sorry." Then he saw my face. "What?" he asked.

I was about ready to hit him. "You bastard."

His eyebrows went up, but his voice was even, half-joking. "My mother would deny it. I take it you think I did something?"

He was going to brazen it out. I lifted my fist and he took several hasty steps back. Not once did it even occur to me that he hadn't sent a report behind my back. I could see the look of calculation in his eyes.

"Look, if it's about the dating — I *did* let the Professor know, but no one else. And I swear that I told him that the idea was yours."

"Yeah, like last time? In a frigging footnote?" I'd taken several steps toward him, and he'd backed away again, even though he towered over me by thirty centimeters. His face was red now.

"You think I'd...?"

"Yes, I do."

Then I turned and walked away. Of course, now I had to send a separate report in, and it would make us look like we were squabbling siblings. Maybe I shouldn't even bother.

When I got a copy of Merrick's report a few hours later, it turned out that he had been telling the truth. Professor Kineson had sent us both a congratulatory e-mail about the dating, and had given me credit for the idea, and Merrick and Sean credit for the computer model.

It did not make me feel any better.

A little while later, Merrick came to find me. His expression was half-smirk and half-contrition. I had no idea why I had once found him handsome.

"Jen," he started. "Listen, I know we have some history, but I *did* tell you that I gave you credit."

"And yourself, I note. I'm pretty sure that Sean did most of the work."

He ignored this.

"Getting our names out there is important. There is interest in what we are doing right now. If we waited until we had every last detail worked out, no one would care. Publish or perish, right?"

"I'd recommend perish in your case," I said. This was an old argument, though. Part of his excuse for pre-empting my Gliese 837c research was that I had been taking too long to get my results out there. As if that were an excuse for stealing my work.

He turned to walk away, obviously annoyed. At the door, he paused. "If you aren't going to let people know what we've found, then why bother?"

"I want it to be right," I said, trying to keep my voice steady. "I want it to be permanent — to last. Not just be some half-baked headline."

He shook his head. "And if you wait too long, then it's going to be someone else's name that's remembered. Not ours. If we don't carve out our own names, no one else will. We work in a tiny, under-funded field. If you don't get your name out there, how many of your projects do you think will get sponsored?"

He walked away. I watched him go, wondering how he and I could have such different ideas about what our work was about. Part of me, though, knew that he was right about sponsorship. I wondered, briefly, whom I was really angry at.

The next two weeks were spent in icy, silent hostility. Most of the crew, who were military, were completely unaware of what was going on, or at least pretended to be. Sean, though, was stuck in the middle, and shuttled back and forth nervously between us.

It helped that my approach and Merrick's were so different. He spent most of his time with the computer scans and models on the ship, while I spent most of my time at the actual site.

Not that I was getting anywhere. Nor, as far as I knew, was Merrick. I'd caught him watching me a few times. The last time, he'd had that look — the one that I used to read as understanding and admiration, and now read as naked calculation. He was probably hoping I'd let something slip.

I pushed Merrick from my mind as I turned my thoughts back to the graveyard. 700 to 1200 years. It was difficult to believe that a culture with the sophisticated stone-working skills needed to make these monuments would have disappeared without a trace in that time.

My working hypothesis — shared with no one else — was that the monument-makers weren't native. Someone had visited this planet, like we were now, and, for whatever reason, had left this memorial here. Maybe to commemorate their visit, or because something unfortunate had happened. I smiled to myself. I was getting really far *ahead of the facts*.

The idea did *fit* the facts, though. There were no visible tool marks, which was consistent with advanced technology, and there were no indications of any remotely higher lifeforms on this planet than bugs, let alone tool users.

In the past, I might have talked this over with Merrick, but that was obviously impossible. He was good at turning my flights-of-fancy into concrete ideas. Now, though — if he agreed, he'd probably steal my ideas, and if he disagreed, he'd probably use them to discredit me.

I sat down in front of *Maggie's* stone on a small stool I'd been using. Part of my reason for focusing on that stone was that I figured the simpler design might be easier to interpret. In theory, the more complex patterns would provide more material to analyze, but the computers were already trying that approach without any notable success.

Another reason was that it was next to one of the larger monuments, which protected me from the continuous howling wind.

To be honest, though, I think I'd just formed some sort of emotional attachment to my mental image of Maggie.

As for figuring out the pattern — I'd tried every statistical and analytic approach I could think of, including some that were desperately random. I still had a neck ache from my attempt to examine the pattern upside down.

My new approach, such as it was, was to stare at the design while letting my mind go blank in the hopes that something would pop into my head. I tapped on my headphones to start them playing. Today I was listening to Dvořák's *New World Symphony*, one of my favorites. The slow *adagio* opening was appropriately grandiose for the austere landscape, and the fast, crashing *allegro* seemed perfectly timed to the gusting wind.

The second movement, the slow, haunting *largo*, was what I'd been waiting for, though. The gentle music, led by the sonorous oboes, was music for a graveyard if any music was. The *largo* movement was also known as *Coming Home*. I wondered if the creators of the graveyard had made it home.

It was chilly, even with the protective clothing, and I shivered. I rested my gloved hand on top of Maggie's stone. Wanting a closer connection, I pulled off my glove and touched the stone with my bare hand.

The stone was ice cold and it burned my hand, but I held it there for a moment before pulling it back. Not quite ready to give up my connection to the monument, I put my finger in the very center of the spiral design, and ran it around the design.

I'd done this before with my thick glove on, but without it, I suddenly noticed something. As my finger thunked between the uneven dashes, it made a sort of tune.

The hair on the back of my neck stood up and a chill went down my spine. It had nothing to do with the frigid air.

I tried it again, slower. This time, the tune was more pronounced. Well, less a tune, and more a rhythm, since it was basically the same note repeated with different intervals. Or was it? I ripped off my headphones so I could hear better, and tried again, this time using my little finger. The slight differences in the lengths of the dashes and the gaps in between were changing the pitch — creating different notes. I could just *barely* hear the differences. Either my ears weren't sensitive enough or my finger was too big — possibly both.

I pulled out my tablet and brought up the detailed scan of the pattern on Maggie's stone, then had it convert the heights and depths into a wave form, letting the computer figure out the most appropriate scale. Holding my breath, I hit play.

It was a short, pleasant, uplifting tune. I found myself laughing in amazement. I played it again, with my eyes closed. The sad image of Maggie I'd held for so long was now replaced by a little girl running through fields, a flower in her hand. I rested my hand on top of her stone again, ignoring the burning sensation for as long as I could.

I had to try some of the others. I went over to one of the larger monuments with a bigger pattern. I tried it with my finger first, again just able to make out the rhythm. Then I had my tablet try. This tune was a bit more somber and dignified — a man of business, proud of his position, maybe. The next monument was quicker, almost lilting — a teenager full of life.

I wiped tears away from my eyes. Yes, I was overlaying my own imagery on these simple tunes, and they were *human* images, which couldn't be right. But I was being talked to by a *people* who had been dead a thousand years. And I could hear them.

By this point my fingers had turned bright red and were aching from the cold. I wanted to listen to every one of the thirty-seven monuments, listen to thirty-seven distinct voices, but that would have to wait.

The lander was over a kilometer from the site, but I'm pretty sure I covered the distance in less than five minutes. I spent the next ten hours in my cabin, in front of my computer.

Eventually, though, I had to find Sean to let him know what equipment I was going to need — after swearing him to secrecy. I wasn't sure he even believed what I'd found.

The last thing I did was send an invitation to everyone on the lander, before collapsing into a deep, dreamless sleep.

When I got to the site the next day, Sean had already set up everything I'd asked for, including a tablet to control it all. His beard had kept growing and now, under the plastic breathing mask, it looked like he was actually wearing a breathing mask made of hair. I grinned at him, and he waved back.

Merrick showed up a little while later, along with several members of the other science teams and the ship's crew. In general, crew didn't mix with the science teams, but they were apparently curious. Merrick must have been curious as well, but his expression was blank.

I cleared my throat, suddenly feeling like I was about to give an oral dissertation defense in front of a hostile examination committee. The howling wind was chilling, but I felt sweat trickling down my neck.

"Uh, thank you all for coming. I, uh..."

I seemed to lose all control of my ability to speak. Desperately, I looked around, and saw Sean, standing behind everyone else. He winked at me, and gave me a brief thumbs-up. It helped.

I took a deep breath and started again.

"For the past several weeks, we've been trying to figure out what these stones represent, and whether the markings are writing. I now have a solid working hypothesis."

As if playing for dramatic effect, the wind dropped, leaving us in temporary silence. Most of the faces in front of me were openly interested, perhaps surprised, but Merrick's eyes were narrowed in a look of frustration so intense that I almost took a step backwards. What could possibly be driving that? Was he *that* afraid of being beaten to the finish line?

I took another deep breath, and held my ground.

"Each stone represents something — a concept, or, possibly, individual entities. If so, then this site *is* a graveyard — or at least a *memorial*. But the patterns are not words about each of these people. They are music."

I tapped something on my tablet, and Maggie's tune played out from the speakers Sean had placed around the site. They were highly directional, so the tune came from the location of Maggie's stone. At the same time, a bright light shone on the spiral pattern, travelling in time with the playback.

Everyone turned to look. It was the same melody from yesterday, but my experimentation with the parameters had improved it — added more depth and nuance. I'd heard the tune dozens of times by now, and it still made me shiver. From the looks on the faces of the others, I was not alone.

After a brief explanation of what I'd found, and how the patterns worked, I had the computer play its interpretation of several other stones — the somber business man. The teenager. A playful tune that made me think of an entertainer. A reserved, powerful tune that I associated with a mayor or a captain.

One of the biologists was laughing with glee. Several people were running fingers over the patterns, although with gloves on, it didn't work.

"If we can hear it," said the biologist who'd been laughing, "then that means that the creators had ears as well — heard sounds like we do."

"Not necessarily," said Merrick, and the anger was gone as he sank into the problem. "Sound is just vibrations. They might have had very sensitive fingers — digits — something — that interpreted the vibrations."

"Or antennae or a long sensitive tongue," I added. "There's no way to really know."

Merrick grinned at the image, and just for a second, I grinned back. Then we both looked away.

"Also," I continued, looking directly at the biologist, "the computer has chosen a pentatonic scale for the notes because it seems to fit, and because it sounds reasonable to us — to humans. That's fairly arbitrary, although with more research, we might be able to figure out how it was originally supposed to be interpreted."

The biologist sighed. "It's beautiful," she said," but I still wish you'd found me a body to examine."

There was general laughter at that.

The tune from the last gravestone had faded away, and for a moment I was a little lost, not quite sure how to get back on the track of my presentation. I was rescued by one of the crewmen, a short man in a blue uniform, whose name I couldn't remember.

"What about the big one?" he asked, pointing to the large stone in the center of the graveyard.

I smiled at him. "Glad you asked. That one took a while to figure out. You have to do both spirals at the same time." I hit the icon on my tablet, and a strange rhythmic pulsing started.

The crewman tilted his head to the side, listening. "That doesn't sound like the others. The others sound, well, sound like people. This is more like a back-beat or something..."

I nodded at him, impressed. It had taken me hours to figure that out. "It makes sense when you do *this*."

I hit another icon to run the program I'd spent most of the night on. The computer started up *all* of the monuments, delaying some, letting others fade in and fade out, then repeating them, little glowing lights spiraling throughout the site.

It was like standing in a busy market square, surrounded by people going about their lives. Children running, vendors hawking their wares, officials strutting around, and beneath it all, the *thrum* of the center monument adding life and depth to it all.

I let it run for several minutes, before allowing the individual tunes to fade away.

No one moved or spoke. The only sound was the whistling of the wind. I noticed that the crewman who'd asked the questions had tears in his eyes, and after a moment, I realized that I did, too.

Finally, Sean walked over to me, and gave me a one-armed hug.

"It's beautiful."

I hugged him back, my lip quivering.

"They're going to love this back home," said one of the biologists.

I nodded, and kept my eyes on him, careful not to look towards Merrick. "I sent a report back a few hours ago. I'd normally wait until after we were done, but we only have a few weeks left anyway."

The biologist nodded back in agreement, as though it were the most natural thing in the world to have done. Perhaps I *had* been too cautious in the past.

Out of the corner of my eye I saw Merrick take a step towards me, stop, and then turn and walk away. At least there wasn't going to be a big argument in front of everyone. That was a relief.

✍

Two days later I was sitting at the tiny desk in my cabin when there was a knock at my door. It was Merrick. I tilted my head at him and raised an eyebrow.

"I just wanted to say congratulations."

"Thank you." I kept my voice toneless.

Merrick took a deep breath and stepped into my cabin. He opened his mouth, closed it, then took another deep breath.

"I wanted to let you know that I sent a note to the college, giving you full credit for your previous work on Gliese 837c, and withdrawing my own name."

My eyes widened. "You didn't have to do that."

He shook his head. "I did. The thing is, with all of our conversations, I'd honestly convinced myself that we'd done that work together, and that you were holding me back by refusing to publish. I realize now..."

He swallowed. "I realize now that my contribution was almost nothing. It was all you, just like it was here. I think I need to find another field."

I think my mouth fell open. I thought back over the arguments that I'd had with Merrick. His old words twisted into different shapes in my mind, and I could suddenly see them from his perspective. It was true that most of the Gliese work had been mine, but Merrick *had* contributed quite a bit too. Withdrawing his name would cause a scandal — possibly end his career, or *any* career based on research. I'm not sure that I would have had the courage to do anything like that. I wondered if all of the strange looks he'd been giving me lately had been because he'd been thinking about doing this.

He turned to go, and I watched him disappear down the hallway.

There was something I'd wanted to do ever since I'd realized about the music. It was a definite no-no, and I could get in a lot of trouble...but on the other hand, courage deserved courage.

✍

I found Merrick in his cabin a few days later. He seemed surprised to see me.

"There's something I want to show you," I said.

He shrugged, but stood up.

We picked up our outside gear and cycled out through the airlock. We'd normally turn left to get to the graveyard site, but I turned right and started walking. Merrick seemed slightly surprised, but followed without comment.

We walked on in silence for twenty minutes, while I worked up the courage to speak.

"I've been thinking about what you did," I said, finally. "You were right — it was my research and my ideas, but you helped me flesh them out, and you pushed them into being published. You were right about that too."

Merrick kept his eyes firmly in front of him, his face a mask. I plowed on.

"I've been communicating with the professor. He's agreed to talk to the committee. The report on Gliese 837c is going to be updated to show both of our names — with mine listed first, of course."

Merrick's mouth opened, then closed a few times.

"I...," he started, then stopped. He gave the shortest of nods.

We walked on in silence. I led him to a spot about three kilometers from the ship, four from the graveyard. There was a small section of cliff that you couldn't see unless you were standing in the exact right spot, facing the exact right direction.

Merrick had kept his blank emotionless expression intact since I'd told him about the report, but when he saw the cliff face, he burst out laughing.

"When I said we needed to carve our names in the field, this isn't exactly what I had in mind."

There were three parts to the carving I'd made with Sean's laser rig. At the top was a star chart showing Earth's location, and another chart that showed the current alignment of all of the planets and moons in *this* solar system — on the theory that an advanced culture could use it to calculate precisely when we had been there. Below that were our names — Jenna, Sean and Merrick, etched in our alphabet, and below each of the names was a spiral like on the monuments.

"I figure that if another alien species comes along and finds this site as well as the other, it will drive them completely crazy. I know I shouldn't have done it, but I had to leave some proof that we'd been here."

Merrick smiled. He tugged off his glove and stepped towards the cliff, then looked back at me for permission. I nodded.

He started with Sean's spiral. As with the graveyard, only the vaguest rhythm was audible. I handed him my tablet, and he pointed it at the pattern and hit play.

Despite loving music, I was no musician, but the computer had helped me. Sean's tune was solid, confident, capable. Merrick nodded before moving on to the other patterns. Mine was inquisitive, changing — a little bit sad. I wasn't quite sure about it, but Sean had sworn that it captured me perfectly.

Merrick's tune was brash and striving, with a deep under-beat — but uplifting, hopeful. When the computer had first played it, I knew that it fit him exactly, although I couldn't have explained precisely why. He played it a second time, running his finger over the pattern as it ran.

When he finally spoke, his voice was so quiet I could barely hear him "Is that how you really see me?"

I nodded.

"Well, then, perhaps I'm not a hopeless case after all."

I smiled. "Don't get ahead of the facts."

✍ ✍ ✍

Initial feedback

I liked the concept, characters, and prose. The narrator needs some kind of musical background, and we need to hear at least handwaving about how a fairly simply coding is converted to music. Merrick's step back comes far too easily, and it seems odd that the narrator is apparently willing to let him withdraw his name even after acknowledging that she might have been in part at fault. I think there's a good story here, but it needs a little more depth and complexity.

Author's intent

What do you think the story's about?
What emotions are you trying to evoke?

As for what the story is about — it is about the desire to leave a mark on the world, and how, ultimately, that is not the most important thing.

For emotions, I would say that wonder and the fear of rejection/failure are at the heart of the story.

Author's note

When I first started the editing process with Morris, I expected there to be the usual stylistic edits and perhaps some tweaks to make some things clearer. Instead, there were numerous back-and-forths about various concepts and details. This was so unusual that many of the details have stuck with me, years (and dozens of stories) later.

"Graveyard" was one of my first short story sales, so I was particularly eager to please, but I think that everything he suggested improved the story. There were also some things we argued about — he was unconvinced on whether a tune could be heard just by running a finger over the pattern on the stones, and I ended up sending him video of the *Asphaltophone* — a section of road that plays a tune when you drive over it — which gave me the original idea for the gravestones in the first place. I did end up making the mechanism more complex, though — implying that the creators of the monuments had some sort of more sensitive pickup mechanism.

The biggest improvement, in my opinion, was making Jenna a music lover and adding the section where she is listening to The New World, which makes her thinking of the idea of music more natural. I chose that piece both because of its name, which seemed appropriate, and because it is one of my personal favorite pieces — I can easily imagine listen to the Largo on an alien world.

Thanks to Morris's suggestions, the relationship between Jenna and Merrick is fleshed out, hopefully making it more believable that she'd forgive him at the end. There are also lots of little tweaks throughout that, I think, add depth to the story. I also expanded on some technical details that Morris thought were needed, such as providing specific measurements vs. just hand-waving, although we did agree to leave some details out in order to avoid info-dumping. But I did have to prove to him that my physics and archeology were plausible!

Morris asks what the author thinks the story is about. To me, this is a story about leaving your mark, and how long you can expect to be remembered. For the monument makers, leaving their sounds was enough. For Jenna and Merrick they are trying to get their names in print, but have different priorities — fast vs. right vs. permanent. But to last, someone in the future has to be looking — or listening.

Editor's note

The revision process is often a learning opportunity for the editor — you have to have a certain confidence (arrogance?) to believe you can offer people advice about writing, and I like to think I have a broad range of topical experience, but there's an awful lot that I know absolutely nothing about. Sometimes, as we've seen before, my small store of knowledge can lead me wrong, and it tried to have its way in this case too. I questioned the ability to date rock so accurately, and Arlen convinced me it was possible. I doubted the likelihood of deciphering a tune from pits in stone, and Arlen introduced me to the asphaltophone. I've said that writers need flexibility, but that goes for editors too. You have to learn when you get the chance.

The emotional side of the story was happily more in my wheelhouse. I felt that Merrick's turnaround was too quick, too easy. The narrator too, though admitting they'd been in part at fault, was too ready to let him withdraw his name. I felt that a more complex resolution would suit the story better. Arlen made changes that I thought made both characters' actions more interesting and more credible.

One of my pet peeves is characters who act for no discernible reason. Authors do it all the time — usually for a reason, but sometimes as a convenient authorial shortcut for a hole in the story. Here, there wasn't a hole to patch, but Arlen had the protagonist touching the gravestone 'for no reason [he] could explain'. That's particularly hard to pull off in a science fiction story, with no suggestion of supernatural, subliminal messages. Arlen fixed it very simply, with 'wanting a closer connection [to the stone]'. It's a small change, but in my view, it's usually better to give the character reasons for action when possible, and this did.

Graveyard

The crew had already started calling it the *graveyard*.

If it was a graveyard, it would be hard to choose a bleaker site for it, on a planet pretty much made up of bleak sites. I walked as close as I dared to the edge of the cliff, and looked down over a thousand meters of sharp gray crags spreading out all around, us under a dark, thunderous sky. I felt the wind tugging at me, and hastily stepped back.

Merrick was watching over the technicians — as though they needed or wanted his help. To be fair, he did know a lot about the scanning equipment.

Not that I wanted to be fair.

I tugged at my breathing mask, trying to make it more comfortable, and turned to examine the site. Thirty-seven upright stones, spread over a clearing about forty meters wide. The shortest stone was 22 centimeters and the tallest was 196 centimeters — almost two meters. From three sides, they just looked like rocks.

It was because of the fourth sides that we were here. They had been carved flat and a pattern had been deeply etched into each. The designs were different from stone to stone, but they all followed a similar design — a spiral of shapes spreading out from a central point. The shapes were circles and rounded rectangles of different lengths. It sort-of reminded me of Morse code, except that there were at least eight different lengths. Unless, of course, the "dashes" all meant the same thing, and the carver wasn't particularly careful about length.

"Jenna?"

I jumped, then turned around. Sean, the other member of the research team, was standing less than two feet behind me. Hard to hear with the wind and the masks and the warm-weather gear.

Sean held up his hands. "Sorry. Didn't mean to startle you."

"No worries." I grinned at him, putting my hand to my chest. "Whatever doesn't make your heart explode makes you stronger. What's up?"

"We're about ready."

I nodded and followed him over to the "command post" which was really just a stack of plastic crates with some ruggedized computers sitting on top. Sean typed something on a keyboard and I felt the thrum as power ran to the imaging lasers, mounted on poles that had been planted, with some difficulty, into the rock all around the site.

For a while we watched the progress display on the screen, then I turned and walked back towards the stones. Not much point looking at a picture when the real thing was right there.

"You know," said Merrick, who had followed me, and was now standing right next to me. "If it is a graveyard, then the inscriptions would make a certain amount of sense."

I took a half step away from him. "How so?"

"Well, the little one there might be *To Aunt Maggie*, while that one," he pointed to the largest stone with two separate swirls of symbols," might be the Grayon-Alpha-3 equivalent of the Lord's Prayer or *Do Not Go Gentle*."

I laughed, though in truth the idea had already occurred to me. "You know what the Professor would say, don't you?"

"Don't get ahead of the facts." We intoned in unison, then both laughed.

Professor Kineson should have been here. He was the world's foremost xeno-anthropologist, but he was now too old for major journeys. Instead he'd sent his grad students — me and Merrick — arguably the world's only *other* xeno-anthropologists. To date, it wasn't a very popular or useful field, although Grayon-Alpha-3 might change that.

Life was pretty common on the worlds that had been explored — plants and insectoids being the most common, but larger forms as well. Grayon-Alpha-3 was no different, covered in small ugly plants and a number of beetle-like insectoids that were currently being intensely studied by the biology team.

On two previously explored worlds we'd found indications of intelligence — remnants of crude settlements, but no actual settlers. Kineson had been the main researcher for both of those.

But writing — that was a first. If the designs on these stones turned out to be a form of language, that would be a game changer. And it had to be writing. How could it be anything else?

"It could be art," said Merrick, as though reading my mind — a very annoying habit of his. "Like Celtic knotwork."

I shrugged. Even artwork would be exciting, but in my gut, I knew that it was writing — an attempt to communicate. Not that I would ever admit to anything so unscientific as a gut feeling.

The hum of the scanners shut down at the same time as a lull in the wind, and for a few seconds it was eerily quiet. That might have been the moment when the reality of what we were doing set in. We were standing on an alien world in the presence of unquestionable evidence of intelligence. Even knowing nothing about who or what they were, when and how they lived, I felt an almost physical connection to the creators of these stones.

I looked up to see Merrick staring at me.

"What?" I asked.

"Nothing. You just had a look."

He reached out an arm towards my shoulder, but I took another half-step away.

Sean came up to us, his hand brushing against his breathing mask, as though he wanted to scratch his chin. It was hard to get used to Sean having a visible face. On the trip here, he'd had a huge, ragged Santa-Claus beard, but he'd had to shave it off so that the breathing mask would fit. Although he was in his forties, he now looked like a teenager. I'd studiously avoided saying anything, although the rest of the crew had teased him mercilessly about it.

"Scan's done," he said. "We only have about another hour of daylight. We'd should probably get back to the lander."

I nodded, but didn't move. I was looking at the smallest stone — the one that Merrick had called *Aunt Maggie*. I'd spent a lot of time in old graveyards, and the smallest, saddest stones were always for babies and children. In my head, I mentally shortened the label to just *Maggie*.

I turned, grabbed my kit, and followed the others back to the lander.

✍

The next day was all about scanning underground. If these were gravestones, then there should be something underneath them. The Ground Penetrating Radar setup was finicky, and we were all sweating profusely by the time we had it working, despite the cold.

Nothing. There was nothing beneath any of the stones.

"It doesn't mean they're not grave markers," I said, although without much conviction. "They could be cenotaphs — memorializing without the bodies."

No one argued, but I doubted that anyone was convinced.

"There is one weird thing," said Sean.

Merrick and I both turned to face him.

"The stones look rough-carved, but they each extend at least twenty centimeters below the surface, and the fit is precise. I mean, *really* precise." He pointed at the display. "I could *probably* do it with a laser and a bunch of time, but it's hard to see how you could do it with primitive tools."

Merrick shook his head. "If they were an advanced culture with lasers, then there would be some other evidence on the planet. Roads, buildings, something. The satellites have found squat."

"That depends on how old they are," said Sean, scratching ineffectually at his breathing mask.

"Maybe they lived underground," I suggested. "That would explain the lack of anything on the surface."

Merrick shook his head. *"Don't get ahead of the facts,"* he said. The satellites would have found some evidence of any sort of sophisticated underground settlements.

I sighed. We'd hoped to find something buried beneath the stones that we could use to figure out a date. Then, suddenly, I had an idea.

"You know, there might be a way of figuring out a date — from the stones themselves."

"The stones are granite," said Merrick, sounding exasperated. "They are the same age as the surrounding rocks. You can't get an age off of them separate from that."

"Thanks for the Geology 101 lecture." I didn't bother trying to keep the sarcasm from my voice. I turned to Sean. "Weathering patterns. The stones further away from the cliff are weathered less than those nearer to it. We know more-or-less how granite breaks down. We should be able to at least get a rough estimate from that."

"Clever," said Merrick, suddenly interested.

Sean stroked at his chin. "Rough is the word."

"The faces and the designs haven't really worn down," said Merrick.

"No," said Sean, thinking, "but the edges have. We'll have to analyze some other rocks as well for control, but...it could work." He looked up. "Yeah — at least within a few hundred years." He grinned at me. "Nice!"

It was four days later, early in the morning, when Sean knocked on the door of my cabin.

"Yeah?" I answered blearily.

He handed me a piece of paper. "Between 700 and 1200 years."

For several seconds I had no idea what he was saying, and then suddenly neurons started firing in my brain. "You did it? You did it!" I gave him a hug, and he turned bright red. I noticed that he'd started growing a beard again, but that it was carefully trimmed to the shape of a breathing mask.

"This is awesome," I told him. "It's the first concrete thing we really know about the site. The post-project report was looking awfully bare."

Sean suddenly looked nervous. "So, you won't report anything until the end of the trip?"

"Of course not. That would be...why?"

"Well, it's just that..."

But I didn't need to hear it. I already knew.

"Merrick? You told Merrick first?"

"I didn't...he was in the lab when the computer spat out the results. I couldn't — "

But I was already halfway down the passage.

My thoughts, though, were on events from a year ago. Me, curled up on the sofa next to Merrick while he read my research notes on the ancient settlement found on Gliese 837c, telling me how great my work was. Late nights, lying next to one-another, endlessly discussing *my* ideas...

I practically slammed into him coming the other way down the passage.

He oofed, then backed away. "Oops, sorry." Then he saw my face. "What?" he asked.

I was about ready to hit him. "You bastard."

His eyebrows went up, but his voice was even, half-joking. "My mother would deny it. I take it you think I did something?"

He was going to brazen it out. I lifted my fist and he took several hasty steps back. Not once did it even occur to me that he hadn't sent a report behind my back. I could see the look of calculation in his eyes.

"Look, if it's about the dating — I *did* let the Professor know, but no one else. And I swear that I told him that the idea was yours."

"Yeah, like last time? In a frigging footnote?" I'd taken several steps toward him, and he'd backed away again, even though he towered over me by thirty centimeters. His face was red now.

"You think I'd...?"

"Yes, I do."

Then I turned and walked away. Of course, now I had to send a separate report in, and it would make us look like we were squabbling siblings. Maybe I shouldn't even bother.

When I got a copy of the report a few hours later, it turned out that Merrick had been telling the truth. Professor Kineson sent us both a congratulatory e-mail about the dating, and had given me credit for the idea, and Merrick and Sean credit for the computer model.

This did not make me feel any better.

A little while later, Merrick came to find me. His expression was half-smirk and half-contrition. I have no idea why I once found him handsome.

"Jen," he started. "Listen, I know we have some history, but I *did* tell you that I gave you credit."

"And yourself, I note. I'm pretty sure that Sean did most of the work."

He ignored this.

"Getting our names out there is important. There is interest in what we are doing right now. If we waited until we had every last detail worked out, no one would care. Publish or perish, right?"

"I'd recommend perish in your case," I said. This was an old argument though. Part of his excuse for pre-empting my Gliese 837c research was that I was taking too long to get my results out there. Like that was an excuse for stealing my work.

He turned to walk away, obviously annoyed. At the door, he paused. "If you aren't going to let people know what we've found, then why bother?"

"I want it to be right," I said, trying to keep my voice steady. "I want it to be permanent — to last. Not just be some half-baked headline."

He shook his head. "And if you wait too long, then it's going to be someone else's name that's remembered. Not us. If we don't carve out our own names, no one else will. We work in a tiny, under-funded field. If you don't get your name out there, how many of your projects do you think will get sponsored?"

Then he walked away. I watched him go, wondering how he and I could have such different ideas about what our work was about. Part of me, though, knew that he was right about sponsorship. I wondered, briefly, who I was really angry at.

✍

The next two weeks were spent in icy, silent hostility. Most of the crew, who were military, were completely unaware of what was going on, or at least pretended to be. Sean, though, was stuck in the middle, and shuttled back and forth nervously between us.

It helped that Merrick and my approaches were so different. He spent most of his time with the computer scans and models on the ship, while I spent most of my time at the actual site.

Not that I was getting anywhere. Nor, as far as I knew, was Merrick.

700 to 1200 years. A long time, but it was difficult to believe that a culture with the sophisticated stone-working skills needed to make these monuments would have otherwise disappeared without a trace.

My working hypothesis — shared with no one else — was that the monument-makers weren't native. Someone had visited this planet, like we were now, and, for whatever reason, had left this memorial here. Maybe to commemorate their visit, or because something unfortunate had happened. I smiled to myself. I was getting really *far ahead of the facts*.

The idea did *fit* the facts, though. There were no visible tool marks, which was consistent with more advanced technology, and there were no indications of any remotely higher lifeforms on this planet, let alone tool users.

In the past, I might have talked this over with Merrick, but that was obviously impossible. He was good at turning my flights-of-fancy into concrete ideas. Now, though — if he agreed, he'd probably steal my ideas, and if he disagreed, he'd probably use them to discredit me.

I sat down in front of *Maggie's* stone on a small stool I'd been using. Part of my reason for focusing on that stone was that I figured the simpler design might be easier to interpret. In theory, the more complex patterns would provide more material to analyze, but the computers were already trying that approach without any notable success.

Another reason was that it was next to one of the larger monuments, which protected me from the continuous howling wind.

To be honest, though, I think I'd just formed some sort of emotional attachment to my mental image of *Maggie*.

It was chilly, even with the protective clothing, and I shivered. I rested my gloved hand on top of Maggie's stone. Then, for no reason I could explain, I pulled off my glove and touched the stone with my bare hand.

The stone was ice cold and it burned my hand, but I still held it there for a moment before pulling it back. Not quite ready to give up my connection to the monument, I put my finger in the very center of the spiral design, and ran it around the design.

I'd done this before with my thick glove on, but without it, I suddenly noticed something. As my finger thunked between the uneven dashes, it made a sort of tune.

The hair on the back of my neck stood up and a chill went down my spine. It had nothing to do with the frigid air.

I tried it again, slower. This time, the tune was more pronounced. It was a short, pleasant, uplifting tune. In my mind, I pictured a little girl running through fields, a flower in her hand.

I moved on to another one of the monuments, this one larger, with a bigger pattern. It was another tune, a bit more somber and dignified — a man of business, proud of his position, maybe. The next monument was quicker, almost lilting — a teenager full of life.

I wiped tears away from my eyes. Yes, I was overlaying my own imagery on these simple tunes, and they were *human* images, which couldn't be right. But I was being talked to by a *people* who had been dead a thousand years. And I could hear them.

By this point my fingers had turned bright red, and were aching from the cold. I wanted to listen to every one of the thirty-seven monuments, listen to thirty-seven distinct voices, but that would have to wait.

The lander was over a kilometer from the site, but I'm pretty sure I covered the distance in less than five minutes. I spent the next ten hours in my cabin, in front of my computer. Eventually, though, I had to find Sean to let him know what equipment I was going to need — after swearing him to secrecy. I'm not sure he even believed what I'd found.

The last thing I did was send an invitation to everyone on the lander, before collapsing into a deep, dreamless sleep.

When I got to the site the next day, Sean had already set up everything I'd asked for, including a tablet to control it all. His beard had kept growing and now, under the plastic breathing mask, it looked like he was actually wearing a breathing mask made of hair. I grinned at him, and he waved back.

Merrick showed up a little while later, along with several members of the other science teams and the ship's crew. In general, crew didn't mix with the science teams, but they were apparently curious. Merrick must have been curious as well, but his expression was blank.

I cleared my throat, suddenly feeling like I was about to give an oral dissertation defense in front of a hostile examination committee. The howling wind was chilling, but I felt sweat trickling down my neck.

"Uh, thank you all for coming. I, uh…"

I seemed to lose all control of my ability to speak. Desperately, I looked around, and saw Sean, standing behind everyone else. He winked at me, and gave me a brief thumbs-up. It helped.

I took a deep breath and started again.

"For the past several weeks, we've been trying to figure out what these stones represent, and whether the markings are writing. I can now answer those questions."

As if playing for dramatic effect, the wind dropped, leaving us in temporary silence. Most of the faces in front of me were openly interested, perhaps surprised, but Merrick's eyes were narrowed in a look of anger so intense that I almost took a step backwards. It wasn't until that moment that I realized what must drive him — that he was afraid of failure — of being beaten to the finish line.

I took another deep breath, and held my ground.

"This site *is* a graveyard — or at least a *memorial*. It is my belief that each of these stones represents an individual entity. But the patterns are not words about each of these people. They are music."

I tapped something on my tablet, and Maggie's tune played out from the speakers Sean had placed around the site. They were highly directional, so the tune came from the location of Maggie's stone.

Everyone turned to look. It was the same tune I'd thumped out with my finger the day before, but the computer added more depth to it. I'd heard it a dozen times by now, and it still made me shiver. From the looks on the faces of the others, I was not alone.

After a brief explanation of what I'd found, and how the patterns worked, I had the computer play its interpretation of several other stones — the somber business man. The teenager. A playful tune that made me think of an entertainer. A reserved, powerful tune that I associated with a mayor or a captain.

One of the biologists was laughing with glee. Several people were running fingers over the patterns, although with gloves on, it didn't work.

"What about the big one?" asked one of the crewmen, a short man in a blue uniform, whose name I couldn't remember.

I smiled at him. "Glad you asked. That one took a while to figure out. You have to do both spirals at the same time." I hit the icon on my tablet, and a strange rhythmic pulsing started.

The crewman tilted his head to the side, listening. "That doesn't sound like the others. The others sound, well, sound like people. This is more like a back-beat or something..."

I nodded at him, impressed. It had taken me hours to figure that out. "It makes sense when you do *this*."

I hit another icon to run the program I'd spent most of the night on. The computer started up *all* of the monuments, delaying some, letting others fade in and fade out, then repeating them.

It was like standing in a busy market square, surrounded by people going about their lives. Children running, vendors hawking their wares, officials strutting around, and beneath it all, the *thrum* of the center monument adding life and depth to it all.

I let it run for several minutes, before allowing the individual tunes to fade away.

No one moved or spoke. The only sound was the whistling of the wind. I noticed that the crewman who'd asked the questions had tears in his eyes, and after a moment, I realized that I did, too.

Finally, Sean walked over to me, and gave me a one-armed hug.

"It's beautiful."

I hugged him back, my lip quivering.

"They're going to love this back home," said one of the biologists.

I nodded, and kept my eyes on him, careful not to look towards Merrick. "I sent a report back a few hours ago. I'd normally wait until after we were done, but we only have a few days left anyway."

The biologist nodded back in agreement, as though it was the most natural thing to have done in the world. Perhaps I *had* been too cautious in the past.

✍

Two days later I was sitting at the tiny desk in my cabin when there was a knock at my door. It was Merrick. I tilted my head at him and raised an eyebrow.

"I just wanted to say congratulations."

"Thank you." I kept my voice toneless.

Merrick took a deep breath and stepped into my cabin. He opened his mouth, closed it, then took another deep breath.

"I wanted to let you know that I sent a note to the college, giving you full credit for your previous work on Gliese 837c, and withdrawing my own name."

My eyes widened. "You didn't have to do that."

He shook his head. "I did. The thing is, with all of our conversations, I'd honestly convinced myself that we'd done that work together, and that you were holding me back by refusing to publish. I realize now…"

He swallowed. "I realize now that my contribution was almost nothing. It was all you, just like it was here. I think I need to find another field."

I think my mouth fell open. Previous conversations twisted into different shapes in my mind. It was true that most of the Gliese work had been mine, but Merrick *had* contributed quite a bit too. Withdrawing his name would cause a scandal — possibly end his career, or *any* career based on research. I'm not sure that I would have had the courage to do anything like that.

He turned to go, and I watched him disappear down the hallway, thinking.

There was something I'd wanted to do ever since I'd realized about the music. It was a definite no-no, and I could get in a lot of trouble…but on the other hand, courage deserved courage.

✍

I found Merrick in his cabin a few hours later. He seemed surprised to see me.

"There's something I want to show you," I said.

He shrugged, but stood up.

We picked up our outside gear and I led him to a spot about three kilometers from the site, in the complete opposite direction. There was a small section of cliff that you couldn't see unless you were standing in the exact right spot, facing the exact right direction.

Merrick hadn't spoken the entire time we'd been walking, but when he saw the cliff face, he burst out laughing.

"When I said we needed to carve our name in the field, this isn't exactly what I had in mind."

There were three parts to the carving I'd made with Sean's laser rig. At the top was a star chart showing Earth's location, and another chart that showed the current alignment of all of the planets and moons in *this* solar system — on the theory that an advanced culture could use it to calculate precisely when we had been there. Below that were our names — Jenna, Sean and Merrick, etched in our alphabet, and below each of the names was a spiral like on the monuments.

"I figure that if another alien species comes along and finds this site as well as the other, it will drive them completely crazy. I know I shouldn't have done it, but I had to leave some proof that we'd been here."

Merrick smiled. He tugged off his glove and stepped towards the cliff, then looked back at me for permission. I nodded.

He started with Sean's spiral. I was no musician, but the computer had helped me. Sean's tune was solid, confident, capable. Mine was inquisitive, changing — a little bit sad. I wasn't quite sure about it, but Sean had sworn that it captured me perfectly.

Merrick's tune was brash and striving with a deep under-beat, but uplifting, hopeful. When the computer first played it, I knew that it fit him exactly, although I couldn't have explained precisely why. He ran his finger over it a second time.

When he finally spoke, his voice was so quiet I could barely hear him "Is that how you really see me?"

I nodded.

"Well, then, perhaps I'm not a hopeless case after all."

I smiled. "Don't get ahead of the facts."

✍ ✍ ✍

COMMON WRITING FLAWS

'Flaws' are, of course, in the eye of the beholder. One writer's (or editor's) flaw is another's strength or stylistic preference. However, some general issues are fairly common across the board. Below are some of the most common problems that I see in submissions. Where possible, I've added cross-references to stories in this anthology that shared the issue in their original form. The issues are ranked roughly by frequency with which I see them, rather than by importance or prevalence in this anthology.

Context. What's the world like? Who are the characters and what's their situation? If we don't know where we are and what the rules are, the story may be hard to follow. We need enough context to understand the immediate setting and issue, but not so much that it overwhelms us with detail we can't use. More often than not, there's not enough context at the right time, at least about some particular issue. Writers often try to solve this problem with infodumps — blocks of exposition that directly set out the rules or background. Sometimes that works, but generally speaking, an infodump is a sign of a problem with context. Ironically, infodumps are rarely successful; not only do they tend to stop the flow of the story dead, they rarely provide the context that's actually needed for the story to work.

> *Stories that had this issue:* "The Dragon and the Unicorn", "Free Hugs", "Wytchen Wood", "The Tick of the Clock", "Hope on the Vine", "The Lonely King", "Graveyard".

Engagement. Very few stories are interesting if we're not engaged by the characters. Very frequently, I find myself a few pages into a story with an interesting concept, clever world, and good prose, yet find myself thinking, "Why should I *care* about these characters?" And if I don't care, why should I read about them? Note that an engaging character is not the same as a likable one. Horrible, cruel villains can be just as engaging as kind, honorable heroes. The key to engagement is for the reader to know what the character values and what they want. If you show me a villain torturing an innocent child, that's mildly interesting. If you show me that that same villain is torturing the child because he wants to extract the information he needs to establish his precedence among evil villains and thus secure his place in history, that's much more intriguing.

Stories that had this issue: "The Dragon and the Unicorn", "Singot", "Free Hugs", "Going Home", "Satyajit Ray's Beard or the Lack Thereof", "The Wife of Fabian Vitalik", "Graveyard".

Interest. Sometimes, I just don't find the premise interesting. That's a more complex issue than it seems, because, with good prose and characters, virtually anything can be made interesting. However, a very familiar trope without any new twist and without interesting characters isn't likely to appeal, especially if it seems the author isn't well read enough to know that it *is* a familiar trope. Sometimes, the problem is simply that the concept isn't introduced early enough, and I'm not sure what the story is about. (Again, engaging characters can mitigate that.)

Direction. Within the first page, in most cases, I should have a sense of where the story is headed — What's the genre? Is it about a clever new gadget? Is it an extrapolation of developing social norms? Is it a coming of age story? Is it about a personal vendetta? If I don't have a sense by page 2 of what the base story is, I'm not likely to continue. Note, however, that subtlety is important here — starting with "I grew up testing my destongulator so that I could get revenge on Binky Marston" won't do the trick. If you're showing us engaging characters, that's likely the place to give the story direction.

Prose. Good prose is a *sine qua non* for *Metaphorosis.* Not all stories we publish have the rich, lyrical prose of Patricia McKillip or the evocative poetry of Roger Zelazny, but without serviceable prose, authors don't stand a chance with us. It's easy enough to fix occasional errors, but the basics of prose construction are an essential building block for any author. It's easy enough to acquire these basics by the simple expedients of reading a lot and writing a lot.

Punctuation. Even more basic than prose skills is punctuation. If you don't know how to use basic punctuation, you may have trouble as a writer. Sure, an editor can fix this for you, but they shouldn't have to, even if it's an editor you're paying. Basic punctuation is just that: basic. It's one thing to miss or overuse the occasional comma, but not knowing how to punctuate dialogue means you haven't even opened your beginning writer's toolkit. Dialogue standards can vary across languages, of course, but if you want to sell in English, you need to master the fundamentals. Poorly punctuated prose is very difficult to read — that's what punctuation is *for*.

Proofreading. Typos are the literary manifestation of the dark matter all around us; find them all and more will spring up out of nothing. You'll never get them down to zero. Yet it is important to catch as many as you can; not doing so suggests that you don't care about your work, and if you don't, why should anyone else?

Opening. There's a bit of a fixation on opening lines in fiction that I don't really buy into. There's nothing magic about them. But they are your first contact with the reader (many readers ignore titles), and there's a lot that a good opening line can do. An ideal opening line will tell us who the characters are, where they are, what they value, what the genre is, what's happening, what the story is about, why we should care, and what the voice of the story will be. It sounds like a lot, but it's actually easier to combine a lot of those than it might seem. I don't suggest you spend all your time crafting the perfect opening line, but don't waste it either.

Start. Beyond just the first line, the first paragraph or two are your chance to establish the themes and the stakes of the story. What are the issues that are going to resonate throughout the piece? A useful writing exercise is to look at your start and your ending or your opening and closing. Do they touch on common themes? Are those themes reflected in the body of the story? If so, congratulations, you've probably got a clear theme and resolution. If not, maybe your key theme isn't what you thought it was, or maybe you can lead the reader to and from it more clearly. Of course, this is a writing exercise, not a prescription; not all stories must have this cyclical feel.

> *Stories that had this issue:* "Renewal", "The Future in a Wash Basin".

Focus. More often than I would expect, stories lose focus as they progress. That is, they introduce a character, situation, or tension, but then go on to talk about something else for a page or a paragraph. If you have a battle cruiser delivering an ultimatum to the rebels, but then spend time talking about the design of the Admiral's uniform, there had better be a good reason why that design is important. If not, put the haberdashery elsewhere. Short stories are generally efficient; if something isn't important, maybe you don't need it at all.

> *Stories that had this issue:* "Renewal", "Satyajit Ray's Beard or the Lack Thereof".

Ending. Closing lines are, in my view, more important than openers. This is your chance to sum up your themes or resolution, to work a little more poetry into your prose, and to leave the reader with one last image, metaphor, or emotion to go out on — ideally, something that will stick in their memory for days, weeks or longer, that will make them stop and think before just going on to the next story. People may not often cite your closing as the key element of your story, but it could well be the part that cements their memory of it. It's often effective (but not essential), to circle back to images or themes you used at the start. The same can broadly be said of endings in general.

> *Stories that had this issue:* "The Secret Keeper", "The Dragon and the Unicorn", "Renewal", "Going Home", "Satyajit Ray's Beard or the Lack Thereof", "Wytchen Wood", "The Future in a Wash Basin", "The Tick of the Clock", "Hope on the Vine".

Overwriting. The flipside of lyrical, metaphorical prose is the risk of overwriting. Metaphor and imagery are most effective in moderation. Too many metaphors at once risks generating a incomprehensible flock of images rather than a flight of fancy. By all means use metaphors, but choose them carefully for effect rather than volume.

 Stories that had this issue: "Sorry, Sorry, Sorry and I Love You"

Worldbuilding. We all hear about worldbuilding all the time, and about how well master SFF storytellers do it, and that's true. It *is* important. But in a short story, efficiency is also important. If the story is about an apprentice clerk, we probably don't need to know that the paper she writes on is made of fiber from the yazu tree, sourced in the Gliana valley where the dragons live, then shipped on the Glinkit river to a mill in Sandertast, the famously military republic, and ground into fiber by troll women whose saliva leaves a distinctive odor of almonds. It's great if the author know all that, but it doesn't need to come into the story. On the other hand, if the apprentice clerk lives on a barren lava plateau with no trees within a hundred leagues, where she gets her paper becomes more of an issue. The key is to remember that worldbuilding is there to *support* the story. In short fiction, it's rarely an end in itself. There's room for a little colour, but generally, if you don't need procedural detail for the story to make sense, you can leave it out — no matter how proud you are of how cool it is.

 Stories that had this issue: "The Secret Keeper", "The Dragon and the Unicorn", "Free Hugs", "Going Home", "Satyajit Ray's Beard or the Lack Thereof", "Wytchen Wood", "The Future in a Wash Basin", "Hope on the Vine", "The Wife of Fabian Vitalik", "The Lonely King", "Graveyard".

Backstory. In some ways, backstory is simply a question of context — providing the right information at the right time. A careful drip of backstory may provide intriguing mystery to your characters or concept. But not enough backstory in the right place may make their motives hard to understand and thus hard to engage with. There's no magic formula for backstory, unfortunately, beyond 'enough at the right time'.

 Stories that had this issue: "The Dragon and the Unicorn", "Free Hugs", "The Tick of the Clock".

Balance. We've all read novels that are rich and captivating and exciting, right up until the end, when suddenly everything wraps up in the last few pages, leaving us feeling vaguely cheated that the complexity vanished. Similarly, we've all read books that reached their resolution early, but limped on with 50 pages of what's effectively epilogue while we wish the author had stopped while they were ahead. The problems in short stories are the same, but multiplied. Once the structure of the story is clear, you need the right beats in the right places, and it's not always obvious either what the beats should be or what the places are. In brief, though, you need a start that's active enough to intrigues, and lengthy enough to give us a foothold in the story. You need a resolution that's substantive enough to match the length of the story, and enough space to work it out.

Stories that had this issue: "Singot", "Sorry, Sorry, Sorry and I Love You".

Length. Any story can be told at different lengths, as evidenced by the number of stories that began as short stories and ended up as novels. Orson Scott Card's "Ender's Game" started as a compact, very effective story and became a full-length novel (as well as a series with I don't know how many books). Story and novel tell the same story, and they're both fulfilling (though I strongly prefer the story). The same is true of many others. The key is to choose a length that suits the resolution you plan (and vice versa). I frequently note that I found a story 'thin', which is my shorthand for "the resolution was reasonable in itself, but would have worked better in a much shorter story. At this length, it's just not rewarding enough to justify reading this long piece." A thin story doesn't necessarily mean one that's too long, but it does mean one that's too long for its ending. It can just as readily be fixed with a more complex resolution as by cutting the length. A different issue with length sometimes arises with complexity not of the resolution, but of the piece itself. If a piece can effectively be boiled down to 2,000 words, but you're telling it in 10,000, why is that? Is there enough complexity in the piece to reward the reader, or will they go away with just the outlines of it, forgetting much of the detail that added color but not plot?

Stories that had this issue: "The Secret Keeper", "Singot", "Going Home".

Guidelines. Finally, a word about submission guidelines. Different venues have different guidelines, and they're often laid out quite differently or hard to follow. It's annoying and tedious, and yet authors need to take the time to read and follow them carefully. Each magazine's editor wants their own set of rules followed, and the fact that a submitter conscientiously followed some other set will not impress them at all. Happily, most SFF venues follow some variant of the Shunn format. Between that and a careful use of templates, it's very easy to comply with guidelines and thus increase your chances of acceptance.

ABOUT THE AUTHORS

First, a note of thanks to all the authors. As you'll have picked up by now, the *Metaphorosis* editorial process is a grueling on, and it takes some stamina to get through. The fact that all these authors have not only done it (some multiple times) and participated in this anthology provides evidence that it's worth it, and that the end product is worth it — not only in my eyes, but in theirs.

It can be difficult to accept critical feedback, let alone act on it. These authors have gone much further — they've been willing to expose their original, unedited work, with all its flaws and strengths — because they believe this anthology can be a useful tool for writers looking to improve. It takes courage to do that, and I applaud them all for their bravery. Every writer wants to improve, but the authors below have stood up to help other writers as well. That's the kind of commitment that helps keep the SFF community strong.

With that, here's a little more about each of them. Now that you've seen what they can do and how hard they work at writing, why not look up their other work as well?

Wade Dargin ("The Dragon and the Unicorn")

Wade Dargin lives in Saskatchewan, Canada. He is an archaeologist and civil servant. He grew up in remote places and this has likely affected him profoundly. He writes whenever he can.

@WadeDargin

Wade Dargin's story "The Dragon and the Unicorn" was published in Metaphorosis on Friday, 1 April 2022.

Gunnar De Winter ("The Lonely King")

Gunnar De Winter is a biologist/philosopher who's now doing science communication. And fiction, of course. Some of his stories have found their way to *The Deadlands, Future SF Digest,* and *Daily Science Fiction*. Find him on Twitter as @evolveon.

Gunnar De Winter's story "The Lonely King" was published in Metaphorosis on Friday, 29 November 2019.

R.E. Dukalsky ("Hope on the Vine")

R.E. Dukalsky writes speculative fiction about memory, change, conflict and what happens afterward. She has been told that she has School House Rock charm and that she would make an excellent rebel leader, among other dubious accolades. She lives in the Pacific Northwest in a house that perpetually needs more bookshelves.

@tiltingwindward

R.E. Dukalsky's story "Hope on the Vine" was published in Metaphorosis on Friday, 4 March 2022.

Arlen Feldman ("Graveyard")

As well as writing fiction, Arlen Feldman is a software engineer, entrepreneur, maker, and computer book author — useful if you are in the market for some industrial-strength door stops. Some recent stories of his appear in the anthologies *The Chorochronos Archives* and *Particular Passages,* and in *Little Blue Marble* and *Nocturne* magazines, with several more coming out soon. He lives in Colorado Springs, Colorado.

cowthulu.com, @arlenfeldman

Arlen Feldman's story "Graveyard" was published in Metaphorosis on Friday, 30 November 2018.

E.C. Fuller ("Singot")

E.C. Fuller grew up in Claremore, Oklahoma and graduated from the University of Chicago in 2016. She is the short story category winner of the 41st *Annual Adult Creative Writing Contest* hosted by the Tulsa City-County Library and received an honorable mention in the young adult novel category of the *Oklahoma Writers' Federation Annual Writing Contest*. She has been published in the *Tulsa Review, Metaphorosis*, and *Hexagon Speculative Fiction Magazine*. She lives and works in Tulsa, OK

ecfullersbooks.com, @birdshapedhat

E.C. Fuller's story "Singot" was published in Metaphorosis on Friday, 2 July 2021.

Michael Gardner ("Renewal")

Michael Gardner is a writer of fantasy and horror who masquerades as an economist by day. His work has appeared in *Writers of the Future Volume 36, Aurealis, Bourbon Penn,* and *Metaphorosis*. He is also a three-time finalist for the Aurealis Awards. You can find out more about Michael and his work at: www.michael-s-gardner.com

Michael Gardner's story "Renewal" was published in Metaphorosis on Friday, 15 September 2017.

Erin Keating ("The Future in a Wash Basin")

Erin Keating earned her B.A. in creative writing and literature at Roanoke College and her M.A. in history at Drew University, mostly so she could continue to surround herself with old books. She currently works as a grant writer at an arts education nonprofit. When she's not reading or writing, she dabbles in rock climbing, language learning, and playing bass guitar. Her fiction can be found in *Metaphorosis, Haven Spec*, and *Luna Station Quarterly*, among others.

www.erinkeatingwrites.com, @KeatingNotKeats

Erin Keating's story "The Future in a Wash Basin" was published in Metaphorosis on Friday, 18 March 2022.

Mariah Montoya ("The Wife of Fabian Vitalik")

Mariah Montoya is a writer and new mother from Idaho. She loves watching movies and losing at chess games on cold, blustery days. On sunny ones, you can find her running with her husband and a stroller along the Boise river. You can't convince her to use Twitter, but she's sometimes on Instagram @mariah_author.

Mariah Montoya's story "The Wife of Fabian Vitalik" was published in Metaphorosis on Friday, 24 November 2017.

L'Erin Ogle ("Sorry, Sorry, Sorry and I Love You")

L'Erin is a writer living in the Kansas City area. She has always loved speculative fiction, horror movies, and all kinds of books. She has short stories and novellas available at various markets including *Metaphorosis, Pseudopod, Daily Science Fiction,* and others.

lerinogle.com, @lerinjo

L'Erin Ogle's story "Sorry, Sorry, Sorry and I Love You" was published in Metaphorosis on Friday, 23 November 2018.

J.C. Pillard ("The Tick of the Clock")

J.C. Pillard is a writer from Colorado. She uses her master's in English literature to write tales where magic is real. She has published numerous short stories, including two with *Metaphorosis*. In her free time, she knits and spins yarn.

www.jcpillard.com, @JCPillard

J.C. Pillard's story "The Tick of the Clock" was published in Metaphorosis on Friday, 8 October 2021.

Abhijato Sensarma ("Satyajit Ray's Beard or the Lack Thereof")

Abhijato Sensarma is a 19-year-old from Kolkata, India. He is currently an undergraduate student at Ashoka University — and while on the verge of stepping into the real world, this does not prevent him from writing about fictional ones whenever he can. His words have been published in Wisden's *The Nightwatchman, McSweeney's Internet Tendency, ESPNcricinfo, Scroll.in, The Quint, The Wire* and *Samjoko Magazine* among other publications.

Abhijato Sensarma's story "Satyajit Ray's Beard or the Lack Thereof" was published in Metaphorosis on Friday, 11 June 2021.

Jennifer Shelby ("Free Hugs")

Jennifer Shelby (she/her) hunts for stories in the beetled undergrowth of fairy infested forests. She fishes for them in the dark space between the stars. As part of her ongoing catch-and-release program, her stories are now available in many fine places that you can discover at jennifershelby.blog Her first novella, *Slipstreamers: Plague of the Dreamless*, is now available through Engen Books.

jennifershelby.blog, @jenniferdshelby

Jennifer Shelby's story "Free Hugs" was published in Metaphorosis on Friday, 16 July 2021.

Lori J. Torone ("Wytchen Wood")

Lori J. Torone (she/her) lives in New York with her two teenagers and a small rescue dog and is an adjunct professor of English and Speech at her alma mater. She writes fantasy and loves all things medieval and mythic. Her independently published works, including the novelette collection *Through the Oak Door*, are available on Amazon under Lori J. Fitzgerald. You can find her on Twitter @MedievalLit.

Lori J. Torone's story "Wytchen Wood" was published in Metaphorosis on Friday, 15 December 2017.

Martin Westlake ("Coming Home")

Martin Westlake has followed parallel careers as a civil servant and as an academic and has lived, studied, and worked in the UK, Italy, France, and Belgium. The only thing he has ever always wanted to do is write creative fiction. Science fiction exercises a special, but not exclusive, attraction in that regard. For the past fifteen years he has been working seriously at it and he thinks maybe he is starting to get there.

martinwestlake.eu, @MartinWestlake

Martin Westlake's story "Going Home" was published in Metaphorosis on Friday, 12 March 2021.

Pauline Yates ("The Secret Keeper")

Pauline Yates lives in Queensland, Australia, and writes horror and dark speculative fiction. She is a member of AHWA and HWA and is an Australian Shadows Awards short fiction finalist. Her stories appear or are forthcoming in publications including *Black Hare Press, Midnight Echo, Black Hart Press*, and *Tales to Terrify*, and she is translated with Riflessi di Luce Lunare (RiLL), Italy.

linktr.ee/paulineyates

Pauline Yates's story "The Secret Keeper" was published in Metaphorosis on Friday, 4 June 2021.

COPYRIGHT

Title information

Reading 5X5 x3

ISBN: 978-1-64076-033-2 (e-book)
ISBN: 978-1-64076-034-9 (paperback)
ISBN: 978-1-64076-035-6 (hardcover)

Library of Congress

Library of Congress Control Number: 2022940468

Publisher

Verdage

Verdage is an imprint of
Metaphorosis Publishing
Neskowin, OR, USA

www.metaphorosis.com

"Metaphorosis" is a registered trademark.

Discounts available

METAPHOROSIS PUBLISHING

Metaphorosis offers beautifully written science fiction and fantasy. Our imprints include:

Verdage

Metaphorosis Magazine

Plant Based Press

Vestige

Help keep Metaphorosis running at
Patreon.com/metaphorosis

See more about some of our books on the following pages.

VERDAGE

Verdage

Science fiction and fantasy books for writers – full of great stories, but with an additional focus on the craft of speculative fiction writing.

Reading 5X5 x2

Duets

How do authors' voices change when they collaborate?

A round-robin of five talented science fiction and fantasy authors collaborating with each other and writing solo.

Including stories by Evan Marcroft, David Gallay, J. Tynan Burke, L'Erin Ogle, and Douglas Anstruther.

Score

an SFF symphony

What if stories were written like music? *Score* is an anthology of varied stories arranged to follow an emotional score from the heights of joy to the depths of despair – but always with a little hope shining through.

Reading 5X5

Five stories, five times

Twenty-five SFF authors, five base stories, five versions of each – see how different writers take on the same material, with stories in contemporary and high fantasy, soft and hard SF, and a mysterious 'other' category.

Reading 5X5

Writers' Edition

All the stories from the regular, readers' edition, plus two extra stories, the story seed, and authors' notes on writing. Over 100 pages of additional material specifically aimed at writers.

METAPHOROSIS MAGAZINE

Metaphorosis is an online speculative fiction magazine dedicated to quality writing. We publish an original story every week, along with author bios, interviews, and notes on story origins. Come and see us online at magazine.Metaphorosis.com

Keep Metaphorosis running! Support us at
Patreon.com/metaphorosis

You can also find us at:
Twitter: @MetaphorosisMag, @Metaphorosis
Facebook: www.facebook.com/metaphorosis

We publish monthly print and e-book issues, as well as yearly Best of and Complete anthologies.

PLANT BASED PRESS

plant
based
press

Vegan-friendly science fiction and fantasy, including an annual anthology of the year's best SFF stories.

Chambers of the Heart
speculative stories
by
B. Morris Allen

A heart that's a building, a dog that's a program, a woman sinking irretrievably — stories about love, loss, and movement.

Best Vegan SFF
of 2020

The best vegan-friendly science fiction and fantasy stories of 2020!

Best Vegan SFF
of 2019

The best vegan-friendly science fiction and fantasy stories of 2019!

Best Vegan SFF
of 2018

The best vegan-friendly science fiction and fantasy stories of 2018!

Best Vegan SFF
of 2017

The best vegan-friendly science fiction and fantasy stories of 2017!

Best Vegan SFF
of 2016

The best vegan-friendly science fiction and fantasy stories of 2016!

Susurrus

A darkly romantic story of magic, love, and suffering.

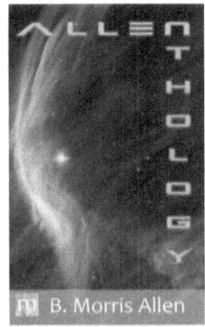

Allenthology: Volume I

A quarter century of SFF, including the full contents of the collections *Tocsin, Start with Stones,* and *Metaphorosis*.

Vestige

Novelettes, novellas, and novels by Metaphorosis authors.

The Nocturnals
Mariah Montoya

Night is Dangerous. Day is deadly.
Where day and night last thirty years, humans move constantly stay ahead of the night and cruel Nocturnals that call it home. But a boy is lost out there.

www.ingramcontent.com/pod-product-compliance
Lightning Source LLC
Chambersburg PA
CBHW050608110726
47899CB00001B/30